MIRA

Jia Lucman

DEDICATION

To my Hooyo, love you mom.

1.

Mira felt the cool sand under her thin straw shoes as she ran to her secret spot outside her tiny village near the large Argan tree. She stumbled on the jagged desert rocks, her mouth watering as she approached. She wondered what her friends would bring her that day. Yesterday was her cousin Fatima's wedding, and her family slaughtered an entire goat to celebrate. After the wedding, Mira discretely collected all the bones she could find from the slaughtered goat and hid them away.

That was when she snuck away from the celebration to her spot under the 20-foot Argan tree that was perched at the edge of the village, away from prying eyes. Mira often found herself sitting under its shade, staring out at her little village. She'd sit there alone, playing with rocks that she'd stack up high to balance, seeing how long they could stand before they tumbled to the ground. She'd also built forts and houses for her straw dolls, all while telling them stories of faraway lands that sat on the outskirts of the desert and beyond.

It was also the spot where she buried the bones she collected, digging a few inches under the sand. She never left so many bones before, so she was excited to see what they would bring her.

That morning, Mira had woken up, brimming with excitement. The *mu'addin* had just finished the call to dawn prayer, leading her father and the rest of the village men to the mosque. After her father's departure, she set out on her mission. She crept quietly through the village as the dawn sky glowed a bright pink and orange color. The air was still cool, a reprieve from the usual scorching heat of the desert sun. Mira looked around suspiciously to make sure no one was watching her and grinned sneakily as she was greeted by an array of figs, sweet berries, dates and a large red pomegranate.

Mira could hardly believe it. She gathered her treats, silently thanking whatever shadow people had left them for her. She couldn't take her treasure home though, because her mother and grandmother would ask too many questions.

In the past, when they caught her eating fruits that were out of season and large, sweet dates that didn't grow in their region, Mira tried to explain that the shadow people had given them to her. Her mother and grandma were furious, "never accept gifts from *jinns!*" her grandma shouted at her. "They will possess you and bring a curse upon our family. Allah separated our kinds for a reason." Mira didn't understand. The shadow people never hurt her; they were terrified of her and every other human. Every time she tried to talk to them or approach them, they vanished, some running off so quickly, she could barely see their form.

So, she learned to keep her interactions with them a secret. Every week, she buried a bone under the Argan tree, and by morning, she'd find food in that same spot. Mira didn't like the food her mama made. It was always the same; sheep milk and porridge with dates—and not the sweet ones the shadow people brought her either.

She needed to find a safe place to hide her treats. There was no way she could finish them all that day, but maybe she could give some berries to her twin brothers, Azule and Hassan. She searched the desert landscape. But there were only rocks, sand and a few scattered trees. She walked further out into the desert and away from the village.

It wasn't safe to venture that far out, but she needed a safe place for her treats. She went to the base of a small rock formation and hid her food between the cracks. Grabbing a few berries and figs, she stuffed them in the pockets of her dress. Satisfied, Mira's hand hesitated over the pomegranate. It looked so red and sweet. She was tempted to have a taste, but she was already late. Mama would probably be looking for her; she hated when Mira snuck off to play in the desert. Thinking quickly, she quickly gathered some firewood and ran back to the village. She kept a mental note of her surroundings so she would be able to make it back to that spot.

Most of the desert terrain looked the same, with scattered shrubs and a few trees. In the distance were rocky mountains that separated her village from the harsh realities of the Sahara; beyond that, Mira could only guess what existed. She lived in a small village outside the Sahara Desert. Her village was nothing more than a few stone homes littered along the rocky desert terrain. The main source of income was the large date grove that most of the village men spent their time tending to. At the yearly harvest, they would send a caravan of these dates out to the cities, along with wool and other Bedouin-made products, to trade for items such as metal pots, spices and other necessities at the bazaar.

Because of its location, her village often hosted caravans coming in from the lands beyond the desert. Among them were merchants, pilgrims, scholars and explorers on their way to Fez, the great Maghrib city, and the capital of the Marinid Sultanate. These strange guests always fascinated her. Along with the other children of the village, she would often trail after them until shooed away by the elders. Still, Mira always found a way to sneak around their camps where they would tell stories of cities made of gold, large oceans and grand mosques.

The air had already grown thick with heat as Mira wiped the sweat from her brow. She tried to control her breathing as she navigated through the small village. She zipped past her neighbors' homes as the village came to life with morning activities. Some dumped their used morning water on the sandy ground, while others swept the area using a short straw broom, removing the ever-present sand from their courtyard. Children were out chasing chickens with sticks, and a goat or two roamed around looking for shrubs to eat.

She grinned as she zipped past it all, inhaling deeply as she tried to control her breathing before entering the small courtyard of her home. Mama was awake, attempting to wipe a wet cloth on her twin brothers' faces as they tried to escape her clutches. She held them tight, shouting at them to stay still. Her baby sister, Sara, was nearby crying for attention. Mira quickly dropped her load and ran to her. She picked her up, cooing at her. Her sister instantly began laughing and smiling.

Mira loved her sister more than anything in the world—especially more than her annoying twin brothers, who were six years old and a menace to everyone in the family and the village alike. Mira wasn't much older, having just turned eight, but she had nearly as many responsibilities as her mother and grandmother. The women in her village were in charge of agricultural activities, which included herding, grazing, fetching water and raising crops, while the men, including her father, spent most of their day working in the date grove under the hot desert sun. They also protected their village from bandits and entertained visitors, mostly the merchant and pilgrim caravans that passed by their village to rest and regroup while heading to the larger cities in the north.

"*Salaam*, Mama," Mira greeted, leaning in to kiss her mother on the forehead. Then, she greeted her grandmother, kissing her forehead and hand. They were all sitting under the makeshift terrace in the courtyard; it was nothing more than a few sticks holding up a roof made of dried date palm leaves. The ground was covered in straw mats. This was where her family spent most of their time when they weren't working. It was where they slept, ate, entertained guests and congregated. They also had a small one-room stone and mud house, which they used for storage in the summer and slept in during winter.

"Where were you?" Mama demanded.

Mira stilled, "I...was collecting fire sticks?" she answered slowly as Mama scowled, looking at the sad pile of sticks she had collected to back up her story.

"You were playing outside the village again, weren't you?" Mama accused.

Mira stayed quiet, knowing Mama would lecture her regardless. "You are too old to be playing these silly games. You should be doing your chores," Mama reprimanded. Mira nodded; she heard all this before. It wasn't fair that she wasn't allowed to play when that was all the twins did, and she wasn't much older than them, but they were boys, and she was a girl.

"I'm sorry, Mama," Mira sighed.

"Clean this place up so we can eat."

Obeying, she quickly swept the terrace and set up the wooden bowls and spoons for breakfast. She snuck some berries into her baby sister's mouth and wiped the sweet juice from her lips to hide the evidence. "You can't tell Mama about the treats, okay?" she told her sister, who just cooed, reaching out for more berries. Mira smiled and gave her the rest of the berries. She always shared with her sister, and when she was older, she would share her secret too, and they would enjoy many treats together.

Mira ran to their water pot, quickly pouring water into the wooden bowl. She watched her reflection in the rippling water, blinking at her strange blue eyes. She once asked her mother why everyone in the village had brown eyes and only her eyes were different. Mama always told her that her eyes were beautiful and there was nothing wrong with being different, but every time she caught their reflection, Mira couldn't help but feel ashamed. Everyone in the village thought she was cursed because of it.

They would whisper insults and say she had the eyes of a devil—and the fact that she often saw strange things didn't help. Mira could see *jinns* for as long as she could remember. She saw them just as people saw cats and dogs. Usually, they were nothing more than shadows lurking in the corner of her eye—always present, but never active. But, sometimes, she saw other things—terrifying things—which gave her nightmares and made her cry out in fear. She saw creatures she couldn't describe. Some flew above her, their large wings casting a shadow over the sun; their loud shrieks making her teeth shatter. However, no one looked up. No one noticed. With time, Mira also learned to not look, to pretend they weren't there.

Some even lived under the sand. She saw their large bodies diving in and out of the dunes. There were smaller ones—fierce-looking ones—the size of a rabbit or dog. Mira treated them as she would any other animal in the desert. She was wary, but she learned not to be afraid. They never went near humans and, more importantly, they were more afraid of her than she was of them.

It took her a long time to comprehend that she was the only person who could see these creatures. Sure, everyone in her superstitious village knew of the *jinn*; they blamed them for everything, from a miscarriage to an ailment. Some even worked with them, collecting coins by casting hexes or offering cures.

Her parents were just as superstitious. When Mira was younger and cried about monsters and spoke of shadow people, they immediately blamed the *jinn*. They took her to different religious leaders who recited the sacred verses upon her, hoping to cast out the *jinns* they believed possessed her. They covered her eyes with rags and tried to expel the 'devils' from them, but every time her eyes were uncovered, they were still that piercing blue hue. But Mira wasn't possessed, so the verses did nothing to dispel her night terrors and 'visions of shadows'.

Eventually, when Mira was six, her family took more drastic measures. They took her to the *Sahir*. That was almost two years ago, and she still feared that if she slipped up—if she acted differently—her family would take her back.

She shivered, at the thought of him and the hellish week she was forced to stay with him.

*Mira was near the courtyard. She saw the small creature hiding in a shrub nearby. She decided to call it 'Iftin'. It looked like a cross between a cat and a rabbit. This one had been lurking in the bush near her home for a few days now, and, every time she pointed it out to anyone, it conveniently disappeared. So, she decided to set the trap, waiting to catch the little beast. She thought that if she finally caught it, her parents might **finally** believe her. Mira propped the basket up with a stick. Iftin liked to eat bones, so she placed a small bone she found under the straw basket and waited. Shortly after, the creature scurried out of its hole, sniffing the air. It cocked its head side to side before approaching the basket.*

She held her breath as she hid behind a tree, watching it inch closer to her trap. She grinned as he entered, and the basket fell upon him. She quickly ran to the moving basket, pushing it down as Iftin wiggled, trying to escape. "Stop moving!" she commanded. Mira placed a large rock on top of the basket to keep Iftin from running off. Iftin tried to move, but the basket wouldn't budge. It was a small creature, but surprisingly strong.

She ran home to find Mama, who was sitting over the fire, chatting with her grandmother as she stirred the large stone cooking pot. "Mama! Mama!" Mira excitedly ran over, pulling her mother by the arm.

"By Allah! What is it this time, Mira?" her mother sighed exasperatedly.

"Come see what I caught!" Mira said, tugging her arm harder. "Please hurry. It's right by the courtyard."

Mama sighed, exchanging a knowing look with her Jida, who just chuckled as Mira continued pulling her mother's arm. "Fine!" Mama gave in, bemused by her excitement. Mama never believed Mira when she tried to show her the creatures she saw. She just kept saying there was nothing there and told Mira not to look for things she shouldn't be seeing. But now, she had proof! She caught Iftin.

Mira dragged Mama to the courtyard. The basket was still there, shaking as Iftin tried to escape. Mama narrowed her eyes at the moving basket. "You have to look fast because it will try to run away once I open the basket," Mira explained.

*Mama gave her a wry smile. "Okay, get on with it," she said with a wave of her hand. Mira removed the basket and Iftin jumped out in a blur, running into the bush and burying itself under the sand. Mira grinned triumphantly at her mother. She **had** to have seen it. There was no way she didn't. "Did you see, Mama? I trapped it using a bone and it just buried itself under that bush!"*

Mama's eyes were wide with horror, but she wasn't looking at the bush where Iftin buried itself. Instead, she was staring at Mira, her eyes filled with concern. "Mira, what

6

have you done? By Allah! Bones, Mira? You could have lured a jinn *into our home!"*

"But it was an animal! Didn't you see?"

"No, Mira, I saw nothing," Mama said, shaking her head, her eyes sad and frightful. Mira frowned. "But it was right there…"

"That's enough!" Mama cut her off. "Enough of this nonsense! Enough talk about shadows and creatures." Mama leaned down, grabbing Mira's shoulders and shaking her. "Seek refuge in Allah, Mira. Seek protection from the jinn!"

"I seek refuge in Allah," Mira whispered, repeating the prayer her mother forced her to recite every day feeling defeated.

Mira blinked away from her reflection, shaking the memory that overtook her. She brought their usual breakfast of porridge, a large bowl of sheep milk, and dates. Her face was pale, but Mama didn't comment on it as she quickly took a few bites before excusing herself to finish her chores.

2.

The next day, Mama asked Mira to collect some more wood for their fire, which meant she got to go outside the village again. Mira swiftly nodded, trying not to look too eager. She really wanted to eat that pomegranate! She ran off before her mother could change her mind, racing through her small village, careful not to bump into anyone.

Villagers scowled as she quickly brushed past them, murmuring her *Salaam*. She ran to the outskirts of the village, past the Argan tree. Mira made her way to the scattered formation of large rocks just beyond her village and searched through its cracks, sticking her small hands in between the rocks, looking for her snacks, but she felt nothing. Mira frowned. She was sure this was where she put it, but, then again, everything looked the same. She walked further out into the desert, eager to find her tasty treasure. But no matter how hard she searched; it simply wasn't there.

Mira huffed a breath of frustration. Without realizing it, she had walked further and further away from her village. Just as she was about to give up and head back, she heard a cry in the distance. She froze, startled at the sound. There shouldn't have been anyone that far out into the desert—especially not her. She shook it off and decided to go back to her village, but then she heard it again; whoever it was, was probably hurt. She paused for a second before following the sound. It sounded like someone was in trouble, and she had to help them.

The crying led Mira deeper and deeper into the desert. The small rock formations gave way to larger formations, and huge rocky hills loomed over her as the crying got louder. "Hello!?" she called. "Is anyone there? Are you hurt?"

She listened, but there was no answer—only crying. She walked even further, entering a valley between two small mountains. She felt a sudden chill rush to her bones as everything in her body shivered, telling her she shouldn't be there. The hot desert air was suddenly freezing, and Mira used her small arms to hug herself. She looked around. The shadows on the rocky mountain seemed to move in unseemly ways. Mira stumbled, suddenly afraid. She knew it was time to head back, but, suddenly, the crying started again— this time, it was louder and so much closer.

Mira swallowed the lump forming in her throat. She ignored the looming shadows and continued walking towards the sound. The shadows continued dancing around, taking shape and then disappearing.

I'm not afraid! Mira thought with a shiver. She remembered what her Jida told her, *"Jinns only have control over you if you let them. Never show them any fear."* It was just the shadow people; they left her food in exchange for bones. They were more afraid of her than she was of them. Mira took a deep breath, calming her nerves. She straightened her shoulders and continued walking to where the crying was growing ever so loud. She finally reached an abandoned well in the middle of the valley, surrounded by what looked like an abandoned town. Mud and stone homes were half-destroyed and sunk under piles of sand as the desert reclaimed her land. It was eerily quiet. The only sound was her soft breathing and the cries that echoed into the air. Mira took a shaky step toward the well.

"H-hello?" she called. The shadows edged closer, dancing in and out of her vision as she tried to ignore them. The crying suddenly stopped; Mira waited for an answer, but there was nothing. "Is anyone in there?" she called again, peering into the black well. It was so dark that she couldn't make out any forms.

"Yes, I'm here," a timid voice suddenly called from inside. "P-please help me." It sounded so scared. So... *alone.*

How long had they been stuck there in the dark, crying for help? Mira suddenly remembered herself alone and crying in a dark corner at the *Sahir's* home, chained and abused with no one to save her. No one investigated her cries. No one answered her pleas for help and mercy. She remembered her father's back as he walked away, leaving her there while she cried for him not

9

to go.

Suddenly, Mira wasn't afraid anymore. She straightened her back in determination. She was going to help whoever was in that well. As if sensing her fearlessness, the shadows fled, sinking deeper into the mountains. *That's right,* she thought. *I'm **not** afraid of you.*

She investigated her surroundings. There had to be something she could use. "Wait. I'll get you out of there. Don't be afraid. I'm here to help you." Mira sent her reassurance into the well. Her only answer was a whimper. She looked around the half-buried homes until she saw a broken wooden bucket a few feet away. Attached to the bucket was a rope, but it was too short. Whoever once lived in that deserted village must have used the bucket to gather water. Beyond the broken stone and mud homes was a tree and a coarse rope tied to it.

Yes! Mira thought, carefully unwinding the rope.

By the time she finished, her hands were chafed and bloody, but Mira barely felt the pain. She was focused on saving whoever was stuck in the well. She tied the rope she found to the bucket, then tied one end to the pillars attached to the side of the well. She hoped it was strong enough to hold. "I found some rope," she called into the well. There was only silence. "Well, I'm going to toss it in. Watch out," she tossed in the rope and held her breath, waiting.

Mira waited for something to happen—for whoever it was to pull on the rope or speak—but silence only ensued. She frowned. Was she mistaken? She definitely heard crying. Maybe the *jinns* were playing a trick on her. Maybe no one was even in the well. Suddenly, the rope stretched, pulling her out of her musing. Someone was pulling on it. She took a step back and the wood groaned as whoever was in the well began climbing up. Mira waited anxiously. Suddenly, there was a hand on the side of the well. It was slender with leathery skin and six long, black fingernails. Mira felt a scream bubble in her chest as the creature shot out of the well, disappearing into the mountain.

She howled in fright, taking off in a run as hot tears streamed down her face. Still shivering with fear, Mira ran away blindly, stumbling and falling until she stopped to catch her breath. It was late afternoon by that point. Her dress was soaked with sweat, but she felt cold. She ran far away from that well and that cursed valley, far away from the shadows and *jinns* that lurked there. Coming here was a mistake. She should have stayed home and ignored the cries. She was a fool for thinking she could help anyone. She was just the cursed *jinn* girl that all the children made fun of. And now, she had been tricked by a *jinn* and lured into the desert—lured to her death.

***

The afternoon sun loomed over Mira's head like a hot lamp. She could see the heat waves before her, shimmering in the distance. Her straw shoes dug painfully into her feet; she felt the skin tearing. The ground was cracked and dry, a labyrinth of jagged lines that showed the aftermath of the drought. She wiped the sweat from her brow, her mouth dry and her stomach grumbling. She had run for so long in the blistering heat that she felt light-headed and weak.

She knew better than to be walking around during high noon; however, she still saw no sign of the village. She found a small desert tree, its branches offered little shade from the sun—still, she decided to rest there and find her way back once it cooled down. She winced as she lay down on the hot sand, shutting her eyes.

She tried to push down her fear and panic. The desert was an unforgiving place, and she didn't know if she would make it back home. She felt foolish for her actions. She wondered if her family was worried about her, or if they were looking for her. Maybe someone would find her. Or maybe they were glad to be rid of their cursed daughter.

What had she let out of that well? What if she released something evil? She shuddered, not wanting to consider that possibility, and forced herself to sleep instead.

Mira eventually drifted off into a restless sleep, feeling the exhaustion of the day. She woke up hours later as the sun drifted west. It was still hot, but not as dangerous as it was a few hours ago. Her stomach growled with hunger. Her mouth was dry, and her skin was red from being out in the sun for so long. Mira sat up and took in her surroundings. Now that she was less afraid—and less panicked—maybe she would make it home before sunset. She definitely didn't want to be alone in the desert at night.

To her right, she noticed something different, then gasped in surprise. There, a few inches away from where she slept under the tree, were date palm leaves filled with nuts, berries and dates, alongside a leather flask filled with water. She quickly grabbed the water skin, forced it open, and gulped its contents down. The cool water trickled down her throat, easing the burning dryness. Mira forced herself to stop drinking; she had to save the rest of the water. She nibbled on some dates and nuts, contemplating her luck: *who had left her this food?*

It had to be a *jinn*, but she didn't see any shadows, nor did she sense anyone around her but the vast emptiness of the desert. A *jinn* must have seen her and brought her food. Whoever it was, she was grateful for this food and water. It meant that she would at least survive the day. Mira silently thanked whoever brought her these substances. She took the remaining food and water and eagerly began walking home.

***

Mira was completely lost. Everything looked the same. She had been walking for hours; the sky slowly darkened, and a cool wind replaced the hot air. The food and water had run out hours ago, and the familiar insatiable thirst and hunger were back. Mira felt despair growing in her heart. She had to find somewhere to camp out for the night because while the day may be blistering hot, the desert nights were often cold. She needed to find wood and build a fire. Perhaps someone would see the smoke and come find her. Or, at least it would keep the animals away.

Her clothing was ripped and torn by the thorny dry bush as she tried to collect its branches, its sharp edges cutting into her hands. She winced in pain and kept pulling until she collected enough shrub for a small fire. Her hand shook as she repeatedly hit two rocks together, hoping for a spark. It was dusk—soon, the entire desert would be engulfed in blackness.

She took a shaky breath, praying deep in her heart. *Please,* she pleaded, *please work.* Mira was raised in the desert, and she would survive this calamity. It was in her blood. Then, after what felt like a lifetime, the rocks released a spark onto the thin twigs. She blew on the spark, urging it to grow. She covered the small fire with her hand and blew into the flame. Thankfully, it grew. Mira sent out a silent, grateful prayer and fed more sticks into her fire. It wasn't much, and it probably wouldn't last half the night; but, as darkness swept over the desert and the stars began shining bright, she was glad for the small victory.

Mira laid down on the sand for the second time that day. She crawled into a tight ball. The fire offered some warmth, and the velvety desert sand was cool against her skin. In the distance, she heard owls and other animals that stalked the night, searching for prey. She felt the tears forming in her eyes as she turned to stare at the brilliant night sky. The stars sparkled in the sky, a symphony of defiance to the darkness. Despite her fear, she couldn't help but marvel at the beauty. She reached her hand up, wanting to catch a star to hold its brilliant light. The crescent moon was dimly glowing—not to be outshone by the millions of stars—and Mira knew she wasn't alone.

Mira was reminded of her mother's unwavering faith, and, now, she held onto that faith more than ever. She prayed deep in her heart to the one that created the stars, asking Him to guide her back home.

As terrified as she was, Mira didn't cry that night. Her feet were bloody from walking and her hand was torn by shrubs. Her stomach rumbled with hunger and her lips were dry with thirst, but she still didn't cry. Mira had not cried since she left the *Sahir's* home two years ago, broken and built anew, and if she could survive that week, she could survive this.

She finally fell asleep, whispering prayers, her small body exhausted from hours of walking.

3.

As Mira stirred in consciousness the next morning, she slowly opened her eyes, expecting to see the dry palm leaves that covered her terrace roof, expecting to hear the soft snores of her twin brothers. Instead, the open pre-dawn sky greeted her. The stars were fading as the light creeping into the horizon spread. She knew from the ache of her feet, and pang of hunger in her stomach that yesterday had not been a dream. She was lost.

Dawn slowly approached, wringing a small sigh from Mira's lips as she stared out into the horizon. Her discomforts were all but forgotten as the beautiful desert sky looked down on her. An ombre of orange, pink and purple spread brilliantly as the sun peeked over the horizon. It was silent; no rooster crowing, no crying baby and no snoring—only the wistful song of the desert.

Mira closed her eyes as she listened to its tune. Sometimes, when she was at home, she woke up early and ran to the Argan tree to listen to the desert's chorus. It only happened at the twilight hour, right before dawn. The song was faint, but it was so beautiful that it always made Mira cry. Now, away from her village, she could fully hear the desert's song, its sweet voice eerie and haunting.

The song came from everywhere and nowhere. She swayed, completely enamored by its beauty. All too soon, the color of the sky faded into pink, then a light blue, as the sun fully emerged, erasing all traces of darkness. The song ceased and she blinked—the trance was broken. She sniffed, wiping her eyes. She didn't realize she was crying, but her tears were not of fear or pain. They were the same tears shed in the face of beauty and peace, capturing your breath and filling your heart with contentment. Getting lost was almost worth it to witness such tranquility.

The embers of her small fire lay dying. Mira blinked in confusion breaking out of the trance. Her fire should have died out hours ago. She glanced around and almost wept in surprise and gratitude. Not only had someone kept her fire from dying out, but someone had left her food again. She almost sobbed in relief as she lifted the water skin. The flask—which had been empty just hours ago—was now full of water. She quickly gulped it down, trying hard to pace herself, and ate the dates, which were large and filling. The berries were so sweet that she moaned at the taste of them. Their sugary juice dripped down her chin. She saved the nuts and figs for her journey and took the rest of the water.

Mira looked around for any sounds of life—a footprint, or even a whisper that someone had been there; someone was helping her, feeding her, making sure she was warm while she slept.

"Hello," Mira called out tentatively into the desert. She waited, but the only reply was her echo. "I don't know if you can hear me, but, thank you. Thank you for helping me." She didn't expect an answer, and whoever it was clearly didn't want to be discovered.

Jinns were as much part of the desert as the sand or rocks. Every village and every caravan told stories of their existence. Except for Mira, they weren't just stories that parents told to scare their kids, they weren't just the fears of superstitious travelers, they were real. They didn't talk to humans or interact with them; however, they were ingrained in the lives of everyone she knew. Mira didn't think they were evil—not until she met the *Sahir*. She shivered at the thought of him and the dark *jinns* that hung onto him like leeches, feeding off his energy.

Good *jinns* kept their distance, repaying kindness with kindness, like the *jinns* who left her food under the Argan tree in exchange for bones. Maybe they were the ones helping her. Her grandmother once told her that Allah separated our worlds and that we should never mix. Good *jinns* never transgress this command. However, she was grateful for the rebellious *jinn* keeping her alive.

Mira began walking again; she tried to map out her surroundings, looking for anything that might seem familiar, but there was only an endless vision of sand and rocks before her, all melding together to paint a monochromatic picture. There was nothing she could use to distinguish where she might be. She had no sense of direction, walking blindly, hoping to stumble upon anything that might help her. Maybe she would happen upon a caravan or a nomadic tribe.

Yes! Mira thought. There had to be someone else out here; and eventually, she would find them. Mira walked for hours, her feet bloodied and full of pain. She stopped only once to cut fabric from her dress and bind her aching feet, but that did little to alleviate the pain. Her water and food were long gone, and the afternoon sun shone directly overhead, covering the desert in waves of heat. Her head throbbed, and not even her tightly wrapped turban could save her from the scorching heat of the sun.

She had to stop again and rest. Hopefully, her friend would leave something to eat and drink. Mira licked her dry lips as she limped to a nearby tree. Though it offered little shade, it was better than sleeping out in the open. She slowly removed her shoes from her pulsating feet. She grimaced as she unwrapped the bloody fabric. She put it on a branch to dry, and laid down, forcing herself to close her eyes and drift off to sleep.

Sleep didn't evade her for long. Exhaustion from walking, hunger and thirst made it hard to worry, so she slept.

Mira awoke a few hours later, still tired and sore from her endless walk. She was greeted once more with fresh water, dried figs, dates and nuts. She gratefully accepted the gift; however, this time, next to her food was a green paste folded into a palm leaf. Mira investigated it, deeply inhaling its scent and wrinkling her nose. She recognized the smell; it was the plant Mama used when she came back from the *Sahir's* house. Mama covered her burns and wounds with this plant. It was medicine!

How? Mira looked around the desert astonished, her eyes tearing with gratitude for her friend whose name and face she did not know. Mira sniffled, leaning down to carefully cover the paste on her swollen and bloodied feet. She then wrapped them up in her cloth and took a shaky breath. No matter how tired and exhausted she was, she couldn't stay there. Who knew how long the *jinn's* goodwill would last? She had to get home. "Thank you," she whispered into the desert, hoping whoever it was would hear her.

The next three days were the same as the last. Her feet didn't hurt as much, though, meaning the medicine had worked. Each day, she walked from dawn to noon, took a nap, ate the food her *jinn* friend brought, and walked again until dusk. On her fifth day in the desert, she felt hopeless. Not even the song of the desert could lift her spirit. She wondered if she'd ever make it home or see her family again.

Mira's chest constricted in pain and loneliness. She missed her mother and sister. She even missed the twins and her father—though he was always distant and cold towards her. She missed her chores and sheep. She just wanted to go home. Mira cried in despair for the first time since entering the desert. She didn't even feel hungry or thirsty; she only felt her loneliness. She curled up in a ball, her wet tears soaking into the sand she slept on. "Mama" she whispered, hiccupping and gasping for air between sobs. "I just want to come home. Please, take me home," she cried.

She was so distraught that she didn't hear the shuffling of feet nearby. She shrieked as a shadow fell over her, crawling away. The shadow—also frightened—disappeared in a blink.

"Wait!" Mira called, not wanting to scare it off, but it was already gone. She wiped her tears with her dirt cloaked hands. "Please, come back," she pleaded, desperately looking for someone to talk to, even if it was a *jinn*. There was still no answer.

"Please..." Mira pleaded into the desert, when, suddenly, the shadow appeared again just as fast as it disappeared. This time, it was a few feet away. She held her breath. It wasn't a shadow, but some type of being dressed in a black tunic and black turban that covered its face. She could only see its large, round, dark eyes and its hands. It had six long fingers with black nails. Its skin was dark and leathery, covered in fur-like hair.

The well! Mira remembered. She could never forget those long, hairy fingers and black claw-like hands. *That's* who her savior was—the *jinn* she came to believe was her friend, was the very thing that got her in this mess in the first place.

Mira's eyes narrowed, "you!" she shouted angrily as the *jinn* took a startled step back, already turning to flee into the desert. "No, wait!" she backed down, softening her voice. "Don't leave..." she whispered, not wanting to endure any more loneliness, even if her only company was the very *jinn* who did this to her.

The creature paused. It looked like it was vibrating. Its hands were held tightly together with nails digging into its skin. It looked like it wanted to run back into the desert where it watched her—where it lurked. "You're afraid," she finally realized as the creature shuddered. Now that she was past the strangeness of its appearance, it didn't look so scary, especially when it looked like it would pass out from fear of her. "I won't hurt you," Mira said softly, feeling a bit sympathetic. She knew *jinns* avoided humans, and even feared them at times, but not to this extent.

The creature's hands loosened its tight grip and its vibration slowed down. She tried not to make any sudden movements, trying to coax the creature. It reminded her of a scared and wounded animal. "What's your name?" she finally asked. She knew it could talk. She heard it in the well when it asked for help.

Mira waited, unsure whether the *jinn* would answer her. Finally, after several minutes, she heard its timid voice, "I-I'm Ayub," the *jinn* stuttered, shifting from foot to foot.

"Ayub," Mira repeated with a smile. "My name is Mira," she said.

"Mira," the *jinn* repeated, as if it were strange to say out loud.

"Do you want to be my friend?" Mira asked hopefully.

The *jinn* froze, cocking his head in an inhuman way. "What is a friend," he asked curiously, his voice still soft and timid. Mira pondered on his question. She didn't have any friends; the kids in the village didn't like her. They always made fun of her, calling her *jinn-girl* or *witch*, laughing whenever she passed them. Her only friends were her dolls and her sheep.

"Friends share stories," she finally decided. Mira loved telling stories to the sheep. Every time she took them out to graze, she told them stories. They were the only ones who ever listened. "And friends help each other. I helped free you from the well, and you are helping me survive in the desert. So, technically, we are friends. I think," she finished. She already considered the stranger her friend, even though she didn't know him.

Ayub crouched down, taking in her words. "Will you tell me a-a story," he finally asked.

Mira grinned, sitting up crossed-legged. She thought for a minute. "Okay! Um, once upon a time, there was a girl who loved pomegranates. But there was only one man in her whole entire village that had a pomegranate tree, except he was very mean and never shared it with the girl."

Ayub's eyes widened in horror. "Why," he asked incredulously.

"Well, because he wanted to hog it all for himself. Anyways, one day, the girl sneaked into his farm and stole a pomegranate from his tree."

Ayub gasped. "B-but stealing is bad!" he said.

"Oh, well...the girl felt bad after she did it, and-and tried to return the pomegranate," she quickly added. Ayub nodded, bobbing his head intently. "But the man caught her. And he was very angry that she stole from him." Ayub gasped again. His doe-like brown eyes were wide and his hand clutched the bottom of his tunic. She bit back a smile, enjoying his exaggerated reaction. Mira deepened her voice and continued, "How dare you steal from me?" She did her best imitation of an angry man. "The girl was very scared. She apologized and offered him her bracelet in exchange. The man agreed and let her go free," Mira finished lamely. She knew her story wasn't very good, but Ayub clapped his hands, jumping up and down, brimming with excitement. Mira grinned at him; his reaction was infectious.

"Wow! I was so scared he was going to hurt her...I'm glad she went home safe," he said happily.

Mira looked at him. He didn't seem evil anymore. She thought Ayub was nice—maybe he didn't mean to trick her. And he *did* look after her and bring her water, food and medicine, keeping her fire alive while she slept. "Can I see your face," she asked suddenly.

Ayub froze. She could hear the frown in his voice. "We're not supposed to show ourselves to humans," he said, unsure.

Mira thought about that. "How many humans have you met who could see *jinn*," she asked. "I'm special, so the rule doesn't apply to me. Besides, we're friends, and friends protect each other. I won't tell anyone about you. I promise. And friends never break their promise."

Ayub hesitated for a minute, nervously vibrating again. "O-okay," he agreed shyly. Mira tried not to look too eager as he slowly removed the turban from his face. She always saw *jinns* as shadows. They never showed their true forms, and she was eager to see what they looked like.

Mira's eyes widened as he gave her a shy smile. He didn't make eye contact with her— instead, looked down at his hand, which was courtly folded together. He looked strange, not human, but not quite animal either. He didn't look scary. He looked kind of cute, like a puppy or a doe. His eyes were large and fully brown with thick lashes. His face was covered in short, brown fur, just like his hands. He had a small button nose and thin lips that caged small canines when he spoke. He looked young—the same age as her, or maybe even younger.

"Your eyes...are brown?" Mira frowned. Ayub cocked his head, blinking his eyes rapidly. Then, he shrugged. "I thought they would look like mine. Everyone said I have the eyes of the evil *jinns*—the *shaytan*," Mira huffed, feeling down. Her whole life she was told she had the eyes of a devil, but Ayub's eyes were warm.

"The *shaytan* has black eyes!" Ayub countered with a shiver. "You don't have his eyes. Your eyes are like the ocean," he added shyly.

Mira frowned. "What does the ocean look like," she asked. She had always heard of the ocean, but living in the desert, she couldn't imagine what it looked like. Ayub turned around, looking at the vast desert landscape.

"It's like a desert of water, as far as one can see, and it's the same color as your eyes."

Mira blinked, bringing her hands to her eyes. "Is it beautiful," she asked.

Ayub gave her a curious look, "Is the sky beautiful?" he responded.

Mira looked up at the cloudless blue sky and sighed, "Yes."

"Your eyes are more beautiful," Ayub stated, giving Mira a small, shy smile.

Mira smiled, feeling relief. She didn't have the eyes of a devil, or the eyes of a *jinn*. She had the eyes of the ocean, and it was as beautiful as the sky.

"Now we are best friends," she declared firmly. Ayub grinned widely, his small canines now prominent; he bounced up and down in excitement. Mira grinned back at his excitement, feeling better than she had in a long time. She wasn't alone anymore.

Mira ate her breakfast and began walking again, Ayub kept his distance, but now that they had broken the ice, he asked her a million questions. "Why are you called Mira? Do you have parents? What's your favorite food? Do you also like pomegranates?" Mira tried to keep up with his questions. His chattering was a great escape from the silence she had experienced over the last five days.

When the noon sun hit, Mira sat down under another shadeless tree, sighing. Her feet were sore again, and, while Ayub was a welcomed distraction, she was still so exhausted.

"Why are you sad," Ayub finally asked after a short silence. Mira frowned, her eyes burning with tears again. No one ever asked her that, and Mira had been sad for a long time. She hadn't felt genuinely happy ever since her father left her with the *Sahir* to be cured. Mira forced the tears back, overwhelmed by the sympathy and pain in Ayub's eyes. He was sad, she realized, because she was sad.

"I miss my family," she finally whispered. "I've been lost in this desert for five days and I just want to go home," her voice broke.

Ayub shifted forward, reaching a hand out to her, then snatching it back, still afraid to touch her. "Where is your home? I can help you. I'm very good at finding things," he offered.

Mira looked at him, hope filling her chest. She didn't think to ask Ayub to lead her home because she assumed he didn't know the way either. "My village is called Imlil," she told him. "It has a very large date farm. My father works there, and it's surrounded by small hills and mountains. There is a small well outside the village, and I go there to fetch water for my family, and there is a huge Argan tree. It's my secret spot. I sit there under its shade when my family sleeps in the afternoon."

Ayub nodded. "I will find your village, Mira. Then, you won't be sad or cry anymore."

Mira's eyes watered, her heart filling with gratitude for her friend. "Thank you, Ayub," she whispered.

Ayub grinned, looking out into the sky. "You should sleep."

Mira yawned, as if right on cue and grinned back. "Will you be here when I wake up," she asked. Ayub nodded feverishly. Mira smiled, laid down on the hot sand, and closed her eyes.

Mira woke up several hours later and, for once, her eyes didn't desperately look for water. Instead, she looked for Ayub. He sat like a statue, several feet away from her, staring out into the desert. He had a defensive stance, as if he were guarding her while she slept. Mira grinned, sneakily creeping up from behind him.

"Boo!" she screamed, making Ayub jump several feet into the air. He reminded Mira of a surprised cat as he landed in a crouch, staring at her in shock. Mira laughed at Ayub's frightened eyes.

Ayub scowled as he relaxed. "You scared me!" he pouted. His face crinkled and she couldn't help but laugh even harder, holding her side.

"I-I'm sorry," she wheezed. Ayub gave a reluctant smile. He looked embarrassed, and Mira felt a bit bad. "What did you do while I slept," she asked, controlling her breathing.

Ayub sighed and came to sit near her—or as close as he was willing to get. "I went to look for something," Ayub replied, not meeting her eyes.

Mira frowned. "What did you look for?" Her heart filled with hope that maybe he had found her village. Ayub reached into the folds of his cloak, pulling out something round and carefully placing it in front of her. Mira gasped, "a pomegranate!"

Ayub played with the ends of his cloak, turning his face away from her. "You said you liked pomegranate, like the girl from your story, and I don't want you to have to steal it," Ayub explained. Mira's eyes grew bright as she grabbed the pomegranate. It was so big and red; she felt her heart fill with gratitude.

"Thank you, Ayub! This is the nicest thing anyone has ever given me." Ayub grinned widely, his eyes bright with happiness. Mira grinned back and smashed the fruit against a rock, offering half to Ayub. He didn't take it. His face was uncertain, so she left it on the ground next to him. She used a bit of water from the water skin to wash her dirty hands and took a bite of the ruby seeds.

The pomegranate was so sweet and juicy. Mira groaned, "it's so good!"

Ayub tentatively grabbed the other half, using his nail to pull out the red seeds, and nodded in agreement. They ate together in silence. Mira's hands and face were red with nectar from the fruit, and she was full by the time she had finished.

She sighed with satisfaction, rubbing her belly slowly. "Where did you find that?" she asked. Pomegranates were not native to her region. She only had it once when a trader bought it from Fez and gave it to her father as a gift.

"I got it from Tunis. They have the best pomegranate," he remarked casually. Mira had only heard of that land once from a caravan that was headed to Mauritania. That caravan had been traveling for weeks before it reached her village.

Mira blinked at Ayub. She knew he was fast—he could be gone in a blink. But to run to Tunis and back, all in an afternoon, was incredible. "Wow! I wish I could run that fast," Mira mused.

"I'm the fastest *jinn* in my clan!" Ayub boasted proudly.

She didn't doubt it. "Why were you in that well," Mira asked, suddenly curious.

Ayub frowned. "My clan put me in there to punish me," he said softly.

"Why?"

Ayub didn't answer, looking into the desert. After a few moments had passed, he finally exhaled and admitted, "I did something I wasn't supposed to do. I helped a human." Mira felt her heart drop. "He was a shepherd boy. He fell off a cliff and his foot was stuck in a boulder. I saw it happen and watched him as he spent days crying for help. One night, when he finally fell asleep, I removed the boulder. A few days later, I found his sheep and guided them back to him. When my clan found out what I had done, they threw me in the well and left me there for a long time."

"W-what will happen if they find out you're helping me," she asked quietly, half hoping he wouldn't answer truthfully.

Ayub averted his eyes. "They will kill me...or worse."

"Ayub...I..."

"We should go," Ayub cut her off. Mira wasn't even sure what she would have said. She couldn't bring herself to tell him to leave her; she had grown too attached and dependent. Not only for survival, but for company, as well.

Mira sighed, not particularly excited to begin walking again. But still, she pushed herself and started in the direction she had been going for the last five days. There wasn't any logic to it; she was just hoping she'd stumble across someone...anyone.

"You're going the wrong way," Ayub called. "Your village is west."

Mira froze, turning abruptly to look at Ayub. "You found it! You found my village?"

"I told you I was good at finding things," Ayub grinned.

"Praise be to God!" Mira prayed. "Ayub you are truly amazing!" He flushed at the compliment, and Mira began walking west with renewed energy.

4.

"How long until we get there?" Mira groaned for the tenth time. It had been two days since Ayub told her that he had found her village. But Mira hadn't realized just how far away she had wandered.

"It's not my fault you walk like an old camel," Ayub shrugged. Mira rolled her eyes, annoyed. She was exhausted from walking, and tired of the desert. The only thing that kept her sane was Ayub's steady presence.

The last two days weren't completely terrible. Ayub was a great companion—when he wasn't talking her ear off, that is. They probably would have gotten to the village faster if they hadn't stayed up so late every night telling stories and playing games until dusk.

Mira sighed dramatically. "I'm just tired of walking," she complained.

"I know," Ayub said quietly, his face sympathetic. It was mid-morning. They had been walking since dawn, but Mira was already tired. "We're almost there," Ayub tried to assure her.

"That's what you said yesterday"

"Well, I forgot how slow you walk."

Mira gave him a sour look. What she wouldn't give to have his *jinn* speed, just for a day.

"When I get home, I'm going to have a long bath." She couldn't wait to get the grime and dirt off her body. Her mother would probably faint at the sight of her dirt-crusted daughter. Mira's dress was brown and stiff from dirt and sweat, places of it ripped from getting caught in the shrub. Her hair was a bird's nest of tangles, and more dirt coated her hands, feet, and fingernails.

Ayub didn't say anything. He was uncharacteristically quiet. "What's wrong with you," she asked after a few hours of silence.

Ayub nervously fidgeted with the edge of his turban, shifting his feet. "Will we still be friends when you get home," he asked quietly.

To be honest, Mira had not given it much thought, but now that he mentioned it... "I don't know. I'm not supposed to talk to *jinns*."

"I'm not supposed to talk to humans either." Ayub's face fell, his eyes shining with tears. Mira chewed the inside of her cheek. It's not that she didn't want to be his friend. She had grown quite fond of the *jinn*. But if anyone saw her talking to him—if anyone found out she was friends with a *jinn*... She shuddered.

Mira's father held her hand, leading her through the village. She was so excited when he told her they were going somewhere special that morning. Baba never took Mira anywhere. "Where are we going Baba," she asked again.

"We are going to see a Sahir.*"*

"What is a Sahir,*" Mira asked, confused, but Baba didn't answer her. He was quiet as he tightly held her hand, guiding her outside the village. She looked back at the small town, her heart racing. Was she in trouble? Was this because she tried to catch the creature? A bad feeling overwhelmed her as they approached a small stone house outside the village. She saw eerie shadows lurking around the house. But these shadows weren't like the ones she saw around the village. They felt dark and menacing. She shivered.*

"Baba, I want to go home," she whispered, trying to pull her arm free. Mira wanted to run away from this place and never look back. He held her hand tighter, pulling her toward the house. As if waiting for their arrival, the wooden door creaked open. Mira hid behind her father's leg and looked up at the man who had emerged from the house. He was older than her father, with a thick, black beard and hollow cheeks. He wore a black kaftan and a tightly wrapped black turban. His eyes were dark and lined with kohl, and his skin wrinkled with a deep tan. But it wasn't his appearance that frightened her. It was the inky dark shadows which clung to his body.

"Assalamu alaykum," her father greeted the Sahir.

"Walaikum Assalam." The Sahir*'s voice was deep when he spoke, as the shadows moved excitedly in and out of his body. Mira closed her eyes. "Is this the girl," the* Sahir *asked with a dark gleam in his eyes.*

"Yes, this is my daughter."

"Come child. Let me look at you." Mira shrunk further back, afraid of the man. Her

father pushed her out. The Sahir *looked at her curiously, as if trying to read her. He leaned down and opened his hand in invitation. The shadows suddenly shot out, clinging to her. Mira screamed, fighting to scramble away when the* Sahir *closed his hand, causing the shadows to retreat from her. Mira shivered, tears streaming down her face. The inky feeling of the shadows still clung to her skin. Her father's eyes were hard, and the* Sahir *clicked his tongue. "You were right to bring her to me," he said as if the display had proven his suspicions. "Your daughter was born possessed. She has the eyes of a devil. But I can help her."*

Baba nodded. "Shukran," he said, pushing Mira forward.

Mira grounded her feet, the shadows on the man were dancing eagerly as if she would be their next meal. "Please, Baba. I want to go home. Don't leave me here!" she cried. Her father ignored her, lifting her off the ground and into the waiting hands of the Sahir. *The shadows began clinging onto her again. She could feel them penetrating her skin, cold and filled with darkness. "Baba! No, please," Mira sobbed, reaching out desperately to her father. "Please, Baba! Don't leave me. I'll be good, I promise." Her father turned around and walked away.*

The Sahir *clicked his tongue, pulling Mira into the dark, stone house. "Baba! Baba!" Mira screamed and screamed until her throat was hoarse! The wooden door confined her into darkness.*

"Quiet girl!" the Sahir *snapped. She whimpered as he placed her on a thin mat in the corner, chaining her feet to the ground. He peered at her curiously and Mira shrunk back, trying to scratch and push the shadows off her body. But they kept coming; their oily blackness, digging into her scalp and trying to enter her mind. She could see the forms of the shadows moving with lightning speed, digging themselves into her body. She felt like she was being stabbed with a thousand knives.*

"No," Mira moaned. She wouldn't let them in. They wouldn't possess her. "Stop!" she screamed with everything in her. Suddenly, the shadows retreated, and she sagged with relief.

"How curious," the Sahir *mused while studying her. Mira had a horrible feeling that she had just done something wrong.*

Mira felt sick as the memories assaulted her. "What's wrong," Ayub asked, his face filled with concern. She shuddered. Ayub wasn't like those dark, evil *jinn*; he was kind. He was good, but she couldn't risk anyone finding out about him. She couldn't risk going back to the *Sahir*.

Mira swallowed. "It's nothing," she said shakily and began walking.

Ayub was quiet for a long time. "D-did someone hurt you," he asked finally.

Mira closed her eyes, trying to dispel the memory. "Yes," she whispered. Ayub was punished for helping a human, and Mira was punished for seeing the *jinn*.

5.

It was just past noon, and Mira was dizzy from the afternoon sun. It had been exactly seven days since she ventured out into the desert; lost and abandoned. While she was grateful for her new friendship with Ayub, she couldn't wait to go back home and reunite with her family. Mira sighed as she peered out hopelessly into the hot, barren desert, the heat waves visible through the dry air.

"You should rest now," Ayub suggested. Mira didn't think she could walk any further, even if she tried. It was too hot, too dry and too exhausting. She slumped down under a small tree, her skin red and blistered, her lips dry and cracked despite the steady stream of water Ayub constantly provided her with.

The awkwardness of their previous conversation had faded as they settled in comfortable silence. Mira laid down on the hot sand as Ayub was perched up a few feet away from her. She studied him while he stared out into the desert. He was her closest friend—the only person that bothered to talk to her, to get to know her, and listen to her stories. She felt closer to him than she did to the children she had grown up with within her village.

"I'll still be your friend," she said quietly. Ayub gave an excited jump, whirling around to face her.

"Truly!?" His face lit up with excitement, and Mira couldn't help but grin.

"Yes but…" Mira bit her lip, "I can't talk to you when I'm in the village, only when I'm outside. I go out every morning after dawn to graze the sheep.

We can play while they eat, but you can never enter the village. There is a bad man there who traps *jinns* and turns them into shadows."

Ayub's eyes widened as he shrank back in fear. He swallowed, "I won't go in the village. I-I don't want to be trapped by a human," he whispered. It was well known that human *Sahirs* trapped and enslaved *jinns* to do their evil bidding, and she didn't want Ayub to fall into that fate. "I'll wait for you every day by your favorite tree. Then, you can tell me stories."

"I'd like that," she whispered.

Mira woke up from her nap earlier than usual. It was still hot, but the sun was as overbearing as before. Mira drank from her water skin and ate the nuts and dates Ayub brought her. He was in a cheerful mood now that he knew she wouldn't leave him. They began walking again and headed west.

A few miles into their walk, Mira began noticing a strange cluster of rocks in the distance. She squinted her eyes—no, not rocks, they were houses. Her village! "Ayub! Do you see that!"

Ayub gave a quizzing look, "The village? It's been there all day."

"Why didn't you say anything?"

"I told you we were close."

Mira rolled her eyes. *Stupid jinn powers.* But her heart fluttered with relief anyways. She didn't want to admit it, but she began doubting if she'd ever make it home. Despite her exhaustion, she hurried her step.

She could see her village draw closer and closer, the familiar rock formation and the sparse shrub which their sheep would graze on. Her eyes watered with relief and her heart burst with exhaustion as she neared her favorite tree. She noticed then that Ayub wasn't following her. He stood several feet away, his eyes sad. Her excitement died as she realized Ayub couldn't follow her into the village. It was too dangerous for both of them.

"It's okay," Ayub said sadly. "I'll wait for you here, Mira, like we promised."

Mira felt her eyes water as she looked at her friend. She nodded; her throat tight. She hadn't realized how much she grew to love the *jinn*. "I'll miss you, Ayub, and I'll come back. I promise."

"And friends never break their promise," he finished, repeating the words she had told him when they first met. Mira grinned, wiping her eyes. She waved as she walked away turning towards her village. This wasn't a goodbye; it was just a *see you soon*. Ayub continued to watch her as she made her way home.

Mama, she thought desperately, as she reached the outskirts of her village, stumbling against the jagged rocks. She heard a gasp and whirled around. It was one of her neighbors, a woman named Um Issa. She dropped the firewood she was collecting and stared at Mira as if she were a ghost.

"I seek refuge in Allah!" the woman prayed. "What are you!" Um Issa took a fearful step back. Mira supposed she looked terrifying, completely caked in dirt, her hair tangled with grime, and her naturally tanned skin, browned from the sun.

"It's me, Mira Al Hussaini."

The woman's eyes widened in surprise. "Praise be to God! Mira!" she rushed over to her, grabbing her shoulders, patting her down as if to make sure she was real.

"We thought you were dead. How…" the woman was at a loss for words.

"Can you take me home, please? I want to go home," Mira cried.

Um Issa's eyes filled with sympathy as she grabbed Mira's hand. "Oh, of course, you poor child, come." Um Issa led Mira through the village. Shocked gasps and silent prayers rang out as everyone gawked at her. Mira swallowed, feeling self-conscious.

As she reached close to her house, she saw her mother running towards her. "Mira!" she shouted.

"Mama!" Mira cried, releasing Um Issa's hands and running into her mother's arms. They crashed into each other, both sobbing.

Her mother's body shook. "*Alhamdulillah, Alhamdulillah,*" her mother prayed as she held her.

Soon, her father, grandma, and even her aunts and uncles, crowded over her, each one taking turns to give her tearful hugs and kisses. Mira had never felt so loved. She had never felt fuller than she did at that moment. "It's a miracle," they called. "Praise be to God."

Mira's grandmother approached her. "Come, Mira. Let me look at you," Jida said, embracing her with shining eyes. "Praise be to God. It is truly a miracle," she whispered, her weak limbs shaking as she held her.

Her Baba picked her up, and she clung to him as he led her away from the excited crowd. "That is enough," he called. "My daughter must rest and eat."

As they entered her home, Mira was greeted by her twin brothers, who rushed into her arms. "Mira, you're back!" they both cried in joy. Mira held her brothers, feeling her eyes water. She hadn't realized how much she missed the twins. "We thought you were dead!"

"Ali said you were probably eaten by *jinns* and Hassan hit him," Azule told her, looking at Hassan who was sporting a black eye.

"He deserved it," Hassan grumbled.

"That's enough, you two," Mama scowled, grabbing Mira's hand and leading her to their stone house. Mama began removing her tattered dress, her hands shaking. Mira swallowed the lump in her throat, unable to speak, and just watched silently as Mama poured water from the large clay vase into a bathtub. She sat Mira in the small, wooden tub, skillfully pouring the cool water over her sand-crusted hair.

Mama grabbed a rag and began cleaning the layers of dirt off Mira's legs, arms and body. Mama held Mira's hand in her own, using the cloth to remove the dirt from her fingernails. Then, she brought the wet rag to Mira's face; eyes bright with tears, she placed a hand on her cheek.

"Mama," Mira whispered, her own tears falling down her face. She didn't realize how much she truly missed her mother's warmth.

"Oh, *habibti*," Mama sobbed, hugging Mira close to her. Mama sobbed even more. "My daughter, my life…" Mira held Mama close, her heart bursting with longing and love. Mama had always been stern, apprehensive. She hadn't seen her mother break down like this since the day she was brought home from the *Sahir*.

"I'm okay, Mama. Please don't cry," Mira told her.

She was tired and homesick, but Mira was happier than she had been in a long time, despite it all. Mama nodded, placing two tear-soaked kisses on Mira's cheeks, then began tackling her matted hair.

After Mira had been scrubbed dry and placed in a clean dress, Mama swallowed, suddenly anxious. She leaned down at eye level, her hand on her face. "Mira," mama licked her lips nervously. "How did you survive, my daughter?"

Mira thought about Ayub and her promise not to reveal him. She then thought about the *Sahir* as fear entered her heart. Mira shook her head, suddenly afraid. What would she tell everyone? How should she explain her time in the desert? "I-I…" Mira was unable to speak, the words lodged in her throat.

Mama placed a comforting hand on her cheek. "Shhh, it's okay. I won't let anyone hurt you. I won't let anyone take you from me."

Mira thought about the day her mother had dressed her in her finest dress and told her Baba was taking her somewhere special. She tried not to think about the horror she felt when she realized her Mama knew. Her Mama knew Baba was taking her to the *Sahir*. Mira blinked, forcing the resentment down. But Mama loved her. She didn't know what the *Sahir* would do to her. She nodded, not trusting her voice, and Mama gave her a gentle squeeze.

It was mid-afternoon when Mira emerged from the stone house, thoroughly scrubbed. Besides a few scrapes and sunburns, she was fine. Mama led her to the courtyard where the twins, Baba, her grandmother and her baby sister, Sara, waited for them. "I finally got rid of those gossiping fools," her grandmother scowled.

"Jida," Mira said, clinging to her grandmother, missing her earthy smell, grateful that she wouldn't have to face any more curious neighbors. Jida's wrinkly face looked even older; dark circles under her usually bright and happy eyes. "My child! Miriam, bring the girl some food. She must be starving," Jida told her mother, examining her body. "I've missed you so much Mira. I prayed day and night for your return. My beloved granddaughter." Jida embraced her tightly. Mira swallowed the lump in her throat overcome with happiness.

Her father gave her a curious look, bouncing her baby sister on his knee. "Sara," Mira whispered, embracing her baby sister who cooed and hugged her back.

"Come," Baba said, sitting her next to him. The twins squeezed between them, chattering while their mother prepared a quick meal of sheep milk, dates and porridge.

Mira grinned, for once, not complaining about the porridge and wolfing it down. "Mira, how did you escape the evil *jinn* that took you into the desert? Did you have to fight it off," Hassan asked with a twinkle in his eye. Mira choked on her milk.

"Hassan!" her father scolded.

"What! That's what Ali said. He said Mira was kidnapped by *jinns*."

"I wasn't kidnapped! I got lost," Mira frowned.

"Enough, we are not discussing this," her father said, ending the conversation. Mama nervously avoided her eyes, and her grandmother muttered a prayer. Mira tried to ignore the strange feeling in her stomach and tried to enjoy the rest of the late afternoon with her family.

6.

The next morning, her home was bustling with more activity than she had *ever* seen. Family after family came by their small home to pay their respects. Each family brought small gifts of dates, butter, milk or wool with them—whatever they could afford to give. They would mutter prayers and gawk excitedly at Mira as if she were some sort of miracle.

Mira felt uncomfortable at the impromptu celebration. This was the most interesting thing that had happened in their village in years. Though she understood their curiosity, she just wanted to be alone with her family. She just wanted things to go back to normal. The women in her family were busy serving milk and dates, while her father chatted with the men of the village. The whole time, Mira was forced to sit with them in the courtyard, accepting their *salaam* and grateful prayers, while all the other children played.

Mira was enjoying a toffee date gifted by one of her neighbors when, suddenly, there was a commotion in the crowd. People gasped and whispered as they parted ways. She looked up and froze, her heart tightening with fear.

Making his way through the crowds was the *Sahir*. He looked just as Mira had remembered him—not that his was a face she would ever forget. Her father stiffened next to her, and his companions frowned. She was no longer basking in the bright mid-morning sun. She was no longer with family and neighbors celebrating her return. She was transported back to the dark house of the *Sahir*.

Mira struggled against the chains at her feet. The air in his small stone home was thick, making it difficult to breathe. It smelled like strange herbs mixed with oil incense, and the stone walls were blackened with smoke. There was a small table lined with jars of spices, and a hanging rope with dried meat, and three beheaded chickens, their blood dripping into the bowls underneath. Splat, splat, splat. *She held her ears to block out the sound.*

The Sahir *was at the table, humming softly as he crushed something in the stone bowl. He poured water into the bowl and mixed it with the herbs.* "Drink!" *he demanded, extending the bowl to her. Mira pushed herself deeper into the wall as the shadows began clawing at her once more. The* Sahir *sighed. He gripped her tightly by the hair, forcing her mouth to the bowl. Mira's eyes watered as her scalp exploded in pain.*

"Open your mouth now!" His dark eyes were bright with warning. Mira whimpered and gagged as he poured the bitter, thick drink down her throat.

Mira coughed, feeling sick. "Do not throw up. I will make you drink more," he cautioned. She forced the bile back, tears streaming down her face. The Sahir *lit an incense and began chanting incantations in a strange language that didn't quite sound like Arabic.*

The shadows danced, growing in size as he sang, clawing at her mind and her body. She felt them seeping through her pores. Mira felt sick. She cried out, balling herself on the ground in a fetal position. She was lightheaded and dizzy, and the shadows kept clawing at her mind. She felt the darkness as they whispered. "No, no, no," Mira moaned with the little energy she had left.

Mira's skin prickled, as if she were being poked with a thousand needles, her heart pounded, and her head felt like it was about to explode. "Stop!" she screamed. And, just like before, the shadows slithered away, and Mira sagged with relief.

Mira blinked, feeling suddenly cold. The man who haunted her nightmares glared at her with open hostility. The shadows danced around him, cloaking him in a dark aura. "Fools," the *Sahir* spat, looking around the astonished crowd.

"Nasir, welcome…" her father stood. Mira still could not move, frozen with fear and assaulted with memories of her time with the *Sahir*. She felt the beatings and the hot coal on her feet, the bitter drink and shadows constantly trying to break her—to take her mind and bend her to his will. Mira remembered her father's shocked face when he finally came for her, her small, thin, battered body unable to move.

The *Sahir* calmly explained that he had to beat and starve the *jinns* out of her. Mira replayed her mother's horrified cries in her mind, and the guilty kindness her family had shown her in the weeks after her arrival.

"You invite a devil into your home and call it family?" the *Sahir* accused, cutting off her father.

Mira shivered as her mother suddenly ran to her side, pulling her close. She snapped out of her haze as she took in the scene that was unfolding before her. Gone was the festive atmosphere, the air now thick with apprehension. "Everyone, please, it's late and my daughter is tired—" her mother began.

"That *thing*," the *Sahir* interrupted, pointing his boney finger at Mira, "is not your daughter." The air filled with audible gasps. "That thing is not even *human*!"

"Nasir, please. Let us speak privately," her father pleaded as he approached the *Sahir*.

"Everyone should hear this, Abu Hassan. Everyone should know what walked into our peaceful village yesterday. How can a child survive for seven days and seven nights in the desert, while our livestock dies from drought?"

Mira's mother stiffened. "Allah provided for her, just as He provides for us all," she challenged.

The *Sahir* laughed, and his shadows danced as if laughing along with him. "Is that what it told you, Miriam?" he said, and her mother sputtered. "Tell us, child," he turned his attention to her. "How did Allah provide for you? Did He send provisions from the sky?"

Mira balked as, suddenly, every eye in the village was on her. She didn't know what to say, or how to explain herself. Her eyes watered as she clung to her mother.

"Do not be fooled by its tears. Look at it! Seven days in the desert with no food or water, and she returned fatter and healthier than when she left!"

Murmurs erupted as the villagers stared in suspicion. The same villagers who were smiling and calling her a blessing just moments ago, now looked at her with fear and suspicion.

"*That's enough!* You need to leave my home, now," her father demanded, his hand on the tilt of the small ceremonial sword he carried on his belt.

The *Sahir* held his hands up. "Do not be fooled, people. That is *not* our daughter who has returned from the desert. That is a *jinn* who has taken over her body. It's a devil, sent here to deceive us so we deviate from God's blessing. If we allow it to live amongst us, we surely will be cursed." The people gasped in fear, whispering prayers.

"Leave now! All of you. Get out of my home!" her father bellowed, his sword now in his hand.

The *Sahir* was already walking out. "I've just come to warn you." His final words drifted among the frightening crowd, who began walking out, casting fearful glances at Mira.

Mira's entire body was shaking in fear. Her mother still held her tightly until everyone slowly left, the mood fully dampened. "Superstitious fools," her grandmother muttered.

"It's okay; you're okay," her mother whispered into her hair. The twins sat subdued. For once, the only sounds came from the senseless babbling of her clueless little sister.

Baba was in a dangerous mood, his face dark as he sulked silently not to be approached. Mira did her best to avoid him for the rest of the day. She ignored the arrival of her uncles and family elders. Instead, her mother took her away from the rising arguments. Mira sat with her brothers, who, innocently, tried to lift her mood, talking about Abu Issa's new camel, and how they watched it give birth to a calf. Mira wasn't listening. She was afraid. Afraid that the people really believed what the *Sahir* said. Afraid that she would have to go back to his home.

"You don't look like a *jinn*," Azule finally commented, snapping her out of her endless tornado of thoughts.

"That's the point," Hassan countered, rolling his eyes.

Mira glared at them both. "Shut up," she snapped.

They had the decency to look ashamed. "Sorry," they grumbled.

But Mira had enough of their company. She left them and went to look for her mama. Mama and her grandmother were sitting near the fire pit. Her mother was rolling out dough while her grandmother slapped them inside the stone pit. Mama gave Mira a small smile. They hadn't yet talked about what happened that morning. "Do you need help, Mama," she asked, wanting to be useful.

"Mira offering to do chores. Maybe she really is a *jinn*," her Jida jokes. Mira balked as her grandmother chuckled softly. "Now, child, I may be old, but I have more sense than those superstitious fools. And I think I'd recognize my favorite granddaughter anywhere." Mira smiled.

"Come, you can help me knead the dough," Mama said, shifting over and making room for her. Mira's smile grew and she sat next to her mama, kneading the sticky dough before making it into a small ball and handing it to Mama to flatten. Mira tried to ignore the rumbling of her father and uncles' angry voices, knowing she was likely the cause of their argument. Mira swallowed, her hands shaking as she kneaded the dough. Her Jida sang an old Arabic nursery rhyme that her mother had sung to her when she was younger. Mama joined in the song, and Mira smiled, joining in, as well.

Once the dough was finished, mama cut vegetables for soup, and they prepared for dinner. Her uncles and father had left to go to the mosque for prayer, and Mama lit the oil lanterns around the terrace and set up for dinner.

Baba arrived shortly after with three men by his side. His face was grim as Mama quickly stood, pulling Mira to her feet. Mira recognized the men. They were their tribe's elders, and the leaders of the village.

"*Assalamu alaikum,*" Mama welcomed. "We were just about to have dinner. Please, join us." The men gave her a curt nod and sat cross-legged on the mats. Baba sat opposite them as Mama offered food and milk. The men declined, and Mama paled. Even Mira knew it was a grave insult to decline food as a guest.

Her grandmother scowled at the men. "Afraid you will catch something," Jida huffed, offended at their blatant disrespect for their customs.

Baba shot his mother a warning look. "Please, forgive my mother," he apologized. "She forgets her place sometimes."

"I forget nothing, and I will not be insulted in my own home. What crime have we committed other than embracing our daughter, whom God has returned to us?" Jida retorted.

"Perhaps it'd be best if the women went in the house and let the men speak," one of the elders finally suggested. He was the eldest of the three, his beard bright orange with henna. He had a red turban, worn only by tribal elders, and his face was stern.

"Perhaps your mother should have taught you some manners," Jida snapped.

"Miriam, take my mother and the children to the house," her father ordered. Mama nodded, taking Mira's hand.

"The girl will stay," the man said coolly, eyeing Mira suspiciously.

Mama's hand tightened around Mira's, and Baba's hands balled into fists as he gave a curt nod to Mama. Mama hesitated before letting go of her hand and walking away from the courtyard with Jida. Mira sat next to her father; her hands folded in her lap. She stared at the ground as her heart pounded with fear and apprehension.

"It seems you have caused quite a commotion in the village today, child," the man spoke. Mira looked at her father, but he didn't look at her. His hard eyes didn't leave the men in front of them.

"I'm sorry, *Sheikh*," Mira finally apologized, not knowing what to say. She didn't mean for any of this to happen.

"Tell us, child, how did you manage to survive in the desert? Even an experienced rider wouldn't have made it seven days without food or water, so how did a young girl not only survive, but find her way back home?"

Mira's hands shook. She was at a loss for words. How was she supposed to explain what happened without getting in trouble? "Allah provided substance for her. Is He not the best of providers?" her father answered on her behalf.

"Allah provides, but one must also tie his camel."

"She doesn't remember much of her time in the desert. She was disoriented and had a serious case of sun sickness when she arrived. You can't expect her to remember everything when she is just a child," her father defended.

Mira closed her eyes, wishing everyone would just disappear, wishing she never went into the desert that day.

"Come now, Ali, we know your daughter has been haunted by *jinns* since she was born. We all warned you when we saw her eyes. We know you took her to every *Imam* in the village to be exercised. And we know you left her with the *Sahir* to be cured. If the devil did not already touch her, then why would you do all that?"

Her father's jaw ticked at the mention of the *Sahir*. "That was a mistake. I should have never taken her to the *Sahir*."

Mira gave her father a startled look. It was the closest thing to an apology she had ever gotten from him after he left her there, all alone. "The *Sahir* tells us he couldn't help her, and that you took your daughter back before he could completely rid the *jinns* from her body."

"He was tormenting her!" her father snapped, losing his cool. "It was a mistake. My daughter is not possessed, nor was she ever," her father said more calmly. The men didn't look convinced.

"These are difficult times already, Ali. Our wells are drying up, our livestock is dying. For the last three years, our harvest of dates was barely enough to trade at the bazaar. The people are worried, and rightfully so. To invite a *jinn* amongst us would only invoke more calamity to our tribe. We can't risk it. The devil deceives, Ali. I know you wish to believe that this is your daughter that clings to your hand and calls you *Baba*, but we believe that it is a *jinn*. You know it yourself; nobody survives the desert." The other men nodded in agreement.

"As you said, *Sheikh*, the devil deceives. Perhaps you are now being deceived. You take the word of a *Sahir* over the word of a father. You are wrong. I know my daughter. I will not be fooled. Please, *Sheikh*, you must understand. I am a father. I spent the last seven nights praying for my daughter to return, and Allah has answered. Would you question your Lord's mercy? Is it not possible for Allah to answer the prayers of a father? Do you not remember the story of Prophet Yusuf, whose brothers cast him in a well? His father prayed for years, and Allah finally answered his prayers. Could my Lord not answer the prayer of his servants?"

Abu Sufyan cleared his throat, shuffling at Baba's passionate speech. "I understand this is hard for you to accept, Ali. I, too, am a father, but just as the Lord is capable of mercy, the devil is capable of deceit. He fooled our Father, Adam, and cast him from heaven. We all see the devil's deceit, ya Ali. You are blinded by fatherly love."

"Then what would you have me do? Castaway my daughter?" her father snapped, slamming his fist on the ground.

The men exchanged glances. "We sought counsel from the *Sahir* on how to rid ourselves of this evil. He says the drought and our tribe's misfortune are all because we ignored the wicked child born to our tribe. We ignored the warning, so God has sent a message. And we must cleanse ourselves of this evil, the way our forefathers did."

"What is that supposed to mean?" Baba's voice was quiet.

Abu Sufyan cleared his throat. "You must bury it in the desert. The dirt will cleanse it and the soul of your daughter will be released into heaven." Mira frowned in confusion, not understanding the conversation, but watching closely as Baba paled. Mira heard a pained shout from her mother, who was listening to their conversation.

"Have you gone mad? That practice was cursed by our prophet—by Allah, Himself—how could you ask of me something so abhorrent?"

Abu Sufyan's mouth thinned. "Your daughter is gone, Ali. We are asking you to bury the evil that plagues your home and save our village from further misfortune." His face softened. "She is just a girl, Ali. Do this and God will bless you with many sons."

"No," her Baba declared firmly. "I cannot, and *will not*, do what you are asking."

Abu Sufyan's face hardened. "If you refuse, Ali, then you and your entire family will be cast out of our tribe, cast out from our protection. You will enter the desert. Will you risk your entire family for one daughter who is already lost to the *jinns?*"

Her father flinched, and Mama quietly sobbed. Mira didn't know what to do. She didn't understand what was happening. Why were they doing this to her? Why were they making her mother cry and her father angry?

"Please, Abu Sufyan. You can't do this. Let us visit the *Imams*, not the *Sahir*. They can examine my daughter. I read the holy verses on her myself, and she did not react. If she were a devil, wouldn't it burn her?"

Abu Sufyan's mouth was grim, his face hard. It was obvious his mind was made even before he had even entered their home. "We have made up our mind, Ali. You have three days to bury the devil or leave." Abu Sufyan stood, judgment was passed, and his companions stood with him.

"Abu Sufyan, please. I beg you! Don't ask me to do this," her father clung to the older man's thobe.

Abu Sufyan gave her father a disgusted look, his companions equally as merciless. "You have three days," he said, pulling his garment from her father's desperate hands and walking out into the dark.

Mira didn't know what to do. Her father lay prostrated on the ground, not moving. Mama came running to her father's side, holding him as he quietly sobbed. Mira was heartbroken seeing her parents so devastated, all because of her. Maybe the villagers were right. Maybe she *was* cursed. Why else would she bring so much misery to her family?

Mira didn't notice when her Jida entered the courtyard, grabbing her frozen body. "Come, child," she said, pulling Mira to her feet. Jida led her into the stone house. The twins and her baby sister were already asleep, oblivious to all that had just happened. Jida tried to feed Mira, but she couldn't eat. So, Jida just held her.

"Jida, what will happen to me?" she whispered.

"Nothing, my child. Nothing will happen to you. Your father loves you. He will not listen to the demands of demented old men." Mira closed her eyes, listening to the calm and rhythmic breath of her sleeping sibling, desperately wanting to believe her.

7.

Mira woke up the following morning to the sounds of her twin brothers playing. For a moment, she fooled herself into believing the previous day had been a horrible dream. But the tension was thick amongst the adults. Mira hadn't seen her father the entire day. Her mother and Jida went about their chores with quiet dismay, neither of them talking much. When her father finally arrived later that evening, she knew whatever he had been doing, didn't get him the results he had hoped for.

His face was stormy, and his body rigid with anger. Jida quietly took Mira away when he arrived, leading her into the stone house. "Is Baba angry with me?" Mira whispered into the dark room after her siblings had fallen asleep.

Her Jida affectionately stroked her hair, "No, *habibti*, he is not angry with you." Jida tried to reassure her, but Mira wasn't so sure.

The next morning, Mira was awoken by a commotion outside the stone house. She could hear her parents arguing and her mama crying. Mira's eyes widened as her Jida entered the small house, pulling Mira close to her. Her father wasn't far behind.

"Please, Ali. Do not do this. Forget this wicked place. Allah will provide for us, just as he provided for our daughter." Mama was crying and clinging to her father's thobe. Mira felt her heart thundering against her chest as her sobbing Jida held her tight, muttering prayers.

Her father's face was filled with quiet rage as his gaze landed on Mira. He painfully pulled her arm, forcing her away from her Jida's clutches. "No!"

Mama screamed, trying to pull Mira away from him. "Do not do this, Ali. You will damn your soul. You will damn us all," her mother clung to his feet, begging him to stop.

"We are already damned!" her father screamed, kicking away her mother. "We were damned the day she was born and opened those cursed eyes!" Mira flinched as his words penetrated her heart. All her fears, all her insecurities about her place in this family were laid bare by her father's angry confession. Her insecurities about her strange eyes and her strange ability were finally put into words.

Mira felt cold, the tears instantly drying in her eyes. She felt numb as her father pulled her away from her sobbing mother who was held by her Jida. Her brothers were crying, as well, holding a hysteric Sara, probably frightened from all the yelling. Mira didn't want this. She didn't want her family to be broken apart and destroyed, all because of her. All because she was born cursed.

The villagers all watched with barely concealed contempt as her father took her away. She didn't fight him, too detached from everything that had happened. The very people she grew up with—the people she had known her entire life—just stared as she was sentenced to death. Some watched wide-eyed as her father carted her away into the desert, some averted their eyes in shame, and others spat on her and cursed as she passed.

Baba didn't loosen his grip on her arm as he guided her away through the village, past her favorite tree where she had enjoyed her secret treats, and past the sparse, grazing land where she took their sheep and told them stories. Mira felt resigned from it all, like an imposter who was finally exposed as a fraud. Baba led her deep into the desert until the village was a long-distance away. She was so numb that she didn't even notice the shovel in his other hand as he sat her down under another shadeless tree.

The last time Mira sat under a tree in the hot sun, she was wishing and praying to find her way home, back with her family. Now, she was wishing she had died in the desert. Mira hugged her knees close to her, trying not to think about her mother's sobs, Jida's heartbroken face as she held her mother, the fear in her twin brother's eyes, and the shameless hatred in the faces of the villagers she had grown up with. Mira rocked her body back and forth.

The only sound she heard was that of metal hitting the earth, and her father's laborious breathing as he dug a hole in the ground—a hole in which he would bury Mira.

But maybe it wouldn't be such a bad thing, she thought. Maybe her elders were right. Maybe the earth would purify her, and when she was cured, her father would come for her and take her back home. Mira held onto that thought like a man dying of thirst holds onto water.

"Mira! Mira!" the sound of her name being called startled her. Her father was still digging the hole, now near his calves. She looked around. In the distance, she spotted Ayub.

"Ayub?" Mira whispered; her voice hoarse.

Ayub inched closer, shooting nervous glances at her father who was still digging. "Are you okay? I was waiting for you and you never came," Ayub said, his eyes filled with concern. Mira's throat tightened at the sight of her friend. Despite everything, she was still happy to see him. Even though Ayub was terrified at being so close to any human other than her, he still came to check on her.

Mira nodded slowly, not wanting her friend to worry. She glanced nervously at her father, but he wasn't paying any attention to her. His clothes were caked with dirt from digging, and his brows glistened with sweat. Ayub frowned, flinching as her father grunted. He looked like he was fighting the urge to flee from the human who was so close. But he didn't. Instead, he sat a few inches behind her, and they fell into a comfortable silence.

"You should leave," Mira finally whispered, barely moving her lips. She didn't want him to witness what was about to happen. She was scared and slightly embarrassed. She had told Ayub endless stories about her village, her family and her father. But she only told him good things. She told him how her father would lift her on his shoulders so she could see the traditional sword dance on Eid, and how he would chase her around the courtyard, pretending to be a wolf. She told him about how she would climb on his back as he prayed, and the sweets he brought her every Friday from the village market after he returned from Friday prayer. She didn't tell him about the man who left her with the *Sahir* to be tortured—the man who didn't look back as she sobbed for him to save her. She didn't tell him about her father who wouldn't look at her for months after he finally took her back.

She only told Ayub good things, and, now, he was about to witness her father's stony face, digging his daughter's grave. Mira was embarrassed. However, Ayub didn't laugh at her like the other children at the village. He didn't curse her like the villagers did as her father pulled her away. He didn't call her a hypocrite and a liar.

"I'm not leaving you, Mira," he whispered. "You're my best friend. My clan threw me in a well and you saved me. I'm not leaving you, even if we have to be buried together."

Mira felt the numbness fade away as her eyes filled with tears. "He'll come back for me," she whispered. "Once I'm cured, he will take me back home."

"I know," Ayub whispered back. "But I'll still stay with you until he returns. You can tell me more stories while we wait."

"Will you tell me about the ocean again?" Mira whispered. Ayub nodded happily, excited to share his knowledge. "The ocean is huge!" Ayub chattered away. Mira found herself smiling at her friend as he spoke.

Suddenly, Ayub flinched, fearfully fleeing into the desert so quickly that he was gone in a blink. She frowned and saw her father climbing out of the hole he had dug. He threw the shovel on the ground and headed for her with a determined look.

Mira felt her body trembling as her father reached for her, pulling her to her feet. He lifted Mira into his arms, leading her to her grave. Mira didn't struggle. Her heart was heavy. She peered at her father, his face caked with dirt and his usually shiny black beard that he always brushed and oiled, was brown with dust and tiny rocks.

Without thinking, Mira lifted an arm to wipe the dust from her father's beard. Her father stumbled, catching himself. She hated seeing him so upset, and she blamed herself. She was a curse upon her family. Her father closed his eyes, his nostrils flaring as his jaw ticked. He reached out, pulling Mira's hand away from his beard, and lowered himself into the hole. Mira swallowed the lump in her throat as she looked around the dark grave her father dug for her. No matter how much she tried to convince herself that he would come back, she was afraid he wouldn't.

Mira blinked. Ayub was already in the hole, curled up in the far corner, shaking with fear as he waited for her, just as he promised. And, suddenly, Mira wasn't so afraid anymore. At least she wouldn't be alone.

Her father still held her, the emotion on his face warring. He looked so hopeless that Mira felt her heart break. "It's okay, Baba," she whispered, trying to console him. "I'm not afraid. I don't want to hurt you and Mama anymore."

Her father let out a strangled sound and let go of her wrist that he was holding so tight it bruised her. A single tear fell from his eye as he stared out into the desert. Mira reached her hand to her Baba's face to wipe his tears.

"I'll get better," she continued, her own tears falling from her eyes. "I'll get better, and then you'll come back, won't you, Baba? You'll come back for me when I'm better, then everyone will forgive me."

A loud sob wrenched from her father's chest as he fell to his knees in the grave he dug for his daughter, more tears falling from his eyes. "Don't cry, Baba, I'm sorry. I-I'm sorry I was born cursed." Mira hugged her father. She was afraid he wouldn't come back, despite what she told Ayub.

"No, no, no," her father sobbed, pulling Mira to his chest. His body shook with grief. "My daughter, what have I done? What have I done? May God strike me. Please forgive me, my daughter. Forgive me, my Lord," her father wailed. Mira could barely breathe as her father clung to her as if the devil himself would rip her from his arms. "Forgive me, forgive me, Ya Allah."

Mira didn't know how long her father held her. She didn't know how long they sat in the grave as he clung to her; eventually, emotionally exhausted, Mira fell asleep in her father's arms.

***

Mira's heart quickened as consciousness tugged at her, pulling her from sleep. She squeezed her eyes shut, wanting to return to a state of slumber where she was at peace. She was afraid of what she would find once she opened her eyes. Mira wiggled one toe, then another. *Shouldn't the dirt feel heavy?* All she felt was a hot breeze. The memories of the previous day came flooding back, the guests smiling and giving gifts and well wishes. The *Sahir's* bold accusation. Her breath quickened as she remembered how quickly everyone had turned on her. Then, her father dragged her out into the desert to bury her, to "cleanse her of her curse," as the elders of her tribe had put it.

After a few minutes of heavy breathing, Mira finally dared to slowly open her eyes. She blinked, her surroundings finally coming into focus. She flattened her hand on the thin, straw mat. She looked around at the heavy clay vases that held water, the small stone walls, and the dried palm leaf roof.

She was at home. *Home.* Mira let out the breath she didn't realize she was holding. Her father had not left her; he brought her back home. The wooden door cracked open and the bright sun filtered into the dreary room.

Mira squinted her eyes while her mother rushed in, coming to her side.

"*Habibti*, you're awake?" Mama pulled Mira onto her lap, crushing her into her chest. "I knew your Baba would do the right thing," she whispered. Mira held onto her mother. She was so sure her father was going to leave her in the desert, but he hadn't.

"What's going to happen, Mama?" Mira whispered, remembering what the elders had said—the ultimatum they gave her father.

Mama swallowed audibly. "Baba went out. He is trading our sheep for a camel, and we will leave this place." Mira froze. She couldn't believe she and her entire family were being forced to leave their village, their tribe, the only home they have ever known, and all because of her recklessness.

"Will we be okay, Mama?" Mira whispered, remembering how hard it was for her to survive in the desert. If it hadn't been for Ayub, she would probably be dead. But Ayub couldn't help them this time. Her family didn't know about him, and they didn't know how she survived. Mira suspected they knew *something* had helped her, but they didn't want to know, choosing ignorance over the fact that their daughter had a cursed gift.

Mama sighed, her hands trembling slightly as she caressed Mira's hair. "Allah doesn't burden a soul with more than it can bear. He will provide for us, my daughter. I truly believe that. We will be okay. Just have faith."

"But this is all my fault, Mama." Mira's voice broke as she finally admitted the truth that had been weighing heavily on her heart. She had done this to them. She had uprooted them; if anything happened, Mira would never forgive herself.

"Shhh, it's just a test. Our lord tests His servants, Mira. We will get through this. Now, come, we have a lot to do." Mama stood, pulling Mira to her feet. Mira wiped the tears from her eyes, sniffling. Despite what her mother had said, she still felt responsible.

Mira, her mother and grandmother spent the rest of the morning in a flurry of activity. There was so much to do, and Mira was happy about the chores, for once, because it kept her mind off everything that had happened the last few days. Jida slaughtered an entire goat, and Mira had to force herself not to steal a bone for Ayub as her grandmother dried meat and figs. Mama washed and dusted and organized all their humble belongings. No one entered their courtyard. No one came to check on them.

Just the day before, the entire yard was full of gawking neighbors and nosy aunties, delivering presents and well wishes, but now, everyone avoided them—even their own extended family.

Nobody came to inquire about what had happened. Nobody offered help or charity. They were cursed. A plague to the village. They probably even blamed Mira for the drought. But because of yesterday's activities, her family had a lot of provisions that would otherwise have been impossible to prepare on such short notice.

Baba returned sometime in the late afternoon looking exhausted. His turban covered his face in shame. With him was a small she-camel, who lazily trailed behind Baba as he led her to a tree with a rope and tied her. He removed the turban from his face. His eyes were red and his face tired. "This is all you could find?" Mama asked, unimpressed by the camel.

Baba scowled. "Nobody would trade with me. Abu Sufyaan finally agreed to give me this small camel in exchange for all our sheep."

Mama frowned in disgust. "After everything we have done for these people, this is how they treat us? May Allah curse them."

"Miriam!" Baba scolded. "We made our choice. We will leave the rest to God. At least this she-camel will provide us with milk on our journey." Mira scurried away, not wanting to hear more of that conversation. She went to her grandmother who was crushing wheat in between the stone slabs. Mira sat next to her, silently watching as her grandmother's expert hands crushed the wheat until it was powder.

"I was born in this village, as was my father and his father," Jida finally spoke, breaking the silence. "I gave birth to your father in this very home. I have never left this village, nor have my children. I know you are scared, but you were always too big for this village, too curious, too smart for your own good. And now you get to leave this place, see something different, build new roots, and, perhaps, even see more of the world."

Mira frowned. She hadn't thought about it like that. It was true. If this didn't happen, Mira would probably spend her entire life here, just like her mother and grandmother. She would get married; her husband's family would build her a stone house somewhere in the village. She would bear children, cook and do all the domestic chores. She knew that would be her life, and she never questioned it or dared to dream of anything bigger. She thought about the caravans that stopped in their village and the stories they told about large cities and oceans.

There was an entire world out there beyond the desert. Mira felt the familiar burn of adventure stir in her heart—the very burn that lured her out, deeper and deeper into the desert, until she finally got lost in it and started this mess. And for once in her life, she didn't know what her future had in store, and she was scared, but underneath that fear was exhilaration.

"Will you come with us?" Mira asked instead, not wanting to admit her dark desires. Her grandmother gave her a sad smile. "The desert is no place for an old woman," she said.

Mira felt her heart break. She knew her grandmother couldn't make it in the desert, and she had plenty of aunts and uncles who would take her in, but the idea of possibly never seeing her Jida again shattered Mira's very being all over again.

"I don't want to leave you," Mira cried.

"And I don't want you to leave, but we must each accept our destiny. This is God's will, Mira. It is not for us to understand, only to accept." Mira thought about her Jida's words as feelings of guilt and excitement formed in her heart. Despite everything, Mira was relieved to leave the village she always felt like an imposter in and forge a new destiny.

***

That night, her uncles arrived. Their faces were cold as they quietly spoke with her father. Mira would never forget how they tried to convince her father into burying her alive, shaming him for not having the strength to do so. They frowned, shooting Mira a look of disgust as they escorted her grandmother out of their home.

"Get your hands off me, you worthless dogs! You spineless cowards! Do you just watch as your brother—your blood—is exiled and thrown out to die? Have you no shame!" Her grandmother struggled against them, cursing. "Leave me to die. I'd rather die than live with you!"

"Mama, please," her father pleaded. Baba got on his knees in front of his struggling mother, kissing her hands and placing them on his forehead.

"My son, you do not deserve this. Allah will curse this village for their ignorance." Her grandmother was now crying. "How could they do this to you? Ya Allah, how could they do this to my son?" Her grandmother wept.

Mira ran to her side, not caring whether her uncles were there, and not caring that they hated her. She held onto her weeping Jida, her frail body shaking as her bony hands wrapped around her. Her mother and the twins joined, and they all wept with their Jida until her uncles finally pulled her away.

8.

The air was thick with the promise of heat. It was just past dawn and the sky was an ombre display of bright pink and orange as the sun peaked from the horizon. There was a subdued sense of acceptance. Mira had not slept that entire night. Her heart was heavy with apprehension. Today, they were leaving their village, the place her family had called home for generations, the place she was supposed to spend her entire life.

Mira listened as the call to prayer rang out, breaking the silence of the night. She pretended to be asleep when her mother gently tapped her awake. Her father didn't go to the mosque that morning. It was the first time he hadn't attended the dawn prayer. Instead, he prayed at home with his family, then spent several minutes in prostration, his shoulders shaking slightly.

His beard was drenched with tears when he finally got up, his face grim. Mira pretended not to notice. There was no joy that morning. None of the usual flurries of activities ensued. Instead, they quietly washed up, ate breakfast and sat in silence, each lost in thought, staring off into the distance. Mira looked at the spot her grandmother used to occupy, her wrinkled fingers working the prayer beads that never left her hand. Mira didn't feel like eating anymore, but she knew she needed her energy, so she forced herself to swallow without tasting anything.

Only her baby sister, Sara, cooed with happiness as she enjoyed a date, blissfully unaware of the coming days. Sara was the only one who could make Mira smile anymore. She was the only one who didn't look at her in fear or with pity. Even her mother and grandmother sometimes looked at her in fear and resentment. They tried their best to hide it, but Mira could see it in their eyes.

After breakfast, Mira helped her mother pack up the rest of their belongings, they couldn't linger long. They had to leave before the afternoon sun. Traveling at peak noon would be impossible, and their time was up. The village elders were already outside their courtyard when they were ready, along with a small, murmuring crowd.

Their belongings were meager: a few straw mats, two wool blankets, a metal pot, and some wooden bowls. Her mother wrapped up their belongings in date leaves, along with wooden poles to build their temporary home in the desert. Baba then attached everything to the she-camel he bought using all their savings and livestock. One camel in the desert was worth more than a hundred sheep, and her milk would provide much-needed hydration.

Mama made them all wear leather socks to protect their feet from the hot sand before putting on their straw shoes. She created a sling on her back for Sara, and they met their father in the courtyard of their home. Mira swallowed as she gave her home one final look. The twins cried, clutching onto their father's thobe as he led his family away. The villagers gawked as Mira and her family traveled its narrow, gravel streets. Some neighbors turned their heads in shame, while others cursed them and spat on the ground once more as they passed.

"Keep your head up," Mama whispered, fiercely squeezing her hand. Mira raised her chin; she would not cower in front of them. They were silent as they passed their neighbors and friends. The people who they ate with, lived amongst and whose weddings they attended were all strangers now. No one came forward. No one said goodbye. No one offered any kind words. Instead, they just watched as her family walked in silence. Mira had strolled through this village a thousand times. She passed smiling neighbors, grumpy old men and scuffing children, but this time, everything and everyone felt foreign.

After what seemed like a lifetime, they finally made it to the edge of the village, near the Argan tree where she had spent endless afternoons. Mira's body came to a complete stop as the *Sahir* stepped in their path. Baba paused, pulling the rope of his she-camel as he glared at the *Sahir* who held up his hands, as if offering peace. The shadows that were always attached to him danced as they filtered like black smoke. She shuddered as her mother's grip tightened. The *Sahir* just smiled, his teeth white against his black beard and deeply tanned skin. His eyes were lined with the usual *kohl* and turban fitted on his head.

"Peace be upon you," he said, raising his hand to his heart. Baba didn't return the greeting which was an insult enough. The *Sahir* brushed it off "Ali, I'm very sorry it came to this, I know how much you love your family. And to be thrown out into the desert without the protection of your tribe..." the *Sahir* shook his head as if the sentence was too much to complete.

"What do you want?" her father demanded, not in the mood for his games.

"An offer of mercy. I understand how difficult it must have been. I don't imagine any father would be able to bury someone who looks like his daughter—"

"She is my daughter!" her father cut him off angrily. "And you know it very well. Don't think I don't know why you did this." Mira blinked in confusion. Was she missing something?

The *Sahir* smiled. "Yes, of course. I was very interested in your daughter's *unique* ability; however, my assessment of the *jinn* now claiming to be your daughter is true."

"You are a *Sahir*, who practices black magic. I was a fool to let you anywhere near my daughter." Her father clenched his hands into fists.

"Yet, you still brought her to be cured. You wanted to fix something that wasn't broken." The *Sahir* looked at her as he spoke, his eyes gleaming with the same obsessed possessiveness he had when he first saw her. "That is the past, I've come to make you an offer. Give me your daughter. I will make sure she is well-fed and taken care of. She will be my responsibility, my apprentice. I will raise her and you can visit whenever you like to check on her well-being."

Mira's heart dropped at his words. *No, please, no.* Mira stared at her Baba, begging him with her eyes as her mind flashed back to the day he left her, the day he walked away while she begged him not to.

"No!" her father's voice was firm and left no room for discussion.

"Don't be a fool, Ali! You and your entire family will perish. You will die out there. Give her to me. I will tell our elders that she is my responsibility. I will expel the *jinns* inside her."

Her father's face was deadly as he took a step closer to the *Sahir*. He grabbed him by the collar of his robe. "I said no the first time you asked, and

I'll say no again. You will never have my daughter. I will kill you before I allow you to ever lay another hand on her. Now, move out of my way." Her father shoved the *Sahir* back. The pleasant mask was erased from his face as his features darkened, the shadows dancing around him furiously. He recovered himself, smoothing down his robe. His eyes didn't leave Mira for even a moment as her father led them away into the desert.

***

The desert sun rippled off the golden dunes, distorting Mira's vision. It had been seven days since her family entered the unforgiving desert, tribeless and homeless. The first three days were the most difficult. Sara wouldn't stop crying and struggling against her mother's body, uncomfortable with the constraint of the sling and consistent heat. Her tired cries echoed through the desert, answered only by the screech of wild hawks that flew overhead, hunting for their prey.

The twins didn't stop complaining. They were always hungry, always thirsty and always tired, even though her mother fed them more than she should and gave them more water than they could spare. Their water skins had run out within the first five days. No matter how much they tried to pace themselves and ration their resources, the thirst was unquenchable. The drought had hit the desert harder than it did her tiny village. They were met with abandoned camps and empty wells. The nomads who once roamed this area, fled south to get water. The sparse vegetation, which camels and sheep once grazed, were gone, leaving only the skeletons of thorny bushes.

Now, they relied solely on their temperamental she-camel for milk; however, her udders were producing less and less milk each day. Sara didn't cry anymore, and that worried Mira more. Mama didn't drink or eat much—instead, gave most of her share to the twins. Her breasts were dry, without much milk to offer the baby. They had to stop multiple times a day because her mother was too weak and dehydrated to walk.

Mira didn't fare much better. Her lips were cracked and bleeding. Her feet were blistered within the leather socks. She constantly had to fight through the darkness that threatened to overwhelm her.

Baba didn't speak much. The only time he spoke was to tell them that they had to keep moving; however, every night, when they set up camp, she heard his tearful prayers. They wouldn't last much longer. Even Mira understood that. Soon, their she-camel would stop producing milk, and it didn't matter if they had food leftover; they would die from thirst.

Mira didn't see Ayub since that fateful night he offered to be buried with her. She supposed he could help her family; lead them to water or people, but she didn't dare seek him out. She didn't dare look for him. Even when Sara stopped crying, stopped eating, her body limp and her lips dry, she knew she couldn't ask him for help. She was too afraid. Too afraid to admit what her family already suspected, and too afraid they would think the villagers were right, that she was cursed, and all this was for nothing.

It was now high noon. Her father had stopped them all for the day. There were no trees to sit under, just a sea of red-orange dunes that stretched over the horizon. Baba built a make-shift tent, impaling four sticks into the sand, and covering the top with a wool tarp. It offered little shade, but her family still crowded under it, eager to receive a small reprieve from the scorching sun. Their she-camel stood nearby, lazily chewing on a small bush.

Baba finally joined them with a half-empty bowl of camel milk. Each time he brought the bowl of milk, its content was significantly lesser. "That's all?" Mama whispered; her voice hoarse. Her sun-soaked face was lined with dirt and she looked like she had aged years, not days. She was losing weight as her *abaya* hung looser. Sara slept in her lap. She slept a lot these last few days.

Baba's face was grim as he handed Mama the bowl. "That's all," he repeated, his voice resigned. Mama swallowed thickly, her hand shaking as she lifted the bowl to Sara's mouth, trying to coax her to drink.

"Drink, Sara, it's milk," Mira whispered to her sister, holding her mouth open. She stimulated her sister's throat urging her to swallow, and mama poured milk into her mouth. Sara coughed weakly, her eyes fluttering open before closing again. Mira sniffled, holding her sister's tiny hand. Hands that once firmly wrapped around hers now barely held on.

Mama offered milk to the twins who drank it greedily. She quickly removed the bowl from their mouth as they cried for more. Mira felt her heart twist at the sight of her exhausted brothers, the mischievous light, almost extinguished from their eyes. Mama then passed the bowl to Mira. There was barely any left for her, her father, and her mother, but she forced herself to take a large gulp, knowing her mother would not allow her to take less.

Mira gave her mother a weak smile and handed her the bowl. She placed the bowl to her lips, but Mira knew she was only pretending to drink. Mama hadn't drunk anything for the last two days. She passed the bowl to Baba who emptied its contents, unaware of Mama's deception. When Mira had confronted her mother the other night, she brushed her off, telling her she was drinking and eating as much as everyone else. However, later that night, she made Mira swear to watch over her brothers and sister, should anything happen to her. And Mira swore with a heavy heart. She swore to watch over her siblings.

Mama passed around the dried meat, figs and dates, and they ate in silence. Mira laid down on the sand next to her baby sister as they took their afternoon nap. She was slowly drifting off when she heard her parent's soft murmurs.

"We won't last another day, my wife," Baba confessed, his voice laced with sadness and pain. "The she-camel barely produces any milk, and if we don't find water soon…" Baba's voice broke.

"We will find something. Allah has not abandoned us. This is merely a divine test. You must have faith, *habibi.*"

"How can I have faith when my children are dying before my eyes? The drought has caused all the nomadic tribes to move south. We come across nothing but dried wells and abandoned settlements. Miriam, perhaps it's best we end things now before…"

Mira flinched as a sharp slap rang out. She slowly opened her eyes and saw her father's shocked face as he stared at her mother. "How dare you! How dare you even think such a thing!" she whispered furiously. "Have you so little faith, Ali?" Mama said, softly sagging in her father's arms as if the outburst had stolen all her energy. Her father held her tight, wrapping his arms around her weak form. "Promise me…promise me you will take them somewhere safe. Promise me you will not give up." Her voice was so low, that Mira had to strain her ears to hear. "I promise, my wife. I promise. Now, sleep."

Mira closed her eyes tight, stifling a sob. *Please*, she begged. *Please don't let my family die.*

9.

Mira woke up with a startle a few hours later. The twins were curled up next to each other, and her parents slept in each other's arms, their faces set grimly. Mira rolled over to peer at her baby sister. Mira felt her heart pound as she gently tapped her baby sister, who slept unmoving next to her. Her skin was cool to the touch, and she didn't look like she was breathing.

"Sara?" Mira whispered, shaking her a bit harder. She lifted her arm and let go quickly, somehow feeling an absence of life. "Sara!" she called louder with more alarm. Mira placed her head on Sara's chest "Sara!" she yelled, waking up the rest of her family.

Mama rushed to her side, pushing Mira out of the way. "No, no, no," she whispered as she picked up Sara's limp body, shaking her to wake up. Mira scuffled back, sobbing as her father approached, his face bleak. "My baby. *Hayati*. My life!" The twins ran over to where Mira sat paralyzed with grief, hugging her tight as they sobbed together. Mama's cries were quiet as she clutched onto Sara's body. She didn't need to say it. Nobody did. Their baby sister—the light of their family—was gone, and it was all because of Mira.

They buried Sara in the desert. Her father led the solemn prayer and her family picked up and kept moving. Mama was growing weaker. She tried to stay strong as the twins clung to her sides, but Mira noticed her hollowed breaths and sullen eyes. That night, as Baba tended to the fire, Mira sat near her mother, laying on her lap. Mama quietly ran her fingers through her matted hair, humming the song she sang to Mira when she was a baby.

"Maybe if I claw out my eyes, I won't be cursed anymore," Mira whispered after her Mama finished her song. She had thought about it so many times that, perhaps, having no eyes would be better than having eyes that were cursed. Eyes that saw that which shouldn't be seen. Eyes that caused people to be suspicious. Eyes that caused her baby sister to die. But Mira was always too scared. She couldn't imagine not seeing another sunset, not gazing up at the radiating moon, not seeing the face of her beautiful mother.

Mama gasped, whispering a prayer, holding Mira tightly against her chest in a burst of sudden strength. "Don't you ever say that again!" she said fiercely, then sunk into her bones, drained. "You didn't cry when you were born," Mama whispered wistfully. Mira blinked up at her. For the first time in days, her eyes were clear, and she looked almost peaceful.

"At first, I was worried something was wrong, then you opened those big, blue eyes. Everyone was shocked. We had never seen such color, and some villagers were convinced it was a bad omen. But then you stared into my eyes as if challenging me, and I knew I would die before I let anyone take you away. You always saw past everything, always asked so many questions, even if it got you in trouble," Mama chuckled to herself.

"I never wanted you to stop being curious, never wanted you to lose the light in your eyes, but then we took you to him…" Mama's voice trailed off as Mira wiped the stray tear from her eyes. "You stopped smiling after that. You stopped asking questions. Stopped being curious. I'm so sorry, *habibti*. I swore after that day that I would never let anyone take you from me. I would never let anyone hurt you, and I failed. Please, forgive me."

Mira didn't know what to say. That dark part of her heart—that unforgiving part that was angry and hurt at her mother for dressing her in a fine dress and sending her off to the *Sahir*—was finally happy to get an apology. "I forgive you, Mama. I love you."

Mama smiled sadly. "Forget all that happened Mira and be happy. Never allow anyone to ever make you feel like you are less than you are. You are powerful and those who sense it, fear your power. Promise me that you will not give up Mira, promise me you will find happiness where you can." Mira swallowed the lump in her throat as her tears cascaded down her cheeks. "I promise Mama," she whispered softly. Mira closed her eyes as her mother leaned down to place a gentle kiss on her right eye and then her left.

"Remember what I taught you Mira, never compare yourself to others, there is no comparison between the sun and the moon, each shine in its own time. And you, my dear, shine brightest of all. You are the light that guides my soul. I love you my sweet daughter and no matter what happens, I hope you never forget that. I pray that you will find happiness in this life, and I pray that I will get to be your mother again in paradise."

Mama did not wake up that morning; instead, joining her baby sister in the afterlife.

***

Mira's mouth felt like sandpaper. Their she-camel barely produced enough milk a day to hydrate one person. She could barely move as she lay under their makeshift tent, wondering who they would lose next. The twins slept, the signs of dehydration marking their darkened features. Their once bright and round faces were now sunken and dry. She used the ends of their turban to try and remove some of the grime from their faces.

Baba sat crossed-legged, chewing tobacco, his face unreadable. His turban was loosely wrapped, and his usual tidy appearance was haggard; his thobe caked in dirt, sand and sweat. The harsh lines on his sunbaked face were prominent, and his cheeks were hallowed. His usually trim beard was overgrown and lined with silver. Mira wanted to comfort him, but she didn't have the words nor the energy. Baba barely spoke since their mother passed two days ago. He set up their camp, built their fire, fed them and made them drink what little milk their she-camel could afford. Then, he sat by the fire and stared at it for hours. Mira turned away and snuggled protectively next to her brothers until she fell asleep.

Later that night, she woke up suddenly to a scuffling sound. Her eyes flew open and she stared into the dark fathomless eyes of her father as he loomed over her. She swallowed as she felt a cold, steel dagger upon her throat. This was the second time her father had tried to kill her.

Part of her wanted him to do it. The guilt and pain from losing her mother and Sara weighed heavily on her chest. But she promised Mama she would live. She promised Mama that she would forget all that happened and that she would be happy.

Baba stared into Mira's eyes, with a look of hopelessness and despair. "Forgive me, daughter," he whispered. "There is no other way."

"You promised Mama. You promised her that we would live. If you must kill me, at least save my brothers." Her father's hand shook as a sob broke free. He dropped the dagger and buried his face into his hands, his shoulders shaking uncontrollably.

"You are your mother's daughter. Her faith is all that kept us alive for this long," he said softly after a few minutes.

"We will live, Baba," Mira told him firmly. They would not die in this desert. They would live. Mira laid back down, the conviction strong in her thundering heart, and went back to sleep. To survive, she needed her strength. If Baba couldn't protect them, then she would make sure she and her brothers lived. She would never give up.

Mira woke up to the distant sound of hoofs. Baba was already in front of her and her brothers, his dagger raised protectively. Mira shielded her eyes from the setting sun as she stared out. There, on top of the dune, stood three men on horses, their heads tightly wrapped with turbans and their faces covered. Hope stirred in her heart as the men slowly approached their small tent. Mira and her brothers hid behind their father while he stood to greet the men.

"God is great! Peace be upon you!" her father greeted the men, his voice hoarse. The men stopped several feet away, their large horses huffing in annoyance. They stared them down. Their eyes were dark and lined with *kohl*, and their features indistinguishable. Baba licked his dry lips nervously when the men did not return his greeting, instead, inspecting their meager camp with an investigative look. "Please, my children have not had water in days," Baba pleaded with the men, gesturing toward them.

The men gazed at each other before one of them removed a water skin from the inside of his robes and tossed it at Baba's feet. "Thank you! Thank you!" Baba hurriedly grabbed the water and ran towards them. Kneeling, he opened the water skin and brought it towards the twins, who drank like camels, choking on the water in a desperate thirst. Mira patted their backs as Baba brought the water to her mouth. She took a giant gulp, not being thoughtful of others for once. The cold water felt like heaven against her sandpaper tongue and dry throat.

Once Mira had her fill, Baba brought the water to his dry lips and took a giant gulp. The men waited patiently, never once taking their eyes off them. Baba returned the water skin to the rider who threw it, thanking them again. The men still did not speak, watching them with guarded eyes. "My family and I have been lost in the desert for ten days. You are only here because of my dead wife's prayer. Please, for the sake of God, will you help us? We need water and direction to the nearest town or village."

The man in the middle who threw the water finally spoke. "There is no village, nor town, for miles. The drought has sent everyone away. There is nothing here."

Baba's shoulders sagged with every word. "Please, I already buried my wife and my baby. I cannot watch my sons and daughter die, too. I don't have much to offer you in terms of payment, but the reward of my Lord is vast."

The men looked at each other again. They couldn't refuse. Baba had invoked God's name, and they were honor-bound to help. "Come with us," the man finally spoke. "You can meet our *Sheikh*. He will decide what help we can offer your family."

"Thank you. By Allah, you will be rewarded ten folds for this charitable act!" The men grunted as Baba excitedly prepared their camel, the light of hope entering his dead eyes for the first time in weeks.

And in the distance, perched on top of the golden-red dunes, was Ayub, smiling brightly as he waved at Mira. It was him. He led these riders to them. For the first time in weeks, Mira felt a genuine smile form on her lips.

10.

The sky began darkening to a blue-black hue as the bright desert stars flickered above. In the distance, Mira spotted a small settlement nestled in between the towering dunes. Small fires lit up the sun-weathered tents scattered before them. Mira breathed a sigh of relief at the first sight of civilization in days. Baba whispered a prayer as the men led them into the Bedouin camp. The men didn't speak throughout the entire journey, silently guiding their horses forward.

Only a few people were still out who gave them curious glances as they made their way through the camp. It was now fully dark, and the people were preparing for sleep. Mira was thankful that not many people were awake to peer and gawk at them. They made their way to the largest tent. It was black, made up of goat and camel hide stitched together. The flaps gently swayed in the light night breeze.

The men gestured for them to enter the tent. A small oil lamp inside a glass casing lit the tent. The entire floor was lined with patterned red and white woven rugs, with a few scattered cushions here and there. Mira was amazed at how warm and welcoming the tent was. The people in her village always looked down on the Bedouins. They considered them ignorant and backward. But this magnificent tent was warmer and more welcoming to her than the dusty, small, mud-brick homes in the village.

Mira settled down on a cushion, feeling the soft wool rugs against her skin. The tent was bigger on the inside than it appeared on the outside and was held by four wooden pillars. Mira thought that at least another three families could fit in the tent with them.

"*Assalamu alaikum,*" a voice finally called. Mira looked up at the young man who stood in front of the entrance.

"*Walaikum Assalam,* brother!" her father rejoiced, standing to greet the man; quickly ushering him inside the warm tent. He was younger than her father—probably in his late teens or early twenties. His skin was richly brown with a shiny black beard and warm, dark eyes lined with traditional *kohl*. His turban was intricately tied on his head, the tail of it hanging over the opposite shoulder.

He wasn't as imposing as the men who led them here. Instead, he seemed warmer and more welcoming. "My name is Zayad BinNazir, my father, *Sheikh* Abdulaziz Al-Nazir, welcomes you to our humble dwellings." He placed a hand on his heart as a sign of peace and welcome.

"Thank you, Zayad. May God shower his blessings upon you. My name is Ali Abu Hassan. And these are my children, Hassan, Azule and Mira. We are very grateful for your hospitality."

"Of course, you all must be very exhausted. You may sleep here tonight and rest. My father will visit you in the morning," Zayad said, smiling warmly at them. Mira found herself smiling back at the kind man. Zayad said his goodbyes before exiting the tent. A few minutes later, two young women joined them with plates of meaty broth, bread, dates and milk. Mira's mouth watered as they set the plates before them, as well as a cup of water to drink and a cloth to clean themselves with. They also left them clean clothing and warm blankets. Mira grinned at the girls; one of them gave her a quick smile before leaving them to eat and bathe.

They ate everything; for the first time in days, Mira was stuffed. She grabbed the water and the cloth and started washing her brothers. They were tired, and much too satisfied with the meal to put up much of a fight. They began dozing off just as Mira finished dressing them in their new robes that were a tad bit too large. Mira frowned at how much weight they lost. She was often angry with them for always complaining during their journey, but as Mira counted their visible ribs, she realized just how close she was to losing her brothers, too.

After her brothers were well-fed and cleaned, Mira covered them with a blanket and used the same cloth and water to clean herself. Baba was perched on the other side of the tent, drinking a warm cup of tea. When Mira finished dressing, she then brought the water to her father to wash his feet, the same way her Mama used to when he came home from the fields. But, Baba grabbed her hands gently. "Sleep, daughter," he whispered. "You've done enough. I can take care of myself." Mira gave him a small smile and joined her snoring brothers, feeling at peace for the first time in ages.

After what seemed like a few hours, Mira woke up to the robust sounds of children playing. The camp was alive with activity, but Mira was still groggy and sour from their long and treacherous journey. She stretched and yawned as the bright morning light filtered into their tent from the small gaps at the entrance. The twins were still fast asleep, completely exhausted. She put her hand under their nose to make sure they were still breathing. Her father was also still asleep on the far side of the tent. Mira stretched her arms, then curiously peaked outside the flaps of her tent.

She saw children running with sticks, and women sitting in front of their tents over open fires as they baked bread, wove carpets and handled babies. Camels sat around in the distance. Beyond the tents was a large fence filled with hordes of sheep and goats. "Hello," a young girl appeared right in front of Mira, surprising her. She fell back into the tent, her heart hammering. The girl poked her head inside and wrinkled her nose. She was a bit older than Mira, with long brown hair that was braided to her side, and big, brown eyes.

She waved Mira forward. "Come on," the girl whispered. Mira looked unsure at her father, who was still peacefully sleeping. She bit her lip as the girl impatiently gestured at her to come out. Mira hesitantly followed her outside, squinting her eyes at the bright sun. The girl began running, urging Mira to follow her. She did just that and followed her through the camp which was a lot bigger than she had thought. There were at least three dozen tents. Mira and the girl ran until they finally stopped at a pen full of camels. The girl led her inside to a young calf nesting close to its mother.

"This is Juju," the girl said proudly. "He is mine. My Baba gifted him to me for my engagement. He says I will recieve a dozen camels when I get married."

"Married?" Mira asked, confused.

"Yes. I just turned twelve, and when I have big breasts like my sister, Aliya, I'll have to get married," the girl explained.

"Oh, when will that happen," Mira asked, curious at this strange girl. Girls in her village didn't tell her stuff—not even her cousin Fatima. All the kids there thought she was strange and avoided her. The girl just shrugged, playing with her baby camel. His mother huffed in annoyance but didn't protest as the girl pet him.

"Want to touch him," she asked, instead.

Mira smiled and brought her hand to his soft pelt. He sniffed her, rubbing his small head on her palm causing her to giggle.

"What's your name," the girl finally asked.

"Mira."

"It's nice to meet you, Mira. I'm Yasmin! You are the first new girl we had in our camp, so I wanted to steal you away and make you my friend before the other girls got a chance. Also, they are nasty, so it's best to just stick with me." Mira grinned at Yasmin. Nobody ever asked to be her friend before—well, besides Ayub, but that was different.

"Okay," Mira said shyly, letting Yasmin lead her back to the camp. She quietly snuck back inside the tent her father and brothers were still sleeping in, hoping they didn't notice her absence. Mira laid down next to her brothers, smiling.

Later that morning, after her father and brothers had woken up, they all washed up and ate the breakfast that was served once again, by the same young girls that had served them the night before. Mira didn't mention her adventures from that morning.

After they had eaten, Zayad returned to their tent. "Peace be upon you," he greeted.

Her father rose to meet him, shaking his hand. "My father will see you now," Zayad informed them. Mira was suddenly nervous to meet the *Sheikh*. He would be the person to decide their fate, and she really didn't want to go back to the desert.

Zayad led them through the camp. The people they passed gave them friendly smiles and offered *salaam* as they made their way to the black tent perched near the end of the camp. Zayad opened the flaps and guided them inside. The inside of the tent was like theirs, with warm rugs of red and white, colorful oil lamps and scattered cushions. There was a short table in front of a man who sat upon a throne of pillows. The man waved them inside. He was older than her father. His black turban was loosely draped over his shoulders. He wore a dark thobe on top of his robes, and his traditional dagger was secured to leather straps across his waist. His beard was gray and his eyes dark. He looked at them with mild interest, but Mira could tell he was watching them with a careful eye.

Baba stepped forward first to offer his greeting, kissing the *Sheikh's* hand. Mira and her brothers followed suit, and they each took a seat across from him. Zayad sat next to his father, giving them a reassuring smile. The *Sheikh* offered them tea and date biscuits. Mira declined, too nervous to form an appetite, but the twins gratefully accepted, wolfing down the cookies. Their father gave them a scolding look, but the *Sheikh* just waved him off, offering more cookies to the boys.

The *Sheikh* reclined back in his seat, turning his attention towards Baba. "Abu Hassan, my son briefly informed me of your situation; however, the details were a bit unclear," the *Sheikh* spoke, not bothering with pleasantries. "What were you doing in the desert with your family? And what is your tribe?" Baba cleared his throat, clearly uncomfortable, and Mira suddenly found it difficult to breathe. Would the *Sheikh* kick them out once he found out why they were banished?

"I was traveling with my family, *Sheikh*. We wished to seek our fortunes elsewhere; unfortunately, we lost our way. My tribe is the Banu Ihsan."

Baba was vague with his answer, and the *Sheikh* narrowed his eyes. "Why have you introduced yourself as Abu Hassan instead of your tribe's name? I suggest you think carefully before you answer, Abu Hassan. I am a generous man. As our traditions dictate, we will welcome guests with open arms and homes. However, if you lie to me one more time, you and your family will be expelled from my tribe." Baba swallowed audibly, glancing at Mira and his sons.

"Forgive me, *Sheikh*. I do not wish to transgress against your hospitality…but I already lost my wife and my young child. I only ask you to host us until we regain our strength, then we will continue on our journey."

"I will decide how long to extend my hospitality, Abu Hassan; and it depends on the answers you give me. I will not judge you on your story, but I must protect my tribe, and I cannot allow you to continue staying in our camp without knowing your situation," the *Sheikh* explained, his eyes hard. Mira dug her fingers into her palm as she tried to shake off the nerves. Baba didn't want to reveal what had happened, but it was obvious he had no choice.

Baba sighed in defeat, "I, along with my family, were banished from our village and exiled from our tribe. The Banu Ihsan do not claim us anymore, so I cannot use that name. I am now simply Abu Hassan."

"Why were you banished," the *Sheikh* asked. Mira couldn't read the expression on his face. He didn't seem surprised by Baba's confession. His eyes were curious, like a man who had heard stories from all sorts of people.

Baba didn't answer for a few minutes, his eyes cast downward. "They wished for me to do something I was unable to do… They asked me to bury my daughter," he finally spoke. His words were soft and laced with pain. Mira tried not to think about that night.

The *Sheikh's* eyes widened a bit. He glanced at Mira with renewed interest. "Why would your tribe ask you to do such a cursed thing! It is a forbidden act from the days of ignorance," Zayad spoke, disgusted at the information.

"They believed my daughter was…possessed by *jinns*, and that her presence was the cause of great misfortunes."

Zayad scuffed at that. "And they call *us* ignorant," he mumbled, shaking his head.

The *Sheikh* stared at Mira now; absent-mindedly stroking his gray beard. "Even if your daughter were possessed, there are ways to cure such *ailments*. Why would they come to such a conclusion?" he said almost thoughtfully.

Mira didn't look into his eyes. Baba shifted awkwardly. "Several weeks ago, my daughter disappeared into the desert. We searched for her for days, but we could not find her. We thought she had died… However, seven days later, she came back unharmed. We were just grateful that Allah had answered our prayers and returned our daughter. We didn't question how a child could survive seven days in the desert. It was a miracle…" Baba's voice broke.

"At first, the villagers also believed it to be a miracle. They celebrated her return with us. Then, one amongst them began sowing doubts. He began convincing the villagers that the girl who returned was not my daughter, but an evil *jinn*—a devil disguised as her. All at once, they turned on us. Our neighbors—even our family—began to believe that she would bring down a calamity. Our village elders were convinced that the only way to avert such a fate was to bury my daughter in the desert, or we would be expelled. I couldn't do it," Baba finished bitterly, his face awash with anguish and his hands white as he fisted them.

The *Sheikh* shifted his attention towards Mira again. "Child, go to that chest and bring me the book inside," he asked Mira. Startled at the sudden shift, she looked at her father, who nodded. Mira stood up and opened the wooden chest. Inside was a mat, prayer beads, and a huge, leather book. The book was heavy as Mira lifted it out of the chest and walked it over, handing it to the *Sheikh*. The *Sheikh* gave her a warm smile and took the book from her hands. He opened the book and began reciting verses. It was a Quran, Mira realized as his melodious voice filled the tent, and Mira smiled. She always loved listening to the recitation whenever it was read in the mosque. The *Sheikh* finished reciting and closed the book.

"If your daughter were truly a *jinn* with ill intentions, she would not have been able to touch the holy book without being burned. Nor would she be able to listen to it, sitting there and smiling as I read its holy verses. This is just a child. You did the right thing, Abu Hassan, and I'm sorry you lost your wife and baby because of it." Mira's eyes suddenly watered at his words. Even though she knew she was still herself, sometimes she wondered if the villagers were right.

"Thank you, *Sheikh*," Baba whispered, his voice thick with emotion.

"However, one question remains. How did this child survive in the desert?"

Mira glanced at her father, even though the *Sheikh* was looking at her when he asked. "I believe our Lord provided for her just as he provided for Abraham's wife and child," Baba answered for her. Mira didn't look at the *Sheikh*, afraid her eyes would betray her.

"Of course, our Lord provides for us in different ways. But I wish to know *how* he provided for you, Mira," he spoke, this time directing the question at Mira.

Mira swallowed, suddenly afraid. She looked at her father, but he was staring ahead, his face expressionless. "Do not be frightened, child. I will not hurt you." The *Sheikh's* eyes were warm, and Zayad gave her an encouraging smile.

Mira took a deep breath. "I was sent by my mama to collect wood when I heard a noise. It sounded like someone was crying, so I followed the sound. It led me far into the desert, but because the cries were so sad, I didn't notice how far I had gone. I finally reached an abandoned town in a valley between two mountains..." Mira paused as she heard an audible gasp from Zayad. The *Sheikh's* eyes narrowed.

Mira froze, confused by their reaction. The *Sheikh* softened his eyes, his expression unreadable, and asked her to continue. "I came across a dried well and I knew that was where the crying was coming from, so I cast a rope inside the well. The crying stopped and...and I think something came out," Mira stumbled on her story, not wanting to reveal that it was Ayub who came out of the well. "It frightened me, so I ran and ran very far. I was tired and couldn't find my way, so I slept. When I woke up, water and fruits were waiting for me."

The *Sheikh* stared at Mira, his hand absently rolling the stones on his prayer bead between his fingers. "That is a very interesting story," the *Sheikh* mused. His voice was soft and warm, but his eyes were shiny with a calculated look as he stared at Mira intensely. "You are all welcome to stay with us as long as you like, Abu Hassan," the *Sheikh* finally turned away from Mira and smiled at her father. "Our home is now your home. Unfortunately, because of the drought, we cannot host you as well as we like, but you are welcome to share everything we have."

Her Baba almost sagged with relief, tension releasing from his shoulders. The twins who were patiently sitting shot their heads up at that, grinning at each other. However, Mira didn't feel relieved. In fact, she had a strange feeling in her stomach—as the *Sheikh* looked at her again, his eyes gleamed with intensity and promise—of what, Mira had no idea.

11.

The Bedouin tribe had completely adopted her family once word spread that the *Sheikh* had welcomed them indefinitely. The members of the tribe began coming with gifts and supplies to get the family started with life in the desert. The men worked together to build them their own tent. It was smaller than the one that they were initially welcomed in, but it was cozy and perfect.

The Bedouin people were extremely kind and generous to the new members of their tribe. Each family brought them something. For weeks, they received gifts from all the members of the tribe. They were given wool carpets, blankets, chickens, pots and whatever each family could spare. They didn't hesitate to give. The *Sheikh* himself gifted her father a female camel and several sheep from his livestock.

At first, they were overwhelmed by the generosity and tried to refuse; however, the tribe insisted that they take what was offered, as refusing a gift was considered a grave insult. So, they began graciously accepting their generosity.

Since they had no mother, the women in the tribe adopted her family; each day, they brought them food from their own kitchens, even though the drought had left each family with barely enough to feed their own. Um Zara was especially attentive. She was a widow with one daughter. She constantly fussed over Mira and the boys, bringing them food and cooking for them.

Mira's friendship with Yasmin had also grown and flourished. Each day, they went out into the desert to graze their herds. They played games, and

Mira told her stories. Yasmin was very lively and did most of the talking. She knew everything about everyone in the small tribe, constantly telling Mira who was doing what. And, although she terribly missed her mother and sister—especially when she saw other children with their mothers—Mira was happy, and that gave her a sense of peace. She had fulfilled her mother's dying wish and lived. God had heard their prayers.

"Hurry up, you old camel!" Yasmin yelled, interrupting her thoughts. Mira looked up at her friend, who was already halfway up the dune they were climbing. She wasn't used to the soft sand of the desert, her feet sinking into its depth as she laboriously slugged forward. The ground in her village was firm and rocky. It wasn't like the fine sand that surrounded the camp. Mira pulled the wooded slab up the dune, struggling to reach the top where Yasmin waited impatiently. She released a heaving breath when she finally got to the top. Yasmin sat on top of the dune, grinning, not at all tired from the climb.

Mira tried to control her breathing as she positioned her wooden slab next to Yasmin's and sat on it. This was her favorite part of this game they played. Once she finally reached the top of the dune, she saw the vast expanse of the Sahara Desert. The golden dunes stretched as far as her eyes could see. A blanket of golden waves. The sun was hanging low, making everything in the desert have a reddish-orange tint. Mira took a deep breath, marveling at the vastness of the open desert. She felt so small and so insignificant compared to its glory. Yet, she also felt like she was part of something beautiful. The desert was alive even with the harshest of conditions. They survived just like the birds, camels, and insects. It was a testament that life could thrive in the harshest of conditions, and Mira was living proof of that.

Yasmin let out a loud sigh. "What's wrong?" Mira asked her friend who let out a frustrated breath.

"Mama got mad at me this morning because I was playing instead of doing my chores. She said I can't play anymore when I get married, and that I should stop acting like a child since I'm already engaged."

Mira frowned. "Why can't you play anymore when you get married?" She didn't like the idea of her friend not being able to play with her anymore.

Yasmin shrugged. "I think something happens to you when you get married because when my sister got married last year, she stopped playing with me," she frowned.

"What happens when you get married," Mira asked innocently. She never thought about marriage. Even though she was only eight, she would be expected to get married in a few years.

"I don't know, she wouldn't tell me. Nobody does. But whatever it is, I won't ever stop playing with you" Yasmin promised. Mira grinned at her friend. They held hands and slid down the dune, giggling as the wind pressed against them.

The two girls decided to race home; as always, Yasmin won and stretched out her hand expectedly. Mira let out an annoyed breath. She reached into the pocket of her dress and pulled out a date, handing it over to Yasmin who grinned as she took a bite. "One day, when I'm as tall as you, you'll be giving me all your dates," Mira promised.

Yasmin just smirked mischievously, "We'll see about that."

Mira said goodbye to her friend and made her way to the tent. She waved at the older women who sat together over a fire before entering her tent. Mira tidied up. Soon, her brothers would be back from playing, and they would be hungry. She grabbed her wooden bowl and headed to their pen to get milk from their female sheep. By the time she got back, Um Zara was waiting outside her tent with a large, covered bowl. Mira knew there would be cooked grains with meat and bread.

Mira smiled. Um Zara entered their tent and set down the bowl. Um Zara lived in the neighboring tent and had taken to cooking for her family. Mira was grateful for her help. With her mother gone, the housework was too much for Mira to do on her own. Her father spent most of his time with the other men of the village; they met in the communal tent where her family had stayed their first two nights. They spent hours talking, smoking and drinking tea. Her brothers had taken well to their new life, as well. They made lots of friends and were out all day playing in the desert.

Mira was left to do all the housework. She cleaned, dressed and bathed her brothers, made breakfast, and took care of the animals. So, she was grateful that Um Zara was there to make them dinner and offer help. "Where did you go today?" Um Zara asked Mira knowingly. Mira flushed. Um Zara was very traditional. She felt responsible for Mira, and that included making sure she didn't get into trouble.

"I was with Yasmin, but we only played for a little bit," Mira explained quickly.

Um Zara shook her head in disapproval. "That girl, her family gives her too much freedom. She shouldn't be running around like that at her age and neither should you." Mira didn't say anything. Why couldn't she play when all she did all day was work? Her brothers weren't expected to do anything, yet Mira couldn't even enjoy a few hours with her friend.

"Make sure your brothers eat well, and give my *salaam* to your father," Um Zara said, her cheeks reddening. Mira frowned, not liking the attention Um Zara gave her father, so she just nodded.

That night, after they all ate and Mira cleaned up, they had a visitor. "*Assalamu alaikum*, Abu Hassan," Zayad called from outside the tent. "May I come in?"

"*Walaikum Assalam*, Zayad," her father greeted him, rushing to let him in. Mira sat in the corner to give them space in the small tent. Zayad ducked into the tent, giving Mira a warm smile. "May I offer you something," Baba asked, looking around the tent.

"No, no. I just came to tell you that my father would like to speak with you."

Baba's eyes widened in surprise. "Right now," he asked warily.

"Yes…and bring your daughter." Zayad stood and waited outside the tent. Mira glanced at her father, apprehension settling in her stomach. What could the *Sheikh* possibly want with her? Her father seemed just as confused as he motioned for Mira to get ready.

Zayad led Mira and her father through the dark, sleeping camp. A few lights were shining from some tents—families who were yet to call it a night. Mira grew more and more nervous as they drew nearer to the *Sheikh's* tent. She twisted her hand in her dress, not sure what to expect. Mira and her father stood outside the *Sheikh's* tent as Zayad announced their arrival. Then, they made their way inside.

Mira had not seen the *Sheikh* much the last few weeks, but that was probably because she actively tried to avoid him. She didn't like the way he looked at her, as if she were a mystery he needed to solve. Mira quickly sat on the wool carpet, folding her courtly hands into her lap. The *Sheikh* was sitting on his cushion, a warm smile on his face as he greeted and welcomed them. Mira kept her eyes down, afraid of what might happen. Had she done something wrong? She was trying so hard to be normal. She didn't seek out Ayub, even though she missed him terribly. She ignored the strange creatures that would pop in and out of her vision when she took their sheep grazing, and she never talked about the *jinns*.

"Don't be afraid, child. You are not in any trouble," the *Sheikh* reassured her, sensing her unease.

"Why did you wish to see us," her father finally asked.

The *Sheikh* didn't answer for a while, his fingers rolling the stones of his prayer beads. "How are you all settling in the camp? We are a simple people. I hope the desert life isn't too boring," the *Sheikh* said instead, ignoring her father's question.

"We are settling in well. The Bedouin people live up to their reputation as the most hospitable, and we are truly grateful," her father answered.

The *Sheikh* nodded. "And you, child? How are you liking it here," he asked, directing the question at Mira.

Mira looked at her father who gave her a slight nod. "I like it very much, *Sheikh*," Mira answered honestly.

"That's good. I'm very happy you like it here. And we are very happy to have you." Mira smiled shyly, relaxing slightly now that she knew she wasn't in any trouble. "Would you like to hear a story, Mira?" the *Sheikh* asked her suddenly.

Mira nodded eagerly. She loved stories and collected them as if they were treasures.

"Once, there was a young Bedouin boy, not much older than you. His father had given him an important job and entrusted him to care for their large livestock. The young boy was always eager to impress and wanted to have the fattest herd in the tribe. So, he traveled far and wide to find the best land for his livestock to graze. However, at that time, there was a drought—not unlike this one—and it was difficult to find good pastures, no matter how hard the boy looked. His sheep were growing thinner, and the boy was afraid that he would soon lose them. One day, the boy decided to climb the highest mountain in the desert. However, the highest mountain stood near a haunted valley, and the boy was warned never to cross into that valley. It belonged to the *jinns*, and humans were never to enter; those who did lost their minds. But the boy, eager to please, did not listen to those warnings. He thought they were tales used to scare children. He thought if he could only see far enough, he would spot some pasture for his sheep.

"The boy climbed the mountain, higher and higher, until he could see the entire desert. It was so beautiful. Consumed in his admiration, the boy lost his footing and fell. He fell between two boulders and lost consciousness. When the boy woke up, it was nighttime, and the desert had grown cold. The boy shivered and tried to pull himself out, but his foot was stuck, and it wouldn't budge. No matter how hard he pulled, the boy could not free himself.

Soon, he began hearing strange noises that didn't belong in the desert, and he grew fearful because he recalled all the stories he had been told. He desperately tried to free himself, but he simply could not. The shadows in the mountain grew, and the boy began reciting the holy verses of his Lord. Each time he read, the shadows would run from him, as if it burned them. The boy read all night until dawn, and the shadows dispersed. Exhausted, he fell asleep.

The boy was stuck for two days without food and water, and at night, the shadows would return to haunt him. He would recite the verses of his Lord the entire night. On the third day, the boy was weak and on the verge of death. He knew he would not be able to recite that night because his voice was gone. His throat dried up from the lack of water.

The boy prayed and prayed the entire night, hoping for someone to save him until he fell asleep. In his sleepy state, the boy felt something move beside him, but he was too weak to open his eyes. He felt a tap on his foot and heard a voice telling him he was free. But the boy assumed it was a dream.

When the boy finally woke up, he realized that he was able to move his leg. It wasn't a dream; something had really freed him. The boy used the last of his strength and pulled himself from the gap he fell into, then climbed down the mountain, limping all the way home. Several days later his flock was mysteriously returned to him"

Mira stared at the *Sheikh*, her mouth agape by the story. The *Sheikh* absently massaged his foot as if he had a phantom pain, and that's when Mira realized.

"The boy was you!" she whispered.

The *Sheikh* laughed heartily. "Yes, clever girl. I was the boy. I survived a terrible ordeal in the desert with the help of God's unseen creature, just as you did. So, I know not all *jinns* are evil, just like not all people are bad." Mira nodded in agreement. He was the first adult that didn't reprimand her. The first person who didn't look at her like she was cursed. Mira smiled at the *Sheikh*, as her respect for him grew and grew.

Baba cleared his throat, looking disturbed. He didn't seem to enjoy the *Sheikh's* story, "*Sheikh*..." the *Sheikh* held up his hand, silencing her father, his eyes still on her. "Mira, you survived seven days in the desert during the worst drought in forty years. The *jinn* you saved returned the favor by saving you, and now I need your help to save my tribe."

Mira blinked in confusion.

"*Our tribe* needs help, and you can help us." The void in Mira's heart slowly started to mend itself at the sound of that word. *Our.* And thinking about Um Zara, Yasmin, and all the people who had welcomed her and her family, she was starting to feel like she belonged.

Baba's eyes darted to Mira, and he frowned. "*Sheikh*, I understand these are difficult times; this drought is not sparing anyone. But Mira is just a child; what can she do," her father asked, echoing Mira's own thoughts.

"She can lead us to water," the *Sheikh* said matter-of-factly. His eyes burned with intensity. Mira swallowed thickly. How would she lead anyone? She didn't know of any water. The *Sheikh* shifted in his seat. "You were lost for seven days, and the *jinn* brought you water. Perhaps it could lead you to the source." Mira paled thinking about Ayub. He would never show up in a place with people. He was too afraid, and Mira couldn't ask him to do that.

"I-I can't," Mira stuttered, not sure how to explain her relationship with Ayub. No one knew about him, and she just wanted to be normal. If the Bedouins found out she could see the *jinn*—that she could speak to them— they would cast her out, just like her village did.

"You don't need to be afraid, child. I know you can communicate with them." Mira stiffened at those words, and the *Sheikh's* eyes narrowed as if she just confirmed his suspicion. "Just ask it to lead us to the water." His voice was soft, but he didn't understand.

"They are not supposed to help humans," Mira whispered, remembering that Ayub told her he was cast in that well for helping a human. No matter how much she wished to help the tribe that saved her, she couldn't put Ayub at risk.

"They helped you."

"That's different. I saved him, and he is terrified of humans. He would never come near this place," Mira said, exasperated. She just wanted to go home. She didn't want to do this. She didn't want to be the *jinn* girl again. She didn't want people cursing her, and children mocking her. She just wanted to be like everybody else.

"He?" the *Sheikh* mused, never missing a detail. Mira bit her lip, realizing she had revealed too much. "Would he help if it were just you?" the *Sheikh* asked.

"I-I don't know. Maybe," she admitted, knowing Ayub would do anything for her. He loved her just as she loved him. That's why she didn't want to ask him about this. She didn't want to use him the way the *Sahir* used and controlled *jinns*.

The *Sheikh* thought about that and turned to Zayad, who sat quietly through the entire conversation, as if he didn't quite believe it was taking place. But it was obvious he and his father had already discussed this proposal. The *Sheikh* and his son whispered quietly for a few minutes, and Mira couldn't hear what they were saying. Would they kick them out if she were unable to help? Would she have to go back to the desert again? Mira's heart pained as she thought of her mother and baby sister whom they had lost to the desert, and her father's desperate face as he tried to take their lives. She didn't want to go back. She didn't want to lose anyone else.

The *Sheikh* finally turned his attention back to Mira; this time, it was Zayad that spoke. "We can send you out alone, and the…*jinn* will lead you, God willing, to the water. I can track your movement from far away and send word back to the tribe who will be following behind me."

"You- you want me to go back into the desert alone?" Mira whispered, afraid. She didn't want to go back. She didn't want to be lost again.

"Zayad will be close behind you, child. Do not be afraid. We won't let anything happen to you."

"*Sheikh*, this is madness. You can't possibly believe that my daughter can communicate with *jinns*. She is not a *Sahir*. She is just a child," Baba finally contorted.

"Abu Hassan, I understand that this is hard for you, but I believe your daughter is capable of saving us. I give you my word that nothing will happen to your daughter, and if she is successful, you and your family will be part of this tribe. You will be granted our protection, as well as twenty camels and forty sheep. You and your family will be well-respected, and you will join my council in all tribal matters."

Baba put his hands through his short beard, contemplating.

"You have my word, Abu Hassan. Once she becomes of age, I will personally secure her marriage to someone from my own family. No one will speak ill of you or your family," the *Sheikh* promised.

Mira frowned. She didn't care if she never got married. She was more afraid of going into the desert alone, despite what Zayad said. Surely, her father would never allow it.

Baba was quiet for a long time, "And if she fails," he asked finally.

The *Sheikh's* eyes darkened. "Then, only God can help us, but you will still receive all I promised, regardless of whether you choose to stay with us or not."

Baba closed his eyes, then gave a slight nod in agreement. Mira felt her heart drop. How many times had her father cast her away? How many times had he let her down? Still, each time, a piece of her heart broke away. She didn't bother pleading with him this time. She didn't beg. Instead, she looked ahead, feeling disgusted. The only reason the *Sheikh* had saved them and allowed them to stay was because he wanted something from Mira.

Mira blinked away the pain; ice forming in her heart. Even if she did this—even if she saved the tribe—she knew no one would look at her the same. She would go back to being the cursed girl—the girl who spoke to *jinns*—eventually, they would grow to fear her. They would blame her for any and every misfortune; eventually, they would kick her out. She knew how it would all play out.

The *Sheikh* reached out as if sensing her fear and pain. He lifted her chin, and her eyes shined with tears that she refused to let fall. "I give you my word, Mira. We will protect you. I'm sending my own son to follow you to make sure you are safe, and if you are ever in any real danger, we will end this and find a new way. If there was any other way to save my people, I would have taken it. But I can't help but believe that God has sent you to save us, just as he sent that *jinn* to save you."

Mira just nodded, not bothering to explain herself. She wasn't afraid of the desert because it didn't discriminate. She didn't fear the sun because it shined bright on everyone equally, and she didn't fear the *jinn*, either. The thing she feared the most were the humans that she was asked to save. The very ones who would eventually turn on her for it. The desert didn't discriminate, but people did.

12.

Mira was filled with anxious energy. The *Sheikh* announced during the Friday sermon that the tribe would leave to find water. He didn't mention Mira's role, but people would know soon enough. "Are you excited to leave," Yasmin asked, putting her arm over Mira's shoulders. Mira struggled with her weight as she carried firewood to her home. She had been distancing herself from her friend, too afraid of what would happen to their friendship when Yasmin found out the truth about her.

"Yeah," Mira said, non-committed.

"What's wrong," Yasmin questioned, arching her eyebrow.

Mira sighed. She knew she was being unfair to her only friend, but she would be leaving with Zayad tomorrow. He would take her into the desert, then leave her there. Mira liked Zayad. She knew he would keep his promise to keep her safe, but she was still scared. She was afraid of getting lost, and she was also afraid of failing.

"Nothing, I'm just nervous."

"Well, just stick with me. We have been moving a lot these last few years because of the drought, so I'm pretty much an expert on nomadic life." Yasmin gave her a playful shove.

"Actually, I'm not leaving with the rest of the tribe," Mira admitted quietly. She didn't want her friend looking for her during the journey. Mira also knew Yasmin wouldn't stop bothering her until she had an answer.

"You aren't coming with us? What do you mean!" Yasmin demanded.

"Well, I'm going with Zayad to…scout, but we'll meet up with the rest of the tribe eventually."

Yasmin stopped in her tracks, her eyes narrowing. "Zayad Bin Nazir? Why are you going with the men to scout," she asked suspiciously.

"I'm good at finding things. The *Sheikh* is hoping I can help find water."

"*HA*! Then why did it take you two hours to find me when we were playing hide and seek? I almost gave up because you were so slow, and I smelled like camel dung from hiding in their pen."

Not sure what to say, Mira just squirmed. "I have to go, Yasmin. I can't really explain." she paused, biting her bottom lip. "I just hope we can still be friends when we meet again." Mira turned and ran to her tent, ignoring Yasmin's calls. Tomorrow, she will leave with Zayad and the other warriors. She just hoped the plan wouldn't fail. Everyone was counting on her.

Sleep evaded her, as Mira tossed and turned, thoughts of the desert consuming her mind. She hadn't seen Ayub in weeks—not since she got to the camp. She wasn't even sure he would be out there. Maybe he went back home. What would she do if that were the case?

Zayad arrived early that morning. It was pre-dawn, and the camp was still asleep. He and her father exchanged words while Mira got ready in the clothes and shoes he brought her. Her leather sandals were soft and firm. They would protect her feet from the sand, and the dress was made of light cotton to keep her cool. She also had a satchel with a small blanket for warmth when it got cold and for shade for when it was too hot. He brought her dried meat and fruit, and a filled water skin, which should last two days, if she was careful.

Taking a calming breath, Mira looked at her sleeping brothers. She didn't tell them she was leaving—they wouldn't understand, anyway. Instead, she placed a kiss on each of their heads, vowing to return. Their lives, as well as the lives of everyone in the tribe, rested in her hands. She had to find the water, or the tribe would perish. Mira stepped out of the tent with a new resolve; she would do this for her brothers, for Yasmin and for the tribe that adopted her with open arms. Regardless of the *Sheikh's* motives, they were innocent and still accepted them without knowing her role.

Zayad stood outside her tent, his head tightly wrapped in a turban. He wore a long, black *thobe*, and a long sword was hung at his waist, replacing his ceremonial blade. He gave Mira a reassuring smile as she stood next to him. She tried to keep her head up and be brave, but she couldn't return his smile.

Baba cleared his throat. Mira looked at him, her heart filled with mixed emotions. Part of her was angry with him for letting her do this alone, and the other part pitied him. Her Baba sacrificed so much because of her—lost his wife and baby girl. He never said anything, but sometimes, she thought he blamed her for what happened to Mama. She blamed herself.

"Goodbye, Baba," Mira whispered, wrapping her arms tightly around him as she swallowed her tears. Baba stood stiffly for a second at her unexpected hug. He wasn't an affectionate man, but he returned her hold. "May Allah protect you, daughter," he whispered gruffly. She sniffled, pulling away from him. Zayad held out his hand and Mira took it hesitantly. They walked into the sleeping camp. Soon, everyone would wake up not knowing that their future was in the hands of an eight-year-old girl.

The sky was blue-black, and the stars were stretched out, brightly flickering like tiny lamps as they made their way to their horses where they were met by four other warriors. Zayad lifted her onto his horse. Mira held tightly onto the reins as the horse neighed. "Calm down, Najma." Zayad scolded the horse and petted its face. The horse neighed, huffing a breath from his nose. Zayad chuckled and climbed on top of the horse behind Mira. "Don't be afraid. She's a gentle girl," Zayad said, taking in her white knuckles as she held on for dear life.

Mira was afraid. The horse was huge, and she had never been on one before. Zayad clicked his tongue and the horse moved forward, its hoofs kicking back sand as he led them into the twilight.

Mira didn't speak the entire time they rode. After the first hour, she finally relaxed and started enjoying the ride. She braved patting Najma's mane every now and then, and the horse huffed in approval, which made her smile. They rode all morning as the camp disappeared from view, widening the sea of sand before them. Mira looked around the golden dunes, wondering how she would ever find water in such a desolate place.

Soon it was afternoon, and Zayad and the other warriors stopped to rest. Their faces were covered. She didn't know what they looked like; only their _kohl_-lined eyes were visible as they rode in silence. Zayad helped her off the horse, and Mira gave him a small smile. He took her blanket and made her a makeshift tent by pushing two sticks to the ground. Its shade would protect her from the afternoon sun. He took her water skin and replaced it with a full one.

Mira swallowed, not missing the fact that he only set up one tent. They would leave her here. Mira knew they would still be out there tracking her and following close behind, but she wouldn't see them.

After he was finished, Mira sat in the tent, removed her satchel, and placed it next to her. Zayad cleared his throat. His eyes were full of pity; he didn't agree with his father's plan. He didn't think she would be capable of doing what her father thought she could do, but he obeyed the *Sheikh*, nevertheless.

Zayad crouched down to her level. "You are a brave girl, Mira. Most warriors would be too afraid to do what you are doing. You fit your namesake well: a leader."

Mira's eyes watered thinking about the words her mother often said to her, *"Your name means leader and it suits you."* But Mira didn't feel like a leader. She felt like a scared little girl who just wanted her mama to comfort her.

Zayad misinterpreted her tears. "You have my word, brave girl. I won't allow anything bad to happen to you. You may not see me, but I will be close by." Mira wiped her tears. She couldn't speak. Her throat was too tight with emotion, so she just gave him a small nod.

Zayad hesitated, sighing. He pulled out a red piece of fabric and handed it to her. "If you decide you can't do this anymore and want to go home, leave this at your camp and I'll take you back." Zayad promised her.

She graciously accepted the fabric, giving him her first real smile. "Thank you," she whispered, grateful for the lifeline.

Zayad returned her smile and ruffled her hair. "May Allah protect you," he said before leaving with the other warriors. Mira watched them as they disappeared into the horizon. She clutched onto the fabric, feeling relief to have this escape. She trusted Zayad would keep his word.

***

It'd been two days since Mira began her mission, her water had run out, and she was beginning to feel desperate. There was still no sign of Ayub. Mira couldn't help but feel disappointed. She tried calling him, but there was no answer. She woke up every morning and afternoon expecting to see him, or at least his offering of food and water, but there was nothing except an empty desert. Mira still had the red fabric Zayad had given her, and even though she was thirsty and exhausted, she couldn't use it. She didn't want to give up. She didn't want to go back empty-handed. She wasn't ready to lose her family and the tribe she was growing to love. The *Sheikh* believed in her. He believed that Allah had sent her to help his tribe; she didn't want to disappoint him.

Mira's throat felt like sandpaper, and her lips were dry and cracked. She drank the last drops of her water, knowing that tomorrow, she would have to go the entire day without it. The sun was setting, and Mira prepared her tent. She was so tired from dehydration, that the dried figs and meat she forced down just made her thirstier. Mira climbed up the dune. She knew she had to preserve her energy, but she simply loved watching the sunset on top of the dunes.

The beautiful sky filled with orange, red, and purple, making the desert shimmer like gold. Being up there made Mira's heart fill with warmth—all her ache and thirst were forgotten. From up there, Mira felt as though she could forgive the desert for being so cruel to her. Up there, she didn't question God's will. Up there, she didn't feel alone.

Once the sky began to darken to a blue-black, Mira lifted her head and wiped her tears. "I hope you are happy, Mama," she whispered into the desert before tumbling down.

The sand was soft and cool as Mira lay upon it. The dunes weren't beautiful golden hills once darkness enveloped the desert; they were dark shadows looming over her. So, Mira always looked up instead, staring at the bright desert stars. Sometimes, she counted each one until she fell asleep, and other times, she just stared at them until she was hypnotized by their light. *Please*, she prayed. *Please don't let me fail.*

***

She woke up the next morning to the song of the desert. She hadn't heard it the first two dawns she was there, but she could hear it now; a soft echo in the wind. Ayub once told her that the song was the voices of the *jinns*. It was the prayer they sang, and it was wistful, filling her heart with both happiness and sorrow. She listened—weeping quietly as the song infiltrated her heart—until the sun fully emerged; chasing away the stars as well as the song. Mira sniffled. She couldn't smile because her lips were so dry they would crack and bleed. Her mouth felt like sandpaper, but she forced herself to eat.

Mira folded up her blanket and gathered her supplies, dragging herself forward. It was so hot that day that she could barely breathe, even though it was still morning. Her tongue felt swollen in her mouth as she forced herself to keep moving. She could see the heat in waves before her, clouding her view. Dark spots began to form in her vision as she swayed with heat. Mira felt lightheaded and nauseous, her feet slugging forward as she strained to lift them. The sand felt like weights on her feet as she tried to drag them through. Mira's eyes rolled back and her vision began to blur. Then, suddenly, she fell into the hot sand, and the world turned black.

"Mira, Mira… Please, wake up!" Mira frowned. She was so tired; all she wanted to do was sleep. But the panicked voice wouldn't leave her alone. She groaned and lifted her heavy eyelids. She had to squint against the blazing sun as huge, brown, doe eyes filled with concern hovered over her.

"Ayub…" her voice was barely audible. Surely, she was dreaming.

"Mira!" It was Ayub. His high-pitched voice was filled with worry as his whole body rang with energy.

"Water," she whispered, unable to lift her head. She felt like a camel was sitting on top of her. Her whole body was so heavy she couldn't lift herself up, no matter how hard she tried. Ayub nodded, his movements animated as he disappeared in a blink. Mira tried to get up to call him back, but she was overcome with exhaustion, so she closed her eyes and let the darkness consume her.

She didn't know how long she was sleeping when she felt wetness dripping in her mouth. *Water?* Mira parted her lips slightly as the water slowly began pouring into her. She coughed, sputtered it out, and blinked her eyes open. Ayub was hovering over her, pouring the water into her mouth. His brown face was filled with worry. Mira coughed again, choking on the water. She lifted herself on her elbows and grabbed the water skin with a shaking hand.

Mira brought the water to her dry, aching lips and drank, the cool liquid easing away the dryness and the burn. She drank greedily until she couldn't drink anymore. She still felt weak and exhausted, but she could also feel some energy returning to her dehydrated body as the water-filled her. Mira wiped her mouth and forced herself to sit up, peering at Ayub, who sat a few feet away.

"Ayub?" she whispered, her eyes instantly filling with tears. Mira didn't realize how much she missed her friend.

Ayub stopped shaking, suddenly still as a statue as he stared at her. Then, his eyes filled with tears. He shifted forward like he wanted to touch her, but then pulled back, crying silently. Mira felt her own tears streaming down her face as they both cried—not talking, just staring at each other. Eventually, they both settled, and Mira started feeling better.

The sun was hanging low, about to set, flooding the desert in golden light. Mira wiped her eyes, "I missed you so much, Ayub"

Ayub's lips shook as he spoke. "I missed you, too," he said, his voice trembling. "I'm sorry I didn't come sooner. I-I thought you were dead. You wouldn't wake up!" he cried again and his whole body shook violently. Mira wanted to hug him, but she knew she wasn't supposed to touch him as *Jinns* were often known to possess humans through touch.

"I'm okay, Ayub, don't cry. You saved me again." Mira gave him a shaky smile. Ayub smiled back shyly, his eyes still bright with tears. "How did you find me," she asked.

Ayub glanced around nervously as if someone were after him. "I felt you leave the camp, so I searched for you in the desert. I should've come sooner. I'm sorry." Ayub slumped his shoulders.

"But how," she asked, naturally curious.

Ayub scratched his head like he wasn't sure how to answer. "You have a color, all humans do, but yours is a very bright violet. I can see it, even from far away. But I didn't see it anymore at the camp, so I looked for your light," he answered.

Mira was confused and fascinated. *She had a light.*

"Where have you been?" She hadn't seen him in weeks.

Ayub shuffled uncomfortably. "I was hiding," he admitted. "My clan wanted to punish me again because I broke the rules when I helped you." Ayub looked down, his hand fidgeting with the fabric of his cloak.

"Oh. What will they do if they find you?"

"They won't find me. I'm too fast!" Ayub grinned, his small canines peeking through. Mira smiled back, feeling guilty. She didn't want Ayub to get hurt because of her. He risked getting caught to save her, and now she had to use him. Mira sighed. The sun was now setting over the horizon, and she was still so exhausted.

13.

The next day, Mira felt much better. She was hydrated, but besides a few bumps and bruises, she was fine. Ayub sat a few feet away from where she had slept, staring out into the desert. Mira shifted forward sneakily, "Boo!" she shouted behind him and Ayub jumped forward in surprise, his eyes wide. Mira began giggling at his wide-eyed expression, Ayub scowled at her, then began laughing along.

"You got me again!" he said, remembering the last time she had scared him.

She grinned, grabbing the water skin to take a drink. "What were you staring at?" she asked, swallowing a big gulp of water and feeling its coolness make its way down her throat.

Ayub shrugged, "I was listening to the desert." Mira nodded and fiddled with her dress, unsure of how to ask Ayub for his help. Even though she was well-rested, her heart was heavy with guilt. Ayub didn't even ask why she was out there. He just accepted her like he always did.

Mira cleared her throat. "Ayub...where did you find this water?" she finally asked slowly.

"I got it from the oasis," he answered nonchalantly, trying to catch a sandfly that kept slipping through his fingers.

"Is it nearby, this oasis?"

Ayub stopped what he was doing, cocking his head to the side. "To me, yes, but you are very slow, so, it might be far for you."

"Will…will you take me there?" Mira held her breath, watching his face for any negative reaction or suspicion at her request.

Ayub frowned, looking suddenly uncomfortable. "We're not really supposed to lead humans there. It's where my kind rests and drinks."

"Oh, what would happen if humans went there?"

"They would take it for themselves," he answered matter-of-factly.

Mira shifted uncomfortably. He was right. That was exactly what she wanted to do—lead her tribe to this oasis, and then take it. "Couldn't they find somewhere else? *Jinns* are more resourceful than humans." She needed a reason to justify this so she wouldn't feel so guilty. If the tribe didn't get to this oasis, they would die. The *jinns* could probably find another one. They were the kings of the desert.

"It's a sanctuary for my kind. It provides us shade under its large date trees and is a place where my kind gathers for peace. Anyone who comes to the oasis is granted safety."

Mira chewed her bottom lip. It wasn't just an oasis, but a sanctuary. How could she take their place of peace from them? "Is there another place with water," she asked hopefully.

"There are small waterholes, but the drought is even affecting us *jinns*." Still, Ayub was not suspicious. He didn't ask Mira why she was so curious. Instead, he patiently answered her questions, and it just made her guilt fester inside her.

Mira rose to her feet, dusting off her dress. "Let's play a game," she said, not wanting to think about the oasis anymore.

Ayub grinned excitedly. "Can we slide down the hill," he asked eagerly.

"How did you know about that game?"

Ayub flushed with guilt. "I watched you play with your friend," he said quietly.

"You're my friend, too, Ayub," Mira responded, knowing an innocent feeling of jealousy was growing inside him.

Ayub lifted his head. "Really?"

Mira grinned. "Yes. You are my best friend," she affirmed.

Ayub and Mira spent the rest of the morning looking for something they could use as a slide. They finally found some large pieces of bark from a date palm tree and spent the rest of the afternoon laughing and sliding down the dunes. When they were all tired out, Mira laid under the shade of her makeshift tent, weighing her options. She didn't want to take away a sanctuary from the *jinns*, nor did she want to hurt Ayub, but she couldn't ignore the tribe's suffering. A tribe she was now a part of.

She thought of how happy her brothers were, and how they were assimilating to life as nomads. She even thought of her father, and Um Zara, who always cooked for them. She thought of Yasmin and Zayad, who had both been so kind. She couldn't let them down, even if it meant betraying her best friend. She was human, after all. She would go to the oasis, and the tribe would claim its water.

Mira and Ayub spent the evening talking. She told him all about the Bedouin tribe, and how they had saved her family. She told him about Zayad and Yasmin, and even the *Sheikh*. Ayub's eyes watered, and he cried silently when she told him about her mother and Sara. She told him about the hundreds of livestock that the tribe had, and how she and Yasmin would play hide and seek.

Ayub listened attentively, laughing, crying and awing at all the appropriate times. He always listened like what she had to say was the most important thing in the world. He was fascinated by her stories and hung onto every word.

They watched the sunset together, which was the perfect end to a perfect day. "Mira today was the best day of my life," Ayub whispered tentatively.

"Me too," she whispered back with a heavy sigh. Then, they both drifted off to sleep.

***

"Ayub, I want you to take me to the oasis," Mira said the following day after she had finished eating.

Ayub raised his left eyebrow slightly and began fidgeting nervously. "I don't think that's a good idea, Mira."

"Why not?" she demanded.

"I told you it's a sanctuary, and different clans meet there to settle things."

"Will they hurt me if I go?"

Ayub scratched his head. "It's against our laws to harm a human, so they won't physically hurt you... But Mira, *Jinns* will always find a way to get around that barrier."

Mira thought about that for a moment. "When I found you in the well, I saw shadows that looked like smoke. I knew they were *jinns*, but I wasn't afraid. When they saw that I wasn't scared of them, they left me alone."

Ayub smiled at Mira. "That's because you are different. They were afraid of you."

"Why?"

Ayub glanced around conspicuously, lowering his voice. "I told you, every human has a color—a light. Yours is so bright it scares my kind."

"Is that why you were so afraid of me when I first found you?"

Ayub nodded his head. "But I'm also scared of all humans—just like humans are scared of *jinns*. Humans don't understand how much more power they have than we do."

Mira thought about what he said and considered his warning, but she didn't have a choice. She had to do this for the people she loved. "Take me there," she finally resolved.

Mira and Ayub walked for eight days. Ayub could have probably traveled there and back a hundred times, but instead, he followed her pace. Ayub had the same excited childlike energy, chatting with her nonstop the entire time, and Mira appreciated it. He kept her mind off her task and the enormity of the never-ending desert.

Eventually, amid the desert and sand, Mira spotted outlines of large trees far in the distance. At first, she thought her eyes were playing tricks on her— that the heat was messing with her mind. But as they approached, she began seeing more and more signs of life.

"Ayub, is that…" Mira began.

Ayub just grinned excitedly. "Follow me," he said as he climbed a large dune. Mira followed him up, the sun hanging low, covering the desert in a reddish-orange tint. Ayub was already there, staring out into the desert, waiting for her.

Mira finally got to the top and released a huff of air. She looked out into the desert and gasped. Before them lay a large oasis nestled in between the dunes. The green-blue water sparkled, and it was surrounded by vegetation, large palm trees and bushes. She smiled as she took in the sight; her eyes narrowed as she spotted people and animals below. "There are people!" Mira announced in surprise. She couldn't make out their faces, but she could see their form.

"Those are not people. Those are *jinns*."

"Oh. Do they live there?" she asked nervously.

"Some do, but others are travelers." Mira's heart dropped in guilt. Soon,

Zayad would track her down and send word back to the tribe if they weren't already on their trail. But they were a nomadic tribe, and as soon as the drought was over, they would leave. *Right?* She felt awful about what was about to happen, but she didn't have any other choice.

Mira spent the following two days camping near the oasis, waiting for Zayad. She was too afraid to enter the Oasis on her own, unsure how the *jinns* would feel about a human being there. Instead, Ayub was the one to enter, bringing her water and dates. On her third day there, she felt someone nudge her. She startled awake, suddenly afraid.

"Shh, it's just me." Zayad was crouched down next to her. His horse stood a few feet away. His face was taut and tanner than usual from being out in the desert.

"Zayad?"

Zayad grinned at her, his white teeth gleaming in contrast to his short black beard. "You did it, Mira, by Allah, you have saved us all." Mira smiled shyly, her face flushing. She wasn't used to being praised. She looked around for Ayub, but, of course, he was gone. "The oasis...it's amazing," Zayad continued, his face awed.

"Did you go into it?" Mira asked cautiously.

"Not yet. I just sent one of my riders back. They will inform our scouts and the tribe will be here in a few days."

"Oh, that's good." Mira didn't sound convincing, but Zayad was too excited to notice. He held out his hand for her, and she grabbed it as he lifted her.

"Why don't we go explore our new home?" he said with a smile. Mira nodded and followed him, along with two of his warriors. Zayad lifted her onto his horse and took his place behind her as they trotted forward.

Mira scanned the area. As they drew near, she saw shadows flying into the desert away from the oasis, afraid of the new invaders. Some of the *jinns* stayed hidden behind the trees. The hair on her arms raised slightly as the *jinns* stared at them in fear. She wasn't afraid. She stared at them until they slithered back into the trees.

"Praise be to God!" the other warriors whispered as they approached the water, unaware of the danger that surrounded them—the shadows that lurked nearby, following them, waiting.

The men and horses approached the water, drinking deeply. They must have been thirsty, out in the desert for several days without water. They set up camp near the shores of the oasis and set a fire after eating dried meat and dates. Then, they drifted off to sleep, exhausted, but Mira laid wide awake. Her eyes narrowed as she saw movement at the edge of the oasis. She quickly closed her eyes as the giant, muscular figure approached their camp.

Mira peaked under her lashes as it stood still, its head cocked, staring down at Zayad's sleeping form.

"Stop!" Mira whispered as the figure's hand snaked out to Zayad's throat. Its hand stilled, its black form unmoving like a statue as Mira stood, controlling her breathing. Her heart hammered in her chest. The *jinn* stared at Mira, as if unsure whether she was addressing him. "Go away!" she whispered, not wanting to wake the men. She couldn't see the *jinn's* face; its features were shrouded by the darkness. But she knew it heard her and understood, cocking its head to one side. "You and your kind must leave this place now," she said.

"This is our home." The *jinn's* voice was hoarse, unlike Ayub's timid speech.

"I know, but now, my tribe is coming to take it. I'm sorry, but you must leave," Mira's voice was firm. She didn't show fear; she knew in her heart that it couldn't hurt her.

The *jinn* glided closer to her, studying her like an insect. "Arrogant human girl. How dare you take what's ours?"

"We take what God has permitted us to take in His book." The *jinn* circled her, his feet not touching the ground as his long, black robes dragged the floor. "And when my tribe comes, they will not ask so nicely. I can see your kind. I know your tricks. I can warn my people of your presence. They have a powerful *Sahir* who can control you, and a *Sheikh* who can drive you out. So, leave now while you still can," Mira threatened, hoping it would fall for her bluff. She knew it had no real power over humans. *Jinns* could not harm humans; the natural law did not allow it.

The *jinn* froze, its body twitching. "We shall leave for now, but we have long lives, and even longer memories. You humans live short lives. Once you are gone, we will return and take back our water," it whispered, its voice carrying in the wind as it disappeared. Mira sagged with relief. She couldn't believe that worked. She pulled her knees to her chest and began shaking.

The *jinn* had kept his word. The next morning when they woke up, there were no shadows, just trees and vegetation. Mira knew the jinns would eventually be back and try to drive out the humans, but their tactics relied on fear and trickery, and they knew she wasn't afraid of them, so they left. For now.

Mira didn't see any sign of Ayub over the next few days, and she didn't go looking for him, either. She was too afraid and too ashamed of what he might think of her. She tricked him into bringing her to this oasis, then took his kind's sanctuary and scared them off. She didn't know if Ayub would ever forgive her, and she didn't dare ask.

14.

1 year later

"I got it!" Yasmin shouted triumphantly, holding the struggling chicken by the neck. It had escaped the pen while Mira and Yasmin were getting her eggs, its wings fluttering wildly.

"Finally," Mira sighed, tired from chasing it around. It had been exactly one year since they arrived in the oasis. While Yasmin didn't seem to care much about Mira's role in finding their new home, the rest of the tribe treated her with cautious respect.

The *Sheikh* had made her father and their family honorary members of the tribe, taking them as his kin, so the rest of the tribe had no choice but to treat them with respect. But Mira heard their whispers, saw their sneaky glances, and took note of the way they all avoided her.

They were afraid of her. Mira knew the rumors that were spread about her, that her mother was a witch and that they were expelled from their village because she cursed people. It was nonsense, of course, but people believed anything. The only people who didn't treat her differently were Yasmin and Zayad, her father had remarried to Um Zara a few months after their arrival. Mira hadn't seen Ayub since the day Zayad came for her. She saw a few *jinns* lurking near the oasis, but they all fled when they saw her. Mira still wasn't sure why, but the *jinns* feared her.

"Are you ready for your wedding?" Mira asked her friend. Yasmin was to wed within the next few weeks.

She scowled at the reminder. "Do I have a choice?" she countered, carefully laying the eggs in her basket. Mira frowned in sympathy. Her friend did not want to get married, but it was customary. She was already thirteen and considered fit for marriage, and her parents wouldn't wait any longer to marry her off.

"Zayad is a good man," Mira said, hoping to ease her friend's sadness.

Yasmin just made a face. "He is an arrogant, goody-two-shoes, and I can't stand his face!"

Mira rolled her eyes. Yasmin barely ever spoke to Zayad, and he was anything but arrogant. "It could be worse, and Zayad isn't as bad as you think. Just give him a chance."

"If you like him so much, why don't you marry him?" Yasmin huffed.

Mira felt her face flush. "I don't like him!" she said embarrassed. Zayad was always kind to Mira, like how she imagined an older brother would be. He always defended her against his tribesmen when they got verbally abusive or left her out, and he always brought her presents. He adopted her younger brothers as his own, teaching them how to ride and shoot arrows, and the twins loved him.

"Ya right! You never stop talking about him. At least you don't have to worry about getting married," Yasmin said, hinting at her unpopularity in the tribe. Even though it was true, it still hurt. Yasmin didn't mean anything by it, but, sometimes, she said things that stung. She always thought her problems were the worst, and never really listened or tried to understand what Mira was going through. She loved Yasmin, but sometimes, she couldn't help but resent her.

Mira didn't respond. Instead, she quietly gathered the rest of her eggs in the basket and headed home. In the one year they had spent in the oasis, the tribe began building mud and brick homes, setting up a semi-permanent settlement, instead of their usual nomadic tents. There was a small farm, a mosque and a large communal courtyard. The *Sheikh* had gifted her father a large plot of land near the oasis, along with two palm trees, twenty camels and forty sheep. Her father built them a modest, three-bedroom home with a large courtyard. The *Sheikh* also took him into his council, so, not only was her father a rich man now, but he was also well-respected within the tribe.

Her father never really acknowledged what Mira had done, but he built her a room with a wooded straw bed and red carpets. It was the first time Mira had her own room, and she loved it. She just wished her mother and baby sister were alive to enjoy their good fortune.

Um Zara was kind enough, but she was strict and was always scolding Mira for everything. Even now, she scolded her for being idle and not returning fast enough with the eggs. Mira just apologized and got started on her daily chores. Now that the twins were old enough, it was their job to take the livestock grazing while Mira and her stepmother did housework with the other women.

"Mira, come here," Um Zara called. Mira placed the makeshift straw doll that she was making on her bed and left to go see Um Zara, who was waiting in the courtyard. Um Zara held up a red dress and new leather shoes. Mira grinned. It was beautiful. She never owned a colored dress before, and wore the only plain, wool dresses from her village. She traced the patterns of the dress with her fingers.

"This is mine?" she whispered in awe.

Um Zara chuckled. "Yes, your father had it made for you. He traded our fattest sheep for it." Mira raised her eyebrows in surprise. "You will wear it tonight for Yasmin's wedding."

Mira's eyes lit up in excitement. She hadn't thought much about what to wear to her best friend's wedding because it didn't seem like a happy occasion, not when Yasmin was so angry and moody the few weeks leading up to this day. She couldn't be comforted, no matter what; still, Mira was happy to have a pretty dress to wear to her friend's wedding.

"Why don't you go bathe so I can braid your hair?" Um Zara suggested, giving her a little shove. Mira smiled and rushed to her room to get ready.

After they both got dressed, Mira and her stepmother made their way through the settlement until they approached the large, black tent set up in the communal courtyard. It was surrounded by decorated camels and lined with fire sticks. Mira's eyes widened as they entered. Inside, the entire floor was covered with carpets. The smoke from the incense covered the tent in a rich, earthy smell. There were dozens of large pillows lined on the floor for the women to sit on, along with a short, wooden table that held all sorts of snacks, from dates, to figs and rice with bowls of camel meat.

The tribe's women gathered. Their hairs were braided, and they wore their finest clothes. Their hands and feet were dyed red with henna. They wore silver and gold coins on their heads, necks and feet, clinging together as they walked. The tent was filled with a hundred different conversations and laughter. Mira sat down with her stepmother on one of the cushions as an elder woman took to the center with a large drum and began beating it.

Conversations simmered down, as the women listened as the old lady began lamenting a song-like prayer. She thanked God for the blessed union and named the lineage of both parties that were about to marry, giving honor to their esteemed ancestry. Her strong poet-like voice carried through the tent, and her drumbeat even louder. Mira was enthralled.

The wedding ceremony of the Bedouin tribe was similar to that of her village, but also a bit different. Its energy was rawer. The drums echoed through the empty desert that their tribe had traveled through over the centuries—a testament to their people. Finally, after the woman finished her song, she began releasing a long, wavering, high-pitched sound representing trills of joy. "*Lolololoeeesh,*" they sang in unison, rapidly moving their tongue back and forth, placing their hands above their mouth to make the sound ring across the space before them.

Soon, the doors to the tents opened, and all the women stood to the sides as Yasmin slowly entered, flanked by female members of her family. Her eyes were downcast as she walked forward. She wore a beautiful, black dress embroidered with red, gold, and green yarn. Her long *sheila* trailed behind her, and two braids fell to her waist. Her head, chest and feet were covered in gold and silver coin chains, rhythmically clacking against one another as she walked.

Her cheeks were dotted with red, and her big, brown eyes were lined with *kohl*. She looked down; her hands clenched in front of her. She was beautiful. She didn't look like the Yasmin she knew, but a radiating, young bride.

The women continued their high-pitched shouts of joy as Yasmin made her way to the center of the tent and sat on an elaborately designed set of cushions. Her mother and sisters began dancing for her as the women musically beat the drums. Yasmin didn't look at them. Instead, she kept her eyes down as the other women joined in on the dancing.

Soon, the energy in the tent picked up as the women danced, sang and talked joyously. This was the first wedding to happen in the tribe since they had moved. The wedding celebrated not only the union of the two most prominent families in their tribe but also their good fortune and new home.

Her stepmother was distracted in conversation, and Mira slowly wiggled through the crowded tent and sat near her best friend. Yasmin was the only person not enjoying this day. In fact, she looked furious. Her eyes were angry as she kept her hand clenched into a fist, her nails nearly ripping through her palm. Mira's heart was heavy at her friend's situation. She reached out and placed her hands in Yasmin's, holding her tight.

Yasmin looked at her friend, her eyes watering. Mira gave her a tight, understanding smile and held her. "I'm scared," Yasmin finally whispered, so low she barely heard her over the drums and conversations.

"I wish I could take you away from here," Mira whispered to her friend, wishing there was something she could do to help, knowing all too well there wasn't. These were their ways, and no one could escape the inevitable.

After a few hours, the women ate, and the party started dying down. There was an announcement that the groom would be arriving, and Yasmin clenched onto Mira's hand so tight it hurt. Mira tried to give her a reassuring smile, but Yasmin's eyes were hard as she stared directly ahead. Yasmin's mother whispered harshly to her daughter, telling her to lower her eyes, but Yasmin ignored her.

Soon, the tent's doors were held up as the groom's family entered, Yasmin's family led them in as they greeted each other warmly. Yasmin's annoyed expression didn't change as she greeted her new father-in-law, despite her mother's seething looks. The *Sheikh* just laughed it off, and formally introduced Zayad to his new bride.

Zayad smiled warmly. His cheeks flushed as he kissed his new bride on the forehead and sat down on the opposite side. Mira tried to give them some space, but Yasmin held her hand even tighter, so she stayed put, feeling awkward. After a few more prayers and speeches, the wedding was officially over. Zayad stood, holding his hand out to Yasmin, who refused to even look at him. Her mother rushed over, apologizing and whispering furiously at her disobedient daughter. Finally, Yasmin let go of Mira's numb hand and hesitantly took Zayad's.

Mira felt bad as she watched her unwilling friend go home with her new husband. Zayad wasn't a bad guy, and this was just how things were done, but Mira still hated that her friend didn't have a choice, and when her time came, she wouldn't have a choice either.

Mira couldn't sleep that night. She was filled with worry. *Would Yasmin change because she was now married?* Yasmin promised her when they first met that she wouldn't change—that she would always be her friend—but Mira wasn't so sure.

***

A week had passed since Yasmin's wedding, and Mira hadn't seen much of her friend. She didn't come to their usual hang out spot on the other side of the oasis. She didn't milk the sheep the same time Mira did. And when she saw a glimpse of her around town, Yasmin pretended not to see her. Mira tried to stay patient, but she couldn't help but worry. She nervously twisted the hair on the straw doll she made for Yasmin as she stood outside her family's sheep pen, hoping she would be able to give her the gift she had made.

She paused as she heard a familiar voice, "Why are you always this grumpy in the morning?" Yasmin murmured to the sheep she was milking as she gently caressed the annoyed animal. She always talked to them like they could understand, which was one of the reasons Mira was so fond of her friend.

"Yasmin?" Mira whispered, rushing to her friend. She threw her arms around her, hugging her tight. Even though it had only been a week, she missed her friend terribly. They had spent every day of the last year together.

Yasmin didn't return her hug. Instead, she just sat there stiffly. "Are you okay?" Mira asked, taking in her friend's appearance. Her eyes were darker than usual, and she looked like she hadn't been sleeping well.

"I'm fine," Yasmin answered gruffly, returning to her task.

Mira stood, awkwardly shifting her feet. "I made you this," she said hurriedly, holding the small straw doll out to her friend with an innocent smile plastered on her face.

Yasmin sighed, irritated. "I don't want it, Mira."

"Oh." Mira dropped her hand. She was disappointed and confused at her friend's cold attitude. "Do you want to play rocks with me today," Mira asked hopefully. It was Yasmin's favorite game. They would skip rocks in the oasis and see who could get it to skip the farthest.

"No," Her tone was clipped.

"We can play a different game…"

"No."

"How about we…"

"I said no, Mira!" Yasmin shouted angrily. "I don't want to play any more stupid games with you."

Mira flinched back at her aggressive tone; her eyes filled with hurt. "Did I do something to make you upset," she asked softly, not understanding why her friend was so angry.

Yasmin laughed bitterly. "You just don't get it, do you? I can't be friends with you anymore," she whispered harshly.

Mira felt her heart breaking, refusing to believe her friend's words. "Why," she asked instead.

"Because, Mira, I'm a married woman now. I can't be seen playing childish games. Especially not with someone like you." Those words devastated Mira so much she could hardly breathe. The other girls in the tribe never made their dislike a secret; they always called her a witch and made fun of her, but Yasmin never treated her any differently. She was always quick to jump to her defense.

Mira shook her head and wiped away her tears. "Yasmin, please don't do this. You're my best friend." Mira dropped the doll, clutching to her friend's arm instead, pleading with her not to cast her away like everyone else.

Yasmin swallowed, avoiding her gaze. Her own eyes were wet with unshed tears, but she hardened her features. She removed Mira's hands from her sleeve. "I'm sorry, Mira, but we can't be friends," she said softly.

"But why? Why can't we be friends? I'm sure Zayad wouldn't mind." Zayad liked Mira. He was the only person in the tribe, besides Yasmin, who didn't hate her.

Yasmin scowled at the mention of her husband. "Of course, he doesn't care! He's a man, Mira! He won't be the one who is looked down upon, the one who is shamed for being friends with the village *freak*." Mira blinked and took a step back, those two words ringing in her head. That was all she'd ever be. She turned around and ran.

"Mira!" Yasmin called her name.

Mira ignored her and sprinted away. She kept running until she was outside the oasis and into the desert. She ran and ran, her eyes blinded with tears. Then, she fell to her knees in exhaustion, her tears soaking into the soft sand.

Mira sobbed quietly and pulled her knees to her chest. "Mama," she whispered into the desert. "Sara…" She called their names over and over again. The pain in her heart made it difficult to breathe. She wished her father had buried her that day. She wished she didn't have to live with the shame and guilt, all because she was born different. Mira couldn't blame Yasmin for not wanting to be associated with her. She was poisonous to everyone around her. She was cursed.

"Mira?" The voice was quiet and timid as it called her. Mira looked up and saw Ayub. He was crouched down in front of her. His warm, brown eyes were filled with pain and worry.

"A-Ayub?" Mira whispered, crying even harder.

"Oh, Mira," Ayub was by her side, awkwardly crying with her. He didn't even know why she was crying, but his entire body shook as he cried for her.

"I'm-I'm so s-sorry, Ayub," Mira hiccupped through her tears.

"Mira, please don't cry. Don't cry anymore."

Mira wiped her eyes, trying to control her hitched breath. "You must hate me," she whispered after her tears had run dry. She couldn't even look at Ayub, ashamed of what she had done. She used him to save a tribe that now hated her.

"Why would I ever hate you? Mira, you're my best friend. I love you. Always," Ayub said, confused and sad.

"But I betrayed you. I led the tribe to your people's oasis, knowing they would steal it," Mira whispered, admitting her guilt.

Ayub cocked his head to the side, looking back at the oasis. "God declared this world to belong to humans. Our kind, we were punished a long time ago for our disobedience. We can live where there are no humans, but we can't claim any land for ourselves. We can't physically hurt any human either, and humans even have the power to enslave us. That is why *jinns* live in abandoned places and in the wild. Once humans begin to settle in a land, we must leave it. You didn't do anything wrong," Ayub explained.

"So, you're not mad at me," Mira asked, confused.

Ayub blinked. "I was waiting for you," he whispered. Mira peered at her friend under her wet lashes. All this time, she avoided the desert because she thought Ayub hated her.

"I missed you so much, Ayub!" Mira whispered.

Ayub grinned, that same light and excitement entering his eyes. "I missed you too, Mira."

Mira didn't tell Ayub why she was crying, and he didn't ask. He never asked her why she was sad. He only cared that she was sad, and he did everything he could to take away that grief and make her happy again. Mira spent the rest of the morning with Ayub. They talked, played and told stories. Mira felt her loneliness filter away, replaced by her love for Ayub.

15.

3 years later

"Ready or not, here I come!" Mira shouted. It was late afternoon, and Mira strolled around the date grove, looking for Ayub. It was winter now, and she spent her afternoons playing with Ayub while everyone else rested in their homes. Four years had passed since Mira led the tribe to the oasis, and even though the drought was over, and it began raining again, the tribe didn't leave. In fact, the small settlement had turned into a lively oasis town. Word spread that a large oasis town flourished in the middle of the desert, and caravans of merchants rerouted their journeys to stop there and replenish their resources.

The tribe, once a band of Bedouin nomads, was now rich in name and power. Their oasis was a rest stop and a trading post. However, while most of the tribe enjoyed their new fortune, Mira was, once again, cast aside. But because her family had the protection of the *Sheikh* and were now honorary members of the tribe, they tolerated her presence, but Mira knew they feared her.

More stories spread of her dark gift, and her little escapades into the desert alone to play with Ayub didn't help. Her father and stepmother tried to stop her from wandering, but they failed. Mira no longer tried to be accepted by the tribe. After Yasmin, her only friend in the village, had cast her away, she had no one left.

Even her younger brothers were too busy with playing with village children and tending to the animals to pay her any attention. Her father was never home, and her stepmother constantly nagged her. Mira's only friend in this world was Ayub, and she no longer cared what anyone thought of her.

She loved Ayub more and more with each day. But she hated the fact that he always won their games. "I give up!" Mira pouted, unable to find Ayub anywhere on the date farm.

"Who hoo!" Ayub shouted, shooting up from the ground. "I win!" he jumped in the air, swooping around in an aerial display.

"Not fair! You cheated!" Mira shouted.

"No, I didn't. You only said I couldn't hide outside the date palms, but you never said anything about the ground!" Ayub retorted, smugly wiggling his eyebrows. Mira crossed her arms, annoyed that Ayub was too good at hiding, tag and all other physical games.

Mira sighed, sat down on the sand, and used a stick to draw pictures. Ayub was always fascinated with the drawings. They weren't much—just rugged sketches of camels, houses and mountains—but Ayub loved each one.

"I wish I could see what was beyond the desert," Mira whispered. While everyone else was happy and content with their new home, Mira was depressed. Each time a caravan entered the oasis town, she was the first to run to them to ask questions and listen to their stories. She listened outside the communal tents when they discussed their travel with the *Sheikh* and other men of the town. She found herself constantly wondering what life beyond the desert was like.

Ayub shrugged. Being a desert *jinn* himself, he had no idea what lay beyond the dunes. He only went to the desert's edge once and saw the ocean. But even that sight terrified him, because of the *jinns* that lived under its waves, and he never went back.

"Aren't you even curious," Mira asked.

Ayub shrugged. "Not really. I think it's scary."

"You think everything is scary," Mira mumbled.

"I'd rather be here with you," Ayub said kindly. Mira smiled at him. Ayub was a simple being, content with his life. He never asked questions, never wondered. He simply accepted everything. Sometimes, Mira wished she were as simple. But her mind and heart were filled with longing for whatever lay beyond the desert.

Mira went home as the sun was starting to set. It was Friday, and no one was at the date palm grove. She had the place all to herself where she could play with Ayub.

"When will you stop this wandering?" her stepmother began as soon as Mira entered. Mira sighed, used to her nagging. While her stepmother was kind to her at first, she increasingly grew irritated with Mira, and was swayed by the women's gossip.

She constantly complained to her father about Mira, who just quietly listened, giving Mira a tired look. A lot of the tribesmen still did not trust him, especially with Mira being his daughter. But they were forced to respect him, regardless. Since her father grew up in a village, he was able to help tremendously in the tribe's transition from nomad to a stationary town and trading post. While the nomads were experts in negotiating and hosting, his opinion was valued in matters of trading and farming.

"Sorry," Mira whispered numbly, not wanting to hear another lecture.

"This is why everyone in the tribe talks about you. Instead of doing your chores, you run off alone, speaking to yourself like a madwoman. How am I supposed to live like this? Girls your age are already married, tending to their husbands. But you're here and unable to find a husband."

Mira had already heard this speech a thousand times. She learned never to talk back and walk away quietly when her stepmother finished talking. Mira entered her small room and sat on her straw bed. She pulled her leather-covered book from under her bed using her fingers to trace the letters inside. She knew how to write every letter in that book as she had copied it onto the sand a thousand times. However, she could not read. The book was given to her by a traveler who stopped at their oasis a year ago. He was the greatest storyteller Mira had ever met.

Every night, the children and adults gathered in front of a fire, and he told the most amazing tales. Mira was always the first to sit in front of the fire. She constantly followed him around, asking questions. He just chuckled every time and pointed out that she was more curious than a *jinn*. When he was leaving, Mira was so sad. She cried and cried and cried until he opened his bag and gave her a book.

It was her most prized possession, but not many people in the tribe knew how to read, and even if they did, she doubted they would read to her. Every night, she came up with a different story that the book might be about. One day, she resolved that it was about a camel herder who found a magical lamp. Then, the next day, she thought it might be a story about a caravan traveler who met a king.

"Mira!" her stepmother called, tugging her from her musing. Mira quickly shut the book, hid it back under her bed, and made her way to the living quarter of their small, brick home. Her father was sitting cross-legged, prayer beads in hand, while her stepmother sat across from him. Mira quickly greeted her father and sat down, confused as to why they wanted to see her.

"We have great news!" her stepmother began, pulling Mira's attention. "We found you a husband!" Mira blinked at the announcement, looking at her father who was idly counting his beads. "The *Sheikh*, may Allah bless him, has convinced his cousin to marry you. He is a well-known man, and you will be his third wife."

Mira frowned. She had given up on the thought of ever getting married. Why would anyone agree to marry someone like her? "Baba?" Mira looked at her father to confirm the news.

Her father cleared his throat. "He will be a decent husband to you, Mira, and you will do as I say," Baba declared. Her stepmother nodded approvingly.

"You can return to your room now," her stepmother said, dismissing her.

Mira returned to her room, confused. To be honest, she hadn't thought much of marriage. Suddenly, she was apprehensive at the prospect. She remembered Yasmin's anger and fear in the weeks leading up to her marriage to Zayad, and now she was filled with the same fear. What would happen to her? Would she change as Yasmin did, and stop playing, stop imagining and wandering? Would she stop being a child once she got married?

Mira felt her heart shatter. Her hopes to one day travel beyond the desert were also shattered. She would live her life like every other Bedouin girl, married, doing chores and raising children. Except her children would be cursed, just like her.

***

Mira spent the next few days filled with apprehension. She walked around the settlements, spying on her betrothed. She had wondered if he was kind and handsome like Zayad, but Mira was horrified to find that he was an old, graying man. She felt like her days were numbered. Every girl got married and had little say in who was chosen for her; however, Mira couldn't imagine being someone's wife. She didn't want to be like the women of the village who never played and never questioned a thing.

She didn't want to weave baskets and gossip over tea. She wanted to see the world. She wanted to go beyond the desert. But as a girl, she knew that dream was next to impossible. Her father and stepmother had not mentioned her marriage after informing her all those nights ago. Her stepmother, however, was in a great mood, excited to finally be rid of Mira, and her father was as staunch and unaffectionate as ever.

"Mira! You're not listening to me, are you?" Ayub grumbled as he sat on top of the dune outside their settlements. Mira blinked, lost in thought. Not even Ayub was able to ease her worry.

"Sorry, what did you say," Mira asked. Ayub rolled his eyes, plopping into the sand. Mira covered her eyes as sand flew around; she gave him an annoyed look.

"I said a large caravan is heading this way!" Ayub grinned. Mira gasped excitedly. It had been months since a caravan entered their oasis.

"Are you sure? Where? How close are they?" Ayub knew how much Mira loved the caravans that stopped by their oasis. He made it his job to inform her anytime one was about to arrive.

Ayub tapped his chin, contemplating the question. "They are still a few days out, I think. They are walking really slow. I got tired of watching them."

Mira clapped her hands excitedly. This was the first piece of good news she had in a long time. She finally felt like she had something to look forward to.

Mira spent the rest of the day imagining the stories her book might hold. She imagined it was about a caravan from a faraway kingdom that had a castle made from sand, and even a river. Mira had never seen a river, but last year, one of the caravans had traveled from a land with a great river. One of them told Mira that the river stretched for miles and miles; it was supposedly a hundred times bigger than the oasis.

She wondered what a river looked like, or a city. But even more so, she longed to see the ocean. She wanted to know if it actually looked like her eyes, the way Ayub said it did. Mira closed her eyes, counting the days until the caravan would finally arrive.

***

The day had finally come. Word arrived from the warriors who patrolled the outer limits of their oasis town that a large caravan was headed their way. There was a thrill of excitement in the air because this would be the biggest caravan to ever stop in their oasis. *Maybe it belonged to a king!* she thought, her excitement growing and growing. She soon forgot that she was about to be an old man's bride and that she probably wouldn't be able to chase around the caravan in excitement with the other children anymore once she got married.

That's when everything would change. This made Mira extremely sad. She wished more than ever that her mother was here to comfort her and tell her everything would be okay. Ayub just wouldn't understand, and her stepmother couldn't wait to be rid of her.

So, she only had one person she could talk to, but she was afraid they wouldn't want to talk to her.

16.

Mira stood outside the small, brick home that belonged to the first friend she ever had—well, the first human friend. She stopped by this house many times, watching, unable to say anything. Ever since Yasmin got married and told Mira they could no longer be friends; they barely shared a few words here and there.

But now, Mira needed someone to talk to. Someone who would hold her hand and understand her fear, just as Mira did for Yasmin on her wedding day, and all the days leading up to it. Someone to calm her nerves and tell her everything would be okay. Mira pulled on the sleeves of her dress, contemplating how she would approach the house. Then, she felt a hand on her head.

Mira ducked down, staring up at Zayad who gave a grin. "What is the blue-eyed princess doing at my humble home?" Mira smiled. Zayad and his father were the only ones in the tribe who didn't fear and avoid her. Zayad went out of his way to be nice to her. Every time a caravan came by, he got her a small trinket and gift, calling her a blue-eyed princess.

However, Zayad and his father were the only ones who really knew her role in finding their new home. Mira gave him a small smile. "I wanted to talk to Yasmin."

Zayad raised his eyebrow in surprise, then quickly recovered. "Of course, I'm sure my wife will be happy to see her old friend," Zayad assured her as he ushered her into the sandy courtyard.

Mira stood outside while Zayad went into the home to inform Yasmin of her arrival. She was extremely nervous, not sure how Yasmin would react. Zayad came out a few minutes later with Yasmin trailing behind him. She was far from the mischievous girl Mira had met a few years back. She looked a lot older and had grown into her body.

"Well, I'll leave you ladies alone. Don't get into too much trouble," Zayad said, excusing himself and giving Mira a wink. Mira felt like a nervous child next to Yasmin, who had grown tall and mature.

"Would you like to come in?" Yasmin asked, holding the wooden door open. Mira nodded and followed her into the cozy home. It was smaller than her house, but warm and inviting. The floors were covered with straw rugs to protect from the dust, and the walls were decorated with woven artwork. There was just enough natural light shining in from the small window. The walls were lined with patterned cushions that were red, black and gold, making the room appear spacious.

Mira sat down while Yasmin went to retrieve water. When she returned, she sat across from her. "How have you been," Yasmin finally asked after a short silence.

"Good," Mira replied, giving her the standard answer.

"We haven't spoken in so long. I was surprised to see you today," Yasmin commented.

"I know you don't want me here, but I didn't know who else to speak to," Mira confessed.

Yasmin sighed sadly. "Mira, I know I haven't been kind to you, but that isn't because I dislike you as a person, I just...as a wife, I can't be seen with you. The other wives already give me a hard time, and if I were seen running around with you...I was scared I would be cast aside."

Mira swallowed the lump in her throat. She understood why Yasmin wouldn't want to be seen with her. The other people in the tribe feared her, and the only reason she wasn't expelled from the tribe was because of the *Sheikh*. But it still hurt her heart to hear it.

"I'm getting married," Mira announced instead, not wanting to talk about her reputation in the tribe.

Yasmin gave her a surprised look, "You are?"

"Yes! He is an important man in the tribe. He's the *Sheikh's* cousin. So, maybe it won't be so bad. Um Zara said she will get me a new dress and shoes, and that my future husband has many camels and sheep," Mira tried to sound enthusiastic.

"The *Sheikh's* cousin? You mean, the old man who has two wives," Yasmin asked incredulously. Mira just nodded, taking a sip of her water to hide the quiver in her lips. "Um Zara said it won't happen until I come of age, but I'm not sure what that means. Also, I'm not sure how to be a wife. I was wondering why everyone changes when they get married. What happens? Will I change, too? Will I no longer want to play and tell stories?"

Yasmin sighed heavily, giving Mira a sympathetic look. "Mira, it's not really proper to talk about these things to unmarried women…"

"Then how will I know anything!" Mira wondered. "If I had a mother, she would tell me…"

"You're right. You deserve to know. I did promise to tell you what happens before my own marriage," Yasmin blushed then began. "Well, first, you have to become of age. That means that you will bleed every month…from your private area." Mira blinked, confused, then remembered she often saw her mother washing bloody rags, and every time she asked why, she said she would tell her when she was older.

"Does that hurt?" Mira asked, horrified.

"Not usually, but sometimes, it can be uncomfortable. It just means that you are a woman and that you can get married and have children."

"Then I hope it never happens to me," Mira whispered to herself, defeated, but Yasmin heard.

"I'm sorry, Mira. You were supportive when I was marrying Zayad. Looking back, I feel so foolish because you were right. Zayad is a great husband, and it could have been a lot worse. Us girls, we don't have a lot of say in who we marry and how we live. Unfortunately, we were born to wed. But you're different," Yasmin said, passionately holding Mira's hands. "You are not bound by the shackles of this society. Why should you follow its rules when it spits on you and casts you aside? I don't know whether you look upon us with pity or envy, but people don't have the same expectations of you as they have of us. So, you have a choice when a lot of us don't."

Mira shook her head sadly. "That's not a choice, Yasmin. I didn't choose to live outside of society. And even as it shuts me out, it expects me to behave according to its rules. I have to live by all of its limitations without any of its benefits." Yasmin stared at Mira with what appeared to be sadness or pity. "I don't want to get married, but I have no more of a choice than you did. At least your husband has all his teeth," Mira whispered, laying her head on the table.

Yasmin slumped in defeat, rubbing her back. Mira closed her eyes. This was the first time anyone had touched her in years. She lifted her head to look at her friend, her heart aching with envy and sadness.

"You know the night before I was to marry Zayad, I was so angry that I packed my bags and prepared to run away. I thought I'd rather take my chances out there than be married," Yasmin admitted.

Mira was surprised her friend had tried to run away, "what did you see," She asked curiosity sparking in her heart.

"Nothing, I barely made it past the first dune. I was too scared," she laughed. "But I'm glad I stayed because I've truly grown to love Zayad. I'm not saying it will be the same for you, but sometimes we realize our destiny when we least expect it."

While She appreciated Yasmin's advice Mira didn't think she could ever accept a marriage with the *Sheikh's* cousin or anyone else for that matter. "But, don't you ever wonder what's out there," Mira questioned, it was all she thought about lately. She found herself imagining day and night what lay beyond the desert. Her mind and soul were no longer present in this oasis.

"No, not anymore," Yasmin admitted. "I've accepted my place here. This is the only life I will ever know. If you could leave, would you do it," She asked.

"Yes," Mira admitted without hesitation if she had an opportunity to leave the desert, she would take it in a heartbeat. If there was a world out there where she wasn't cursed, she would find it. If there was a place where Mira could be happy, she would search for it until she reached the ends of the Earth. But, unlike Yasmin, Mira did wander the desert for days and nights and all it brought her was pain and misery. She wasn't sure a world where she could be happy even existed.

"Yasmin, would you still be my friend if my eyes were brown like yours?" Mira wasn't sure why she asked, but she often wondered how different her life would be if she had normal eyes.

Yasmin moved to sit next to Mira and pulled her in for a hug. "I'm so sorry, Mira. I've been so awful to you! Everyone has. Zayad told me what you did. You saved us all. I wish it were enough to make people listen."

Mira just cried, holding onto her friend. She was so tired of being hated, tired of being feared and misunderstood, and tired of being a burden. But

Mira knew after she walked out of this house, they would go back to being strangers. She didn't want Yasmin's reputation to be dragged down. She didn't want the tribe to hate Yasmin like they hated her. Yasmin deserved to be loved.

Mira pulled away and wiped her eyes. "Thank you, Yasmin." Mira appreciated this kindness, and even though they would never be friends like they used to, she still loved her

"Mira, I will tell Zayad to speak to his father. Maybe he can convince him to stop this marriage," Yasmin tried to assure her. Mira just gave her a small nod, knowing that it would be pointless. *Her* father wouldn't change his mind. And now she had to decide if she would accept her fate like Yasmin did, or take a risk to see what lay beyond the desert.

17.

Salim

Salim struggled as he led his heavy camel across the soft desert sand, his feet sinking into the ground, each step more staggering than the last. It had been several days since they passed their last Bedouin village, collecting water and other provisions. Since water was so scarce in this portion of the journey, each man only took a few sips each day, enough to keep them hydrated.

Word had spread of a large oasis town that seemed to spring up out of nowhere over the last few years. The tribe had a friendly and hospitable reputation, often hosting travelers and caravans for weeks at a time, trading precious Bedouin goods, such as wool, leather, and woven carpets.

Stern men with covered faces set upon high horses stalked them as they journeyed across the desert. This meant that the oasis was close, and these men would protect them from bandits. The men never neared them, instead, they kept their distance as the caravan slowly moved along the desert.

Salim was eager to reach the town, not just to rest and replenish his resources, but to practice his trade. While Bedouins were known for their superstitious and suspicious nature, they were also some of the most hospitable and generous people, often overpaying for small services with what little they had, and from what Salim had heard, this tribe had plenty.

Salim licked his dry lips and squinted his eyes, loosening the turban around his mouth and nose. He peered before him, letting out a relieved sigh. In the distance, he saw the great desert oasis glittering like a jewel nestled between the dunes. There were large date palms surrounding it, covering the many scattered sandstone homes in its shade. It was an astonishing sight to see such life flourish after weeks in the desert.

Salim trotted forward with the rest of the weary caravan. Once they neared the oasis, they were greeted by three men standing tall on their horses. They all had their faces covered, except one young man, who climbed down his horse to greet the caravan.

"Peace be upon you!" the young man shouted cheerfully. He looked to be in his twenties with dark, tanned skin, dark brown eyes, thick lashes and a short black beard. Salim gave him a quick assessment, as he often did with anyone he crossed.

"My name is Zayad Ibn Hussain Al Nazir, and I will be your host." The leader of the caravan and their guide, Abdullah, walked forward to return the greeting while Salim and the others waited behind him patiently.

"Peace be upon you as well!" Abdullah answered. "Your oasis is like a paradise for the weary traveler! May our Lord protect you from the evil eye."

The man laughed heartily. "Yes, it is a paradise in our hearts, and a blessing from our Lord! From where have you come?"

"We traveled from Fez, the great walled city. We are heading to the land of the Nile, trading silks, spices and metals," Abdullah told him.

The man nodded. "Well, Bani Nazir welcomes you to our oasis. You shall be our guests here for as long as you need. However, we cannot allow any weapons into our oasis," the man said, gesturing at the men behind him, who quickly began searching the group.

Salim tried not to be too irritated as they took his sword. He knew he would get it back eventually, but he hated being without a weapon. Instead, he gave the stern men a smile and a polite nod. When it came to Bedouin tribes, Salim knew to play by their rules.

The men waited patiently while all their weapons were seized. "You shall receive these back at the end of your stay. Now, welcome. We have prepared tents and food."

"Thank you!" Abdullah said gratefully, following the man along with the rest of the group.

The oasis was quite large—more like a small town than a Bedouin camp. Salim heard the *Sheikh* of this tribe was guided here through a dream during the seven-year drought. Their people went from being a small, relatively unknown nomadic tribe to a well-respected, wealthy tribe, even among some of the more well-known tribes. Their name and status quickly rose in rank as the custodians of the great oasis. Salim began hearing of the oasis weeks before they arrived. The other trading town and villages nearby often spoke of the miracle oasis and the blessed tribe that settled there. They said the oasis was protected by a powerful *jinn*, and that its water had healing properties.

Salim huffed at that, chalking it up to Bedouin superstition. He was a man of logic and science. But looking around at this burst of life surrounded by a sea of sand, he could understand why they thought it was a miracle.

He wasn't quite sure how they managed to find such a gem in the desert, but from the look of their many camels, fattened livestock and towering date palm, they must have been truly blessed.

Salim and the rest of the caravan passed many small homes scattered around the oasis, its dwellers curiously watching them from the courtyard while the children chased them, only to be shooed away by the covered women.

They walked behind the men to an area meant for guests. There weren't any residential homes nearby. Salim stared in awe at the oasis, it's clear, sweet water sparkling in the sun. The man led them to a small camp with scattered tents. In front, there were several large clay pots filled with water and a section to feed and tie the animals.

The men quickly tied their camels; finally, with a nod from their host, they rushed to the pots of cool water, each taking a deep drink. Salim had never tasted such sweet, crisp water. He closed his eyes as the cool liquid went down his parched throat. Shortly after, Salim, along with a few other men from the caravan, were shown their communal tents.

The tents were very spacious. Inside, there were bowls of nuts and dates, along with water and camel milk for them to drink. There were also several blankets, pillows and straw mats for them to sleep on. Having been traveling with the caravan for almost three weeks now, Salim was used to sharing small spaces with other men. However, this was nicer than most of the places they had stayed.

Outside the tent were several tubs, already filled with water for the men to bathe and clean themselves. Salim bathed and wore fresh clothes. He washed his thobe and turban, as well as his leather socks and hung them on a nearby tree. By the time he was finished, the afternoon prayer was being called out, and Salim returned to his tent, desperate for sleep.

Salim woke up later that evening. The caravan was invited to a feast hosted by the *Sheikh* to welcome them to their oasis town. At the end of the feast, each man would pay his respects to the *Sheikh*, giving him a gift to thank him for his hospitality.

He straightened his thobe, then oiled his beard and combed his hair, finally feeling like himself after a long journey. He followed the rest of the caravan down a path lit with torches which guided them to the feast. Salim's mouth watered as the smell of roasted meat drifted in the air, making the men hurry their steps as they entered the gathering.

They were led by another young man from the tribe to a large communal area set up with thick wool carpets that were lined with cushions for the men to sit upon. The ground was lit with colorful, glass oil lamps covering the area in a soft glow of gold, green and red. Salim sat next to his fellow roommates, impressed with the life these Bedouins had built, all the while taking notes of the riches he could earn. Unlike the rest of the caravan, Salim wasn't a trader. He was a locally trained physician and spent the last few years working for his uncle at his family's apothecary.

After years of saving, he finally earned enough money to fund his travel to Damascus, where he hoped to study medicine at Nur al-Din Bimaristan, the most prestigious hospital in the Islamic world. However, Salim didn't have nearly enough to pay for his board and tuition there, which is why he spent the last few weeks working in different villages along his journey. He set up a make-shift hospital and treated patients at each stop, earning money along the way.

Salim watched as a line of young men dressed in Bedouin ceremonious clothes arrived with large trays of food consisting of camel meat, roasted goat, bread, dates, soup and camel milk. Everyone waited hungrily as the *Sheikh* arrived with his entourage. The *Sheikh* entered with a determined walk. His *kohl*-lined eyes were watchful as his guests stood to greet him.

He waved his hand, encouraging everyone to sit, "Welcome, friends, to the Banu Nazir. We have a Bedouin proverb, 'A visitor comes with ten blessings, eats one and leaves nine,' and it was the blessing left behind by weary travelers that has kept my tribe prosperous. So, eat, drink, rest and trade," the *Sheikh* announced as the men clapped and cheered.

A young boy read a short prayer aloud, and the men began to feast. Hands and arms were entangled across the spread that lay before them, each man grabbing a portion of the delightful food that was offered to them.

After everyone had eaten, they were served tea with date biscuits and hash to smoke as the men chatted. Soon after, the *Sheikh* and his entourage stood, making their way to a black tent perched at the end of the communal gathering. As was the custom of the Bedouin tribes, each traveler entered the tent and presented the *Sheikh* with a gift. Salim waited patiently as the traders lined up to enter the tent one by one, each eager to personally greet the *Sheikh*.

Salim cleared his throat, dusting off his garments. He stood outside the great tent with the other merchants from his caravan, each chattering as they held their gifts of spices, silk, silver, metal and other goods. But Salim held something different in his small, wooden box. He waited quietly until one of the guards motioned for him to enter.

Salim gave the man a nod as he entered the large tent. The *Sheikh* sat upon red embroidered cushions; one knee was perched up while his other leg was folded under him. His posture was relaxed as he held prayer beads in his hands, his fingers lazily working the beads, one by one. The *Sheikh* was old, but his eyes were keen and watchful as he observed Salim with limited interest. His gray beard was stained red with henna, and his head was wrapped with a simple black turban, one end hanging loosely over his shoulder. Next to him were three other men, one of whom Salim recognized as Zayad, the man who had welcomed them earlier that morning.

The *Sheikh* lifted his hand to his heart to acknowledge Salim who gave him a warm smile, bowing low in a display of respect. "*Shiekh*, thank you so much for your hospitality. The Banu Nazir have surely exceeded their reputation as the most hospitable tribe in the desert. My name is Salim Al-Zuhair from the great city of Fez, and I'd like to present you with a gift, if you would please accept." Salim opened his wooden box, presenting its contents to the *Sheikh*.

To the untrained eye, Salim's gift wasn't as flashy or as grand as what some other merchants had presented. Inside the box were several tablets of medicine Salim had manufactured. The desert folk had no doctors and used only local herbs to treat themselves, so Salim knew they had likely never seen medicine before.

The men beside him looked unimpressed as they began to murmur. "What is this?" one of the men proclaimed. "Do you insult our *Sheikh*?" The others nodded in agreement.

The *Sheikh* raised his hand, silencing them. "Please, excuse my brethren. They are but simple Bedouin folks. Ask them only of camels and war," the *Sheikh* chuckled. "They do not recognize a learned man when they see one, and this medicine will be of benefit to my health."

Salim raised his eyebrow, impressed with the *Sheikh's* wisdom and knowledge. To be honest, he didn't expect him to recognize the medicine, assuming he was just an ignorant nomad. "Thank you, *Sheikh*, you humble me with your wisdom. Unfortunately, I do not have gifts of silk and gold. I only come with my knowledge and experience, and if you would allow me, I would be honored to treat your sick and elderly," Salim declared, repeating his practiced speech with another bow.

"Tell me, Salim, what do you hope to gain by treating our sick and elderly? As you know, he who focuses on the snake will miss the scorpion," the *Sheikh* said, quoting the Arabic proverb, and hinting at his lack of trust in Salim's words.

Salim swallowed nervously, clearing his throat. This *Sheikh* was not like the uneducated villagers he was used to encountering. He spent the last few months traveling with different caravans and setting up temporary hospitals to treat the sick—or pretend to treat them. In exchange for his services, he received many goods, which he then traded for silver and gold in hopes of funding his education.

"My reward is only with my Lord," Salim said instead, giving the *Sheikh* his most charming smile.

But the *Sheikh* was not so easily swayed, "and where did you learn such knowledge?"

"I was an apprentice for many years under my father, who was a skilled physician. I also ran his apothecary for many years after he was called to return to our Lord," Salim said, hoping to sound sincere and dutiful.

"Your camel is quite heavy for a man seeking only the reward of his Lord. I almost mistook you for a merchant," the *Sheikh* laughed. Salim chuckled nervously. Sure, he took advantage of the uneducated people to fulfill his own gain, but he *did* actually help them—well, he helped some of them.

"My Lord is truly bountiful, and the people of the desert are the most generous," Salim responded, offering a strictly political answer.

"Our generosity is vast like the desert, and our justice is swift like the wind. I have seen many deceivers try to come to my oasis and sell people cures that do not exist. They think because we are simple Bedouins, we do not know anything of the world beyond our desert. So, you can appreciate my wariness."

Salim rubbed his sweaty hands on the fabric of his thobe. He wasn't expecting an interrogation. He had imagined this playing out much differently. Perhaps it was best to abort the mission. Clearly, this *Sheikh* was more distrusting than the other tribal leaders Salim had come across. "*Sheikh*, I apologize if I gave you the wrong impression. With your permission, I will reflect upon myself and learn from your humility."

"Don't be ridiculous! It's not often we have a physician in our part of the world. Our people will surely benefit from a man of your standard. A tent is being set for your practice as we speak. You will treat my people, and if you are sincere, you will be rewarded plenty... However, if you are being deceitful and wish to take advantage of the ignorance of the people, then you will face our justice," the *Sheikh* proclaimed.

"*Sheikh*, as you know, not all sickness can be treated. I can only try my best and leave the rest to God," Salim persisted, suddenly afraid. He was used to temporarily minimizing the symptoms of those he treated with poppy, cannabis or simple placebo plants. He did not actually treat anyone. He did not have the means nor the time.

"Good health is a crown worn by the healthy that only the ill can see. You will be judged on your sincerity. Be sincere and all shall be well," the *Sheikh* said, motioning for his guards. The conversation was over, and Salim was given his task.

Salim gave the *Sheikh* a heartfelt smile, bowing low, "as you wish."

Salim left the tent, trying hard to keep his features pleasant as he tried to make his way back to his communal tent. "This way!" his guard said gruffly, leading him in another direction. "Your living quarters were moved."

"But my things..."

"Your things are in your new tent," the man said, leading him to a large, black tent near the oasis, and away from the other members of the caravan. "You will sleep here, and your first patients will arrive in the morning, so be prepared," the man warned.

"Ah, that's very kind of your *Sheikh*," Salim murmured, eyeing the two guards who were placed not so subtly a few yards away.

The man stood unmoved, waiting for Salim to enter his new home.

Salim entered his tent with a curse, rubbing his temple; things didn't go as planned. He was supposed to set up a little hospital to give people some small and temporary cures to numb the pain, then, he was supposed to be on his way as a hero with his treasure. But now, with this sharp-eyed *Sheikh* on his back, he would have to actually practice medicine. He would have to use techniques reserved for the rich and the royals to treat these desert fools, all for a few pieces of wool and grains!

18.

The next morning, Salim was awoken by the murmurs of the tribesmen and women who stood outside his tent, patiently waiting for the doctor to treat them. Salim gave them a tense smile as they began piling in front of him, shouting their ailments and begging him to cure them. Salim held up his hands. "Please, people, calm down," he said, trying to quiet the rumbling crowd, but it was useless. Mothers pushed their sick children toward him, and old men and farmers yelled for his attention.

"Enough!" came a shout from behind them. The crowd immediately quieted and moved back, giving the man room. "We have not been properly introduced. My name is Zayad Bin Nazir, and I'm here to assist you with your tenure. Anything you need to help treat my people, you will get it," the man said. It was obvious he was greatly respected in this tribe.

Salim gratefully took his hand, "Thank you, Zayad. I am Salim. It's a pleasure to meet you. Unfortunately, I won't be able to treat this many people without proper facilities."

Zayad nodded to his men, who immediately dispersed the crowd. "Now," Zayad said, "Tell me what you need so we can prepare it for you."

Zayad and his men built beds, prepared water for sanitation, and gathered whatever medicinal herbs they had in their proximity—and it was pitiful. While some ingredients could be used to stop bleeding and treat certain ailments, he wasn't sure how much he could actually do. But he would have to try his best and hope the *Sheikh* saw his sincerity.

***

Salim spent the next few days along with his newly assigned assistant treating people from the tribe. Most suffered from diseases of the lung caused by the harsh desert climate, and from a lifetime of inhaling sand particles. Some children had the pox, date palm harvesters had broken limbs from falling during harvest—their bones would have to be reset—and old men and women had clouded eyes.

By the end of each day, Salim was exhausted. This was the most he practiced medicine since his father had died. He planned to save his skills for the elite cities he crossed, not these nomadic nobodies. However, if he wanted to keep his head, he would have to make do with what he had.

After a few days in his makeshift hospital, Salim was called to see the *Sheikh* and give him an update. Even though he was trying his best with what little he had to treat these people, he was still nervous, not sure what to expect from the *Sheikh*. The stern guard who seemed to be following Salim everywhere escorted him to the *Sheikh's* tent.

Salim entered the smoky tent, respectfully greeting the *Sheikh* and his entourage. He couldn't read the *Sheikh's* face, and he was usually good at reading people and charming them into spending their money. But this *Sheikh* was different. He was hawk-eyed and not easily trusting, and he seemed to see through Salim, which made him nervous.

"*Sheikh*, I wish to thank you for the facility you built. I have spent the last few days tirelessly treating your people, and I hope that you can see my sincerity," Salim said, placing his hand on his heart.

"A camel does not need to remind the rider he has two humps, and sincerity is not something that can be declared. However, the people have been pleased with your service—for the most part—especially our young men who unfortunately fell from the date palms. However, I hear you turned away many of our old who are struggling to breathe."

Salim cleared his throat, prepared for this question. "*Sheikh*, I don't mean to turn anyone away. But as you know, these men suffer from sand sickness. It affects many people living in the desert, and I simply do not have the medicine to treat it," Salim tried to explain.

The *Sheikh* gave him a discerning look, motioning at one of the guards standing by the entrance of the tent. The man stepped forward carrying a wooden box, and Salim's heart sank. The *Sheikh* grabbed the box, opened it, and placed it in front of Salim.

"The most common sickness for my people is sand sickness. At a certain age, we begin coughing up blood and struggling to breathe. The desert gives us life, then takes our final breath. However, many years ago, a great scholar came to our tribe. I was just a boy at the time, but I will never forget this man. He had a tent, much like yours; for weeks, he treated our sick and elderly. Back then, our tribe was not the affluent people you see here today. We did not have material wealth, gold and silk; we didn't welcome caravans of silver and spices. We didn't even have goods to trade. We lived in a simpler time," the *Sheikh* said, almost longingly.

"However, one thing I always remember about this scholar, may Allah be pleased with him, is that he was able to cure sand sickness. He used a special plant that he smoked, and those affected would inhale the smoke of the plant. In a few short weeks, they would be breathing better. Curiously enough, that plant looked just like this one right here," the *Sheikh* finished, looking directly at Salim.

Salim cleared his throat, trying his best to look sincere, hoping the *Sheikh* couldn't hear his hammering heart. "Ah, *Sheikh*, these plants are not mine. They belong to my uncle. I was just delivering it for him," Salim lied smoothly. "Surely you can understand. A man cannot eat bread from a table that isn't his."

"Hmm," the *Sheikh* stroked his beard thoughtfully. "We are in communication with all the trading towns nearest to us, and you have left quite the impression. Word is that you pretended to cure people with poppy, demanded their life savings, then took off."

"I demanded nothing, *Sheikh*! I am appalled at these accusations. I am a doctor, not some swindler!" Salim stood, outraged. He slowly backed down as a blade appeared at his throat. Salim held out his hand. "Please, *Sheikh*, you must believe me. I am not here to swindle you. I'll treat the patients."

"Then prove it. I will give you two weeks to heal my people. If you are able to do so, I will allow you to leave; however, if you are a swindler taking advantage of the weak and the needy, then you shall face justice!" The threat was clear. If Salim did not treat all the patients, he would die.

Salim swallowed, bowing at his waist. "Of course, *Sheikh*. I will do my best."

All that work for nothing! Thought returning to his tent with a curse. Once

Salim discovered that villagers would pay any price to see a doctor, he played the part pretended to them, leaving with both treasure and honor. But now, this *Sheikh* was threatening everything he was hoping to build for himself.

Salim stared at the precious medicine the *Sheikh* had taken from him. "Damn old man!" The *Sheikh* was right. This medicine could be used to treat sand sickness and ease the lungs of his patients who were suffering. That's why he wanted to keep it and sell it at a high cost. He paid a lot of money for those precious and rare medicines and was expecting to make back his investment tenfold. After the seven-year drought, wild medical herbs that once grew in the desert were a rare occurrence. Their prices were astronomical, and now he had to waste it all on these camel herders! Salim couldn't believe his luck.

The next day, all the patients he had sent away returned, each suffering from sand sickness, their loud coughs ringing through his makeshift hospital. Salim felt himself die a little as he ground his precious medicine into a fine powder that he would burn, allowing his patients to inhale. The medicine would break apart the mucus that formed in the lungs to catch the sand particles.

Salim did this for several days before realizing his medicine was running out too quickly. There were too many patients, and not enough herbs. Salim crushed the last of his herbs, looking at the young boy who was wheezing before him, too young to have this disease. But the boy explained that he got lost in a bad sandstorm last year and was barely surviving.

His tearful mother stood by his side, crying and begging Salim to save her son. The world was full of sick and dying people, all begging to be saved, so, Salim had long ago shut his heart to the tears of a patient. But as he looked into the eyes of this brave, young boy, he couldn't help but feel a twang of sympathy.

"I have administered the medicine for your son. He will begin to cough out thick, yellow mucus in the next few days. Make sure you give him lots of water."

The mother cried and touched his feet. "Thank you! Thank you! May Allah reward you manifold!" Salim awkwardly patted the boys head. He was used to these tearful displays of gratitude, but this was the first time he actually did something to deserve it.

Salim took stock of the remainder of his medicine. He was almost out and hadn't even treated half of the cases. He had a feeling that the *Sheikh* would not be so understanding of his predicament. Perhaps the *Sheikh* knew he would never be able to treat all these people. "Dammit!" he shouted, kicking the box. This was useless. He was going to die, just like the patients he pretended to save.

Everything he worked for over the last few years—all the sacrifices, all the lies—for nothing! He would die in this desert instead of fulfilling his dream of reaching Damascus. He would be a failure, just like his uncle had predicted. Salim fell to the ground in despair.

"Here you go!" a timid voice whispered, holding the box that he had just thrown. Salim lifted his head, and a young girl stood before him, holding out his wooden box. Annoyed, Salim grabbed it and cast it aside. "Get lost, kid. The hospital is closed," he muttered, not in the mood to entertain any more curious Bedouin children.

"Why are you sad," the girl asked instead of leaving.

"Hah! Why am I sad? Because your beloved *Sheikh* is going to cut off my head for being unable to treat his backward tribe!"

The girl just frowned, and Salim finally noticed her strange eyes. They were bright blue with a sprinkle of gold. They were the strangest eyes he had ever seen, unnerving but beautiful. There was something old about her eyes that looked odd in contrast to her childish face.

"Why can't you treat them," the girl asked, ignoring the rest of his outburst. Salim sighed, not sure why he was talking to a strange Bedouin child, but since he was probably going to die tomorrow, he didn't have the energy to shoo her away.

"You see that," he asked, pointing to what was left of his medicinal herbs. "I need it to treat people, and I don't have any more of it. And since I can't treat them, I'm going to die tomorrow. So, forgive me if I'm not in my usual, charming mood. Impending death has a way of making a man forget his manner."

The girl just blinked at him, and instead of saying another word, he walked into his tent to sleep before his execution the following day.

19.

The next morning, patients were already lined up outside the tent. Salim took a deep breath. He barely slept. He contemplated escaping since his guards were no longer outside, but the desert was an inevitably slow death. Surely, the *Sheikh* was an understanding man. There was truly nothing Salim could do for these sick people, unless a miracle happened, and Salim didn't believe in miracles.

Salim sat in front of an old man who was wheezing loudly. This would be his last patient. He gave the man a tight smile. He at least had enough medicine to save one more patient. His hands shook as he opened his medic box, unprepared for what he was about to find.

"Dear God!" Salim couldn't believe his eyes. The box that had been empty yesterday was now full of the exact herbs he needed to treat his patient. The old man sitting in front of him, waiting to be treated, gave him a strange look. Salim was so sure he would die that day. Perhaps the *Sheikh* found some medicine and refilled his stock.

Salim took a deep breath. "Are you ready, uncle," he asked the confused man.

***

A week had passed since the *Sheikh* ordered Salim to treat all the cases of sand sickness in his tribe, and by some miracle, Salim had done it. The caravan was getting ready to leave, and Salim was permitted to join their goodbye feast. The tribe spared no expense, lavishing them with an array of spiced meat, bread and even rice. They drank camel milk and spent the night smoking hash and talking.

Salim was in a joyous mood. He had survived and healed all his patients; now, it was time for the *Sheikh* to keep his word and free him. Later that evening, the *Sheikh* called for Salim.

"*Sheikh!*" Salim greeted him cheerfully. The *Sheikh* nodded, gesturing for him to sit. Salim sat cross-legged across from him.

"I was quite skeptical when I heard a healer had entered our oasis, and when I sent word out to confirm your identity, I heard some sinister tales. However, you have proven to me that you are truly a skilled healer, and you have my thanks." The *Sheikh* slightly bowed his head to Salim in the ultimate display of respect.

"*Sheikh!* I couldn't have done it without you. Had you not replenished my medicine; I would surely have failed in my task." Not only had the *Sheikh* replenished his medicine, but he had given him extra to take.

The *Sheikh* raised his eyebrows slightly. The other men began to murmur. "Your medicine was replenished," he asked.

"Yes. Twice. You even gave me extra to take," Salim looked around at the empty faces. "Perhaps I am mistaken." *If it wasn't the* Sheikh, *then where had the medicine come from?* he thought.

"Leave us," the *Sheikh* demanded. The men began piling out of the tent, leaving only himself, Zayad and the *Sheikh* remaining. "Did you happen upon a little, blue-eyed girl," the *Sheikh* asked after the men had cleared out. Salim frowned. He remembered the curious little girl he had briefly vented to, but what did that child have to do with anything?

The *Sheikh* suddenly began laughing, along with Zayad, as if some secret joke had erupted between them. "If you see her again, make sure you thank her. That child saved your life!"

"How—" the *Sheikh* cut him off, raising his hand and gesturing at his son to bring over a wooden trunk. The *Sheikh* opened the trunk, turning it around for Salim. Salim coughed. He couldn't believe his eyes. The trunk was filled with silk, gold, silver and spices. It was more treasure than he had ever seen. "*Sheikh…*" Salim had no words.

"It's payment for your service."

"I don't know what to say…" Salim stammered, hypnotized by the treasure. "This is too much."

"You saved my people, and that is priceless. As the head of Banu Nazir, you have my gratitude. Please accept this humble gift."

"Thank you, *Sheikh*! Your generosity is greater than the sky!"

***

Salim whistled as he prepared his camel, following the routine he had practiced for the last few weeks as a traveling physician. He finally had enough to board a ship to Cairo, his final stop before Damascus. While Salim had no formal medical education, he worked under his father who was a gifted physician for many years. His father had attended medical school in Damascus before settling in Fez and working there for many years at his apothecary. However, after his father's death six years ago, Salim had no choice but to hand over the struggling apothecary to his uncle, who was tasked as guardian over him and his sisters.

His uncle pretended to care for them, using this painful time to convince him to hand over guardianship. Unbeknownst to him, his uncle used his claim to steal everything his father had left for them. He then took control of his father's apothecary and forced Salim to work there in exchange for food and shelter for him and his sisters.

It was during those hard years that Salim decided he would take his life into his own hands. If it were up to him, he would have left years ago, but Salim couldn't abandon his sisters. His uncle often used them to get Salim to do his bidding, using him to grow rich with the apothecary in a way his father never could.

So, Salim waited until his sisters were old enough to marry, spending his time working and saving, hoping to finance his journey to Damascus. After his last sister wed several months ago, Salim packed his bags and departed. It was time for him to fulfill his life mission and become the man his father wanted him to be.

He spent months traveling with different caravans, realizing he could earn money as a healer in rural trading towns and villages. Salim had a great aptitude for creating medicines for different sicknesses. While his father approved of Salim's gift in medicine, he often disapproved of his ambitions, often saying, "when ambitions end, happiness begins," but Salim knew he would only be happy when the world was at his feet. After years of trying to live up to his father's expectations, he wanted nothing more than to succeed and to Salim, success was money.

When he left Fez, he only carried his bags and a few precious medicines with him. He knew graduating from Nur al-Din Bimaristan would finally cement his place in the world of medicine. It didn't matter how skilled Salim was, without the proper qualification, he would be forced to spend his life treating the poor for pennies, when he really wanted to treat the wealthy and elite in his city. Treating the poor may have been enough for his father who was obsessed with medicine, and, for a time, Salim tried to care for the struggles of others, but he couldn't see beyond his own pain.

He tried to connect with his father, but, beyond medicine, there was nothing else that bound them together. And it was his father's lack of drive that forced Salim to go out and provide for his sisters. It was no wonder Salim wanted wealth.

Salim thought about his father's open-door policy, where no one was turned away. He often felt his father was wasting his talents on the poor. He barely made enough to feed and house his children and they often argued about money. However, not one person, who his father showed kindness to spoke up for Salim and his sisters, even though they knew of the abuse they faced at his uncle's hand. People were inherently selfish, and only those willing to take what was theirs would survive in this cruel world.

Now, Salim had greater ambitions, and as he pulled the ropes under his camels to secure his treasure, he got a taste of what his life would be like once he finally reached Damascus. He didn't need the apothecary; Salim would build his own legacy; he would accomplish all the success his father failed to achieve.

"Are you leaving?"

Salim blinked, pulled out of his thoughts by a soft voice. He looked down at the strange, blue-eyed girl who seemed to always be watching him. Her eyes looked sad as she stood a few feet away. He didn't pay much attention to her when she came by the makeshift hospital. There never seemed to be an end to the curious children watching him as he treated his patients.

Salim sighed, giving the ropes one final tug. "Yes, I must leave your wonderful oasis and continue my way," he told her, checking his water skins to make sure they were filled for the journey. He didn't know where the next town would be, so he always made sure to have extra water on him.

The girl stood, watching him silently as he secured his turban and led his camel to drink her fill before they headed out. It was dawn; soon, the caravan would return to the desert to resume their journey.

"Where is your home," the girl asked after minutes of silence. Salim looked at the girl again. Usually, he had no patience for children, but he was in a good mood that day, and he had a few minutes to spare while the rest of the caravan finished getting ready.

"I am from the great Maghrib city of Fez, and soon, I will be the most respected and sought-after physician there. Your tribe is lucky they got to be treated by me," he told her with a wink.

"What's it like," she asked, her eyes bright with curiosity. Salim smiled. There was something about this child, old yet young. He couldn't help but feel a bit fond of her. He noticed she didn't sit with or talk to other children when they stopped by his tent. She often sat alone, silently watching him with those curious eyes, observing him like a student. She reminded him of the eager boy he was before leaving his home to follow his dreams.

"It's beautiful chaos, thousands of people, huge *souks* lined with colorful spices, and merchants from all over the world, each seeking to trade. Tall brick buildings with balconies that overlook the cobblestone streets…"

Salim closed his eyes, feeling overwhelmed with homesickness, which was strange since he was so desperate to escape that city. Having lost both his parents while he was still a young boy, and his entire inheritance stolen by his uncle, besides his two sisters, he had little to return to.

However, Salim planned to take back everything his uncle had stolen from him. He wouldn't return the lonely penniless boy he was when he left. He would return as a capable and educated man, ready to build his wealth.

"You miss it?" It was phrased as a question but felt more like an observation.

"Yes, I guess I do." Salim cleared his throat as the caravan leader began announcing their departure. "Goodbye, kid," Salim said, pulling his camel. After a few steps, Salim felt a small hand pull on his thobe. "Will you take me with you," the girl asked sincerely as she stared at him.

Salim blinked, taken aback by the request. He pulled his thobe free from her hand. "No, now go home, kid."

"I can help you," the girl said, undeterred.

Salim raised his eyebrow at her. "Oh yeah? How so?"

"I can find things—things you may need," the girl said looking at his medicine box.

Salim was surprised. "That was you? The medicine...you found it. How?" There was no way. This medicine was nearly impossible to find in the desert, especially after the drought. And they didn't even grow in this region. The girl just shrugged; Salim looked around. This had to be a joke, or maybe it was a test from the *Sheikh*.

"Listen, kid, I don't need your help. And I'm definitely not taking you anywhere with me, so run along and go home."

The girl looked crushed, her strange blue eyes watering at his rejection. Salim cleared his throat and looked at the caravan which had already started leaving. He didn't have time for this. Salim turned around and paused, cursing. He dug into his pouch, pulling out the small glass-stained sun catcher—the possession he kept with him for many years, which reminded him of his past. His mother was an artist, often creating and selling glass art. He held the sun catcher in his hand. He didn't need the reminder anymore, and for some reason, he knew it would be in better hands with the child.

Salim turned around holding the sun catcher out to the girl, who just stared at it in amazement. Her eyes were bright with excitement. He thought it would be better off with her. "Here, take this."

The girl slowly reached out her hand, as if afraid to break it. "Some of the homes in my city have windows that look like this, so I kept this to remind me of home, but I don't need it anymore. It's yours."

The girl grinned as she held the glass to the emerging sun, creating a colorful shadow. "Thank you!" she screeched, suddenly throwing her arms around Salim in a tight embrace. Salim pushed her away, uncomfortable at her unadulterated joy. She looked at him like he was some kind of hero. Salim wasn't a good person; he was an opportunist, but he couldn't help the little joy that grew in his heart from seeing her happy smile.

"You're welcome," he said gruffly, patting her head. He gave her a genuine smile, pulling his camel to catch up to the caravan. He didn't have to look back to know she was watching him leave.

20.

It was past dawn, and several days had passed since they left the oasis. This portion of the journey was the most grueling and draining. The fine sand made it difficult for both the men and the heavily loaded camels to move, slowing down the entire caravan. Salim pulled his feet out of the sand, his breath haggard, each step heavier and more laden than the last. Because of the drought, several trading towns were abandoned, and the journeys rerouted. While they were able to rest and take ample supplies to prepare for this difficult walk, Salim couldn't wait until they got out of this desert. He couldn't wait to board a ship to Cairo, which would be the final stop before heading to Damascus.

Salim was not as accustomed to traveling like the rest of the caravan, which was filled with experienced traders. He often trailed behind the other men, focusing on his breathing and steps. So, it took a while to register the shouts and frantic scrambling of the rest of the caravan as they traveled. The caravan leader yelled as the men hurriedly moved toward the higher sand dunes. Salim looked around in confusion. Behind him loomed a large cloud of sand, bigger than anything he had ever seen before.

The camel protested as Salim desperately tried to lead it toward the high dune that the rest of the caravan was climbing. He frantically tugged the rope, but his camel resisted, distressed by the onslaught of sand and wind. He realized he wouldn't make it, and with a curse, pulled free his cloak from the camel and fell back as the roaring wind pushed him to the ground. The sand felt like a million tiny razors as Salim covered his head and body with the cloak.

Salim moved around blindly, trying to find his camel, but each time he took a step, he was knocked back down by a vicious gust of wind. Salim coughed, blinded by panic. He forced himself to get up, trying to escape from the assault, until he could no longer stand. Salim covered his entire body with the cloak, laying down in a fetal passion as the sandy wind continued to batter him. For the first time in years, Salim found himself praying.

It felt like hours since the storm began—so long that he had lost consciousness. Salim finally woke up feeling a heavy load on his body constricting his breathing. Panicked, he tried to dig himself out of the heavyweight of sand that buried him alive. Salim gasped for air as his head emerged, coughing as he crawled out.

The storm had buried him in a thick layer of sand. He grabbed his water flask and gulped down its contents, sputtering as he drank too fast. Salim tried to control his hammering heart, and finally looked around his surroundings. It seemed like the entire layout of the desert had shifted. He stood up, squinting his eyes. He assumed it was late in the afternoon. The caravan couldn't have gone far. He spotted a high sand dune and decided to climb up to get a better vantage point.

His body, still weak from the assault, protested as he forced himself to climb up the dune. By the time he reached the top, his throat was dry, and his muscles strained. He knew he had to be smart with his water, now that he had no idea where his camel or the rest of the caravan was. Salim sat down on top of the sand dune, his head between his knees. He took a small sip of water, which only made him thirstier.

Please, Salim thought. *Please don't let this be the end.* Salim looked around the vast expanse of the desert, miles and miles of uneven sand. The typical layout of dunes was disturbed and rearranged by the massive sandstorm. Salim looked and looked but could not see a single trace of life. The caravan was nowhere to be found. Perhaps they had all perished, buried deep within the desert. Salim had no idea how he survived, but as he looked around the empty, bleak landscape, he knew it was only a matter of time before the desert took him, as well.

***

Salim wandered about the desert, lost for two days, each minute more depressing than the last. He pulled out his water flask, raising it high, and hoped to get at least a drop of water. A few drops dripped onto his parched tongue, a lack of spit making it hard for him to even swallow. He contemplated saving his urine, hoping it might save him, but dehydration made it impossible to pee, and, as a physician, he knew it would only speed up the process.

He licked his cracked and bleeding lips, the heat creating a pattern of waves in front of him as he swayed on his feet taking a few short steps before he collapsed on the sand. He knew his determination not to die was the only thing keeping him alive, but he also knew that wouldn't keep him going for much longer. Salim had lost hope in finding his caravan; he began crawling with a small burst of hopeless energy. He couldn't die. Not like this.

He worked too hard to just have it all end this way; he had to make it to Damascus, and he had to reclaim his life and live up to his father's expectations. He needed to take back everything his uncle had stolen from him, but as he crawled on the sand in the middle of the desert a dying man, that ambition became less and less worth living for. Salim collapsed once again, his body finally giving out. He lay on his stomach and turned himself around to look up at the blue, cloudless sky as the sun beat down on him. Suddenly, he started laughing hysterically; if he had any fluid left in his body, he knew tears would be flowing from his eyes at that moment.

Salim was determined to become a well-known and respected physician, but as he lay there in the open desert, staring at the sky, he knew he would die both nameless and penniless. At least when he treated the poor, they had someone who cried for them, someone who pleaded for them, someone who loved them. Would his sisters even know of his demise? Or would they think he abandoned them? They thought he was selfish for leaving them to fulfill his dreams in the first place, but they didn't know how much he did for them. They didn't know how much he had to sacrifice so they could live decent lives and be cared for. Was he wrong for leaving? Was he wrong for wanting to forge his own path? Perhaps this was the fate a man like Salim deserved. In his selfishness, he would die alone.

This was the end, Salim reached toward his belt, pulling his blade free. He refused to die slowly from dehydration. So, he mustered up the little energy he had left and lifted his arms to slit his wrist, hoping it would speed up his eventual demise. He watched as the blood pooled around his wrist and then stopped; dehydration clogged his veins, making it impossible for him to put himself out of his misery.

Salim laughed even louder—this time like a madman. He couldn't even die. Was this his punishment for his pride and ambitions? For not caring about the needy and the sick, only himself? Another man would plead with God, make promises he would never keep, and pray that God saves him from this disaster. But not Salim. Instead, he cursed, screaming into heaven until he could no longer make a sound and his throat was raw.

He closed his eyes, falling into darkness. *Please*, he thought *just let me die and take me to whatever hell is waiting for me.*

***

Salim groaned. He was too exhausted to open his eyes and make sense of what was happening. He moaned in pain, trying to twist his head away from the cold liquid that was dripping into his open mouth. It took him a minute to recognize that it was water. Salim tried to open his eyes but failed. Exhaustion had overtaken his body. Instead, he opened his mouth wider.

He didn't know whether it was all a dream his mind had conjured from dehydration. Perhaps he already died. He felt a hand working his throat, forcing him to swallow. The cool water slowly traveled down his parched throat. Salim forced the water down greedily, wanting to grab the source and continue pouring it to his mouth, but he couldn't move his hand. He slowly lifted his heavy eyelids and found himself staring into the blue eyes of an angel. He weakly lifted his hand to touch its beautiful face, but his hand fell back, hitting the sand as he began to lose consciousness once more, questioning whether it was just a dream.

Salim stirred from his sleep. His muscles were weak and achy. He was awoken by a whisper and the flickering of a fire. Salim was exhausted—both physically and mentally—but he could no longer feel the effects of dehydration, meaning someone had been giving him water for a while now. Salim squinted his eyes open, and the whispering immediately stopped. Across from him, sitting still with her legs crossed beneath her, he met the eyes of a little girl who stared back at him, unblinking. Salim flinched, scooting back. This must be some kind of *jinn*, he thought. The caravan always told stories about them, but he soon recognized those strange, piercing, blue eyes.

"You!" Salim sputtered as he pointed at the little girl from the oasis. He looked around desperately. How was she there? Had he wandered back to the oasis?

It was nighttime, and too dark to see anything past the glow of the fire, but he was sure he heard her talking to someone. "Who is with you," Salim asked, confused and agitated. *Where did this child come from?*

The girl simply stared back at him, without blinking. Her braids hung below her shoulder; she was the picture of a perfectly innocent child—except for those cunning, watchful eyes. Those ancient eyes seemed to observe his every move. "I thought you were dead," the girl said, speaking softly. "I found you passed out on the ground, so, I saved you like you save the people who are sick. I wish to be a healer like you, so that way people will love me, and they won't be afraid of me anymore," the girl explained.

But Salim was even more confused. How had she found him? "Are we near your home," he asked, sitting up, now fully conscious and taking note of his situation.

"No, we are far away."

"How did you find me then," Salim asked, swallowing.

"I followed the caravan," the girl shrugged nonchalantly. "I wanted to see your home. Is it true people in the city have homes for books? I think it's called a library. I really want to go to one... even though I can't read." The girl frowned and crossed her arms as if her illiteracy was their biggest issue at that moment.

"Wait, so, you followed the caravan? What about the sandstorm? How did you survive that? And *how* did you find me," he asked again, trying to make sense of everything that was happening.

"Oh um... I sheltered before the storm came; then, I looked for you and found you sleeping. You looked like my mama did before she went to heaven with baby Sara, so, I thought you were dead. But then you moved! So, I gave you water. I was happy you didn't die," the girl grinned.

"You just happened to find me? Just like that?"

The girl nodded, avoiding his eyes. She pulled out some dates and nuts from her bag; suddenly, Salim's stomach grumbled. He couldn't even recall the last time he had eaten. He gulped as the girl passed him a handful of dates, nuts and figs.

Salim accepted the food while keeping an eye on the strange child, who was now humming a song while using a stick to draw on the sand before yawning. "Who were you speaking to earlier," Salim asked after he had finished shoving the food into his mouth.

"No one," the girl whispered, staring into the desert. But Salim was sure he heard her talking to someone, and he wanted to know who. However, the girl just unfolded a small blanket from her pack, and turned her back on him, going to sleep.

Salim watched her for several minutes, trying to make sense of everything that had happened. He almost died—no, he would have surely died if this child hadn't saved him. But Salim couldn't deny that there was something strange about the little girl sleeping peacefully before him. He even began wondering if she was a *jinn* herself. But he quickly dispelled those ignorant thoughts as she peacefully snored, as if they weren't stuck in the middle of a desert.

21.

Salim stirred early in the twilight hours of dawn. His body was still sore and stiff; however, he was alive. He looked up to glance at the star-scattered sky, the darkness slowly giving way to light. He sighed. The small fire lay dormant to his right, the ash flickering away with the soft breeze. He was surprised to find the girl awake. Her back was turned to him as she stared into the desert. Her body gently swayed as if she were listening to the most beautiful song. Salim strained his ears and was only met by the eerie silence of the twilight hour.

Soon, the emerging sun would sweep the darkness away as the sky exploded with a vibrant purple, orange and blue. Salim cleared his throat as he sat up and dusted his thobe. The girl turned around and offered a warm grin. "You're up!" she sang as she stood and stretched her body enthusiastically.

She grabbed her water and took a long drink as if she had an endless supply. Salim grabbed his own water skin and took a few small sips.

"You should slow down on the water. We don't know how long we will be out here," the girl just shrugged nonchalantly. Salim rubbed his temple, then started chewing on some dried meat. Now that his head was clear of the near-death haze, he had to take a more realistic view of his situation. By some strange miracle, this child had saved him. However, they were still stuck, and, soon, they would run out of water.

"Is that all the water you have," Salim asked, wanting to take stock of their supply. The girl held up her water skin and shrugged again. Salim closed his eyes in frustration. How this child had survived this long alone was beyond him—perhaps she knew of a well somewhere.

"Do you know where we are? We need to find a village, or maybe we can head back to the oasis if you can take us there," Salim tried again.

"I can't go back there," the girl whispered.

"You can't or you won't?" The girl just shrugged again, nibbling on some nuts. "This is serious!" Salim snapped, tired of her nonchalant attitude. "We need to get out of this desert to survive. Do you understand that?"

The girl frowned and looked to her right, glancing back at Salim, and then hurried away as if she needed privacy to consult someone. What the hell? The girl started whispering furiously, sneaking glances back at him, then waving her hand around before pouting stubbornly and turning away. She kept turning her cheek in different directions, crossing her arms, and then grinned, clapping her hands.

Salim blinked. *She was insane.* He was stuck in a desert with a mad—possibly possessed— child. The girl finally started back towards him, giving him a small, shy smile, as if she didn't just argue with the empty desert sprawled before them. "There might be a trading town nearby," she announced.

"Okay… do you know how to get there," he asked skeptically. The girl looked embarrassed as she shook her head. Salim rubbed his temples, annoyed. "Let's just go. Maybe we will stumble across some Bedouins."

Salim did not have a compass. He hated himself for not keeping it on his person. Instead, it was on his lost camel. He picked a random direction and began walking as the girl trailed happily behind him. She was a chatty one, going on and on about nothing, and when Salim wouldn't entertain her with his input, she would talk for him.

Salim sighed, frustrated and thirsty. He felt like they were just going in circles. He grabbed his dwindling water and took another small sip. Next to him, the girl also stopped, taking a large gulp of water. "What are you doing?" Salim snapped, snatching the water from her hands. He shook the almost empty bottle, but the girl just stared at him in wide-eyed confusion.

"We need to save water. Do you not understand what is happening here? We are lost in this *damn* godforsaken desert! And we are going to die if we don't find people!" Salim shouted, waving his arm frantically.

"That's a bad word," the girl whispered.

Salim threw his arms in the air, giving up. "You're right, that is a bad word, and I don't care because we are going to die. And you, my child, are entirely unhelpful."

The girl just crossed her arm with a huff and walked away. She sat with her back turned to him. "What are you doing," he asked. The girl just turned her cheek, looking the other way, giving him the silent treatment. "We don't have time for this, kid. Come on, let's go," Salim reached his hand out to help her up, but she just ignored him and scooted further away.

"Fine! If you want to act like a spoiled little brat, you can stay here and die by yourself. I'll be better off without you." Salim threw her water skin next to her, rearranged his small pack, and stormed off.

He sighed heavily a few feet away from the girl. He expected her to follow him, but she just sat there stubbornly. Salim walked back to the girl, unable to leave her. After all, she had saved his life, and Salim hated owing a debt. It wasn't her fault they were in this situation. He dropped his load and sat next to her with a sigh. It was probably a good idea to rest since the afternoon sun was out; walking now would only make them thirstier.

"Look, kid. I'm sorry I snapped at you," he apologized, rubbing his sore feet. "I'll try to be more patient with you, okay?" The girl softened her posture, but still had her back turned to him. "I won't say any more bad words," he offered.

The girl slowly turns around. "Promise," she asked, her innocent eyes making him feel even worse about his outburst.

"I promise."

"And friends never break their promise!" she finished with a smile.

Salim rubbed her head affectionately and smiled. "Sure, kid."

"Mira."

"What?"

"My name is Mira," the girl corrected.

Salim hadn't even thought to ask her name but was glad she offered it. "Ah, well, you have a very beautiful name, Mira. Now, let's get some rest. We have a difficult journey ahead of us."

Mira grinned happily, and Salim couldn't help but feel a small sense of satisfaction at her happiness.

He stirred a few hours later, woken by a soft whispering. By now, he was used to Mira's strange talks with herself, but it was still a bit unnerving and sad seeing such a bright child fall to madness.

As soon as he began moving, the whispering stopped, and Mira just stared at him blankly. He hated it when she did that. It felt like he was interrupting a private conversation, but there was no one else there.

"You okay, kid?"

Mira nodded enthusiastically. He thought about how she was probably scolded at home for talking to herself, which was why she stared at him, trying to gauge his reaction. Salim gave her a reassuring smile, and Mira grinned. She had her water skin in her hands, playing with the string.

"I thought I told you we had to save the water," Salim commented, reaching to take it from her. At this rate, their water supply wouldn't last the day. However, Salim was surprised to find her water skin heavy. *How?* he thought.

Salim quickly opened the cap and peered inside. Surely enough, it was filled with clear drinking water, but he was sure it had been nearly empty just hours ago. "Where did you get this water?" he demanded, frantically looking around. Had someone visited while he slept? Had she found some kind of well or another oasis?

Mira avoided his eyes, "Answer me," he snapped, grabbing her shoulders. "Who gave you this? Where did you find it? Tell me now!"

Mira's eyes watered as she stared at him in fear, her small body shaking. Salim let go, willing himself to calm down as she wrapped her hands around her knees and rocked back and forth.

Salim retreated, her terrified reaction pulling him out of his desperate need for answers. She was scared, and Salim didn't understand why.

"What are you?" he finally whispered. She seemed so ordinary. Besides her eyes, she looked like a normal Bedouin child.

Mira froze and looked up at him with haunted eyes. "My name is Mira. I'm not cursed. I'm not a *jinn*. My name is Mira. I'm not cursed. I'm not a *jinn*. My name—"

"Okay. Okay, please," Salim interrupted. "I won't ask any more questions. Just stop saying that."

Mira quietly wiped her tear-stained cheeks. "Are you afraid of me?" she whispered after a while.

Salim was a bit frightened of this child who had altered everything he believed he knew about the world. He was a man of science and was often bemused by the superstitious ramblings of the uneducated. But he would be a fool not to see that there was something supernatural about her.

"Why would I be afraid of a little girl, huh?" he scoffed instead. "Come on, we should get going, kid."

Mira grinned, hopped up and dusted off her dress. Salim grabbed his pack and paused as he reached for his own heavy water skin. He swallowed, deciding to no longer question the child about these strange happenings. He was alive, and as long as he was with her, he would not die of thirst. But he had made up his mind. As soon as they reached the next town, he would ditch the kid and find the first caravan out of this desert.

Salim sighed, no longer as fearful or as daunted as he was by the vast desert before them. He had hoped that he would make it. This child would be his guiding light. Salim started walking in the same direction they had walked all morning. This desert can't go on forever, he thought. Everything must eventually come to an end.

"You're going the wrong way", Mira called from behind him. Salim raised an eyebrow. "There is a trading town that way," she said, pointing in another direction.

"Are you sure? How far is it?" Salim asked, hope blooming in his heart. The girl shrugged, but Salim believed her. He had no reason not to trust her. He grinned, picked up the child, and spun her around as she giggled in childish excitement.

"You, my dear, are an angel," Salim proclaimed, kissing her on the forehead. The girl's eyes brimmed with happiness as he tousled her hair. Salim would survive. He would make it to Damascus and fulfill his destiny. And as for this child, he would ditch her as soon as they reached the town, and he would never utter a word of it to another soul.

22.

Salim spent the following two days traveling with the child. It felt strange to not limit himself to sips of water and ration food because, by some miracle, each time he awoke, he found his water-skin full and his pack filled with fruits, dates and nuts. The child appeared to be used to such abundance, not even batting an eye at the food and water. Now that she knew he wouldn't abandon her or fish for her secrets, she was even more talkative than before.

He had never met anyone who could utter that many words in such a short time. She told him stories, some of which were interesting, and took the boredom out of his journey. Other times, she asked countless questions about Fez and other cities.

"Will I have my own room when we go to Fez? I had my own room in the stone house my Baba built. I'm the only girl in the oasis with her own room. That means I'm special, right? But Samia said it was because my family didn't want me staying in the same room as them. But she is a jealous liar."

"I'm not going to Fez. There is nothing for me at my home," he said, uncomfortable with where the conversation was going. Salim had no intention of taking Mira with him, but he couldn't tell her that now in case she decided to leave. He needed her—for now, anyway.

"Were you cast out," she asked sadly. Salim cleared his throat, not wanting to think about the past. "No, I was not cast out. I simply wished to follow my own path. There was nothing left for me in Fez."

Mira smiled. "You are just like me!"

"I'm nothing like you."

"Yes, you are! We both left our homes because we didn't belong there. My Jida told me I was meant for bigger things, and I never wanted to live my life in the desert anyways. I want to see the world!" she said with a happy twirl. "It was fate that we met."

"More like a curse," Salim muttered.

Mira rolled her eyes. "That's okay," she grinned. "I will prove to you that I will be an excellent friend. I've already helped you a lot."

Salim sighed and rubbed his neck because he couldn't refute that claim. "Why did you run away from home, anyways? Your family must be worried."

Mira's face fell, her shoulders slumping down. "I think they will be better off without me there."

"You don't know that," Salim insisted. He hoped to convince her to return home. "I know family can be harsh at times, but you must forgive them."

"You can only forgive someone so much before you start to hate them," she whispered, a shadow coming over her face. The pain behind that statement shocked Salim, but he couldn't imagine someone like her hating anyone.

"You hate your family?"

"No, I love my family. That is why I left, so I can still think good of them and cherish their memory."

Salim swallowed; his heart unable to comprehend the little girl. It was okay to hate people that hurt you. Salim had his share of people in this world that he hated. The fact that she still found a way to love so deeply after all her pain was incomprehensible to him.

Salim shook his head and dropped the subject as Mira chatted obsessively about other nonsensical things, as if the intensity of their conversion was nothing to her.

"Hey kid, how about we play a game?"

Mira's eyes lit up. "I love games!"

"Trust me, I know," Salim said, rolling his eyes. She was always trying to get him to play a game with her, but he never gave in.

"Why don't we play the silent game? Whoever talks loses."

Mira frowned. "That doesn't sound fun."

"Ah, you just lost! Let's try again. This time, if you win, I'll grant you a wish."

"Really?!" Mira gasped, then quickly covered her mouth and began frantically signing with her hands.

"Fine, I'll give you one more chance. Starting... now."

Mira made a zipping motion with her hands to her lips and pretended to throw away the key. Although Salim was amused by the child, he was looking forward to some quiet time.

They walked in silence for several minutes. Salim was exhausted, but at least he was well-fed and hydrated. But as he calculated the distance they'd traveled, he started to doubt whether this town was even real, or if he was being deceived by a mad child. But even he had to admit, Mira was not mad. Someone—or *something*—was with them on this journey, but at least whatever it was, was a friend and not a foe.

Sometimes, in her ramblings, Mira talked about her life in the oasis, and while there was not a single negative or even a resentful bone in her body, Salim felt bad for the kid. Her life sounded lonely and awful; he couldn't imagine having her gift and living with a bunch of Bedouins. Even in the city among the educated, she would struggle to be accepted.

He felt for her, but this was her life. Everyone had their struggles, and no one was truly happy in this world. She would have to return to her life because Salim couldn't take her; she wasn't a part of his plans.

Salim heard a loud giggle, pulling him out of his daze. He quickly looked back at Mira, who just stared at him with an expressionless mask. Salim narrowed his eyes at her and continued walking. A few minutes later, he heard another giggle.

He quickly looked back again to catch her in the act, but once more, he was met by an expressionless face. Salim shook his head with a small smile. Technically, she had lost, but her overly innocent face every time he looked back was too good to stop the game.

After walking in silence for a few hours, except for the occasional giggling and whispers from Mira and whoever it was whose company she was enjoying, they had made good ground. With the afternoon sun shining, it was time for them to rest.

"Alright, kid. We'll rest here for a few hours," Salim announced, breaking the silence.

"Does this mean I won?! Do I get a wish," she asked with excitement.

"Hmm," Salim stroked his beard. "With all the whispering and giggling that was happening, I wouldn't say you won anything."

Mira's face fell as she pouted, looking at him with her big eyes. "Stop that." Salim pushed her face lightly, not falling for her puppy dog eyes.

Mira stomped her foot, annoyed. "Not fair," she grumbled as she prepared her rest area.

"Well, next time, try harder, and you might get your wish," Salim said, unmoved, as he prepared his own area. He took out his cloak and laid it on the ground, using a stick to create a makeshift tent to give him some shade.

Salim laid down and covered his eyes with his arm. But as he did so, he felt Mira watching his every move. "What," he asked without budging.

"Will you at least hear my wish," Mira asked earnestly.

Salim didn't want to hear it; he already knew what she would ask for, and he knew he couldn't give it to her. But she was only a child, and he needed her for the rest of the journey. "Fine. What is your wish?" Mira didn't answer for a long time. Curious, Salim removed his arm from his face to look at her. In her arms, she held a book, hugging it close to her chest as if it were the most precious thing she owned.

"I wanted you to read this book to me," she whispered.

Salim blinked, surprised. He was sure she would ask to go with him, but this was all she wanted.

Salim sat up and grabbed the book from her arm. It was in Latin. He had studied Latin and Greek in school; he and his father translated ancient Greek and Roman books into Arabic many times before.

"*Orthographia Bohemica*," Salim read the title of the old Latin spelling book. Whoever gave it to her was studying the Latin language. Salim tossed the book back to her. "Nothing interesting is in that book, kid. Now, go to sleep," he told her with a yawn.

Salim laid down, turning his back to her. He was exhausted from their walk. He hoped they would reach the town soon, and he couldn't wait to eat some real food and find a way to continue his journey.

"I think it's interesting!" Mira snapped angrily. Salim was confused as he watched her stomp back to her little tent, open her book, and pretend to read it.

Salim swallowed his guilt and tried to ignore the feeling, forcing his body to relax, but Mira's pathetic whispering wouldn't let him sleep. He blew out a breath of air. "How about I tell you a story instead?" he offered reluctantly.

Mira's head perked up like a rabbit coming out of its hole, "Really?!" she beamed, sitting cross-legged, eager for him to begin.

Salim cleared his throat and sat up as well. He wasn't much of a storyteller, but he remembered a few stories from his childhood that his father always told, and his favorite story was *Alibaba and the 40 Thieves*.

"Once upon a time, there was a poor woodcutter named Ali baba…"

23.

"Open sesame!" Mira shouted for the thousandth time after they continued their walk. Salim rolled his eyes, regretting telling her the story. Ever since that afternoon, she wouldn't give him respite, constantly asking questions about Ali baba, the thieves and the treasure. She was amazed at how the slave, Morgina, saved Ali baba from the thieves and married his son. "I want to be like Morgina and save everyone!" she decided.

"Well, how about you start with saving yourself because, if you ask me another question about that story, I will feed you to a tiger," Salim threatened.

Mira paused, giving him a quizzical look. "A tiger? What's that? Is it like a camel? Have you ever seen one?"

"It's more like a giant cat, and no, I haven't seen one," he corrected.

Mira's eyes widened. "Once, I caught an *Iftan*. Mama didn't believe me, but it's true. I caught it with a trap!" she boasted.

"An *Iftan*?" Salim asked, confused, as he had never heard of such a creature.

"Well, I made up that name for it," Mira admitted.

"And why did you catch this little beast," Salim questioned, bemused by the tale.

"Because nobody believed me. No one ever believes me," she whispered, falling into sudden silence.

Salim rubbed his chin, baffled by the girl. She was a walking enigma. Sometimes, she seemed childish and naïve, but other times, she was mature and soulful. She came across as very insightful, yet she saw so little of the world. For a simple Bedouin, her dreams were greater than the desert, and her heart bigger than the sky.

He appreciated her curiosity, even while he hated her endless questions. Salim wasn't a patient man, but something about this child made him less and less annoyed with her presence. He was starting to grow a bit fond of her, which wasn't good for anyone. Salim decided not to ask her any more questions, allowing the silence to stretch.

Soon, the sun began to set over the horizon, and they got to work setting their camp for the night. Salim lit the fire, silently poking the flame with a stick, urging it to grow. He grabbed his notebook, using the flickering light to scribble down his thoughts. Salim often wrote in his journal; he wrote about medical thoughts that occurred to him throughout the day, and when he had time, he would experiment with his ideas. He would sketch out the different plants he used throughout his travels, and the herbal medicines he found in the villages he passed.

Mira mimicked his drawings, making her own in the sand. She asked him plenty of questions about his work, but Salim already made it clear that he didn't want to be bothered while he wrote; thankfully, she respected his wish.

Salim was deep in thought with his journal when he heard singing. He looked up to find Mira in her small, open tent playing with a straw doll, singing a slow, Arabic nursery rhyme. He only recognized it because it was the same song his mother sang to him when he was a child.

Salim closed his eyes, and, for the first time in years, dared to imagine the kind woman who had given birth to him, only to be snatched away by death when he was no older than Mira. It was then that his happy family became broken. His father took it the hardest, losing himself in his work and becoming a recluse. The only time Salim had access to his father was when they were discussing medicine. His father often blamed himself for not being able to treat his wife and became obsessed with healing.

So, Salim made it his life goal to learn all there was about botanical herbs, just to connect with his father. The only time his father paid attention to him was when they worked together, and the only time he praised him was when he came up with different herbal solutions.

Salim sighed as the girl started to hum. He swallowed the lump that had formed in his throat and decided to call it a night. In the short time he had been with Mira, she had already opened memories and wounds he wished to keep as closed as his heart.

***

Salim stirred from his sleep the following morning to what sounded like hoofs. He moved abruptly from his position, realizing that he was hearing the sound of a horse trotting towards him. A few feet away, perched upon large, Arabian horses, were three men whose eyes were lined with dark *kohl*. A tattered, blue turban covered their heads and faces. They silently stood watching him and Mira, who was still asleep snoring lightly.

"Get up!" Salim whispered to her, nudging her with his foot before he stood in front of her to greet the men. "Peace be upon you!" Salim called. One of the men pulled out a long, curved sword, warning Salim not to get any closer. Salim held up his hands to show them he was unarmed. His excitement quickly turned to dread. It was more than possible that these men were bandits, a dangerous group that took no mercy on anyone, often slaying the caravans they looted.

Mira grumbled and sat up, yawning as she rubbed her eyes. Her face was caked with dirt, and her hair a tangled mess. Salim quickly blocked her from view, feeling a sense of protectiveness over the child. He turned his attention back to the men who silently observed him. Salim didn't miss how their eyes lingered on his pack—which lay near the dead embers of his fire—and the gold ring that gleamed on his right index finger.

"Please, brothers. My daughter and I got lost in the desert during the sandstorm. By Allah, we thought we would surely die. I apologize if we accidentally ventured onto your land. If you could just point us to the nearest town, we will be on our way." Salim offered his most charming smile, hoping to appeal to the bandits.

The men looked at each other before the one in the middle with the curved sword jumped off his horse. Salim stiffened and felt Mira behind him. The man used his sword to lift Salim's pack from the ground. His meager belongings—his notebook, a few loose coins, and his spare leather socks—fell onto the sand. Salim cursed to himself as the man bent down to pick up the coins. It wasn't much, but it was enough to buy him a spot with the next caravan.

The man stuffed the coins in his pockets, turning to face Salim. "Please, brother. That is all we have," he pleaded as the man approached with his sword pointed towards him. Salim froze. The man used his sword to lift the side of his thobe, demanding the small, ceremonial blade he kept on his body. Salim nodded, and with shaking hands, he removed the clasps of the belt that held his only weapon, handing it over to the man who tossed it to his companion.

"Please," Salim pleaded again, holding his hands together. "Just let us go in peace." There was a very real chance that the men would simply slay them and be on their way, as bandits were known to do in the past. These thugs weren't just robbers; they were cold-blooded killers, and everyone did their best to avoid an encounter with them.

The man ignored his pleas, lifting his chin toward the gold ring that gleamed on Salim's right hand.

Salim fisted his hand. "This is worthless, my friend. Listen, I-I'm a doctor. I'm sure some of your companions are injured or need medical attention given your line of work... I can treat them if you would just..." Salim grunted, falling as the man struck his head with the butt of his sword. His eyes darkened, and he heard Mira quietly whimpering.

"Off," the man demanded again. Salim nodded, pulling off the ring with shaky hands. This was his father's ring—the only connection to him he had left. It was the only thing his greedy uncle had allowed him to keep.

Salim swallowed, hesitating slightly, unable to raise his eyes as he tossed the ring over. The man grunted, shoving the ring in his pockets, along with the coins he had stolen from Salim.

Salim heard Mira's soft cries, but he didn't dare turn around. He didn't want to risk bringing any attention to her, in case these men tried to take her.

"Please, you have taken all we have. We are already lost. Allow us to take our chances in the desert and be on your way," Salim pleaded with the men, hoping they would finally leave now that they had taken anything of value. However, the man's attention was no longer on him, but on Mira, who peeked from behind his arm to look at the men. This was what Salim was afraid of.

"Move," the man demanded as Salim quickly used his body to hide Mira's.

"Please, brother. Don't do this. She is just a sick child. She won't be worth anything to you," Salim begged on his knees. They couldn't take Mira. He needed her to survive; he needed her to lead him to the town.

The man grabbed Salim by his thobe and tossed him aside. "She will be worth much on the slave market," he threatened, fiercely grabbing Mira by the arm. Mira screamed and pulled away, but the man yanked her forward.

"Please, don't do this," Salim begged desperately, grabbing the man. The man kicked him, forcing Salim to fall back, as he continued pulling Mira, who was screaming for him. Salim felt his heart shatter as she reached her hand toward him, begging him to save her.

"I have gold. Please, just lead me to the next village, and I can get you all the gold you want. Just don't take her!" His pleas fell on deaf ears as the man dragged Mira toward his horse. Salim felt his hope crumble; they would take her from him and sell her as a slave and he would die in the desert alone.

"Mira," Salim whispered, unable to do anything but watch as she was carried away.

"No!" Mira suddenly shouted. Salim watched in horror as she bit the man's hand and caused him to yelp in pain, quickly dropping his arm as she fell back and scurried away. The man's eyes filled with rage as he raised his sword. "*Khallas*," his companions yelled out for him to stop, but the man ignored them and charged toward Mira. Salim pushed Mira behind him and stood tall before her. He couldn't let the child die. Her death meant his death.

Salim stood on shaky legs as the man raised his sword, a murderous rage in his eyes. His hand was bloodied from where Mira had bitten him. "No!" he heard Mira scream before he was pushed back by a sudden burst of angry wind and blinded by a sandstorm that appeared out of nowhere. Salim coughed and covered his eyes with his arm, using the outer layer of his thobe to cover himself and Mira as she clung to him desperately.

He heard the frightened shouts of men, and the uncontrollable neigh of horses. "*Jinn*," was the only word picked up from them as their desperate screams were cut off while they hurried away.

Salim kept his body covered as the wind suddenly stopped. The air cleared and the desert returned to normal, almost like that sandstorm hadn't happened at all. The bandits were long gone, and Salim shook the sand from his body. Mira sniffled, her small body shaking as she covered her face and hugged her knees.

"Mira, are you alright?" Salim whispered, gently shaking her. She looked up, wiped her eyes, and gave him a mischievous smile. She uncurled her fist, and inside her hand was Salim's ring, the one his father had given him. Salim choked back a laugh as she grinned.

"Has anyone told you that you are insane," he asked her in disbelief.

"People tell me that all the time. They also say I'm possessed," she joked.

Salim chuckled, pulling her in for a hug. He was relieved the child was safe—that they were both safe.

"Did you do that," he questioned her.

Mira shook her head and turned to her left with a triumphant smile. "Ayub saved us!" she whispered.

25.

"So, let me get this straight. Ayub is a *jinn*, who happens to be your best friend," Salim asked a few hours later, still feeling the effects of their latest incident.

Mira nodded, bobbing her head. "I'm not supposed to talk about him, but I told him we can trust you, even though he doesn't like new people—especially humans."

"Right. And Ayub is the one who was leaving us food and has been guiding our journey?"

"Yup!" Mira agreed. Salim was surprised she was finally talking about her strange ability; the fear and suspicion she displayed anytime he asked about her odd happenings were almost gone. It was as if their latest incident built an unquestionable trust between them. Being the opportunist he was, Salim saw the benefits of having such a rare and exciting gift. As a Moroccan, he was all too familiar with his people's obsession with *jinns*, and he knew certain *sahirs* would do anything to possess her gift, even if it meant ripping out her eyes. He suddenly felt uneasy at the prospect. He didn't want anyone to use her, even though he was doing just that.

He was using her gift to survive, and if he were a lesser man, he probably would take her with him, if only to further his own interest. But not even Salim could stoop that low. He couldn't take this child with him. She needed to go home, at least she was safe there.

"Mira, I know I don't have to tell you this, but you can never speak of this to anyone. There are bad people in the world who will try to use you if they find out what you can do. Or they will fear you and try to destroy you."

"I know," she whispered with a defeated sigh. It was obvious she already had her share of pain because of this ability. Mira disclosed that she could see *jinns* her whole life, but she didn't interact with them until she met Ayub. She saved him, and, for that, he saved her, and now he followed her everywhere. Salim was both fascinated and horrified. The logical part of him wanted to understand the *jinn*, interview her, and write books on what she knew. But the cautious part of him knew that some things were better off undiscovered.

"Do you think there is a cure for my eyes? Can they one day be brown like yours?" Mira asked suddenly. Salim glanced at her; her face was covered with dirt, her hair a disheveled mess, her body small and marked with youth. But her *eyes* were ancient. Salim always prided himself on looking people in the eyes. It made it easier to read them, and it's what made him able to charm almost anyone. There was power in the eyes and looking directly at people showed them you had that power. However, even he was unable to look the child in the eyes—they were too strange.

Salim knew there were people in the world who had her eyes. He met a few traders with strange tongues, yellow hair and piercing blue eyes along his journey. They were people from far away, more uncivilized lands, but her eyes were different. They looked like blue orbs. It was as if a light were shining from behind them, and they had specks of gold. They were intelligent and cunning, a strange contrast to her youthful face.

"If there were a cure, would you want it," Salim questioned.

Mira hesitated, looking to her left, at what he assumed was Ayub. He was still a bit unsure of himself knowing there was a creature following them, but he tried his best not to show it.

"If I'm cured, that means I wouldn't be able to see Ayub anymore," Mira whispered softly, a heartbroken look on her face. Salim saw that she wanted more than anything to be normal. And for some reason, she associated her ability with her eyes; however, Salim wasn't so sure. He wanted to study her, but he knew he shouldn't, and he doubted whether he would even find answers if he did.

Mira sighed. "No, I don't want to be cured. I want to be with you and Ayub forever."

Salim nodded, taking in her words. Despite her wishes, Mira was loyal to a fault. She was a fierce and clever child. It was a shame her life would be wasted away in the desert.

It was now almost sunset, Salim squinted his eyes; in the distance, he could see tents and structures. The town! Salim glanced at Mira, excitement forming in his heart. He was a bit skeptical despite everything he had seen those last three days traveling with the child, but she did it. She led him to the town.

No wonder they came across bandits. Bandits were known to follow the trail leading to trading towns; it was the route most caravans took, and they could be easily ambushed. *"Ah-hah!"* Salim laughed, raising his arms in the air. He turned around, picked up Mira, and spun her in a circle as she giggled happily. "You did it! You saved us!" Mira smiled shyly, her eyes gleaming with happiness. "Come, we must hurry before the sun sets."

They finally entered the outskirts of the town. It was small with scattered tents and tables filled with vendors run by local Bedouin merchants hoping to trade with the passing caravans. Salim smiled as he entered; he was penniless and had almost died many times over, but he made it. He knew the port of Tunis was only a few days' journey from this point, and from there, he would sail to Cairo. Though he might not get there with the wealth he had acquired during his long journey, he would still make his way in the world and fulfill his dreams.

Salim ignored the persistent vendors who came up to him with their products, urging him to try this and that. However, the child stared at everything in amazement. She stopped by every table in the small makeshift bazaar, carefully analyzing each item before being shooed away by the annoyed vendors.

Taking in her tattered appearance and clueless gaze, Salim didn't blame them; however, he didn't look much better. Salim sniffed his clothes and groaned. He was usually very particular about his appearance and hygiene. As a doctor, being clean meant life and death for his patients; however, he looked like a haggard beggar, rather than the distinguished physician he was.

Salim followed the path of vendors until he reached the entry to the town. They were stopped by guards and asked to state their business. Salim told them that he was lost in the desert after the sandstorm and had been cut off from his caravan.

"And the child?" the man asked.

"I found this child wandering and half dead. She had lost her family, so I saved her," Salim explained.

"Hey…" Mira protested as Salim nudged her and gave her a glaring look. She frowned but didn't speak another word.

"You may enter," the man said as he opened the gates.

As soon as they entered the town, they were greeted by another wave of activity; merchants and vendors, all mixed along with goats and wagon-led donkeys. There were shouts for warm food, a bed and other more discrete activities. They were in the middle of a souk, where men traded spices, garments, metals and other goods. Children ran around with plates of dates and packs filled with hot teas.

Though this was just a trading town, he missed the chaos; however, Mira looked extremely uncomfortable. They hung off to the sides of the activity as Mira desperately clung to him, matching his steps.

Salim pushed her away. "Find your grip, kid. This isn't the oasis. There is no peace in these places, and there is less peace in the city. You will see many strange things you are not used to. Perhaps you do not belong in places like this."

Instead of being frightened by his words, as Salim had hoped, a look of fierce determination set upon her face. "I'm not afraid!" she said somberly, crossing her arms. Salim shook his head, though he could see the apprehension in her eyes. Her chin was set with determination, even as she jumped back, nearly colliding with a boy pulling a wagon.

Salim patted her head, impressed with her fortitude. He needed to find a familiar face, or at least someone he could charm into helping him. But first, he needed to get clean. Salim looked around the town, searching through the faces. If his caravan survived, they would be here. Salim quickly turned around as he heard a familiar laugh. "Abdullah!" he shouted, waving his hand.

Abdullah looked up, confused, his jaw dropping in shock. "Salim?"

Salim grinned, making his way to the short, Bedouin man who guided his journey earlier. The man gave him a quick embrace.

"Brother, we thought you were lost to the desert," the man said, perplexed. "After the storm, we searched for you, but we were only able to find your camel."

"You found my camel? Oh, Abdullah!" Salim grabbed the man and kissed his forehead. "You have given me the greatest news."

Abdullah chuckled and patted his arm. "Come, brother. You must share with us how you survived the desert."

"Oh, it is quite the story, my friend. I am truly a favorite of our Lord," Salim winked at the older man who scoffed.

"If you are our Lord's favorite, then perhaps the pious need not pray anymore," Abdullah jokes. "Now come, you must be exhausted," he said, pulling his friend.

"Salim?" Mira whispered.

In his excitement, he had almost forgotten that the child was hiding behind him. Abdullah raised his eyebrow. "You must have an interesting story indeed. Who is this child that clings to you like a lost sheep?"

Salim looked down at the frightened girl and sighed. Despite her bravado, she was afraid. "Mira, wait here a moment. I must have a private chat with my friend."

Mira looked at Abdullah before reluctantly releasing Salim's thobe. He gave her a reassuring smile, then led Abdullah away by the arm, ensuring they were out of earshot.

"Brother, I found this child after the sandstorm half-dead, so I took her with me. Believe it or not, she belongs to the Banu Nazir tribe," Salim said to him discreetly. The man looked shocked.

"What was she doing so far away from the oasis?"

"I know not, brother, but the Banu Nazir were very hospitable, so I had to save their child. Perhaps there is a way to safely return her?"

"You did well, brother. They will be most thankful to have their daughter returned. I know some local Bedouins here who are trading with the Banu Nazir. I will find someone to host her until she can return."

Salim nodded, grateful that she would be safe, and returned to her home. "I appreciate that, brother. Now, where is my camel?"

26.

Mira

Mira stuffed her face full of chicken stew as she sat outside of a hostel with Salim. She was still jumpy because of all the activity around her. No wonder Ayub didn't want to enter the town; he was probably scared out of his mind. But Mira wasn't afraid. Well... she was a little scared, but at least she had Salim as her friend and guardian.

"Slow down, kid, or you'll choke," Salim reprimanded as Mira gulped, chugged her cup of water, then wiped her mouth with the back of her hand.

"I never had this kind of food before," she admitted. It was very spicy and delicious. The Bedouin diet was very heavy on meat and grains, and they usually ate the same type of food every day.

"Yeah, well, you are a long way from home," Salim muttered as he ate his own food. He sat in front of her cross-legged, and, even though he was tired of nuts and dates, he didn't rush his food. Instead, he took dignified, measured bites.

Mira sat up, trying to mimic him; she didn't want to be viewed as a feral child. She had to learn to act more dignified if she wanted to stick with Salim.

However, looking around this strange town full of people and animals, she was nervous. Mira spent her entire life in a desert, so getting used to the rest of the world would take time. She kept close to Salim and lowered her eyes, hoping nobody would notice them, but no one seemed to care. It was as if they were used to seeing strange people from all over.

Some had very dark skin—smooth and rich. It reminded Mira of tree bark. They were dressed in rich garbs and robes, flanked by men who catered to them. Though Mira also had dark skin, hers looked like the desert—tan and sometimes red. She had never seen anyone with black skin.

"Are they kings?" Mira whispered to Salim, amazed at the men who ate quietly beside them.

Salim raised his eyes. "They might as well be," he muttered.

"Wow!" Mira was amazed. She had never seen a king before.

"Stop staring," Salim snapped, pulling Mira's attention.

"Will you tell me about them?" she asked earnestly. She hoped he was in a good mood. Sometimes, at night, before the fire would go out, he told her stories of the places he visited through his journey. Mira cherished those stories, locking them up in her memory, so she could pretend to read them in her book. However, most often than not, Salim was annoyed with her, but that didn't bother Mira. He was the only person in the world she told her secret to, and he didn't abandon her, nor did he fear her.

"They are salt traders from the kingdom of Mali," Salim finally gave in.

"Have you ever been to Mali? What is it like," Mira asked, curiosity blooming in her heart.

"I have not been there, but from what I hear, it's a wonder, filled with riches, and its people blessed with salt and gold."

Mira's eyes gleamed. Salim was being very nice to her that day. He bought her a new dress and food, he answered all her questions, and he didn't tell her to be quiet when she talked too much. Maybe now that they were free from the desert, he wouldn't be so moody all the time.

"Listen, kid," Salim said as he cleared his voice. Mira looked up, diverting her attention from her surroundings. "I found a family you will stay with for a little while. I already met them, and they are good people."

Mira frowned. "But I want to stay with you."

"You can't stay with me. It's-it's not proper. I am a single man, and people would talk."

"What will they talk about," Mira asked, confused.

Salim sighed, scrubbing his face. "I need to stay in the men's quarters. You are a girl, so you will stay with a family. They will help you get cleaned up and watch over you."

"No, I don't want to leave you!" She cried in panic.

"Hey, calm down," Salim whispered, quickly looking around to see if anyone heard. "Do you remember the wish you had in the desert," he asked suddenly.

Mira's head perked up and she nodded. "Well, if you're good and listen to what I say, I will fulfill your wish and read your book to you."

"Really?! You'll really read my book?" Mira clapped her hands in excitement. She was so happy she could spin. She wished Ayub were there so she could tell him the good news.

"But you have to stay with the family. You cannot leave their side until I come for you. Do you understand?"

Mira nodded frantically. She would do anything to finally know what was in that book. She was so angry when Salim said it wasn't interesting. It was the most interesting thing in the world to her. It was her escape from reality. She read it a thousand times, and each time, it was a different story.

"But you'll really come for me, won't you?" Mira asked again just to be sure.

Salim gave her a tight smile and nod.

"Do you promise?"

"Sure, kid. I promise."

Mira grinned. "And friends never break their promise."

***

Mira waited outside the small, sand brick home, nervously holding the new dress Salim bought her. The house was like the house she occupied in her old village, but bigger. It had wooden windows that open outward and wooden doors. Mira was a bit curious to see the inside of the house as Salim spoke to the man and woman near the door. The woman was holding a baby and had a scarf over her mouth and nose. Salim pulled a few coins out of his pocket, giving them to the man. The man nodded and they shook hands.

Nervous energy filled her as she stood waiting; she didn't know these people, and she didn't particularly like new people. Salim was the only person she trusted in this world besides Ayub. He was her savior; he was going to take her from this place and into his world.

Salim walked over to her, leveling himself to her height. "Remember what I told you, kid," he asked. She nodded slowly, looking behind him at the waiting family.

"Don't leave the house under any circumstances," she whispered, repeating his words from earlier.

"Good, Zaynab and her husband, Khalid, are very nice people. They will watch over you for a few days. I want you to behave and listen to what they say. Okay?"

She swallowed the lump in her throat and was unable to speak. She missed Ayub, and was scared, but she had to listen to Salim. Now, she had to prove to him that she could be good so that he would take her with him.

"When will you come for me," Mira asked, needing reassurance.

Salim dusted off her shoulders. "I'll come in three days," he said. "Will you wait here until then?"

Mira nodded, her eyes watering. She didn't want Salim to leave her—not even for a day.

"Hey, don't cry, you hear me? Everything will be okay," he assured her.

Mira nodded again, not trusting her voice.

Salim stood, leading her to the family. The woman smiled and greeted her warmly, while the man shared a few more words with Salim.

27.

The family prepared a warm bath for Mira to clean herself. She smiled and waved at the baby who reminded her of Sara. Mira closed her eyes as she entered the wooden tub. She was caked with dirt and grime. If her mother were there, she'd scold her for her appearance. And if Jida were there, she'd make a silly joke to calm Mama down.

Zaynab poured the water over her head, and Mira imagined it was her mother who washed her, scrubbing her body and hair. She imagined it was baby Sara on the floor cooing as Mama took care of her. The water dripped from her hair and mixed with her warm tears. *I miss you, Mama. I miss you, Sara. I miss you, Jida,* she thought while the stranger finished washing off the soap.

"Get dressed and I will prepare you some warm food," the woman said, interrupting her thoughts.

Mira shook off her longing and gave her a small smile. "Thank you," she whispered, wrapping the towel around her body. She put on the new dress Salim got her. It was black with red embroidery. The material was soft against her skin, not the plain scratchy wool she was used to. He even gave her new shoes and leather socks. Mira grinned as she spun around in her new dress. The woman, who introduced herself as Zaynab, called her outside and began skillfully braiding her hair before leading her to a room in the back of the house. The room was sparse with only a cot, a small table and an oil lantern. After spending days in the desert sleeping under the night sky, it felt nice to be on a cot.

"You are not to leave this room for any reason. Do you understand? You can only leave to use the toilet outside. I will bring you your food and take it when you are done," Zaynab instructed her sternly. She then closed her door, leaving her to her thoughts.

The air was still warm even though it was now dark out. The soot covered oil lantern shined dimly as she sat on her cot. Mira wondered what Salim was doing at that moment. Was he scribbling in his journal as he did when he couldn't sleep? She asked several times what he wrote there, but he always brushed her off, never disclosing the content of those pages. But Mira didn't mind being ignored, so long as he stayed by her side and didn't leave her.

Digging in her small bag, Mira pulled out her book and began reading. Today, the stories were about the kings of Mali and their epic trades. Mira imagined they had magic powers that turned salt into gold. She imagined they lived in large, clay palaces and had lots of date groves and camels.

Exhaustion finally took over as Mira yawned loudly. There was so much excitement that day that she could barely keep her eyes open. "Goodnight, Ayub. Goodnight, Salim. I love you, Mama. I love you, Sara," she whispered, just as she did every night before dozing off.

The following morning Mira was awoken to the sound of Zaynab entering her room to deliver her breakfast. "Thank you," she whispered, but the woman ignored her and left without a word. Mira sighed. She remembered the fearful glare Zaynab had given her when she first saw her eyes, as well as the whispered prayers.

But Mira was used to this adverse reaction, and she was used to spending endless hours alone in her room. Mira had a world inside her head; oftentimes, that world was her only escape. Were it not for her overactive imagination, she would have been overcome with despair years ago.

Mira was playing with her straw dolls when the door slowly creaked open. It had been a few hours past lunch, and Mira had kept her promise not to leave the house. She looked up and frowned when she didn't see anyone at the door. But then she grinned excitedly when the baby crawled into her room on chubby hands and knees.

"Hi!" Mira cooed, approaching the baby. She pulled out some berries she had saved from Ayub, offering them to the baby who giggled, grabbed one and stuffed it into her mouth. Mira laughed as the juice dripped down the baby's chin.

"My baby sister liked berries, too. Her name was Sara," Mira told the baby who blabbered incoherently. "Do you want to play with me," she asked as the baby reached for her doll.

"You have to be careful with it," she scolded as the baby tried to eat the doll.

"I'll be the mama, and you'll be the baby, okay?" Mira told her, dancing her doll side to side. The baby giggled, lifting her fingers to squeeze Mira's face. Mira laughed, covered her eyes, and said, 'boo!' The baby cackled every time Mira revealed her face, clapping excitedly.

"What are you doing?!" Mira flinched as Zaynab stormed into the room, pushing Mira away from her baby.

Mira fell back, scrambling away. "I-I'm sorry. She came into the room, and we were just playing," she tried to explain.

"You stay away from my child, demon! You will return to the Banu Nazir soon enough. Until then, stay here," Zaynab shouted, making the baby cry. Mira looked down as the woman stormed out and slammed her door.

Confusion hit her as she thought about Zaynab's words. She wasn't going to Banu Nazir; she was going with Salim. They would see the world together, and he was coming to get her. *Zaynab must be mistaken*, Mira thought.

She tried to distract herself the rest of the day by telling stories and drawing pictures in the sand, but she couldn't get Zaynab's words out of her mind. *Why would she say that?*

The entire night was filled with apprehension as Mira tossed and turned. She finally decided she would have to leave in the morning and find Salim. Zaynab had the wrong idea, and Salim needed to explain to her that Mira was going with him; this was all a misunderstanding.

28.

The next morning Mira woke up bright and early to pack her things, just in case they had to leave. She paused as she held her book in her hand, frowning, Salim would probably refuse to grant her wish now that she was about to disobey him, but she had to explain what Zaynab said so that he could correct her. Zaynab thought she was going back to Banu Nazir, but that was wrong. Mira was going with Salim.

Careful not to wake up anyone, she slowly tiptoed out of the house. The dawn sky was bright as the sun lazily rose from the west, basking the desert town in its colors. Mira had already memorized the way to the caravan camp; she was always very good at remembering things. She walked through the sleeping town; a few merchants were up already, quietly drinking tea and setting up their tables for trade.

It was hard to believe that this was the same bustling town she had entered two days ago. Back then, it was much scarier and intimidating. The new sights and foreign sounds amazed Mira as much as they scared her. But she was happy to know that dawn's peace stretched everywhere. Mira quietly crept her way through the town, careful to keep her gaze down and her footsteps swift. She was used to sneaking around undetected, slipping unnoticed through the people.

As Mira reached the edge of the caravan's camp, she noticed that everyone in the camp was already awake and alert; each man was busy preparing his camel and tearing down his tent.

Mira frowned, confused. She knew that caravans only tore down their camps when they were about to journey out. She grinned, suddenly excited. They were leaving today! Salim would probably be at Zaynab's house any minute now to fetch her. Mira clapped her hands excitedly. Part of her wanted to run to Salim and ask him if they were truly leaving, but she remembered she wasn't supposed to be there in the first place.

She thought about turning around to head back but paused; she always enjoyed watching caravans come and go, fascinated with the details that went into preparing for such a long journey. It probably wouldn't hurt to watch them for a while and then run back before Salim went to get her. She could probably still get her wish.

Liking the plan, Mira rubbed her hands together devilishly. She had grown bored of being cooped up in that room anyway. She looked around for somewhere to hide and found a small tree a few feet away from the camp. Mira grinned, ran to the tree and quickly climbed its branches. From there, she knew she would be able to see everything that was going on in the camp.

"What are you doing?"

Mira gasped, almost losing her footing. Her heart thundered as she held on tight, barely avoiding a fall. She narrowed her eyes at Ayub, who came out of nowhere, hanging upside down on one of the branches of the tree.

"Ayub! What did I tell you about sneaking up on me? You scared me half to death!"

Ayub smiled sheepishly, "Sorry, Mira. I didn't mean to scare you."

"It's okay," Mira said, quickly climbing the rest of the way up and perching herself on a branch. Ayub did a little flip, crunching down on the branch above her. His feet folded under him. "Show off," Mira muttered.

"Why are we sitting in a tree?" Ayub asked.

"I'm watching the caravan. They are getting ready to leave," Mira told him.

"Cool!"

Mira grinned at Ayub, her excitement growing. Soon, she, Ayub and Salim would all be a family. Ayub wasn't so scared of Salim—well not as much as he feared other humans; he even gave Salim food and water when they were in the desert. Ayub still wasn't comfortable with the idea of traveling with another human, but he trusted Mira, and that's all that mattered.

"Do you think cities will be this scary?" Ayub shuddered. Ayub hated the town. There were a lot of humans in it, and a lot of bad *jinns*. Mira saw them lurking around in every corner; some of them were attached to the caravans, and some attached to people. Mira always avoided people who had *jinns* attached to them. They reminded her of the *Sahir*.

Mira frowned. She assumed the city would be like a town, but from what Salim told her, a city was bigger. "I'm not scared of the city, but there might be a lot of humans and bad *jinns* there too," Mira admitted, even though she was a little scared.

"Do we have to go?" Ayub grumbled. "Why can't we stay in the desert?" Ayub hated the idea of leaving the desert. He was born there and lived there for a very long time. He was a desert *jinn*, and the desert was in his blood.

Mira sighed heavily. "I already told you, Ayub. We will go to the city and be a family there—the three of us—and we won't be sad and lonely anymore."

"Okay," Ayub muttered.

Knowing how much Ayub loved the desert she felt bad taking him away from it. She knew Ayub would never abandon her; he was her best friend, and she could never imagine being without him. "It'll be okay, Ayub. Trust me."

Mira watched silently while the caravan prepared for their journey. They tied up heavily loaded camels, refilled their water skins, and tied the goats that they would slaughter on the road for food. She grinned as she spotted Salim talking to one of the other men. He was already dressed in his traveling robes, and had his turban secured to his head. He looked clean, just like he did when she first saw him in the oasis.

Back then, Mira was mesmerized by him—how he skillfully healed the people of the oasis. She watched him daily as he prepared medicine, checked the people and wrote in his notebook. She was fascinated by his ability. She went home every night and pretended to heal her dolls, repeating things she had heard Salim say. She ground up dry shrubs and pretended to give them medicine. Mira secretly hoped that Salim would teach her how to heal people as he did. She imagined people waiting for her, thanking her and praising her for helping them. They would no longer fear her, and they'd finally see that she wasn't evil. Mira was good, and she loved to help people.

The caravan was just about ready to depart, and Mira anxiously watched, wondering why Salim hadn't gone back to retrieve her yet. Soon, the caravan leader started calling out their departure, "*Yallah! Yallah!* Move out!" he shouted as the caravan formed a train. Mira frowned, confused as Salim joined the back of the train. *Did he forget her?*

Mira quickly climbed down the tree, her heart racing as she chased after the caravan. Her tiny feet kicked the sand behind her as she sprinted to catch up with them. "Salim, wait!" she shouted, waving her hands frantically.

Salim paused and looked back; surprise written all over his face. Mira stopped in front of him, breathing hard. "You forgot about me!" she accused.

He closed his eyes and took a deep breath. The caravan didn't pause, but a few men looked back before proceeding. "I thought I told you not to leave that house," Salim whispered harshly.

"Well, Zaynab got angry with me for playing with the baby, and said I was going back to Banu Nazir. I came to find you so that you could tell her she's wrong. I'm coming with you!" She explained in a rush, puzzled at his attitude.

"You are not coming with me."

Mira blinked, not sure whether she heard him right. "Yes, I am. I'm going with you. You have to tell Zaynab that she's wrong!"

Salim sighed, frustrated. "Listen, kid. I can't take you with me, okay? You have to go back home."

Mira shook her head. What was going on here? Salim promised he would take her. "B-but you *promised*. You promised you would come get me. And friends never break their promise!"

"I'm not your friend," Salim snapped. "Now get lost, kid."

He turned his back and grabbed the rope to his camel. Mira felt her heart shatter as Salim walked away. She felt the tears roll down her cheeks as she followed him, grabbing his robes.

"Please, Salim. I'm sorry, I'll be good. I promise I won't talk too much or ask you to play with me. Please don't leave me" Mira pleaded, not sure what she did wrong. She couldn't understand why he was being so mean to her. Salim turned around, pushing her hand off his thobe. Mira stumbled and landed on her back. She looked up at him in shock.

"I don't want you to come with me. Don't you get it, kid? I'm not your father, and I'm definitely not your friend. *You* are no one to me. The only reason I tagged along with you this far was because I needed your help to survive. I don't need you anymore, so I'm leaving. And if you follow me, I'll expose your secret. Do you understand? Now, go back and leave me be!"

Hot tears streamed down her face, as Mira scrambled back in disbelief. She stood and began running blindly back to the tree she sat in with Ayub.

By the time she collapsed under its shade, Mira was shaking and sobbing into her dress. "Mama," she cried. She wanted to be with her mother and Sara. She wished she were with them in heaven, and she wished she no longer had to live in this cruel world.

Mira sniffled, angrily wiping her tears. She couldn't believe Salim abandoned her. They were supposed to be a family. She told him her secret, and he used it against her. She should have known humans were cruel and treacherous creatures; they hated anything that was different. Perhaps Mira didn't belong in this world; she was tired of being used and discarded.

"Mira, are you okay? Why are you crying," Ayub asked, his face pained as he helplessly watched his best friend break down before him. He was vibrating with energy; his body shook.

"I'm not okay, Ayub. I hate it. I hate everyone. People are mean and cruel. And I hate Salim. He is the worst person in the world!" Mira cried as betrayal burned in her heart.

Ayub started crying. "Please don't hate me. Mira, I love you. You're my best friend. I'll never leave you! You don't need anyone else, only me."

That only made Mira cry harder. She loved Ayub more than anything, but he was a *jinn*. He could never understand her feelings, her loneliness, or her desire to be normal. As much as she loved Ayub, Mira was human, and she wanted nothing more than to be accepted by her kind.

"You keep crying like that and you will flood this entire town," a voice said, standing over her. Mira looked up, sniffling and hiccupping and she calmed her crying.

"Salim?"

Salim gave her a small smile as he stood awkwardly in front of her. "Listen, kid. I'm sorry I was so harsh earlier and…" Salim grunted, huffing out a breath of air as Mira slammed into him with a tight hug, crying into his thobe. Salim awkwardly patted her back. "Hey, enough of that. You're getting your boogers all over my clothes."

Mira ignored him, not letting go. "You came back! I knew you'd come back!"

"Really? Because I heard you telling Ayub how much you hated me."

She finally let go looking up at him. "Sorry, I was just angry," she said, embarrassed.

"Well, I guess I kind of deserve that," he admitted, giving her a small smile and a handkerchief.

Mira returned the smile, wiping the snot and tears from her face. "Does this mean you will take me with you," she asked hopefully.

Salim sighed, "no, but I'll take you as far as Cairo. After that, you are on your own," he said finally. Mira's face fell as disappointment filled her. "If you don't want to go, then it's probably best you head back home,"

"No!" Mira interrupted. "I'll go to Cairo!" She decided she'd convince him to keep her on their way there.

"Are you sure, kid? Life in the city isn't all sunshine and rainbows."

"Yes, I'm sure. I want to go to the city"

Salim rubbed the back of his neck, as if regretting this decision already. "Alright, kid. I'll take you there, but no more. Once we reach the city, we go our separate ways. Got it?"

"Got it," Mira nodded. At least this was better than being left behind. If she couldn't convince Salim to keep her, she would find her own way in the world.

"Come on, Ayub! We're going to see the world!" Mira announced as she grabbed her things.

"Really? Is the world scary," Ayub asked, confused about what was going on. One minute Mira was crying her heart out, and the next she was almost giddy with excitement.

Salim cleared his throat. He was always uncomfortable when she talked to Ayub. "Hurry up! The caravan is already gone. We'll have to follow them."

29.

Mira and Salim traveled together following the trail of the caravan. Salim told her that they couldn't join the caravan directly because he didn't want to explain her presence. Mira was okay with this arrangement; she preferred it being just the three of them anyway. She spent the last few days glued to Salim's side; she was so paranoid he would disappear that she refused to give him even a little space.

Salim rolled his eyes as Mira accidentally bumped into him for the third time. "Kid, you are attached closer than my shadow," he grumbled, having long given up on telling her to back off.

Even at night, Mira woke up countless times paranoid that he would be gone. She was jumpy and nervous the entire trip. Her heart still ached from his hurtful words, even though she tried to convince herself he didn't mean it.

"How will we get to Cairo," Mira asked, tired of walking. Mira still couldn't believe Salim was taking her; she never imagined she would go somewhere so far. She didn't even care that he was planning on leaving her there. She was brimming with excitement; soon, Mira would get to see the city she had been dreaming of, ever since she met that traveler who told her stories of Cairo.

Salim looked up into the distance. "First, we will head to Tunis. Then, we will board a ship to the city."

Mira's mouth gaped open and she shared a look with Ayub. "We will board a ship! Will we see the ocean," she asked in disbelief.

Salim chuckled. "It's not like ships sail on land."

She squealed and jumped up and down. "Hey, stop that," Salim said with a smile and shook his head.

"Sorry," Mira whispered. She just couldn't contain her excitement.

Taking off her pack, she quickly dumped its contents into the sand before retrieving the triangle structure given to her by that kind merchant. "They have something like this in Cairo," she declared, holding up the tiny, wooden pyramid. "They are ancient structures built by the people of the Pharaoh, and they have a huge river called a Neel," Mira boasted her knowledge.

"Nile," Salim corrected. "But yes, you are right. We will head to the land of the Nile and the Pharaohs."

Mira grinned ear to ear, clutching the small pyramid, and imagining what it would finally be like to see it all in real life.

"Listen, kid. Once we get to the port, I will have to tell everyone that you are my daughter. It will look strange if I try to board a ship with a random child. Okay?"

None of that mattered, she was going to Cairo, and that was the only thing on her mind. "Can I call you Baba," she asked.

"No."

Mira pouted. "But you said I'm your daughter."

"No, I said you will pretend to be my daughter."

"Wouldn't it be more convincing if I called you Baba," she asked hopefully.

"Just stay quiet and don't speak to anyone."

"Fine," Mira grumbled.

"That means no talking to Ayub either. I don't want people to think I have a mad child."

Ayub stuck his tongue out at Salim, not liking that one bit. Mira giggled at his reaction, earning a scolding look from Salim. She quickly shut her mouth and looked around to avoid eye contact. She knew he hated it when she laughed at something Ayub did. But she couldn't help it. Sometimes Ayub was just too silly.

***

The next morning, Mira woke up feeling an uncomfortable cramp in her abdomen and rolled to her side groaning. Was she sick? She sat up, then felt a wetness on her dress. She turned it around gasping when she saw blood. Mira's heart hammered as she began to check her legs for wounds. She thought an animal had bitten her while she slept, but she soon realized where the blood was coming from, and that was worse than being bitten.

Mira had finally come of age. This is what Yasmin had warned her about, and the dreaded day had finally come. Mira began crying as she held her stomach, experiencing a piercing pain. She felt like a knife was being inserted into her gut.

"What is all this crying about?" Salim grumbled from his spot across from her. She began crying harder. Salim blinked into focus, realizing something was wrong, and hurried to her side, touching her forehead. "Mira, look at me. Tell me where it hurts," he demanded.

Shame filled her as she shook her head. She didn't want him—or anyone—to know what had happened.

"Mira, I can't help you if you don't speak to me. Tell me what's wrong so I can fix it."

"Can you fix it," she asked, wiping her eyes. "Can you make it stop?"

"I can't do anything if you don't tell me what's wrong."

Mira hiccupped. She stood, still clutching her abdomen. The sand where she sat was red with her menstrual blood, which made her cry even more. "Can you make it stop, please? I don't want to get married. I don't want to have babies. I just want to be a kid forever. Please, I don't want to marry that old man!" she begged incoherently.

"Calm down. What are you talking about? What old man," Salim asked, trying to make sense of her rambling. "What you are experiencing is normal for every girl your age," Salim tried to calm her.

"Yasmin said when a girl becomes of age, she bleeds from her private parts, and she has to get married and have babies. And I don't want to marry the *Sheikh's* cousin. He is old and doesn't have any teeth. I don't want to marry anyone!" Mira cried, too blinded by her fears to listen.

"Hey, look at me," Salim ordered, grabbing her shoulders. "You are not at the oasis, okay? you don't have to marry anyone if you don't want to. From now on, what you wish to do with your life will always be your choice. Do you understand me?"

Mira blinked and looked at Salim. He was telling the truth—she could tell by his face. She wiped her eyes, calming down. In all her life, Mira never expected to have a choice in anything. She was always told to do what was expected of a girl, but now, Salim was telling her she had a *choice*. Her life would no longer be determined by those around her. Mira was *free*.

"Do you feel any pain in your abdomen?" Salim asked, pulling Mira from her thoughts. She nodded. Salim went to his camel and pulled out a small tablet and some rags from his medicine box, handing them to her. "Drink this with water. It will help with the pain. And use this cloth under your dress to catch the blood. It must be dry. Do you understand? When you change it, wash it and wring it. This tablet will help with the pain and minimize the blood flow."

Mira grabbed his offering, her cheeks red with embarrassment. "Hey, there is nothing to be ashamed of, kid. I've had many patients who suffered from menstrual pain. They come to me for help, and I never judge them. There should be no shame in such a natural occurrence."

She nodded and gave him a small smile. "Thank you, Salim," she whispered before running out of sight to clean herself and follow his instructions.

31.

The closer they got to the port city of Tunis, the more people they encountered. There were all sorts of people following the worn path to the great city: merchants from all corners of the world, farmers carting their loaded wagons into the city and carriages pulled by horseback. Mira could hardly believe her eyes. There were street vendors lined up selling anything from food to clothes and other knick knacks, each persistent in their trade.

Mira's eyes widened as the large stone towers came into view; they were queued outside with other people hoping to make it into the city.

The city was surrounded by lofty stone walls. In between the walls were large towers, each manned by guards. The walls were so high, Mira swore they could touch the sky. Her heart hammered as they went closer to the arched entrance. She grabbed hold of Salim's robes and, for once, he didn't push her away.

"Remember what I told you, kid. Do not say a word."

Mira nodded. She doubted she could speak, even if she tried.

As they got closer to the city, Ayub disappeared, too afraid of all the commotion. Mira didn't blame him. She, too, was afraid of what was to come.

The queue into the city got shorter and shorter. Soon, Mira and Salim were standing in front of the large, intricate, arched gate. There were two stern guards armed with spears and covered in leather armor, the likes of which Mira had never seen.

She quickly hid behind Salim, suddenly fearful of these men. "Business," the man asked curtly. Salim quickly pulled out some papers that Mira couldn't read. "My name is Salim Al-Zuhair. I am from the city of Fez, here to board a ship to Cairo." The man took the papers, glancing at her before handing them back to Salim. He nodded, and Salim thanked him as they moved forward.

"Halt!" the man suddenly stopped them. "Who is the child?" he said, pointing at a shaking Mira.

"This is my daughter. Unfortunately, we lost her documents while traveling," Salim quickly explained.

The man raised his eyebrow. "Is this your father," he asked her curtly.

Mira nodded frantically, wanting to get away.

The man was unmoved. "She needs documents."

Salim sighed, pulling out a few coins from his pocket to give the man who, then, motioned for them to enter as he pocketed his coin.

"Thank you." Salim grabbed Mira's hand and led her into the city. Mira was so frightened by the confrontation that she didn't look around her until they were inside an enormous bazaar.

Mira's eyes widened as she froze in place, looking around the packed alleyways. She looked down at the cobblestone floor lined with eager vendors. The sights and sounds were too much for her to take in—she was completely baffled by what she was seeing. Mira sniffed the air, her stomach grumbling as they passed the many dessert and food stalls. People were crammed everywhere, trying to buy their bread, meat and other goods. Butchers called out meat prices while covered women stood nearby to purchase their share.

Salim led a dazed Mira by the hand, pulling them out of the bazaar. She sniffed as the scent of salt and fish infiltrated her nose. She was too overcome with sensation; soon, the excitement of the souk and its chaos was overshadowed as they entered the port. She blinked in awe as they made their way past a maze of merchants, fishermen and other people, each yelling and buzzing with activity.

The port was lined with great ships. Mira had heard of ships, but to finally put a picture to the word was unbelievable. The ships were so big, Mira had to cram her head to look at them. Lined in front of them were stacks of crates filled with all kinds of goods that were to be transported to different cities, as well as stalls of fish and other sea creatures.

"Mira! Snap out of it," Salim was suddenly in her line of vision.

She blinked, transfixed by all she was seeing. "Huh?"

Salim sighed. "Are you really that amazed by all this?" Mira nodded, shifting her attention back to the towering ships. Salim chuckled, "I don't know what I was thinking when I plucked a desert flower, but please don't make me regret this."

Mira nodded again, not really listening to what he was saying. Salim grabbed her by the shoulders and led her to a stone step. "You sit here and have your fill. I will buy us passage on one of the ships. Hopefully we can board for Cairo today."

"Sure" she whispered absently before realizing his words. "Wait! we are actually going on a-a ship?" she stammered.

Salim raised his eyebrow at her. "Yes. Why? Have you changed your mind and wish to return home? I'm sure I can find a caravan—"

"No! I want to go with you," Mira immediately interrupted. There was no way she was going back to that oasis. It was never her home, and no matter how daunting the experience, she wanted to go on that ship and see the ocean—something that, until now, she had only ever dreamed of. Mira had a taste of adventure, and now she was addicted, helpless to its lure.

"Of course," Salim grumbled. "Well, it was worth a try. Stay here, and no matter what, do not leave this spot."

"Okay," Mira agreed.

"I mean it, Mira. Do not leave this spot."

Mira wrinkled her nose as Salim squeezed his way through the busy port. The smell of fish wasn't sitting well with her. She had dried fish before, but Mira wasn't much of a fan. She preferred camel meat.

"I don't like this place. It's loud and scary."

Mira yelped as Ayub appeared next to her, staring at the activity around him. "Ayub! You scared me again."

"Sorry," he apologized sheepishly before going back to sulking.

"Guess what? We are going to board a ship and sail on the ocean! Can you believe it!" Mira grinned.

Ayub crossed his arms, unimpressed with the ships. "I don't like ships, and I don't like the ocean. I like the desert," he asserted.

"Well, if you like the desert so much, why don't you go back?" Mira snapped, annoyed with his lack of excitement and negativity.

"No, I want to stay with you forever, Mira. I'll follow you to the ends of the earth, and even if you go to the sky, I'll grow wings and follow you there," Ayub retorted with a serious expression on his face.

Mira felt bad. She didn't mean what she said. She knew Ayub would never abandon her. "I'm sorry, Ayub, but Salim says Cairo has a great desert—bigger than the one we came from. Perhaps it won't be so bad," She tried to cheer him up.

"Really," he asked, his interest peaked.

Mira nodded, enthusiastically. "Mhm, they have dunes that touch the sky. You can slide down them all day and night. It will be so much fun."

Ayub's eyes lit up with excitement. "And you'll play with me," he asked eagerly.

"Well, I'll play with you sometimes, but I might have some grown-up responsibilities too, so you will have to learn to play by yourself as well."

"Okay," Ayub sighed, sagging down on the step next to her. Mira sat silently with him, watching the ships, she watched as the hungry birds scooped down to eat bread, and the endless people who filtered in and out of her sight.

"Mira!"

Mira looked up at the sound of her name and grinned brightly when she spotted Salim. She didn't want to admit it, but she was worried he wouldn't come back, that he would board the ship without her. However, seeing him now, she was glad she had kept her promise and stayed put.

"We must hurry. I found a ship to Cairo, but it's leaving now," Salim urged, waving her towards him. Mira scrambled to grab her bags and follow Salim.

She paused. "Ayub, let's go," she called to her friend.

Ayub huffed. "I'm faster than any old ship," he bragged.

Mira rolled her eyes. "Ships are scary. I will run fast and meet you there," he promised.

"Mira!" Salim called again impatiently.

"I'll see you there," she called out as Salim grabbed her arm to rush her to the departing ship.

32.

The large ships hovered over them like mountains as they approached. She couldn't comprehend how such a large structure was able to float and was fearful that it would sink. Her legs quivered as they walked on the narrow plank. Mira paused, unable to take another step. Salim grabbed her hand and gave her a reassuring squeeze. "You're okay, kid. I won't let anything happen to you," he promised.

Mira swallowed, appreciating the reassurance. The ship was firm—not as shaky as she imagined it would be when they stepped onto its wooden deck. She looked up at the large, striped, red and white sails that were held together by a large pole and many ropes.

Salim led her to the edge of the crowded ship as more and more people piled on. She held onto the rails, her knuckles white with apprehension as she finally stared out into the deep blue ocean. Mira's breath left her body as the salty winds of the sea greeted her, welcoming her into its domain. She felt her eyes water as she took in the magnificent sight, "Praise be to God," she whispered in amazement. Ayub was right. The ocean was like the desert; vast and imposing, as far as her eyes could see. Even the waves that gently crashed into the ship reminded her of the waves that often formed on the sand dunes.

Mira closed her eyes, deafening herself to all the chaotic sounds of the port. She breathed deeply as the wind caressed her face, inhaling its sweet scent. Mira smiled, her heart beating peacefully, content with the beauty it was introduced to. This was truly the greatest day of her young life.

"I must secure our things below deck. Do you want to see your quarters?" Salim asked, breaking Mira out of her trance.

"No, I want to stay here," she told him, not looking away from the ocean that had her hypnotized.

Salim chuckled, "well, enjoy it for now. You will not like it much when the boat starts to move and seasickness begins," he warned as he headed below.

After about an hour, the ship was boarded, and the men began shouting instructions, preparing to sail. Mira tried to look for Ayub on land but couldn't see him anywhere. She hoped he was being truthful and would follow the ship to Cairo. Her feet began to sway as the ship creaked and moved out to sea. She held the railing so tightly her fingers hurt as the ship launched forward. Mira frantically looked around for Salim, her heart hammering. She saw him on deck a few steps away, chatting with another man. She let go of the railing and, with shaky legs, scurried to his side, attaching herself to his thobe.

Salim patted her back. "Not enjoying the view so much now, are you?" he commented as Mira's stomach lurched.

"I don't feel good," she whispered.

"It's just seasickness. Let's go below deck. I will make you a tea that will help calm your stomach and you can lay down for a bit." Mira nodded, grudgingly following Salim down the swaying ship into the tightly packed underdeck.

***

It took Mira two days to finally get used to the seasickness and stop vomiting. The teas Salim made helped with her nausea, but she was glad to finally be able to spend her days above deck, obsessively watching the sea. Mira looked down into the water, grinning; she could see large fish swimming with the ship as they jumped in and out of the water. She looked around at the other passengers to see if they too could see the creatures. She was relieved to see that they were all pointing and smiling excitedly.

Salim told her they were called dolphins, and she reached her hand out to them, giddy by their mischievous smiles as they raced with the ship. But she also saw other creatures that weren't as pretty. She could tell that no one else could see the leathery skin creatures that idly swam in the water. Their tails were like that of a fish, but their upper body was that of a human; however, their faces were scary, and Mira didn't like looking at them.

Her favorite part was the sunset, when the entire ocean would glow yellow, orange and red. She loved seeing the sun's reflection on the soft waves before it tucked itself behind the water like a curtain being pulled down. Sometimes, she snuck out of her bunk bed at night and went above deck to watch the moon and stars. She was happy to find the moon so far away from the desert where she grew up. She always assumed that's where it lived, but the moon was for everyone.

On their last day at sea, Mira was a bit disappointed to find out they were about to disembark, but part of her missed the feeling of soft sand between her toes. As much as she loved the ocean, she was also eager to go back to land and see Ayub; she had so much to tell him.

The ship finally made it safely to port after a week at sea. The Nile delta port was even busier than the port in Tunis, and, for once, Mira wasn't happy. She felt disoriented with all the chaos around her; she hoped Cairo would be calmer.

"We will take the delta Nile into the city of Cairo," Salim informed her as they stood in line to board the smaller ships upriver to a port near Cairo. These ships were narrower than sea ships; they also had brightly colored sails and red-tinted bodies. There were men with large oars rowing the ship and forcing it to move. Mira jolted from her seat as the boat took off. This ride was a lot shorter than the one they just landed from, and the river was much darker and murkier than the sea, but Mira was still amazed by the sights they passed.

The ride was peaceful as people chatted quietly, followed by the heavy breathing of the men who rowed them. She had never seen such greenery, the likes of which they passed on the Nile. Mira gaped at the towering date palms and the endless vegetation they passed. She blinked as she spotted a strange creature lying lazily on the banks of the river; it crawled on four feet and had scaly skin with a large mouth lined with sharp teeth. She shuddered, looking away, until Salim pointed to them and said, "They are called crocodiles. Strange-looking beasts, are they not? I was just as surprised my first time seeing one."

Mira grinned happily. She wasn't the only one witnessing the animal. She knew all the animals in the desert—the seen and the unseen—and could easily distinguish between them, but the creatures she saw on this trip were different.

33.

After a few hours on the Nile, the boat finally stopped at a tiny port outside the city. Mira stepped off the rocking boat, feeling exhausted. She quickly looked around, hoping to see Ayub, however, he was nowhere in sight. Salim pushed her towards a line of double carted wagons attached to different animals. He approached one of the riders, asking him to take them into the city. Mira stepped onto the covered cart next to Salim. "Are we almost there," she asked.

"Not so excited anymore, are you, kid?" Salim quipped, taking in her fatigued expression.

"I am excited," Mira protested. "Just tired."

"Don't worry, kid. We're almost there. Once we get to the city, we can finally part ways."

Mira didn't like the sound of that. She wanted to stay with Salim forever, but he couldn't wait to be rid of her. She fell asleep on the bumpy ride, too exhausted to take in much of anything around her. She wanted to rest. Mira jolted awake as the wagon made an abrupt stop.

"We're here." Those two words were enough to wake up Mira, expelling all previous fatigue as the excitement of finally seeing the city she only ever dreamed of came into view. She stepped off the wagon and was thrust into the dusty streets outside the city walls. She looked around the chaotic scene with wide eyes as she grabbed onto Salim's thobe.

There were lines of people, merchants and travelers, all seeking entry into its walls. There were mule-drawn wagons and trains of caravans with heavily loaded camels. The air was thick with fine sand, basking the entire city in a muted dusty color, matching the walls and ground.

By the time they made it to the great gates of Cairo, Mira was shaking with apprehension. She looked at the city astonished. She thought the walls of Tunis were grand, but these walls and gates were even bigger. Mira gaped as they made their way into the great city, following the never-ending crowd. As they walked, her senses were flooded by sights, sounds and smells beyond that which she had ever witnessed. From the gates, they entered a packed marketplace. Lines and lines of merchants stood in front of colorful stalls, selling everything one can imagine. Packed in front of the busy stalls were tons of people, each yelling and shouting, looking for a bargain and seeking a trade.

Mira didn't like all the chaotic energy that surrounded the city and was confused when she saw all the raggedy children that ran up to Salim begging for help. She didn't know what to say to them, never having encountered beggars in the desert. The tribes took care of everyone, but the people in the cities were different.

Hungry children surrounded them, begging for money and food, Mira watched as Salim shooed them away. She didn't understand what was happening and didn't know what she could do to help. "Why doesn't the Sultan feed his people," she asked as they passed a group of beggars with tattered clothes and injuries sitting on the ground with empty bowls.

"Not even the Sultan can feed everyone. As you will soon learn, Mira, the world is a dark place. You were shielded from it by the bubble of the desert, and the warm embrace of your tribe, but life is not the same for everyone else. If you think your life is bad, remember, there is always someone who has it worse."

Mira felt guilty thinking about her own trivial problems. Though simple, she always had food in her belly. Though harsh, the desert was always a safe place for her. Seeing how people live in the city made her appreciate the life she had. She assumed everyone in the cities were blessed and happy. She definitely didn't think it would be this stinky and dirty.

"Not what you were expecting, is it, kid," Salim asked, noticing her apprehension. She didn't respond, unsure of how she felt. It was not what she imagined.

Shortly after, they made their way out of the packed souk and entered a more residential neighborhood. Mira looked up at the shaded street. Ropes of fabric hung between tall houses with overlooking balconies. The streets here were cleaner; they were lined with cobblestone, and not the fine sand she was used to. There were food stalls with old men sitting on stools chatting while they drank their tea. There were wagons filled with fruits and vegetables Mira had never seen before, and restaurants whose smell of meat and other food filtered into Mira's nose, causing her stomach to grumble.

Salim cleared his throat and avoided her eyes. "Alright, kid. I guess this is where we part ways," he announced. Mira felt her heart drop as she looked around. It wasn't as chaotic here as in the souk, but it was still alien to her. "Do you have somewhere to go," Salim asked. Mira nodded, somber. Salim had fulfilled his promise. He brought her to Cairo, and now he no longer owed her anything. It was she who failed to convince him to keep her by his side, and now it was her responsibility to find her way.

"Thank you, Salim, for everything. You've done more for me than I could have ever prayed for. I wish you well on your journey, and I hope we will meet again one day," Mira told him in earnest. Salim spent weeks caring for her. He tended to her when she was ill, protected her from nefarious people, and became her companion, even if it was only for a short time. She was grateful for him, and would allow him to live his life, and she would live hers—whatever that life may be.

Mira walked away—for once, not looking back. She didn't know where she was going, but determination fueled her path. She found her way to the citadel and was astonished by its size, many arched doors and towering minarets. She explored it with a curious glance. She never knew humans could build such wonders. Mira made it to the gate of the building, where she saw many men dressed in strange ceremonial garbs and holding books, followed by servants rushing in and out of the building that was guarded by stern men.

She cautiously walked up its step, hoping to enter its doors unseen, when she was stopped. "What are you doing here, kid," a man shouted. Mira backed away from the doors and ran from its premises in fear. She looked back, her heart hammering, but no one was following her. It was as if she didn't exist. No one even looked at her. She kept walking around the city until she reached a beautiful mosque. On its steps was an old woman who gave her a toothless smile.

Mira approached the person who reminded her of her grandmother.

"Come, child," the woman called to her warmly. Mira approached with a smile. "What do you have in that bag?" the woman asked, pointing to the bag she clutched in her arm.

"I have a book, a sleeping mat, a wooden pyramid and a glass suncatcher," Mira told the woman.

"Do you have any money," the woman asked Mira, who shook her head. She never had money.

"Then be gone!" the woman shouted, suddenly angry. "You cannot beg here. This is my spot," she snarled. Mira stumbled away from the woman in shock and ran in the opposite direction.

In her haste, she bumped into a few people who cursed at her, dusting off their clothing as if she were vermin. Some even spat on the ground in front of her, and everywhere she went, people told her to get lost. Mira felt her apprehension growing and her stomach grumbling in hunger. She ate a few pieces of dates and made it to a residential part of the city, where it wasn't so chaotic. There were a few tea shops with old men who smoked and talked loudly; some children played with a ball.

The alleyways were dark and curved, Mira looked around the narrow passage; besides a few stray cats, it was empty. Too paranoid to approach anyone, she cleared a spot and used her bag as a pillow to lay her head. Mira cried softly, afraid and alone in this strange place. She missed the empty embrace of the desert and regretted entering this cruel, heartless city.

***

She jolted up the next morning as she felt a hand caress her face. She cowered back, blinked, and stared up into the face of a man. Her body sagged in relief when she realized it was Salim. "What the hell, kid. I was searching for you all night."

Relief flooded her as she slammed into Salim, holding him tight. He came back for her again. Salim patted her back and gently pushed her away. "Why did you say you have somewhere to go, kid," he asked.

Mira frowned, "I didn't want to burden you," she whispered.

Salim shook his head in disbelief. "What, did you think that you would just come to a strange city and live happily ever after? I told you the world was a dark and evil place, and you didn't believe me."

Mira looked down in shame. Salim had warned her of the ugliness of the world, but in her childish naivety, she didn't imagine people in the city could be so cruel. Mira didn't know what she thought she would accomplish by coming here, but it was obvious she wouldn't make it in this world.

"Then I will just return to the desert. I will live my life there with Ayub," Mira whispered sadly. The world didn't want her, so she would have to remove herself from it.

Salim sighed heavily, rubbing his face with his hands. "What the hell am I going to do with you, kid?" he whispered. "Come on. You are not going to the desert. I will stay in Cairo until I find a safe place for you."

That statement brought joy to her heart. Mira looked up at Salim, her eyes watering. When she went to hug him tightly once more, he blocked her advance. "That's enough hugging, kid. Grab your things, and let's go."

Mira gave him a sheepish grin and followed behind him like a lost puppy. Salim led her through the twisted alleyways of the city, until they finally approached a modest stone building where there were straw baskets filled with all kinds of herbs and hand-dried plants. It was still early, and shopkeepers were just preparing for the day.

"Where are we?" Mira asked, studying the strange building.

"We are here to visit a friend of my father's. His name is Faisal, and he is a good man," Salim explained.

He pulled open the wooden door, triggering a bell, which made Mira jump as she tried to locate the sound. "We're closed!" a man called from inside as he sat hunched over a table scattered with all different types of herbs. Mira wrinkled her nose at the strange smell inside the dimly lit shop.

"Uncle are you closed to old family friends, as well," Salim asked the man with a smile.

The man lifted his head, a huge smile forming on his face. His eyes wrinkled as he bellowed out a laugh. "Salim!" he called, standing to greet them, and pulling Salim into a great embrace while kissing both his cheeks. "It's so good to see you, son. Look how big you've grown! I have not seen you since you visited with your father all those years ago. Back then, you were thin as a twig, growing into adolescence."

Salim chuckled and patted the man on the back, "it is good to see you too, Uncle."

Mira peered at the old man suspiciously. He was round and short with gray hair and a short gray beard, but he had a kind face, and his eyes twinkled each time he smiled.

"Come, sit," the man ushered them inside, pulling out two chairs. Mira liked the man only because Salim seemed to smile a lot when he was speaking to him. "I was so sorry to hear about your father. May Allah have mercy on his soul," the man commented while sitting down.

"Yes, it was a very difficult time for us," Salim nodded.

Faisal began pouring cool water into a bowl. He handed a cup to Mira, who took it with a shy smile, thirsty from her adventure yesterday. "Tell me, son, what brings you to Cairo? And who is this strange child who clings to you? Don't tell me she's yours."

Salim chuckled. "No, Uncle, she is not. I have yet to find a woman who will marry me, let alone, give me a child."

The man laughed heartily. "Then whose child is this," he asked, examining Mira with a new light. "She has strange eyes," he observed. Mira looked away, focusing on her cup.

"She is a child I found on my way here and decided to look after her until I can find a more permanent solution," Salim explained. Mira felt ashamed to be burdening him and didn't like the fact that Salim was still trying to get rid of her. But she didn't say anything, instead taking another sip of water.

"Ah, very interesting. It seems you have grown a lot if you look after a stranger's child," the man said, assessing Salim now.

Salim gulped his water, "Yes, it is a bit of an inconvenience for me, but I couldn't just leave her."

Mira squirmed in her seat, uncomfortable with this topic. She needed to convince Salim to keep her, and she still didn't know how. It was clear how he felt about her, and she needed to find a way to make him feel otherwise. The man noticed her discomfort and changed the subject. "Tell me, child. What is your name," he asked her.

"My name is Mira," she whispered shyly.

"You have a very beautiful name, Mira. Do you like sweets?"

Mira's eyes lit up. She looked toward Salim, who gave her a nod. "I love sweets," she said excitedly to the man who chuckled, pulling open a drawer.

"Well, lucky for you, I keep these in my desk. My grandchildren are always coming and demanding something sweet."

He pulled out a plate of treats covered in white powder. Mira grabbed one and looked at it suspiciously. The white powder transferred on her hand, and the texture was squishy in between her fingers. "They're called Turkish delights. It's a treat common among the Ottomans," Faisal explains.

The sweets were strange and smelled like roses. She took a tiny bite and chewed. It was much sweeter than the hard date biscuits she was used to eating at home. Mira's eyes widened the more she chewed. "You like it," Faisal asked. She nodded, eating the rest of the candy in one, big bite, and chewing it with her cheeks full. Salim and Faisal both chuckled at her expression.

Mira took another candy, then another, ignoring the men's conversation. "That's enough," Salim said, stopping her from reaching for another as he grabbed her hand mid-air.

"But, it's yummy." She pouted, wanting another bite.

"It will give you a stomachache, and I don't want you keeping me up all night. Here, take this," he said, handing her a handkerchief.

Mira sighed dramatically and Faisal chuckled at their exchange. "I must say, your relationship is very peculiar."

"I'm not sure what you mean. I'm only watching over her until I find a safe place for her."

"Sure," Faisal said, giving Mira a wink. "Tell me, child, how do you like the city so far? It must be quite different from the desert, right?"

Mira frowned when she thought about his question. While she was very impressed and astonished by the scale of the city, she missed the quiet peace of the desert. "I am happy anywhere I can be with Salim," she answered honestly. She didn't care where she lived, so long as she was with him and Ayub.

Salim shook his head, not surprised by her answer. "It is not proper for a young girl to live with a strange man, Mira. You can only live with a male family member or a husband," Faisal told her.

"Then I will marry Salim, and we will be a family," Mira decided, pleased with her answer.

Salim choked on his water and coughed. "No one is marrying anyone, so, you can forget about that," he said incredulously, surprised at the audacity of her statement.

Faisal laughed, amused. "Forgive her, Salim, she is just a child and does not understand what she is saying," Faisal said, laughing at Salim's distraught expression.

"Now you understand what I'm dealing with. Hopefully, you can help me find a solution to this problem," Salim said.

"All I see is a child who loves and respects you. Give her a break."

Mira nodded in agreement. She did love and respect Salim, which is why she wanted to stay by his side.

"Well, then, you must both stay with me until you figure out what you will do next," Faisal declared, hitting Salim on the back.

"Uncle, I cannot burden you. You barely have enough space for your own family. Mira and I will find our own lodging," Salim countered with a grateful smile.

"Nonsense. Your father was like a brother to me, and you are like a son. If you will not stay with me at my house, then stay here. There is a spare room upstairs. We can part half the room for the child, and you can take the other half."

"Uncle, I don't know what to say."

"You don't have to say anything." The man placed his arm on Salim's. "I'm just happy I got to see you again."

"Then I will earn my keep. I will man the shop for you in the morning, and you can spend more time with your family," Salim suggested.

The man nodded in agreement. "Then we have a deal."

34.

Mira and Salim spent the next few days cleaning out the packed and dusty room they would be staying in. Mira cleaned while Salim organized the stuff. Salim was an orderly person, so the state of the shop was riling him up. He spent his days covered in dust, organizing everything in the shop until it was perfect. Faisal apologized, explaining he had no help running the shop after his son died, and he was growing old and couldn't manage things the way he used to.

Salim just brushed him off; he enjoyed organizing things, and Mira believed Salim was obsessed with tidiness. He often scolded her for not brushing her hair, always telling her to wash her hands and feet. He was very nitpicky. Sometimes, he made her drink herbal teas to help her immune system, saying she would be exposed to diseases in the city her body wasn't used to. He always made sure she finished her plate of food, and even gave her a bedtime. He was worse than a mother hen, but Mira didn't mind. She spent the last few years without any proper parenting, and it made her a bit feral.

After cleaning, she would go upstairs to draw on paper with the pigments Faisal gifted her while Salim tended to the customers.

Mira was busy drawing when she heard a loud commotion from the shop. She lifted her head and listened to the muffled voices when she heard a crash. She hurried down the ladder to see what was happening and gasped at the sight before her. An old couple were holding a young girl who was thrashing wildly while Salim and Faisal tried to calm her. "Please, help us," the parents were pleading while restraining the girl.

"We can give her something to calm her," Salim said, quickly grabbing some poppy powder from the shelf. The girl stopped fighting as the medicine calmed her down. Her parents sagged with relief.

"What happened to her," Faisal asked the grieved parents.

"We believe she is being afflicted by a *jinn*," the father explained, caressing the girl's hair. "We took her to a *Sahir* who said a *jinn* is possessing her, but none of the religious leaders were able to free her of this demon. Each time they tried, she hurt herself, and when we tie her up, she bites her tongue. So, we decided to end the treatment so we could preserve her life. Now, we just use medicine to calm her."

Faisal tsked sympathetically, but Salim was unconvinced. "Perhaps she suffers from something medical. Not every ailment is the work of *jinns*. You need to take her to a doctor."

"We tried everything!" the father said, exasperated. "We spent thousands of dinars trying to treat our daughter, and nothing has worked."

Mira frowned, she was touched by the father's pain, and Salim was wrong. The girl was, in fact, possessed. Mira could see the *jinn* that was attached to her head. It was calm now because of the drugs, but earlier, it had been using its long, thin arm to dig into her skull, which is why she was thrashing about.

The *jinn* had a small body and was hunched over her head. It was hurting her. "Let us at least try to treat her medically," Salim suggested, trying to convince the father.

"You can't treat her. There's a *jinn*. It's on her head and it's hurting her," Mira whispered, stepping forward. Everyone froze and stared at her.

"You can see it!" the mother demanded, rushing forward in desperation, grabbing Mira's arm. "You see it! You see the *jinn*!" she accused.

Salim stepped in between them. "Please excuse the child. She doesn't know what she is saying," he said, pushing her back.

"She can help us!" the mother pleaded. "Please, help my baby," she begged.

Mira's eyes watered with sympathy. No mother deserved to see her child suffer.

"She can't help your daughter. Please, it is best you leave," Salim said firmly.

The mother began sobbing.

"I can try," Mira finally whispered, unable to watch this family suffer any longer.

"Mira," Salim warned, but she ignored him. For too long, she had wondered why God had given her this ability, and if she could use it to help just one person, then everything she suffered in her life because of it would have been worth it. If she could help people, then she had to at least try. She had to prove to herself that she wasn't cursed, and that there was goodness in her gift.

Mira stepped in front of the girl. The effects of the drug were wearing off, and the *jinn* began digging into the girl's scalp again, causing her to moan and hold her head. Everyone seemed to be holding their breath as Mira looked at the *jinn*, studying its form. It was thin and black, its arm blurring as it dug faster and faster. The girl groaned in pain.

"Stop!" she whispered. The *jinn* paused for a minute, then continued.

"I said, *stop it!*" Mira said, louder this time. The *jinn* stopped and lifted its head. Mira took a step back, startled at its appearance. It had large, black eyes, a small face, and a large mouth with pointed teeth. Its nostrils were two slits, and its face wrinkled. Mira swallowed back her fear and whispered the prayers her grandma taught. The *jinn* screeched, losing its physical form as it became absorbed into the girl's body, but she could still see its shadow form above the girl's head.

Mira raised her voice, reciting the prayers her grandmother taught her to protect against the *jinn*. The *jinn* screamed louder, but this time, it screamed through the girl who began shouting and thrashing. Salim and Faisal rushed forward to hold her down.

"Stop!" the girl screamed, but it was the *jinn* speaking.

"You need to leave this girl alone. What you are doing is bad, and if you don't leave, God will punish you!" Mira threatened the *jinn*.

"I won't leave. I must punish her," the *jinn* screeched.

Mira frowned, confused, "why are you punishing her? What could she have done to you?"

"She killed my child," the *jinn* screamed, causing everyone but Mira to flinch. "This human child was careless and stepped on my baby!"

"It was probably an accident," Mira tried to explain to the jinn. "I'm sure she didn't mean to hurt your child."

"I don't care! She has to be punished," the *jinn* screamed.

Mira sighed. She felt sorry for the *jinn*, but she couldn't let it keep hurting this girl. "You've punished her enough. Leave now, or I'll make you leave," she told it.

"Let me be, *Al-nazar*," the *Jinn* pleaded, calling her the sighted one. "I'll leave once she has paid the price!"

"You have one last chance," Mira warned, stepping toward the girl who shrunk back. "Leave this girl or I will drag you out of her."

The *jinn* screamed and tried to escape with the girl who began fighting against Salim and Faisal. Mira reached out towards the shadowy form and grabbed it. It was cold and oily against her hand. She forced herself not to shudder as she began pulling the shadow. The *jinn* screamed louder, and the girl's own voice became hoarse as Mira pulled, harder and harder. "Get out now!" she yelled between clenched teeth.

Mira grunted as she stumbled back, pulling the *jinn* free from the girl's body. She heard it scream once more before it disappeared into the air. The girl's body sagged to the floor. Mira breathed hard as her heart hammered against her chest. Her hands looked normal, but she still felt the sticky coat of the *jinn* as it enveloped her hands. She wanted to scrub the feeling off in hot water and burn it away.

"Mama," the girl whispered hoarsely, opening her eyes. Both parents fell to their knees beside their daughter. "*Habibti!*" the mom cried, clutching her daughter to her chest. The father wiped his tears and held his family. Mira smiled, pleased with the sight.

"Are you okay?" Salim asked her with a look of shock painted on his face. Mira grinned and nodded. She saved someone. She used the ability she often thought of as a curse to help someone. She wasn't cursed; she was the sighted one. She could see all those afflicted with evil eye and black magic, and God had given her the ability to cure them.

"Mira, what you did…" Salim was at a loss for words as the mother stepped forward tearfully kissing her hands in appreciation. "Thank you! Thank you! May God reward you, child. You saved my baby," the woman cried.

Mira felt awkward with her praise and simply nodded. The father pulled out a coin bag filled with money and handed it to Salim. "I know it's not much, but please accept this payment," the man said.

"Thank you, Uncle," Salim responded, still in shock as he handed the coin purse to Faisal, who stood dumbfounded while the family left.

"In all my years, I have never witnessed such a thing!" Faisal finally said, breaking the silence and staring at Mira with a new admiration. "You, my child, are truly blessed. What you did today for that family was incredible!"

Mira smiled shyly. She wasn't used to people praising her ability; she was used to people cursing her and running away from her. She felt a happy bubble start to form within her after years of ridicule. It felt good to finally be accepted.

35.

Mira was in deep sleep the following morning when Salim gently shook her awake. She groaned, feeling groggy. The excitement from the previous day depleted her energy, making her oversleep. Mira rubbed her eyes, staring at a fresh-faced Salim who stood over her with a strange expression. "What," she asked, feeling self-conscious. Did she have something on her face? She rubbed the dried drool from her mouth as she sat up in her cot.

"Are you okay," Salim asked, concerned. "You never sleep in."

Mira yawned, stretching her body. She felt kind of weird, but overall, she was okay. "I'm fine," Mira shrugged, shaking off the drowsiness.

"Well, look out the window," Salim said cryptically. Mira frowned as she made her way to the small, wooden window that overlooked the cobblestone street. She peeked out the window and was surprised to find a long line of people standing outside the shop. Mira quickly shut the window, frightened.

"Who are those people? Are they here to take me away?" she gasped, paranoid. The woman yesterday must have told people what she had done. Were they here to expel her from the city?

"Mira, calm down," Salim urged, interrupting her racing thoughts. "They are not here to expel you; they are here to see you."

She narrowed her eyes. People ran away from her anytime she was near, and she couldn't quite understand why, suddenly, there were lines of people waiting to meet her.

"Why," she asked, stunned.

"Because they say you are blessed. Word spread about what you did yesterday, and now all these people want you to treat them," Salim explained with an expression of awe. Mira frowned and looked out the window again. She saw a few *jinns* among the people, but most of them looked fine. "What do you think?" Salim asked. Not sure what to say, she just shrugged.

"Come on, kid. It's your choice. If you don't want to see anyone, I'll tell Faisal, and we will leave this place. However, if you wish to help these people and earn us some wealth, then we can use the income for a more permanent placement."

Mira's head perked up in surprise. "You will stay," she asked.

Salim sighed. "I guess I could stay with you a while longer until we get this sorted out. I still haven't figured out what to do with you…uff…" Salim grunted as Mira hugged him tight, not wanting to hear another word. He was going to stay, and she was happy to have him, even if it was temporary.

"I'll do it, Salim. I'll help those people!"

Salim gave her a small smile and shook his head as he patted her back. "Alright, kid. Don't get too excited. This isn't permanent; I still plan on leaving."

"I don't care. I'll cherish every moment you stay with me," Mira whispered. She hadn't seen Ayub in weeks; not since they left the port in Tunis. She wasn't sure if he was even in the city, and her heart was heavy with worry. She couldn't bear to lose Salim, too.

The next few weeks were the busiest the shop had ever been. Every day, people lined up, hoping to see Mira. They came even if they weren't sick, just so they could ask her to pray for them. Mira felt uncomfortable with this though because she didn't believe there was anything holy or special about her. She told them what her grandmother had taught her: prayers only belonged to God. She encouraged every person to ask God, and He will answer. But people didn't listen. They insisted that she pray for them, touch them or heal them from their ailment.

Salim started filtering out the people who could see her, giving priority to the sick. Most of them had medical ailments that Salim and Faisal could treat with herbs and other medicine, but even they insisted that Mira touch them and read them a prayer. Mira was baffled by humans and their lack of faith. Just as the people in the desert were extreme in their belief that she was cursed, the people of the city were extreme in their belief that she was blessed.

Mira was just a child; she didn't want to be seen as a blessing or a curse;

she just wanted people to look at her and see a kid. To give her a kind smile and reassuring words. She just wanted to be treated normally.

While most of the cases were medical, there were a few *jinn* possessions. Each time, she repeated what she had done the first time. First, she asked the *jinn* to leave. Some of the weaker ones would listen and run away almost instantly. However, some *jinns* were stubborn, and Mira had to force them out.

Each time she forced out a *jinn*, it left Mira feeling strange and icky. She would go to her room afterwards and try to scrub the feeling away, but it wasn't something that could be washed off. It was inside her, attacking her with its oily char. The only thing that gave her relief was repeating the verses her grandma taught her.

***

Mira groaned as she woke up. It was almost noon; she had slept in longer than usual, but today was Friday, and the shop would be closed, so Mira had time to rest. She felt drained, and her energy had been at its lowest this past week. Salim kept telling her to take time off, but she kept insisting on working, hoping that if she made him rich enough, he would stay. She thought she could work through the fatigue, but it was getting difficult to hide the stabbing pain that would enter her chest at random times. It only lasted for a few seconds but that was enough to leave her shaking.

"You're up," Salim whispered from across the room. "I was starting to get worried. How are you feeling," he asked, handing her a cup of tea.

She was grateful for the warm tea. "I'm fine, just tired," she said as she took a sip. She gave Salim the same answer every time he questioned her.

Salim sighed heavily. "Mira, I know you want to help people, but I think you are putting yourself through too much strain. Perhaps we should stop this. I have enough money to find a good home for you, and Faisal agreed to watch over you."

"No!" Mira shouted in a panic. "No, please! I can work!" Mira insisted, jumping up and forcing her body not to sway. "See," she said, squatting up and down. "I'm fine!"

Salim shook his head. "If you are doing this to get me to stay, then this isn't the way."

"Then what's the way," Mira asked, her shoulders slumping. "Ayub is gone, and I don't want to lose you, too. Then I'll have no one."

"How do you know he's gone," Salim asked, sitting down on a chair. "Perhaps he is out there looking for you."

Mira sniffled. "You think so," she asked hopefully.

"I know so. Do you really think Ayub would ever leave you? He is more obsessed with you, than you are with me."

She pondered upon that thought for a moment, and decided Salim was right. Ayub loved her; he was her best friend, and he would never abandon her.

"Where do you think he might be," Salim asked her.

"Well, he might be at a date grove. When we lived in the oasis, I always met him there and we played and told stories," Mira remembered with a smile.

"Then, let's go to the date grove!" he said as he stood.

"Right now," Mira asked, grinning. She didn't expect this at all today.

"Now is a perfect time. It's noon, so the streets will be relatively empty, and the date grove workers will be on a break," Salim told her with a smile.

Mira jumped. She didn't need to be told twice.

36.

Friday was a day of rest, so the chaotic streets of Cairo were almost deserted. Its residents were lounging at home seeking respite from the afternoon sun. Shops were closed, and the only places open were a few tea spots with old men sitting about engaging in conversation. Mira hadn't been out much during her time here. She was still cautious and a little afraid of the big city. However, now, as she walked down its narrow streets, she could see its charm. It was a bright day, and the towering buildings provided shade to the people below. Colorful canopies connected the buildings providing even more shade from the ever-scorching sun. There were street cats lazily lying under large pots, and extravagant carpets were displayed upon balconies to lure in shoppers.

Mira followed closely behind Salim as they walked through the city. Soon they reached the outer wall of the city and beyond it was the biggest date palm grove Mira had ever seen. Directly across the grove, she spotted the Nile; its small waves gently swayed in the wind.

Hundreds of date palm trees towered above them; each tree had a cluster of brown fruits hanging from it as harvest season neared. However, the grove was empty, its workers off for the day, resting at the small residential stone homes built on the outskirts of the farm. Mira took a deep breath, feeling better than she had in days. She just needed something fresh to reset her; and hopefully, she would find Ayub here waiting for her.

"Ayub!" Mira called out loudly as she eagerly looked for her friend. It was hot and she was tired of walking around this endless maze of date palms. She saw a few *jinns* here and there, but they scattered away anytime she was near. It seemed that word about her had spread, even among the *jinns*.

Mira sighed. The heat was getting to her, tiring her out and making her lightheaded.

"Mira!" she heard someone cry as she slumped against a tree. Mira's head shot up instantly. Ayub was standing in front of her. "Mira," he cried again, his huge eyes filled with tears.

"Ayub!" Mira jumped, crying as well. She missed her friend. For weeks, she felt constricted. The air was too hot and thick, but now, it was suddenly sweet and fresh. Ayub was her oxygen. "Why are you crying," Mira asked, even though she was crying, as well.

"I missed you so much!" Ayub said, crying even harder. "I looked and looked, but I couldn't find you!"

How could she ever think Ayub had abandoned her. Of course, he searched for her. "I'm sorry, Ayub. I missed you, too. I'll never leave you again!" she promised.

Ayub grinned happily, jumping in the air like an excited puppy before stopping to assess her. "What have you been doing," Ayub asked her suddenly. "You seem different."

Mira looked down on herself. She didn't feel different. "I've been working with Salim and Faisal at the apothecary," she explained.

"Something's different," he repeated with a frown, studying her with an intense glare.

Mira shifted her feet, uncomfortable with his assessment. She felt something was in fact off with her, but she couldn't put her finger on it. However, she didn't want to think about that right now, she barely had any energy these days, and walking around had drained her.

"Well, I've kind of been helping people," she admitted. "I was pulling out bad *jinns* from possessed bodies."

Ayub gasped dramatically, placing his hand against his mouth. "Mira! You can't do that! You can't! The *jinns* will hurt you!" he cried.

"I thought you said *jinns* can't hurt people. Stop crying! I'm fine! See," Mira stood and twirled, which made her dizzier than she expected, so she sat back down.

"Yes, they can Mira, *jinns* can't physically hurt people, but they always find a way! And it's hurting you in here," Ayub said, pointing to his chest.

"Ayub, I'm fine! I just need to work hard so we can be a family."

"But we are a family," he said, clearly hurt.

"I know that. But what about Salim? He is part of our family, too! Maybe if I work hard and make him a lot of money, he will stay."

Ayub frowned. He didn't like Salim much because he was jealous and wanted Mira all to himself, but Mira loved Salim. He was her hero. "I don't like it," he huffed finally.

Mira picked up a stick to distract him. "Want to see something cool," she asked instead.

Ayub's head perked up as he bounced up and down nodding "Yes!"

Mira smiled and began writing his name in the sand. Ayub's eyes widened as he watched her. "What are you drawing," he asked curiously.

"I'm not drawing, silly. I'm writing," she said as she finished. "This is your name. A-Y-U-B."

"Woah! That's so cool! How did you learn how to write," Ayub asked, amazed.

Mira grinned pridefully. "Uncle Faisal is teaching me. He is Salim's friend, and he says I'm really smart!" Mira explained, spelling her name next to Ayub's. "That is my name. Ayub and Mira are best friends forever!"

Ayub grinned widely, clapping his hands. "I wish I was smart like you," he said in awe.

"Well, you're good at a lot of other things, like running and hiding," she encouraged him.

"I'm the fastest runner in my clan!" he boasted in agreement. Mira giggled while writing a few more words that Faisal had taught her.

"Mira, we have to go," Salim interrupted suddenly.

"No!" Ayub whined, sticking his tongue out at Salim not wanting Mira to leave. He was still too scared to enter the city.

"I'll come back, Ayub," she assured him. "I promise!"

***

Mira skipped happily next to Salim. She felt better than she had in weeks, like a huge weight had been lifted off her shoulders. With all that was happening, she didn't realize how much she missed her friend.

"Are you that happy you saw Ayub," Salim asked her with a chuckle.

Mira nodded, "I'm very happy," she told him.

"Why don't we get some sweets and walk around the souk? We don't have to be back right away," Salim suggested.

Mira grinned and nodded in agreement. This was the best day ever.

They returned to the city center, making their way through the crowded market. Friday prayers had just ended so the souk was now back to life. Mira wasn't as afraid as she was her first few days here, having gotten used to the loudness and chaos. Salim led her to one of the many sweet stalls, and Mira stared at the array of desserts, trying to decide what to get. They all looked so good.

"Peace be upon you!" The shopkeeper greeted them with a hand on his chest.

Salim returned the greeting, "I wish to treat my daughter to some sweets. What is your best dessert here," Salim asked the man.

Mira looked up at the shopkeeper, anticipating his response. But the man gasped when he noticed her eyes. "It's-it's you!" he stammered. Mira frowned at his reaction. Did this man know her? "You are *Al-Nazar*, the blessed child. Please, anything you like, it's yours." The man rushed to collect different sweets into a box. Salim cleared his throat as more people began whispering and staring at them.

The man handed Mira the box of sweets, "If you could pray for my business and sick mother, I would really appreciate it," he whispered. "Please," he begged.

Mira backed away, uncomfortable with all the attention as people stopped to gawk at her. "*Al-Nazar*...it's her...look at her eyes," they spoke to one another in hushed whispers. "Please, my son, he is bedridden. Pray that God will heal him!" a woman suddenly shouted from the crowd, grabbing Mira's arm. Panic set in Mira's heart as more people gathered. She tried to pull away from the woman, dropping her sweets.

"Hey, don't touch her," Salim shouted, pulling Mira to him as she hid behind his cloak, afraid to look at the people who were all screaming and shouting at her. Salim tugged her away from the crowded stall as more and more people stopped to take in the scene. He kept her close, pushing people away and yelling at them to part the way. Mira clung to him, her hands shaking and her heart hammering. People tried to pull her away, but she held on tight.

Soon, Salim freed them from the clutches of the crowd and hurried her down the narrow alleys, hoping to escape unscathed. But everywhere they turned, people yelled for her, calling her to pray for them and heal their ill ones.

Finally, they made it to a small house, and Salim rapidly knocked on the door. Faisal opened the door, surprised to find them there as Salim quickly pulled her inside. "Is everything okay? What happened," Faisal asked, concerned as his wife, Um Asma, entered, equally confused. She gave them a worrying look.

"We have a problem, Faisal," Salim breathed out as Faisal's wife urged them to sit in the *majlis*.

She held Mira's shaking hands into her own, handing her a cup of water. Mira gave her a small smile. Um Asma was always kind to her every time she visited the shop.

Salim took a deep breath, drinking his own glass of water. The incident shook him, as well. "What happened," Faisal asked again after they were all seated.

"I took Mira to the market to get her some sweets, and we were overrun by people, each begging her to cure them. It was ridiculous. I feared someone would snatch her away from me," he explained.

Faisal *tsked*. "I knew something like this would happen. With all the people we turned away, and how the story of the child had been spreading, I was worried people would begin to harass her."

"This is much worse than we thought, Faisal. You should have seen them. They acted as if an angel had descended among them, each hoping her touch would save them," Salim shook his head.

"People are easily misguided, brother. They see her as a miracle. It doesn't make sense, but they see her as hope."

"Damn their hope! She is my ward, and I will not allow her to be threatened like that again. I'm sorry, Uncle, but we will be leaving your shop. I must secure a home for us; I just need you to watch over her for a few days while I settle some affairs," Salim announced as he stood to leave.

Worried he would abandon her, Mira chased after him, not wanting to stay there alone. She was still in shock about what happened earlier, and she needed him. "Hey, I'll be back, kid. I promise. Okay? I just need to find a safe place for us so we can live together. Isn't that what you wanted," Salim said, trying to calm her.

Mira nodded slowly. "Does this mean you'll stay," she asked him hopefully.

"All this is my fault, so your safety is now my responsibility. We will figure this out, kid. You have my word," he promised. Mira nodded, stepping next to Um Asma who pulled her close. He gave her a small smile before ducking out of the house.

37.

Um Asma led her to a small, sparsely decorated room. "I'm sorry for the mess. We just moved in recently," she explained. "The old house was just too small for all my children and grandchildren, so this house has been a blessing. And, to be honest, it's all thanks to you that we were able to buy it."

"This is fine," Mira assured her. She liked Um Asma and didn't want to trouble them.

"Well, you must be tired from all the excitement today. Get some rest, and I'll call you when dinner is ready," she said with a warm smile. Mira nodded and sat on the bed. She closed her eyes, feeling her fatigue return. Now that the adrenaline of the day was gone, she could barely keep her eyes open.

Mira jolted awake as someone shook her. She jumped up, her heart hammering "It's okay! It's just me," Um Asma said, her face coming into focus. "I was knocking, but you were too deep into sleep to hear me," she explained.

"I'm sorry," Mira apologized sheepishly. She wasn't even sure when she fell asleep or how long she'd been asleep for.

"That's okay. Why don't you wash up and join us in the *majlis* for dinner," Um Asma asked her with a smile.

"You want me to join you," Mira asked, unsure if she heard her right. "Of course. You are our guest," Um Asma said, giving her a strange look.

"Oh, okay," Mira smiled. She wasn't used to this kindness. Back in the oasis, she usually had her meals alone in her room because her stepmother wasn't comfortable with her in the main house. She was never invited into anyone's home, even during Eid celebrations she had to watch from the outside.

Next to bed was a small pot of water. Mira quickly washed up and tiptoed to the *majlis* where Faisal and his family were sitting on the floor, their dinner spread before them. "Mira! Come on! We are waiting for you. Soon, these little ones will start eating my fingers," Faisal laughed. Mira gave him a shy smile and sat next to Um Asma. Faisal recited a prayer, and they began eating. Um Asma piled her plate with food, even though she protested. She told her she needed to eat more, and that she had grown too thin.

Displayed on a woven mat were plates of rice and meat, as well as a few side dishes. Mira took a few small bites of rice but could barely taste the food. Instead, she was too focused on watching the family as they laughed and ate together. How Faisal told jokes loudly while his wife rolled her eyes, trying to feed her young children and grandchildren. Mira felt her throat tighten at the sight of seeing such a happy, carefree family. It reminded her of her own family, back when they lived in the small village on the edge of the Sahara.

She imagined herself on the sandy courtyard, enjoying a modest meal of porridge, camel milk and dates. She imagined Mama fussing with the twins, and Baba chatting with Jida while he ate his food. She imagined baby Sara cooing next to her so that Mira would give her a sweet date. Mira closed her eyes, her imaginations transporting her the simple life she enjoyed just a few years ago.

"Mira, what's wrong. Why are you crying," Um Asma asked, suddenly breaking her out of her daze. She looked up, startled to find the entire family staring at her. She felt her cheeks burn with embarrassment as she stood, quickly running to the room, ashamed. Mira slammed the door quickly laying on the small bed, her body shaking.

It wasn't envy that moved her to tears, she loved that they had such a great family. But seeing them like that was just too much pain for Mira to bear. She never really got over her mother's death, or Sara's, and each day they were gone felt like a piece of her was dying.

Mira lay on the bed hugging the thin pillow; the back of her hand was red from her bite as she tried to keep from crying. Mira sniffled, quickly sitting up as Um Asma knocked on the door. "I brought you some cake," she said with a gentle smile, sitting next to Mira.

"Thank you," Mira whispered, taking a bite of the cake so she wouldn't have to talk. Um Asma didn't say anything, just quietly observing her. "Thank you, that cake was delicious," She whispered after finishing.

"Really? The kids tell me it's not sweet enough," Um Asma said with a chuckle, taking the plate from her hands.

"No, it was really good!" Mira insisted, even though she barely tasted anything—still too raw with emotions. Um Asma nodded, and they sat in a quiet silence for a while.

"Mira, I'm sorry for being so insensitive today. I should have known you would be missing your family. I didn't mean to hurt you."

"You didn't hurt me at all!" Mira said, quickly giving her a huge smile. "See, I'm fine! I just remembered a sad story," she lied, trying to lighten the mood. But Um Asma wasn't buying it and offered her a sympathetic smile.

"You are a good kid, Mira, but you don't have to put on a brave face all the time. You have people who care about you. You can burden them with your tears and sorrow. Perhaps it will make the pain lighter."

Mira swallowed the knot in her throat. "I'm fine," she whispered unconvincingly, avoiding Um Asma's eyes.

"Mira—"

"I said I'm fine!" Mira shouted, not wanting to hear anymore. She just wanted to be left alone. She didn't want to be around anyone. And Um Asma sympathy was triggering something in her that she didn't understand.

Um Asma sighed sadly. "Okay, I will leave you for now, but if you need anything, just call for me, okay?"

She nodded, clutching her dress to keep her hands from shaking. What was wrong with her? Mira was never so short-tempered or emotional. She could handle a lot, but lately, everything seemed to trigger her. She felt bad for shouting at Um Asma. She knew she was just trying to help, but Mira didn't want to let anyone in. She didn't want to share her pain, nor did she wish to speak of her sorrow. Um Asma gave her a reassuring smile before finally leaving and shutting the door behind her.

38.

Salim returned to the house two days later; Mira was relieved to see him. While Faisal's family had been warm and welcoming towards her, she felt awkward and out of place living there. She tried to apologize to Um Asma for her rudeness, but she just brushed her off, telling her there was nothing to apologize for.

The other children in the house tried to include her in their games and conversations, but Mira couldn't bring herself to enjoy their company. She felt restless and found it hard to stay focused. The only thing she enjoyed was Faisal's reading lessons. He was always surprised at how quickly she was learning to read and gave her first storybook. Mira spent hours poring over the book, slowly trying to unravel the words. She was immersed in the world the book had created. She couldn't wait to read it to Ayub. She knew he would be so impressed.

Excited for Salim's arrival, Mira ran to his side, curious about his whereabouts. She wondered how he had spent the last three days. And while she had a respite from working, she was still tired. "Hey, kid," Salim greeted her, patting her head. "How have you been? Are you feeling okay?"

Mira nodded, "I feel fine."

"Um Asma told me you haven't been eating much."

Mira shot Um Asma with a look of betrayal, but she just shrugged. "I haven't had much of an appetite," Mira confessed, which was strange because she loved food.

Salim gave her a concerned look. "Why don't we all sit in the *majlis* and talk," Faisal suggested, guiding everyone onto the floor-length sofa. Mira took a seat next to Um Asma, while everyone looked at Salim for answers.

"Well, first off, I just want to thank you, Faisal, for hosting us these last few weeks. Your help has been immeasurable for us. However, I don't think the shop is a safe environment for Mira anymore. Every day, it is crowded with people seeking her audience, and it is best we move somewhere safer."

Faisal nodded. "Salim, you are like a son to me, and I have grown to love Mira like a daughter. Your presence has been a great blessing to my family, and I am happy I was able to host you. I agree with your assessment. I believe it is in everyone's best interest if we move you."

Salim nodded, placing his hand over his heart. "We will also no longer be taking everyday clients. Mira's popularity has grown among the elite of the city, and many are seeking her help. We will take a few clients a week to give respite to Mira, and only treat those who can afford her fees."

Mira swallowed, looking at Um Asma who squeezed her hand. "Perhaps we should ask Mira if this is something she wants to do. The events of the last few days have shaken her," Um Asma said in her defense.

Salim glanced at Mira. "Of course, I apologize for my assumption. Mira can decide if she wishes to go down this route. If not, I will find a safe place where she can live peacefully."

Mira licked her lips, overcome with the decision she had to make. On one hand, her ability could help save people; on the other hand, she didn't like the effect it was having on her. Perhaps with time, she could get used to its effects and find ways to combat it. If she refused, Salim would probably leave for Damascus. Maybe if she agreed, he would stay.

"If I do this, will you stay here," Mira asked earnestly.

Salim cleared his throat, everyone now looking at him. "Of course, your safety would be my responsibility, so I can't just leave. I was looking into the hospital here, and they have an excellent medical school that competes with the one in Damascus. I could pursue my studies here."

"Then I will do it," Mira declared happily, realizing her wish was coming true. She would work hard and be a family with Salim and Ayub.

Um Asma shared a disapproving look with her husband. "Are you sure, Mira? You must also think of yourself and your health. Maybe this isn't the best thing for you," she offered.

"I'm fine. I will eat more and read all my prayers. I will take care of my health. I want to do this," she told her. Um Asma sighed, shaking her head, clearly unhappy with their plans.

Salim cleared his throat, giving her a small smile. "Then I guess it's me and you, kid" he concluded.

And Ayub. Mira thought with a smile.

***

Salim led Mira away from Faisal's home after she bid farewell to the kind family. Um Asma hugged her tightly, telling her to approach her if she ever needed anything. Mira felt guilty for being a bad guest, and appreciated Faisal and his family, however, she wasn't used to such kindness, and didn't know how to react to it.

A covered wagon was waiting to take them to their new home, a necessary precaution so that people wouldn't recognize her. The home was situated in a different part of the city that Mira had never been to. The streets here were quiet and clean, the buildings were also in better shape with windowed arches and surrounding desert plants. It was a very pleasant neighborhood. It was peaceful, and Mira liked it.

Salim led her towards the back of one of the homes, and they climbed up its steps. "I couldn't afford a house of our own, but we will get one soon, God willing. This is just a temporary rental," he told her. Mira was quite impressed with the space. It had a small *majlis* and a balcony overlooking a small garden. She imagined that Ayub would be okay living there. There were two rooms, and Mira gasped with happiness when she saw hers. It wasn't the large bed, nor the full closet that caught her attention, it was the small shelves filled with books that excited her most.

Mira ran to the shelf, touching each book, feeling the bindings, and trying to sound out the titles. "You like it," Salim asked with a knowing smile.

"Is this all mine," Mira asked incredulously

Salim chuckled, "yes, kid, it's all yours."

"Forever!?" she asked, wanting to be sure.

Salim laughed at her, "yes, it's yours forever."

Mira squealed in excitement, jumping up and down. "I love it, Salim! Thank you! Thank you!" she cried. Salim rubbed his arm awkwardly. He was always uncomfortable with her emotional outbursts, but Mira couldn't help it, she was just so happy.

"Wait here. I have another surprise," he said suddenly. Mira's eyes widened. What more could he possibly give her? Salim returned to the room holding a small blanket. Mira curiously peered inside and gasped when it started to move. Mira backed away as Salim slowly opened the blanket. She saw a small face with whiskers. A tiny kitten revealed herself with a quiet meow.

Mira stood frozen as she stared at the animal. "Do you want to pet her," Salim asked. Mira took a cautious step closer, lifting her hand to the kitten. It sniffed her finger, meowed and rubbed its face on her hand. "I think she likes you," Salim whispered.

Mira grinned widely. "What's her name," she asked, awed by the adorable cat that was squirming before her.

"I thought I'd let you decide since she's yours," he said, giving her a wink.

"She's mine," Mira gasped in excitement.

"Yeah, kid. She's yours."

"I love her," Mira cried, her eyes tearing as she held the cat. It purred, her warm body-hugging Mira's as she got comfortable. "I'm going to name you Sara," she whispered.

"Oh, one more thing. I hired a tutor for you; she will be here every afternoon to teach you how to read. Her name is Ms. Leena"

Mira's eyes widened. This was all too much. Salim was fulfilling wishes she didn't even know she had. "I will have a teacher," she shrieked in disbelief. This was the best day of her life. "Thank you, Salim. I promise to work really hard," Mira declared.

"Just make sure you take care of yourself," Salim cautioned before leaving her room. Mira danced in her room, opening the wide windows to take a deep breath. Soon, Ayub would be with her in that beautiful garden. Salim wouldn't leave her, and she would learn how to read and, hopefully, write. And she even had a cat. Mira couldn't be happier; all her dreams were coming true.

39.

1 year later

"How did the rose ever open its heart
and give the world all its beauty?
It felt the encouragement of light against its being,
otherwise, we all remain frightened."

"Very good, Mira!" her teacher, Ms. Leena, approved of her recitation. "I still can't believe how fast you are picking up your lessons." Ms. Leena offered a warm smile, causing Mira to beam with happiness. It had been a year since Mira and Salim settled into their new life. And, every day, she looked forward to her lessons with her tutor. In the last year, not only had Mira learned to read and write, but she discovered her love for poetry, the rhythmic words of those before her filling her mind and heart.

She spent hours everyday pouring over books, and even more time pondering their meaning. She also discovered a love for calligraphy. Salim always made sure there wasn't anything she needed, constantly keeping her desk stacked with books, pens, ink, and parchment. "I want you to think about that poem— next lesson, you can tell me what you think Hafiz was trying to convey."

"Okay," Mira nodded, her thoughts already filled with the poem.

"Also, I won't be coming to teach you next week. My mother is ill, and I must care for her," Ms. Leena informed her with a sad smile.

Mira frowned, "what happened to your mother," she asked.

"She's been having health issues for a few months, and it just got worse. The doctor said it's her liver, and there isn't much that can be done now," Ms. Leena explained sadly.

Overcome with sympathy, Mira quietly rubbed her teacher's arm, trying to comfort her. She had once felt the pain of losing a mother. Ms. Leena gave her a tight smile, looking at the door behind them. She bit her lip in thought, then leaned forward to whisper to her. "I know I shouldn't be asking you this, but perhaps you could visit my mother. People say you are blessed and can heal with a touch of your hand," She desperately grabbed Mira's hands into hers.

Mira tried to pull her hands away, feeling uncomfortable with the request. Meeting her mother would not change her fate. "I'm sorry, teacher, but I can't," she tried to explain.

"Mira, please. I can't pay you much, but after all our time together, couldn't you just—" Ms. Leena quickly pulled back, interrupted by a knock at the door.

Salim quietly entered the room, raising his eyebrow. Mira tried to hide her unease as Ms. Leena stood and composed herself with a smile. "Is everything okay," he asked, taking in the tension.

Mira nodded tightly, not wanting to get her teacher in trouble, while Ms. Leena waved her hands. "I was just saying goodbye to Mira. As you know, I won't be coming in next week due to my mother's illness," she quickly explained.

"Ah. Of course. Did you take her to the hospital I referred you to? The doctors there are the best in the city— as I said before, I will cover the cost of her treatment." Mira gave Salim a surprised look. She didn't know he offered to have the mother treated.

"Yes, well, the doctors are trying their best, but they said it was now in God's hands."

Salim nodded sympathetically. "I'm very sorry to hear that. She will be in our prayers. Now, if you are finished, perhaps I can walk you out," he suggested.

Ms. Leena paused and looked at Mira with desperate eyes. Mira looked down, her heart heavy with guilt, but unless it was *jinn*, there was nothing she could do. "Salim, I was actually hoping Mira could visit—"

"No," Salim cut her off, not leaving any room for discussion.

"Please, it would only be a few moments," her teacher begged desperately. It was obvious they already had this conversation.

"It's time for you to leave," Salim said calmly, undeterred by her pleas. Her teacher sighed, giving Mira one last look before leaving with Salim, who followed close behind. Mira knew without being told that she would never see her again.

Salim was very protective over her and limited the people who had access to her, she was more popular than ever, having a waiting list that went on for months. They were able to move out of the small rental and buy a villa with a huge garden. Ayub lived in the garden, and each day, Mira played with him, read him stories and listened to his own little adventures.

Sara had grown from a small kitten into a well-fed, and somewhat spoiled, cat. Ayub didn't like anything that took Mira's attention away from him. But Mira adored her, so Ayub tolerated Sara for her sake.

Salim wasn't home most of the day. He took her to different appointments when she treated people, however, her clients were only from the city's elite. She had never seen so many cases of the evil eye and she was performing several exorcisms a week. Salim was now a wealthy man, but Mira didn't care much for wealth. He provided her with everything she could ever need.

Unfortunately, he was unable to make it into the medical school in Cairo; they were not impressed with his reputation, calling him a perpetrator of pseudo magic. However, he told her it no longer mattered. Managing her affairs was taking up all his time, anyway. Mira felt a bit guilty for keeping him from his own dream, but he assured her he was happy.

However, not everything was great with Mira. The sticky sick feeling that came with performing exorcisms didn't go away. In fact, it only got worse. She did a good job of hiding her constant discomfort. Salim didn't seem to notice the differences in her, but Ayub did. Every day, he begged her to stop, but she would just distract him with a new story or a game. However, lately, she couldn't bring herself to visit him as much as she did before.

She preferred spending time in her room, practicing calligraphy or reading. She would miss her teacher, knowing Salim would never allow her to come back, and Mira didn't have the energy to argue with him. She wasn't sure how much longer she would be able to keep this up, but she didn't want to disappoint Salim and still feared losing him. She felt as if she were fighting to keep the pieces of her that she knew intact. Each day, another piece of the puzzle that made up who she was would fall away and dissolve, leaving her surrounded by the darkness that fought to take her.

She was obsessed with Salim. He was her role model, her hero, and her father figure. The thought of losing him made her even sicker. So, she hid the effects performing the exorcisms had on her, and Salim was too busy to notice the changes in her, assuming it was just puberty.

Mira leaned against her chair, staring out into the garden. She smiled to herself as she watched Ayub blissfully climb a palm tree before attempting to jump onto another. Suddenly, she gasped in agony as a piercing pain entered her chest. Mira quickly put her head between her knees as she tried to ride out the pain. She experienced this symptom often, ever since she started doing the exorcisms. It only lasted a few seconds, but now it happened more frequently. Mira took a shaky breath as the pain finally subsided.

"Hey, kid," Salim called from her door, Mira looked up, fisting her hands to hide the shaking. "You okay," he asked, cautiously taking in her ashen face.

"Yes, I'm fine," she whispered hoarsely.

"I told her not to bother you with this," Salim admitted with a frustrated shake of his head, misinterpreting her discomfort. Mira was grateful she didn't have to explain herself, but she understood why Ms. Leena did that. Hope was a dangerous thing—a demon worse than fear itself.

"I'm sorry, Mira, but I cannot allow her to see you anymore."

"I know," she shrugged, too tired to put up a fight.

"That's it? Who are you, and what have you done to Mira," Salim joked at her subdued response.

Mira gave him a small smile. "I trust your judgment," she told him sincerely. Salim had taken her from a lonely life in the desert to a palace in the city. She should be grateful to him for saving her, but sometimes, Mira couldn't help but mourn the life she left behind.

Salim sighed. "Well, maybe this will make you feel better," he said, pulling out a small box. Mira gave him a puzzled look, slowly opening the box. Inside were a set of beautiful, gold bangles, glittering in the light. She took them out and placed them on her wrist. "Do you like it? They're from the finance minister. Some say he's the richest man in Egypt. He was very grateful after you treated his wife last week and sent this as a gift."

Mira watched as the bracelets jingled on her wrist. "They're beautiful," she said, trying to sound enthusiastic, but, truthfully, she knew they were just going to be another addition to her growing pile of jewelry that she didn't care much about.

"He invited me to dinner next week. I'm hoping I can find an administrative position. It won't be easy, but with all the connections we've made this past year, I think it's possible."

Mira nodded, holding the box tightly. She was happy for Salim. He was fitting in well with his new life. He was well-spoken, charming, and never out of place in a world of elites. He was born for this life while Mira was just trying to survive it. Sometimes, she wished he would see her and comfort her, she was silently crying for help, too afraid to say the words. But she was grateful to even have this much, Salim was with her and that was enough.

Thankfully, a loud knock on the door interrupted their conversation. The servants rushed to answer. Mira was surprised because they never had visitors, Salim was paranoid about letting anyone near her, and spent weeks vetting the two servants that lived with them. Salim hurried out of the room, and Mira quietly crept out behind to see what was happening.

At the door stood three men dressed in the ceremonial robes of the Sultan's court. Mira knew this because she visited the homes of many administrators and watched them as they returned from the citadel. "Peace be upon you," one man said. Salim returned the greeting, asking them to enter the house and sit, but the men declined. "We are here on official business of the Sultan Al-Malik Al Nasir. He invites you and your ward to his palace. There will be a wagon sent to bring you to his home," the man declared, handing Salim the official decree.

Salim placed his hand on his heart as a form of respect. "Thank you, we shall heed the Sultan's call and arrive as appointed." Salim stared at the door for a while before looking up at Mira, who was eavesdropping on their conversation. Salim called her down and told her that they would be visiting the Sultan's palace.

40.

Mira felt the familiar thrill of adventure turn in her heart as she gazed upon the Sultan's vast and beautiful palace. She wore her finest dress and was filled with anticipation. In her stories, she often told tales of just Sultans living in huge palaces. But this wasn't a story. This was real. Mira was about to meet the Sultan, and she didn't know why. Salim assured her that there was nothing to worry about; the Sultan probably heard whispers of the blessed child and wished to meet her. But Mira couldn't help but feel anxious and excited all at once. Despite her fears, it felt good to actually feel something again.

She fixed the silk scarf that covered her head and fidgeted with the gold bangles she received that adorned her wrist. Mira took a deep breath, looking up at the magnificent palace. They stood in front of 2 large, bronze arched doors decorated with interwoven mosaic patterns that glimmered like gold against the sun. Near the doors were two large towers with golden domes. The walls were covered in beautiful Arabic calligraphy and colorful patterns. Mira loved calligraphy; it was her favorite pastime, and she was quite good at it, but she could never imagine producing something as intricate as what she was seeing before her at the Sultan's palace. The Sultan's servants ushered them inside, which was even more beautiful than the outside.

There were large windows covered with wooden mosaic patterns that cast the entire space in a shadow of different shapes and designs. Thick Persian carpets covered every inch of the ground, as well as a small fountain in the center of the palace's main entry room. Mira looked around, her eyes growing wide as she took in the scene before her. Often, in her imaginative stories, she dreamt of palaces and brave Sultans, but not even her imagination could create such beauty.

They were led to a formal meeting room, where each of the walls were lined with beautiful, woven cushions and dozens of purple silk pillows. The middle of the floor was covered in a large, turquoise Persian carpet. There were two low tables in the center that had a gold water jug and golden cups, as well as a bowl of large dates. Mira felt one of the pillows under her hand; she marveled at its softness. There were two open doors that led to a balcony that overlooked a magnificent garden. Mira stood on the balcony to take in the garden. She couldn't help but think that Ayub would be very impressed with it and couldn't wait to tell him about it later.

"Are you enjoying the view," a strong voice called from behind her as she stood with Salim. They both turned around, and Salim bowed low, placing his hand over his heart.

"Sultan, we are honored to be in your esteemed presence, and humbled you called upon us to enter your beautiful palace," he said without missing a beat. Salim was very political and did well among people, however, Mira had no such manners as she studied the Sultan with a curious glance.

He didn't look like a Sultan. He wore a simple, white robe, and he didn't dress as flashy as some of the officials whose homes she had visited. His eyes reminded her of the *Sheikh* from the Banu Nazir, wise and calculating. However, she also spotted kindness in him. He was shorter than Salim but carried himself with strength. He had a thick, graying, black beard with signs of aging around his eyes. His head was lightly wrapped in a simple, black turban, and his hands were littered with scars.

Salim gave Mira a warning look, and the Sultan chuckled at her bold stare. "I must say, child, you are not what I was expecting. It seems the stories about you were a bit exaggerated. I have been told your eyes glowed, and that a bright light shined from your face. I was worried you might be more angel than human," the Sultan commented, offering his own assessment.

"I am not an angel, nor am I a devil. I'm not blessed or cursed, as people think. I am simply a servant of my Lord, and a human, just like you," Mira told the Sultan.

He raised his eyebrow at her. "You compare yourself to me when I am a Sultan, and you are but a Bedouin?" He challenged.

Salim shuffled on his feet, shooting Mira a stern look, however, she ignored him, accepting the Sultan's challenge. "The Sultan rules over a vast kingdom, and the Bedouin rules over the vast desert. The Sultan worries for his people as the Bedouin worries for his herd. The Sultan looks behind him to count the blades in his back. However, the Bedouin looks up to count the stars in the sky. So, is it not better to be a Bedouin than it is to be a Sultan?" Salim choked back a cough, his eyes widening at her boldness.

The Sultan gave a strange look, then began to laugh heartily. "I knew my people were exaggerating, but I had to see you for myself. I must say, I am far more impressed with your wisdom and sharp tongue than I was with anything I've been told. Come, sit," the Sultan said, inviting them to the *majlis*. Servants started piling in, carrying trays upon trays of fresh fruit, dates, countless sweets and exotic teas.

Mira quickly grabbed a large pomegranate. Reminded of Ayub, she slammed it against the ground to break it open. "Mira!" Salim scolded, grabbing the now leaking pomegranate and wiping its juice from the ground. "Please forgive my ward, it appears I have failed in teaching her manners," Salim apologized to the Sultan, who was staring in bemusement at Mira.

Mira licked the juice from her finger. "Mmm," she grinned. "It's sweet!"

The Sultan grabbed his own pomegranate and slammed it on the ground, breaking it apart and handing half to Mira. She smiled and accepted the fruit. "I have not seen anyone break a pomegranate like that since my days with the Bedouins," he said with a wink.

Surprised, Mira grinned and picked out the ruby seeds, engrossed in their sweetness. "I guess that fruit is more interesting than your Sultan," he observed with a light chuckle.

"Please forgive her, Sultan. She doesn't mean any disrespect," Salim said, quickly coming to her defense. But Mira didn't see what the big deal was. Sultan or not, they were all just humans.

The Sultan waved Salim away. "It's good to be humbled every now and then. It appears the Sultan is no better than a Bedouin," he concurred. "Tell me, child," the Sultan continued, pulling Mira's attention from the fruit. "Is it true the things people have been whispering about you?"

Mira frowned in thought. There were many true things—perhaps, even more, false things; that people had been saying about her. Everyone she met came with their own expectation based on preconceived notions. Some people even reacted violently when she didn't meet their expectations or standards. So, instead of answering, Mira posed her own challenge.

"I have also heard many things about you, Sultan. However, out of the 99 things I have heard, I can only believe one," she said.

"Which is?" the Sultan asked curiously, raising an eyebrow.

"That you live in a palace," Mira finished.

Salim coughed, covering his mouth. The Sultan stared at her in surprise, then looked at Salim as if to confirm what he had just heard. He then began laughing loudly while holding his side. "Because that is the only thing you have seen?" he asked with a hearty chuckle.

Mira nodded. "You can't believe everything you hear," she added. "You can only trust what you see with your own eyes."

The Sultan shook his head in amusement. "Today, not only was I humbled, but I was taught a valuable lesson. You have a bold tongue, child."

"Perhaps your mercy emboldens my tongue, Sultan. If you had received me with harshness, I probably wouldn't have spoken a single word," Mira confessed honestly.

The Sultan was not what she expected; he was well-natured and lenient. He wore humble garbs and entered alone without an entourage. His eyes were dark with worry, and his beard graying with stress rather than old age. When he smiled, the movement did not reach his eyes, and when he laughed, it was as if he hadn't laughed in a long time.

"Then I would have been at a loss, not having witnessed your wit." He offered with a warm smile his eyes softening for the first time. Mira smiled back, enjoying her conversation with the Sultan.

The Sultan grabbed his water and took a sip before setting it down. "Now that I met you, Mira, I must say, I am quite impressed with your wisdom and foresight. However, I didn't call you here just to chat. It seems you are capable of understanding, so I will be frank. My entire sultanate is in danger, and I need your help."

41.

Mira looked up at the Sultan, taking in his serious tone and grim face. She dropped the fruit on a plate, giving him her full attention. This was not the man laughing with her just seconds ago. Rather, this was the Sultan of the Mamluk dynasty, and he needed Mira's help. "Whatever it is, I will try my best and leave the rest to Allah," Mira whispered fiercely.

"Then follow me. It is best I show you," the Sultan commanded, leading them out of the room, away from the main visiting area, and down a dark corridor. They stopped in front of a large, arched door guarded by two soldiers who stood attentively as soon they saw the Sultan. The Sultan nodded at them, and one of the men opened the door to a dark room. Mira immediately felt her step falter as the door opened. A whiff of dark energy, unlike anything Mira had ever felt, had drifted from the room, causing her to shudder. Even Salim had goosebumps on his arm as he felt the shift in energy.

The Sultan bravely walked into the room. The curtains were drawn, and the only light came from a few flickering candles. It was impossible to know whether it was day or night from the vantage point of that room. "He doesn't like the light," the Sultan explained as he headed towards a large canopy bed in the middle of the room. On it lay a young boy who looked to be a few years older than Mira. His face was pale, and his breathing labored. Mira frowned as the Sultan knelt beside the boy, taking his limp hand and placing a gentle kiss on it. His face was so full of sorrow that Mira's heart hurt just witnessing it.

"This is my son and heir, Prince Al-Malik al Mansoor. My other sons died, either in infancy, or in childhood. He is the only one of my sons to live to adolescence. Several months ago, he fell ill. It happened so suddenly. I imported all the best doctors in the world to treat him, from Damascus to Baghdad, but no one could tell me what was wrong. They said it was a spiritual illness; someone had done black magic on my son—on all my sons—causing death. I consulted the greatest Islamic scholars in the city and beyond—yet, each time they tried to rid him of this sickness, my son convulsed and bit his tongue. I worried the treatment would kill him, so I ended it," the Sultan paused, stroking his son's face. The boy was barely breathing.

Mira felt her throat tighten, saddened by the Sultan's tale and the boy's unfortunate fate.

"If he dies, my sultanate will die with him. I have no other heirs, and I fear my nation will fall into civil war if a successor isn't named. You are my last hope, Mira. Help me save my son. Help me save this nation," the Sultan pleaded.

Mira shook. The boy was definitely afflicted by a *jinn,* beyond what the Sultan and Salim could even begin to understand. Mira saw an incredibly large, dark shadow upon his chest when she studied the boy. The *jinn* was not in his physical form, but even his shadow nearly reached the high ceilings of the room. He was darker and more powerful than anything she had ever encountered— she wasn't sure she could vanquish such a demon. The *jinn* sat on the boy's chest, constricting his breathing and slowly killing him.

Salim looked at Mira, taking in her uncertain stance. He stood behind her, whispering in her ear, "You don't have to do this, Mira. Just say the word, and I will take you from here. I will deal with the Sultan."

Mira appreciated Salim's concern, and while she was indeed frightened, she could not leave this boy to suffer as such. "He is indeed afflicted by a great and evil *jinn,* Sultan. It's sitting upon your son's chest, and it's making it hard for him to breathe," Mira explained, having decided she will do what she can to help.

The Sultan looked at his son's barely moving chest, as the attendants started whispering hushed prayers. "He often complained of chest pain before he became bedridden," the Sultan commented. "Can you save him?"

Mira cleared her throat, unsure whether she could, but she gave her word that she would try. Mira approached the bed, and the *jinn's* shadow began to move erratically, getting absorbed into the boy's body. Mira took the boy's hand. It was cool to the touch, but it was also soft. She recited the prayers and sacred verses her grandmother had taught her—words that burned the *jinns* with their purity. The boy's red-tinted eyes flew open and he began to groan.

The Sultan stepped forward, but Salim stopped him from approaching. This was not his son looking at them with burning hatred, it was the *jinn* that had taken possession of the boy's body. "Leave me, human," the *jinn* hissed in the boy's raspy, adolescent voice. Mira paused, looking at the *jinn*. She could still see his shadow luring over the boy's chest.

"You are the one that must leave," Mira countered. "You are making this boy suffer and hurting his father. Leave his body, or God will punish you."

The *jinn* began to laugh. "Do you know who I am, girl? I am of the great *Ifrit*. I have roamed this earth for a thousand years, and I will not be cast out by a little human girl." Mira ignored the gasps and prayers from the audience behind her. This *jinn* would not leave so easily, he was a cunning liar and would say anything to frighten Mira into giving up. Ayub had told Mira of the *Ifrit*. They were a powerful *jinn* species—arrogant and dark. They weren't usually the type to possess humans, so someone must have sent this particular *jinn* to make this boy suffer.

"Who is your master," Mira asked the *jinn*. "Who sent you to possess this boy?"

"I serve the devil. His disciple sent me!" the *jinn* hissed. The Sultan nearly collapsed at this announcement, but Mira doubled down.

"Tell me where the spell is," she commanded. If this was black magic, then that meant someone used a spell to curse the boy. The *jinn* would not leave until it was found and burned. It had to be somewhere close by in this palace.

"I cannot tell you," the *jinn* said, turning away. "Now, leave me!"

"It seems it is you who does not know who I am," Mira told the *jinn*. "You are an *Ifrit*, one of many, but I am *Al-Nazar*."

The *jinn* glared at her, fear entering his eyes. "I am not afraid of *Al-Nazar*," he hissed but his shadow's erratic movement gave away his lie.

Mira looked at the boy's chest. "I can see where you entered the boy; I will grab you by the hairs on your chin and pull you out of his body by force, then you will perish," she threatened the *jinn* whose eyes widened at the thought.

"Please! If I leave, they will kill me."

"If you stay, *I* will kill you," she promised. "Tell me where the spell is. The one which binds you to this boy." She could try to perform the exorcism without the spell, but it could greatly harm both her and the host. The *jinn* screamed, thrashing his body about. The boy's attendants rushed to hold him down. "Fine. You want to do this the hard way." Mira placed her hand on the boy's chest— the darkness from this *jinn* was worse than anything she had ever felt.

She had to swallow back the bile as she hardened her grasp upon him and began to pull. Mira's hands burned as the *jinn* screamed louder in agony, the boy's body seizing up in pain. "Okay! Please, stop! I will tell you!" the *jinn* pleaded. Mira let go of it, wiping the sweat from her brow. The boy's pale hand slowly lifted up as he pointed to the great chandeliers above his bed. Everyone's eyes immediately shifted toward the ceiling.

The attendant quickly grabbed a ladder and began searching the huge chandeliers. There, wrapped in wire and hair, was the dark spell binding the *jinn* to the boy. Everyone in the room started whispering prayers more aggressively this time as the spell was presented to Mira, who instructed them to burn it right away. Now that the *jinn* was not held by a spell he could volunteer to leave the boy.

"I gave you what you asked for. Now, please leave me alone," the *jinn* begged.

"Tell me who did this!" the Sultan commanded, jumping forward. "Who has cursed my son?"

The *jinn* spat in his direction, causing an uproar among the attendants.

"Please, Sultan, let me handle this," Mira told him gently. She didn't want anyone to interfere with her process. "Who has cursed the boy," she asked the *jinn*.

"I can't tell you!" the *jinn* screeched. "They will kill me." The boy's hands seized in different directions, the strain of the possession severely hurting him.

"You will die anyways, *Ifrit*. You can die a believer and seek God's forgiveness, or you can die an unbeliever, and face His wrath. Now, tell me who sent you!"

The *jinn* screamed angrily, "Leave me!"

"I can't do that. You must tell me who sent you, and you must leave this boy," Mira demanded.

"If I tell you, will you let me stay? I won't hurt him anymore. I promise. Just let me stay," the *jinn* cried, trying to negotiate with Mira.

Mira glanced back at the Sultan who gave a worried look. "Yes, if you tell me the truth, you can stay," she lied.

The room fell silent, except for the laborious breathing of the boy. "It was the *Wazir*. He sent me to possess the boy, and he sent my brothers to kill the Sultan's other offspring. He made a deal with my master—a deal that must be honored."

Everyone in the room gasped in horror. Mira looked at the Sultan, darkness clouding his face. Mira didn't know who the *Wazir* was, but, judging from the reactions in the room, the Sultan was betrayed by someone very close to him.

"There is no honor among devils," Mira told the *jinn* as she grabbed hold of him once again, bracing herself against the dark, oily feeling that crawled up her arms and into her mind. She had learned how to protect her mind from the darkness, but this *jinn* was unlike anything she had ever faced before.

Mira told everyone in the room to recite the prayers and sacred verses as she pulled on the *jinn*, needing all the help she could get at that moment. The *jinn* screamed and screamed, the boy's voice going hoarse. His veins popped as he twisted and turned, his body seizing once more. "You promised to leave me! You promised!" The *jinn* screamed as Mira grit her teeth and continued to pull with all her strength.

Soon, Salim joined her, holding her up as he helped her pull. The Sultan and his attendants joined in as well, all using their combined force to pull the *jinn* out of the prince's body. After a fair amount of tugging and pulling, the *jinn's* spirit was free from the boy, evaporating into the air as it perished. Mira, along with everyone else, fell to the ground, all of them breathing hard. She stood on wobbly feet, clenching her chest as a sharp pain engulfed her. She felt a dark energy wrap itself around her heart, gasping for air before she collapsed into darkness.

42.

Light filtered through the small gaps in between the heavy drapes. Mira stirred awake with her head pounding and body aching. She slowly opened her eyes, expecting to be in her room. Instead, she was greeted by a brightly decorated room as she lay on top of a massive canopy bed with silken sheets. Mira looked around the grand room, gasping as she spotted a strange man hovering over her. She cringed, cowering back on the bed. "Please, don't be afraid. My name is Ali Hussein. I am the Sultan's lead physician. He asked me to personally look after you," the man explained, introducing himself.

Mira relaxed, calming her hammering heart and sinking back into bed. Her body was still sore. She felt like she was trampled by a herd of camels, and her head hurt so bad she could barely see. "How do you feel," the doctor asked as he checked her pulse.

His touch was light, but Mira still pulled away from it. "Everything hurts," she admitted. "My head...my body." The doctor began digging through his bag, pulling out some medicine, "this will help with the pain," he told her. Mira nodded slightly, she would take anything to stop this ache, the doctor held her head up to the water as she swallowed the bitter tablet. She groaned, the pain slowly starting to ebb away. Her body relaxed.

"Mira, I'm afraid there is some irregularity with your heartbeat. You are very sick, my child," the doctor concluded. Mira turned her head and stared out the window. She had known she was sick since the first day she pulled out that *jinn* in the shop a year and a half ago. "You already know," the doctor accused. "Tell me, what are your symptoms?"

There was no point in hiding the truth anymore. Mira let out a small sigh "I feel tired all the time," she whispered. "I have no energy, and I can barely sleep at night. Sometimes, I feel a sharp pain in my chest," she finished, rubbing away at the phantom pain.

"Do you know what's making you sick?" the doctor asked.

"The exorcisms. Every time I perform one, it affects me," she admitted.

"Have you told anyone this?"

Mira shook her head. "Mira, I'm afraid your condition is not good, if you continue performing such dangerous acts, it could one day kill you. You can't do unnatural things and expect natural results. What you're doing goes against nature."

Mira sat up, after her encounter with the *Ifrit*, she feared it might already be too late, however, she still didn't want anyone to know of her condition. "Please. I don't want anyone to know, I'll-I'll stop" she pleaded, thinking about Salim and Ayub.

The doctor sighed heavily and frowned. "I understand and will respect your privacy, but you must give your body time to heal itself and never perform an exorcism again," the doctor commanded.

Mira nodded solemnly. "Will I get better," she asked in a whisper.

The doctor sighed, "only time will tell."

He handed her some more medicine to help with the body aches, advised her on how to take it, and left the room. That was when Mira sighed and slumped into the bed. Moments later, Salim rushed into the room and sat beside her. "How do you feel," he demanded, his face laced with worry as he mimicked the doctor, checking her pulse and her forehead for a fever. Mira squirmed away from him.

"A bit tired, but I'm okay," she lied, pulling herself up. "Is the prince okay?" She was concerned about his state. He was so weak, there was a possibility he didn't make it.

"The prince is fine. In fact, he is awake and speaking to his father," Salim assured her.

Mira smiled with relief, even though that small movement made her face hurt. "How long was I asleep," Mira asked. It was still daylight outside, so it couldn't have been long.

"You were asleep for an entire day, Mira. We arrived at the palace yesterday," Salim explained.

"Oh," she whispered, falling back into bed.

Salim sighed, "yesterday's event must have taken all your energy. The Sultans' physicians said you collapsed from exhaustion, but they didn't find anything else wrong. I was thinking perhaps we should pause our work for a few weeks. We can go on a trip—anywhere you like, I hear Alexandria is beautiful this time of year. You could see the ocean again. You really enjoyed it the first time."

Mira smiled, a trip sounded like a perfect idea, but she didn't think she was in any shape to travel, and after what the doctor said, she wasn't sure could ever go back to work. She nodded, still worried, and Salim squeezed her hand reassuringly. Mira was exhausted. Removing that *jinn* took everything in her, and she would be feeling the repercussions of that event for days to come however, she was still glad the doctor didn't reveal her secret.

She rolled her shoulders as the door opened and the Sultan entered with his attendants, giving Mira a sympathetic smile. Salim quickly stood, greeting the Sultan, and Mira tried to sit up, but the Sultan asked her to stay as she was. He pushed her back down on the bed gently and urged her to rest. "How are you feeling, Mira," he asked.

"I feel tired, but I'll be okay in a few days or so," she told him.

The Sultan smiled at her and grabbed her hand, placing a kiss on the back of it, and touching it to his forehead—the ultimate sign of respect. "You have saved my son and my sultanate, and you have revealed a great snake within my court. I shall forever be in your debt, Mira." The Sultan clapped his hand, and a train of servants entered, each carrying cases of treasure.

They presented her with trunks of gold, silver, silk, and jewels. Salim sputtered at the sight of it all. However, Mira wasn't so impressed. Salim loved money and used the money she made to take care of her, but Mira didn't care much for material things. She came from the vast emptiness of the desert and was unimpressed with the city's obsession with wealth.

"You do not like it," the Sultan observed.

"You are very generous Sultan," Mira said, not wanting to seem ungrateful, but she was too detached from this world to enjoy its treasures.

The Sultan chuckled, "I had a feeling you would not be fulfilled with gold and silk, so, tell me Mira, what is your wish? Anything you want—I shall make it happen. Ask for the moon and I shall retrieve it for you."

"If I ask for the moon, then who will guide the stars," Mira pondered.

"Yes, clever girl. I cannot give you the moon, but if your wish is within my power, I shall grant it."

Mira paused and looked at Salim, who gave an encouraging nod. She bit her lip before speaking. "I wish to enter a *madrasa*, somewhere far from the city, near the desert where I can live, and learn until my days on this earth are finished," she told him, revealing her secret wish.

The Sultan shook his head in surprise "Had you asked for half my kingdom, I would have made you its keeper. Had you asked to be my daughter, I would have wed you to my only son. Had you asked for the Nile, I would have given you all its riches. But you ask to go to a *madrasa* and spend your days learning? You both surprise and impress me, Mira. Your wish shall be granted. I will sponsor your education and make sure you live a peaceful life," he promised her.

After saying his goodbyes, he left the room, commanding Mira to rest. Salim stood silently, his face set in an expressionless mask. However, his hands were clenched to his side. "Are you angry with me," Mira asked him. It wasn't her intention to blindside him with this spontaneous decision, but it was time for Mira to leave his side and begin her own journey. She needed to heal—and, for that, she needed to leave.

"I am not angry. I am confused. Have I done something to offend you that you asked the Sultan for an escape? Have I not treated you as my own daughter? I sacrificed my dreams and ambitions just to be your guardian in this world. Was that not enough, Mira? Tell me, what have I done that you would rather spend your days in boarding school? Tell me, where have I failed in making you happy," Salim asked, hurt and betrayal lacing his words.

"Yes, you have treated me like a daughter. Yes, you have sacrificed your dreams and ambitions to be my guardian. And no, you have not failed in making me happy—not even for a day," Mira confirmed.

"Then why do you wish to leave me," Salim whispered, his voice breaking.

"Because you are not my father, and I am not your daughter. You shouldn't have to sacrifice your dreams and ambitions to be my guardian, and my happiness shouldn't be tied to you. I don't want to leave you because I hate you; I *have* to leave you because I love you more than I love myself, and that's not a burden you should carry."

Salim looked away, scrubbing his face with his hands. He was never good with emotions, and this was the rawest conversation they had ever had.

"Take these treasures, Salim, and go to Damascus. Become a great physician and return to your family. Get married to a beautiful, kind woman, and have many children. I will no longer hold you back. I appreciate every moment I have spent with you, but I am no longer in need of a guardian."

"So, that's it? Thank you, Salim, now get out of my life?" he scoffed. "Fine. If this is your wish, then it shall be." He stormed out, leaving her to her thoughts.

43.

Mira stood over her bed, looking at the belongings she planned to take with her. Organized into a small pile, she packed a few simple items from her wardrobe and then went to her desk where she kept her trinkets. She grabbed the small, wooden pyramid gifted to her all those years ago by that kind merchant from Egypt, and now she was here, living in the city that, for so long, only existed in her imagination. She smiled as she remembered the first time she saw the pyramids— she was standing on the balcony of the finance minister's house, and in the distance shrouded in dusty air, she could make out the triangular structures.

Even though she could barely see it, she still marveled at the sight, wishing she had brought her small pyramid to compare it to. It didn't look so big being that far away; it looked just like the small replica she held in her hand, but just the sight had warmed her. Mira carefully put the pyramid in her bag, the same tattered bag which she had left the desert with. She then went to her bookshelf. It was filled with all sorts of books, but the only one she decided to take was the one she still couldn't read yet told her a thousand stories. While she could now read and write in Arabic, this book was in Latin, and its contents were still a mystery to her. She pushed the book into the small bag, which was already full, but she needed to grab one more thing. Hanging on the door of her open balcony was the glass suncatcher Salim had gifted her when he was leaving the oasis.

It hung, gently swaying in the hot wind, the sun penetrating its glass as it released a colorful light on the wall across from it. She carefully removed it, meticulously wrapping it in fabric before placing it in her bag.

"What are you doing?"

Mira jumped in surprise at the sound of Ayub's voice as he perched himself on the rails of her balcony. "Sorry," he immediately apologized. Mira should have been used to him popping out of nowhere by now, but he still got her.

Mira released a breath, giving him a small smile. "I'm packing," she informed him.

"Really? We are finally leaving?!" he beamed, fist-pumping the air. Mira rolled her eyes, unable to share his excitement. This wasn't a happy moment for her. She still didn't want to leave Salim, but she had no choice. "Salim isn't coming, right," Ayub asked, just to be sure.

"No, he's not coming," Mira grumbled, not liking the gleam in his eyes. Ayub nodded, lowering his head and pretended to be disappointed. But she could see the satisfaction painted all over his face.

Ayub was ecstatic to leave the city, having whooped and danced when she told him the news. He was even happier that Salim wouldn't be tagging along. He was awfully jealous of Salim and wanted Mira all to himself. Even though Mira had grown and matured in the years since meeting him, Ayub hadn't changed at all—neither physically nor mentally. He was still the wild, playful, loyal friend she had met in the desert a lifetime ago.

Ayub sighed heavily, "I'm sorry, Mira," he whispered genuinely. As much as he didn't like Salim, he hated seeing Mira sad. "It's okay if he comes," he offered reluctantly.

Mira shook her head firmly. "It will just be us from now on, Ayub," she told him, swallowing the lump in her throat, willing herself not to cry. She will leave this villa with her head up and enter her new life bravely.

Ayub grinned happily. "We will have a world of fun, Mira. You just watch," he promised before jumping off the balcony, distracted by a pigeon.

Mira chuckled. Ayub never failed to brighten her mood—even with the heavy load sitting on her heart, he was able to make her smile. She gave her room one last look—the dozens of dresses in her wardrobe, the growing pile of gold jewelry on her vanity, and the library of books she enjoyed. She never had so many things in her life, but the only things that held any real value to her were the things in her small bag.

With a heavy heart, she slowly closed the door, having already instructed the servants to donate everything she owned to the local madrasa, and made her way down the hall. She stopped in front of Salim's office. She had barely seen him these last few days as he hid away in that room. She hated that he was upset with her, and part of her wanted to beg for forgiveness, but she couldn't bring herself to knock on his door. Salim wasn't an emotional man, and she knew if she saw him, she would break down. So, Mira took a brave breath and descended the stairs, not stopping until she was outside the villa.

Pausing, she took a final look at the villa she called home for the past year. Ayub was already perched on top of the carriage the Sultan had sent, trying to catch a locus with his hands. Mira bid farewell to the servants, who cried and hugged her tight, promising to visit her at the boarding school. And now, it was time to leave. She fidgeted with the stem of her dress, wondering if Salim would come out, then swallowed her disappointment. She took a shaky breath, turning around to face the carriage.

"You'd really leave without saying goodbye, kid?" Mira whipped her head around at the sound of Salim's low voice.

"Salim," she called, hot tears springing to her eyes as she stared at him.

He stood near the door of their villa, a sad resigned look on his face as he watched her. She really thought he wouldn't see her off. "Come here, kid," he finally called to her, opening his arms for a hug. Mira ran into his arms without thought, slamming into him with a tight embrace. She didn't care that her tears soaked his robes—and for once, he didn't push her away. Instead, he held her just as tight.

"You were a thorn in my side for so long. I can't believe you're actually leaving me," he said. Mira laughed and wiped her tears as she stared up at him. She had so much she wanted to say, but the words failed her. How could she convey the immense love and gratitude she had for him? There were no words to describe what Mira was feeling at that moment as she stared at the man who had saved her. The man who pulled her from the dark, lonely hole she was living in and introduced her to the world. Nothing would ever be enough. So, Mira just stared at him, fresh tears springing to her eyes, each telling a story as it slid down her cheek and cemented itself into the soft sand below.

Salim looked away from her, using his arm to wipe his glistening eyes. He cleared his throat, avoiding her intense stare. "Don't look at me like that, kid. I don't deserve it," he whispered, his voice hoarse. Mira was still unable to speak, but lowered her eyes, respecting his wish.

Salim sighed heavily, capturing her small face between his hands as he used his thumb to wipe her tears. He leaned down, placing a gentle kiss on the top of her head. "I'll miss you, kid. Make sure to take care of yourself. Don't spend too much time in your room, and try to make some friends," he advised.

Mira held onto his hands, not wanting to let go. She didn't want to walk away from Salim, but she knew this was the only way to save herself, or else she would sacrifice her life just to see him smile. "Hey, you'll be okay, kid. You're still young. Soon, you will forget all about me."

"I'll never forget you," she whispered somberly.

"Then, I guess I will just have to visit you often, so you don't miss me too much," he chuckled.

"You'll really visit?" Mira grinned happily.

"Of course, I'll visit," he said, ruffling her hair one last time. "I promise. And friends never break their promise, right?" he quoted.

Mira laughed, wiping her tears. This was a bittersweet moment for them both. It was time for Mira to close this chapter of her life, and for Salim to begin his. She had stolen the first few chapters of his book, and now she was handing him back the pen so he could write the rest. She would miss him terribly, but it was time for Mira to move on.

With a heavy heart, Mira slowly stepped away, a piece of her breaking as she turned around. She cried silently with every step, her shoulders shaking as she made her way to the carriage. "Mira!" Salim called out suddenly. She quickly turned around "I-" he swallowed hard, unable to say whatever he wanted to tell her. "Goodbye," he said instead, turning his head. Mira clenched the door of the carriage, unable to say the words back. She would see him again, so there was no point in goodbye. She entered the carriage, her tears an endless stream. Sara crawled up her lap as if to comfort her. Mira wiped her face with shaky hands, taking deep breaths to calm herself.

"I'll be okay. I'll find my own happiness," she promised herself fiercely.

She looked out the open window at Salim one last time. He stared into the distance, and on his face, she saw a single tear roll down his cheek. Mira looked away, not wanting to peer into his vulnerable moment.

44.

6 years later
Salim

The rocky boat finally came to a stop and Salim stepped off onto the sandy bank of the Nile. He journeyed for ten days at sea from Damascus, and now he was finally back in Cairo—the city that changed his life. He had finally returned after six long years; he was able to fulfill his dream with the money the Sultan had gifted them. He studied medicine in Damascus, and now he was back to visit the little girl who had forced her way into his life— and into his heart.

Salim was a different man today than he was when he left Cairo. When Salim left, he was confused and hurt. He was sad that Mira had decided to leave him because he had gotten so used to her presence; he didn't think they would ever part ways. But had she not made that decision, he would have stayed by her side forever, and he would have never realized his dream. When Salim first decided he wanted to go to Damascus, it wasn't for a noble reason. He wanted to earn wealth and respect. He wanted to prove that he could be better than his father and richer than his uncle. But after attending the prestigious school, Salim finally understood his father.

While studying at the medical school, Salim grew to love medicine; he was no longer the smartest person in the room, and that forced him to work harder than ever. He no longer cared about wealth and status, but the pride that came from producing medicine and using his mind to solve problems and investigate sicknesses. He loved the art of medicine. He enjoyed studying amongst the greatest scholars and creating cures from plants. And now, he was ready to share his knowledge with the world.

The banks of the river were lined with a familiar sight: rows of vendors selling their goods to the new arrivals, and trains of carts ready to transport people into the city. Salim walked by the vendors when something caught his eyes, "What is that," he asked, pointing to a blue medallion that looked like an eye. He had never seen it before, and every vendor seemed to be selling some variation of it.

"This, my friend, is *Al-Nazar*," a merchant said cryptically, holding the medallion. It was made of glass, a dark blue circle with a light blue circle inside, imitating a blue eye.

Salim smiled as he held the medallion, "*Al-Nazar*, you say?"

"Yes. This will protect you from the evil eye and the accursed *shaytans* evil *jinns*," the man explained.

Salim raised his eyebrow. "How will this object protect me," he challenged the man.

"It was blessed by *Al-Nazar* herself," the man claimed. "It was fashioned after the blessed child's eye. I will give you a discount on it. Just four dinars."

Salim chuckled, tossing the money at the man, he held the medallion and scoffed in disbelief. Merchants would do anything for a profit. He was kind of annoyed that he didn't think of the idea first. He could have made so much money selling these trinkets. Salim sighed, wondering whether Mira would find it as amusing as he did.

He chartered a horse to take him to the town where Mira was studying. The school was located outside a small village. It was surrounded by desert and a few sparse vegetation. There was a large well for the students to gather water, and it was surrounded by a wall to keep visitors out.

As they reached the simple gates of the school, Salim couldn't help but feel that Mira would love this place. It was quiet, open and close to the desert she knew. She never truly fit into the city, no matter how hard she tried. She was a Bedouin at heart. Salim looked at the amulet he found littering the stalls of the marketplaces. Homes and vendors alike had it painted on their doors and displayed it on their stalls, hoping it would protect them from the evil eye.

He was amazed at the legacy Mira had left this city; tales of her had grown into a trend where people wore her eyes as amulets to protect them from evil. It was all hocus, of course. Just some merchants trying to capitalize on her infamy. However, he still wanted to give it to Mira to show her the impact her presence had.

It was hard to believe 6 years had passed since he last saw Mira, and he suddenly felt nervous. Would Mira even be happy to see him? He wouldn't find the same lost and lonely child he had met in the desert a lifetime ago. No, now, Mira would have grown into a beautiful, young woman. Would she look upon the time they spent together with fondness, or would she see it as a childish attachment? Salim cleared his throat, combing his fingers through his now overgrown beard. His hand felt sweaty; he didn't know why he was so nervous. It was just Mira. But as he knocked his fist against the iron doors, he couldn't help the anticipation.

The gates were pulled open by an old guard who gave him an assessing glare. Salim cleared his throat and greeted the guard respectfully, placing his hand on his heart, stating his business. The guard asked him to wait while he rushed back inside the school.

Salim wiped his sweaty hands against his *thobe*. Soon, an older woman rushed to open the door, and greeted him. "Peace be upon you brother. My name is *Ustada* Aisha, and I am the head scholar at the school. I'm told you are here for Mira," she said.

"Yes, I've come to visit my ward. I know I'm a little late, but I was away in Damascus, busy with my studies," Salim explained.

"Of course, I'm just happy you are here now. I was worried no one would ever come to visit our dear Mira. Come, please. Let us talk in my office," the woman said, leading him through the courtyard of the small school. The school was one story and had many arched doors with students of all ages milling about. It had a beautiful courtyard with a fountain and lots of plants; it looked well maintained, and Salim was glad to see all the money he had sent here every year went to good use.

After Mira had left, Salim sold the house and used half the treasure the Sultan had gifted them to invest in a few local businesses. He tasked Faisal with sending money, food and other supplies to the school every year, in hopes that Mira would benefit from it. And when she was ready to leave the school, she could take the wealth from the businesses, and use it to fund whatever life she wanted to lead.

The *Ustada* led him to a small, brightly lit office. It was spotless, with a few books scattered on her desk. She urged him to sit, bringing him water and offering him tea. Salim declined the tea, but took the water, "I must say, *Ustada,* you are running this *madrasa* very well. I was worried at first when Mira said she wanted to study here, but now, I am happy to know she has been in good hands this entire time," he told her honestly.

The woman smiled. "It is your Mira who was a blessing and a joy to our school—a very clever child, indeed. We benefited much from her presence here. There was not a single student nor teacher who did not adore her."

"Yes, I've missed her greatly. Where is she now? Is she in her classes," Salim asked.

The woman paused, clearing her throat. "Unfortunately, brother Salim, Mira departed from this world four years ago," the woman started. "I've waited a long time for someone to come and look for her. It made me sad to think no one was searching until you arrived this morning. I must say, she spoke of you often."

"Wait," Salim held up his hands, trying to digest what he had heard. Surely, this woman was mistaken. There was *no way* he had heard her *correctly*. "What do you mean, 'departed from this world?' What are you saying? Where is Mira? Where have you taken her," Salim demanded angrily, his heart racing.

"Please, brother, Mira was sick. She—"

"She wasn't sick! She was fine! What the hell have you done to her? Tell me now, or I will turn this school upside down," Salim slammed his hand on her desk, causing the older woman to flinch back.

"Brother, I will need to ask you to calm down. I understand this is hard to accept, but I have done nothing to Mira. There isn't a single person in this school who didn't love her. She was a light from our Lord, and we have all mourned her death, and will grieve for the rest of our lives."

Salim shook his head, refusing to believe a word the woman was saying. *How could Mira be dead?* Not his Mira—she was too full of light to be taken so young.

In a panic, Salim stormed out of the office. "Mira!" he screamed outside. The students gasped, running away as he shouted like a madman. "Mira, where are you!" he yelled, running around the school, looking through the many closed doors.

Girls hid from him running in fright, as he shouted until his throat was raw. "That is enough!" *Ustada* yelled, grabbing his arm. "You will control yourself or leave this place. You are scaring my students," the woman said fiercely.

Salim tried to pull his arm free, looking through all the frightened and sympathetic faces staring at him. "Mira, where are you? It's me, it's Salim...please..." Salim collapsed to the ground, his entire body going numb. "Let us leave this place. Let's go home..." he whispered as the *Ustada* knelt beside him, rubbing his back.

The *Ustada* ordered someone to bring him water, but he couldn't even move his hand to take it, nor could he move his lips to decline. The woman set the water down next to him and pulled him off the ground, leading him to a chair in her office like a zombie.

"How? How did she die," he whispered hoarsely. "How did my Mira die?" He couldn't make sense of it all.

The *Ustada* sighed heavily. "Mira was sick, Salim."

"Then why didn't you take her to a physician? She was under the Sultan's care. Why didn't you seek help for her," he demanded angrily. *How could they let this happen, how could they let her die?*

"This was not a sickness any physician could cure, Salim. It was a spiritual sickness—a sickness of the heart. Mira was performing dangerous exorcisms, which should only be performed by an experienced spiritual leader who studied possessions. She was physically pulling *jinns* from a possessed person's body, and it made her sick. At first, I was not aware of these actions. Each week, the girls volunteer at the local hospital. I noticed that each time she went there, she visited a person suspected of suffering from a spiritual illness. After a few moments with that person, they would be cured. Once I realized what she was doing, I urged her to stop, but she refused. She said if I stopped her, she would leave the school and treat the sick on the streets. The Sultan was the one sponsoring her, so I couldn't allow her to leave."

Salim clenched his jaw. *The exorcisms made her sick. How did he miss it? How didn't he notice it was killing her?* The air was suddenly too hot, and Salim couldn't breathe. He felt like his soul had been snatched from his body. There was a dark shadow hung over the sun, which shined brightly for everyone else. He felt as though the light breeze was taunting him while cooling others. The water in his cup rippled with accusation, and the ground spun, trying to expel his sinful feet. They all knew what Salim refused to admit: he was the culprit for her demise.

"I need to leave," he said abruptly, cutting off whatever the *Ustada* was saying. He could no longer hear, incapable of comprehension. His vision was cloudy. He was hot and cold at the same time. He needed to leave this place. He should have never come in the first place. He should have gone straight to Fez. He should have continued loving her in ignorance, rather than face the reality of her death.

"Wait, please! Before you go, there is something I must give you," the *Usatada* said, hurrying to her drawers behind her desk. She pulled out a small bag, and Salim immediately recognized it as the pack Mira carried with her when they first met. "These are the last of her belongings. She ordered that we donate everything else, and she asked us to give you this, should you ever visit. I held onto it for four years, hoping, one day, you would come to collect it." She handed him the tattered pack; it was old and full of holes. In the end, she kept the only things she left the desert with.

"Where is she? I wish to say goodbye."

"She is buried under the weeping tree. It's in the back of the school, a few feet past the gate."

"The weeping tree," he was confused. *Why would they bury her under a tree instead of in a cemetery?*

"Ah, that's what the students call it. They swear each time they pass the tree; they hear it weep. It was her favorite place on campus. Every day, she went to that tree, read stories, and sat under its shade. I often caught her talking to herself there. She asked to be buried there, so we granted her wish," she explained.

Salim nodded, pulling the pack over his shoulder. "Thank you, *Ustada*. I apologize for the disruption I have caused," he said, distant and detached. Salim walked out of the school and went around it to the back gates. He walked on the sandy path until he saw a large Argan tree perched in the distance. Under it, he saw her grave. It was meticulously cleaned—not a single leaf nor branch lay on it. Her grave was only marked with a small, white stone. Even in death, she lay here, all alone in the desert.

45.

Salim leaned down, placing his hand on her grave. He was still numb, guilt and anger battling inside him. He was so self-observed and blinded by greed that he couldn't see his ward dying before him. But now his eyes were wide open. He remembered her haggard breaths and the dark circles that had a permanent place under her eyes. He remembered her lack of appetite, and, most of all, her silence. Mira was never quiet, but now that he thought about it, she barely spoke during their last month together—probably too overcome with her sickness.

He convinced himself it was just puberty, that she was growing up and leaving her childish babbles behind. But this whole time, she was battling a sickness the eyes could not see. She was pretending she was okay while facing the pain of death alone. Salim knew that the exorcisms tired her, but he didn't realize the extent; he was too blinded by the money she brought in and the status he basked in. He deluded himself into thinking that he was taking care of her—that he was all she had in this world—and that he was the one sacrificing his dream for her.

But it was she who sacrificed her life for him. Salim scoffed angrily. He was angry at Mira. He didn't see her sacrifice as a noble act of selflessness to save others. It was stupid. She sacrificed herself, *for what?* They didn't care about her. They made their amulets, profiting off her service.

She lay here alone for four years, waiting for someone to visit her, someone to mourn for her, and for four years, Salim was nowhere to be found.

Salim opened her meager bag and pulled out her belongings. Inside, he found a small, wooden pyramid, and was assaulted with memories of her proudly showing it off to him, spilling her knowledge of Cairo and its monuments. It was probably her dream to see them one day, and Salim never thought to take her. She wanted to see the world, and Salim locked her up in a villa, paranoid that someone would snatch her from him.

Did he want to keep her because he loved her, or because he loved the wealth she brought him? Was he afraid of losing her, or losing his generator of gold? Salim pulled out the suncatcher he had given her when he was leaving the oasis. At the time, he didn't know it, but she had saved his life by finding the medicine he needed to treat those people. Were it not for her, he probably wouldn't have left that oasis with his head attached. And how did he thank her? With a stupid suncatcher. Still, it was meticulously wrapped and in better condition than when he had given it to her. It was obvious she treasured it and took great care of it.

Salim then pulled out the book she was constantly pretending to read— the one she begged him to read to her—and he couldn't even give her that much. He couldn't even read her a simple book.

"How could you do this to yourself, kid," he whispered to the dry patch of dirt where his Mira lay. "Was this your way of getting back at me? Did you do this to punish me? If you wanted to punish me, then you should have punished *me*! Me!" Salim shouted, slamming his fist to his chest. "But you didn't have to die, Mira…. You didn't have to die just to prove a point."

He angrily threw the book against the tree, scrubbing his face before collapsing next to her grave. He was angry at her for dying and angry at himself for not being better to her. Better *for* her. It was he who plucked a rare flower from the desert, failed to care for it properly, and now it was dust in the wind.

Tears clouded his vision as he looked up at the sky, blinking them away. "Had I known you would have done this, then I would have never looked back that day. Had you drowned the world with your tears, I would not have taken you with me. Had I known you would enter my heart just to rip it out, I would have run far away from your cruelty."

Salim stood on wobbling knees; he wouldn't apologize to her. She was the one who had attached herself to him. He was selfish to his core, and a greedy bastard. She was the fool for choosing to love him.

The book lay open sprawled face down near the tree, and Salim went to retrieve it. As he picked it up, he noticed that a piece of paper had fallen from it. He picked up the folded paper and saw his name written in the most beautiful calligraphy. He traced the letters and smiled. He knew she was good at calligraphy, but this was more beautiful than anything he had seen her write.

She didn't like to share her work with him and screamed at him to leave anytime he tried to peek at her calligraphy, insisting it wasn't good enough. Salim leaned against the tree and carefully opened the letter.

Dear Salim,

You must be surprised to see me write so eloquently. I've grown up a lot since you last saw me. Last night, I had the most wonderful dream. My hands shake even now as I recall it. I dreamt I was lounging in a magnificent garden—not even the Sultan's *gardens could compete in its beauty. I sat there all by myself—a clear, blue sky overhead, and bright, colorful flowers all around. Suddenly, I looked up, and I saw Mama. She was holding baby Sara, and on her face, was shining a brilliant light. Sara reached out to me with the most joyous laugh, but Mama grabbed her hand and smiled at me. I knew then I would soon be joining them in paradise and returning to my Lord. If you are reading this letter, then that means you kept your promise to me. You came back to visit. I imagine you have a lot of stories to tell me, and I also have a lot of stories to tell you.*

I made friends here—sisters who saw me as a person. Here, I was not a blessing nor a curse. I was simply another student. I got to learn so many new things, Salim. I didn't realize how much knowledge there was to learn in this world. Remember that book I asked you to read? Well, guess what? I learned Latin just to read it, and you were right. It was boring. But had you read it to me, I would have never sought the knowledge for myself, and with that knowledge, I read a lot of other magnificent books in both Latin and Arabic.

I want you to know that I fulfilled my mother's promise. I was happy in this madrasa, *and here, I also found my purpose. You may never understand why I continued helping people even when I knew it made me sick. It was no longer about wanting their praise or acceptance. I came to the realization that I will never truly be accepted in this world. I did it because I wanted to. It was my choice. You once told me that I had a choice. That I could decide my life. And, at that moment, it was as if I was born again. You may not realize the profound impact your words had on me, but it was as if I opened my eyes for the first time, and the world was mine.*

Even I, with the wildest of imagination and the greatest of longings, have never dared to imagine that one day I would have a choice, that I would get to decide who I wanted to be, and how I wished to live my life. All I ever hoped for were small joys—so small that no one would care to take them from me. But, instead, I found true happiness. So, of course, in my childish naivety, I worshiped the ground you walked on. You were my savior and my friend. And when the heart loves something—the eyes see it as paradise, and in your own way, I believe you loved me, too.

For too long, I carried a blanket of despair. Its weight held me down, suffocating me, as I sweat the tears of sorrow. However, with you, I was able to cry, laugh, and be my true self because I wasn't at my saddest when I was crying. My sorrow was deepest when I was silent—a silence that concealed the darkness of the soul because, sometimes, everything inside you but the eyes cry.

I have now come to realize that happiness was within me the entire time and loving you taught me to love myself. So, with that knowledge, I have departed from sorrow and embraced content. I have never forgotten you, Salim—not even for a day, however, even if I had never received the honor of meeting you, my fate would not have changed, for it is not in my nature to watch my brother suffer.

If forgetting me is a form of freedom, then I pray to never plague your thoughts. But if you can bear even the smallest thought of me, then I pray you remember me. May we meet once again in paradise.

Your friend, Mira.

Salim clenched the letter in his hands, his beard drenched with tears, his breathing shallow; and his heart still. Has a more beautiful soul ever walked this earth? Should the sky not weep and the earth not shake, lamenting at this loss? Had people truly known the heart of this child, they would bite the tongues that cursed her and envy the eyes that gazed upon her smile.

Overcome with emotion, Salim covered his face as he wept and wept. Suddenly, the wind began erratically blowing around him, Salim raised his tear-stained face. It reminded him of the angry roaring wind that had saved them that day in the desert, but this wind wasn't angry, it was gentle—

caressing his face as if to wipe his tears. This wind didn't roar, it wept—the sorrowful sound piercing his heart. Mira wasn't alone, nor was she ever, and Salim knew this *jinn* would be with her till the earth shook and the seas dried. For Ayub loved Mira more than the arid ground loved water, and he would never leave her side.

Salim wiped his tears and whispered, "I don't think I can ever forget you, Mira. Not because I have a strong memory, or because you profoundly impacted my life, but because I have a heart that never denies those who enter it. I don't know how you made your way into my heart, but you have settled in my soul. Be at peace, my friend. May we meet again in paradise."

ACKNOWLEDGMENT

First and foremost, I want to thank you for reading Mira's story; I hope you enjoyed reading it as much as I loved writing it. Book after unpublish book, story after story buried in my mind; it was all leading up to this moment— for Mira's story to be told. This story is for everyone who felt different and misunderstood, whose good intentions didn't get translated and who felt underrepresented. Growing up with the dream of being a writer, it always felt impossible because I never read stories about people who looked like me and I never felt represented. Mira is a part of me, she is the vision of the little girl I used to be. So, thank you for coming along this journey and discovering her story. Thank you to my sisters who supported me and listened to me rant about Mira and thank you to my mother, the incredible women who inspires me every day.

Made in the USA
Las Vegas, NV
13 August 2024